ASCENDANCE

SCIENCE FICTION STORIES ABOUT REACHING
FOR THE STARS

ALEXIS GLYNN LATNER

**AVENDIS
PRESS**

"Wanderers" was first published in the June 1990 issue of *Analog Science Fiction and Fact Magazine.*

"The Listening-Glass" was first published in the February 1991 issue of *Analog Science Fiction and Fact Magazine.* It was republished in the online astronomy anthology Diamonds in the Sky, *http://www. mikebrotherton.com/diamonds/*

"Trinity Bay" was first published in the July/August 2003 issue of *Analog Science Fiction and Fact Magazine.*

"Quickfeathers" was first published in the May 2009 issue of *Analog Science Fiction and Fact Magazine.*

A Pillar of Stars by Night Chapters 1 and 2 were first published in the September 1992 issue of *Analog Science Fiction and Fact Magazine* as "Chrysalis."

A Pillar of Stars by Night Chapters 3-5 were first published in the January 1996 issue of *Analog Science Fiction and Fact Magazine as* "A Pillar of Stars by Night."

A Pillar of Stars by Night Chapter 6, "The Life-Blood of the Land," was first published in the January 1997 issue of *Analog Science Fiction and Fact Magazine.*

"Cloud Sky City" was first published in the September 2000 issue of *Analog Science Fiction and Fact Magazine.*

"Glorystar" was first published in the December 1990 issue of *Analog Science Fiction and Fact Magazine.*

The Fair Game is excerpted from *Witherspin* (Avendis Press, December 2019).

Ascendance cover image is "The launch of Soyz" © Kostyan FILE ID 15814462 License: Royalty Free at| Dreamstime.com. The cover typeface is Diavlo by Exljbris Font Foundry.

Published by Avendis Press, Houston, Texas.

❀ Created with Vellum

For Stanley Schmidt, long-time editor of Analog Science Fiction and Science Fact Magazine

CONTENTS

PART I

Stories originally published in *Analog Science Fiction and Fact*

WANDERERS

This was my first published story, in the June 1990 issue of *Analog Science Fiction and Fact*. As with a lot of other near-future science fiction, it has since turned into alternate history; and here it is.

Even though the Chinese word for crisis isn't actually composed of characters that mean danger and opportunity, it's a persistent legend because, yes, danger and opportunity do tend to be packed into any crisis —on the Moon as on Earth.

It had been months since John Clay took time away from the project for a three-hour lunch. He waited for Ramona in the restaurant's foyer. Globes of glass, aquaria, set in the dark paneled walls, contained vivid coral reef fish. John watched the fish swim around in their little worlds. For months, he thought suddenly, he had been immersed in the project like a fish in the water—as immersed and as oblivious.

Ramona rushed in and greeted him with an affectionate kiss. They were lucky enough to get a table by the glass that constituted one entire wall of the restaurant. She ordered crab legs. "You can pick over them for a long time and not look like you're just sitting around waiting for something dramatic to happen," she said practically.

"But we are."

The restaurant bustled now, filling up with patrons, all attentive to the view past the glass wall. People walked up outside, too, going to stand by the pilings at the edge of the Indian River. The wide expanse of the river shimmered in bright hot June sun. Ramona pointed toward the water. "Oh, look, there's a dolphin—two of them."

As soon as he discovered the pair of dorsal fins, John nodded.

"They've come to watch it too!"

Ever since Shuttle, two routes led to space: one for human and other delicate payloads, one for heavy and durable goods. The Argosy I vehicle represented the latter in a massive way. Unmanned, relatively inexpensive because it did not have to be man-rated, Argosy would carry the stuff of the future into space on the multiple shoulders of its booster rockets. It stood on Launch Pad 39C, towering over Merritt Island's ragged rug of trees and sea marsh. John could see the apex of Argosy from here.

It reminded him of Apollo 11. On that occasion he had taken his first tour of the Center, with his parents. They saw dolphins in the Banana River from the window of the tour bus. That night they camped out beside the car, on the sandy shore of this same Indian river, with a million other people. Pumping in the liquid oxygen had made frost form on the Saturn V's skin: illuminated by floodlights, the moon rocket shone in the night.

"They know what it's all about," said Ramona. "The old-timers will tell you that the day they threw a wreath onto the sea, for the Challenger people, seven dolphins showed up, and they circled it."

He did not want to think about that old disaster. Not today. "Maybe the dolphins like the sound," John suggested, gesturing toward Argosy I. "The way it vibrates in your blood."

"How come you didn't scare up a visitor's pass?"

"This—is close enough for me. This time."

Excavating in the recesses of her last crab leg, she gave him a puzzled glance.

"I got some news this morning. I—"

The waiter materialized just then. Young, very blond, very chipper, he said, "There's a ten-minute hold! Can I interest you folks in Key Lime pie?"

As far as Ramona was concerned, he could. She accepted it with a radiant smile. As he walked away the young man gave her an admiring look over his shoulder.

Tart lime and dense sweet cream, the pie delighted Ramona. It had been a long time since John had taken her to a restaurant, split a dessert. He had been immersed in his work. He was lucky that she had not left him for a younger and more attentive man. And that might not be a good context for what he had to say today. Worried, he ran his fingers across the tabletop, plexiglass, under which lay an assemblage of seashells on white sand.

"What news?" Appreciatively, she took up a creamy flake of crust —invited it onto her fork. "Is that why you invited me out for lunch and launch?"

"First the good news," John said slowly. "The situation looks good for getting durable goods into space—thanks to Argosy! So—the Array's been put on the launch schedule."

Ramona nodded vigorously. "Good—good! It's about time!"

"Then the—not exactly good news. Not for Phil Taylor. He was diagnosed with heart disease. Meanwhile I passed the major physical with flying colors. Now it looks like I'm going to be promoted—to project manager. That means—on site. Being there."

Ramona's eyes widened. She put down her fork. "That's great for the project. And for you. But I'll miss you."

"No. I'll marry you. Then you can come too!"

But she shook her head, abruptly pushed the pie plate away. "No."

That jolted him. He protested. "But you know what the Array means—you know what it means to me!"

"Don't you know what the sea and the sky and birds and wind mean to me?!"

"The Moon is nature too!"

"You're a scientist. For me nature means this living world. I will not move to the Moon!"

He felt sharply upset. He had presented to her a solution as neat and necessary as that of an equation. She had immediately negated it. And unless another hold developed, the vehicle would take off now in the middle of this argument, spoiling the spectacle for both of them.

The ambient background music broke off; the management had elected to pipe in the last seconds of the countdown instead. A cumulus plume of steam rose out of the fire and water under the vehicle. Voices in the restaurant chorused, "Come on!", "Go, baby, go!" Silver, tridentine on multiple booster rockets, Argosy mounted the air.

Ramona exclaimed, "It's not flying right!"

"What—" He saw it now. The angle of ascent. It tilted to the north. But Argosy was not aimed toward a polar orbit! Reflexively he leaped to his feet. Sound rolled across the river and rattled the window. The vehicle slanted into the sky, the distance, leaving a jagged trail. The building's roof blocked the line of sight. The restaurant emptied, people streaming outside, lining the pilings beside the river to strain their eyes peering north of east.

Smoke stained the sky.

A radio-equipped exercise walker with antennas on his head announced, "They blew it up!" His hearers groaned. The antennas bobbed with the agitated motions of the man's head. "They blew up deliberately because it would have hit Charleston!"

Military-type helicopters raced northward along the coast.

This seemed patently unreal, the smoke, the crowd, the copters. The young waiter happened to be standing next to John with a linen towel still tucked into his belt. It fluttered in a light breeze. Winds aloft were no stronger than this: the weather had absolutely nothing wrong with it today. Except too much heat for June in

Cape Canaveral. "Looked like a goddamn malfunction," John muttered.

Unhappily, the waiter agreed.

"She's down!" the walker with the radio informed them all intently. "In five or six major pieces, hitting the sea."

Under his suit, John sweated. Maybe heat had precipitated the malfunction.

Ramona had tears in her eyes and hands on her hips. "Why did the big dumb bastard have to DO this?"

Early the next morning, the Internal Information Office held a conference. Saturday or no Saturday, people crowded the auditorium. Researchers mingled with NASA managers, space industry reps and astronauts. No lives had been lost, but a dear payload of hardware and hopes had been blown up with Argosy.

On the big monitor, live television came in from search ships offshore. Seas seemed calm, sky clear, weather as hot and fair as yesterday. Karl Kaminsky of the Info Office gave a running slideshow commentary, like a fugue to the slow tempo of the underwater search as displayed on the monitor. This part of the intact vehicle—slide #1 —corresponds to an object located by sonar, lying on the seafloor. Divers spiraled down toward it.

Stress tied knots in John's stomach. Yesterday promoted to project manager. Today this. He helped himself to one of the local newspapers floating around the auditorium. Page One looked more garish than usual, the orange sunrise logo juxtaposed with a big, black end-of-the-world headline announcing Argosy's downfall. "Mullet wrapper!" John tossed the paper away.

Then he found a copy of |Pravda~, today's faxedition fresh from Moscow, shoved into his hands. Phil Taylor demanded, "What are they saying?" Phil jabbed a finger at the front-page photo of Argosy flying to pieces.

John skimmed the Russian text. "Looks like the truth to me," he replied. "Fairly accurate facts. Here's a sidebar about Apollo. The writer wonders whether the United States just suffered bad luck yesterday—or whether we have lost the art for designing big rockets over the past forty years."

Phil nodded dourly.

For the third or fourth time, Karl replayed the launch videotape. The magnificent rocket thundered into the sky. It veered sickeningly on a jagged column of fire. Exploded into a pinwheel of smoke. John caught himself chewing on a knuckle.

"Sabotage?" Karl Kaminsky shrugged. "Of course it's a possibility. Terrorists of three different persuasions have already taken credit, in fact!" Then he fielded another question. "Frankly, yes. Not only was Argosy not man-rated, but the technical specifications of not-man-ratedness fluctuated through two administrations and four times that many budgets."

"And as a result the design had goddamn fatigue," said Phil with bitter certainty.

"The future?" Karl replied to another question. "First we fix the vehicle." A thin laugh trickled through the auditorium. "Until then nothing's gonna go up that doesn't have L-5 written on it!" Too true: no laughter. "As you all know, construction has started on the space base at L-5. Canceling or delaying L-5 is no longer an option. It can make do with the Spaceplane plus Titan VII's. Maybe recommission a few obsolete boosters. Plus buy rides from the Europeans and Chinese. The Soviet Union has its own big fish to fry.

"Unfortunately, the L-5 base will tend to monopolize all available vehicles. Among many other likely casualties of this situation—" John found Karl looking his way. "The Lunar Radio Array got approved only this week, and put on the priority launch schedule. Now ... "

In an unwanted glare of attention, John and Phil extricated themselves from the auditorium. But not before several people zeroed in on them to make sympathetic remarks. Then they had to explain that that Phil was not out of a job and a ticket to the Moon. John was.

They walked across the mall to their office in another building.

"Goddamn," said Phil.

"I'm sorry."

"Sorry for me? Cancel that."

"I'm sorry about the project. All the work we've sunk into it. Now a royal setback."

"Remember the Hubble Space Telescope?"

"How many years before it finally got off the ground? Yeah."

A few purple wildflowers, stragglers from spring, punctuated the grass. So far the sea breeze kept the morning from being unpleasantly hot. Phil said, "Just between you and me, I wasn't looking forward to the part about being stuck on the Moon for however long it took to build the Array." Then he asked, "How about you?"

"Hadn't considered that. Til yesterday my expectations were in the lark mode." Every radio astronomer in the world had fantasized about using the Lunar Radio Array. A precious few weeks' worth of opportunity for highly productive work, with an admixture of fun, a lunar extrapolation of the traditional trip to Puerto Rico to use the Arecibo dish and get in some slivers of Caribbean vacation. It would be a much different experience for the project manager.

In the office, John checked the electronic mail that awaited him in the computer. The e-mail included distressed remarks from his colleagues in the Space Radio Consortium, requests for inside information from various acquaintances, a sympathetic note from his elderly parents. Using the computer, John reviewed the Argosy-related items in the electronic media. That transection contained no information that Karl had not imparted. There was one scary picture of a broken booster rocket falling out of the sky. Some freelance photographer had been out on a shrimp boat in the right—or nearly very wrong—place at the time.

Then the signal for incoming mail flashed. This one came from Schropfer, the director of the Consortium. Terse, it called a conference at the Center tomorrow. MAKE EVERY EFFORT TO ATTEND IN PERSON OR ELECTRONICALLY. DROP EVERYTHING FOR THIS. BRING ALL REPEAT ALL TECH SPECS FOR PLANNED

SPACE RADIO ASTRONOMY FACILITIES. DO NOT BRING ROSE COLORED GLASSES.

The details of space radio telescopes occupied most of the rest of John's weekend. He stayed late in the office Saturday, got up late Sunday. By that time Ramona had left the house to go to the beach. He felt slightly guilty. When he brushed it off, the guilt circled and came back to settle on another perch in his mind. He was still neglecting her. Yet had the project gone up on schedule and he with it, he would have missed Ramona more than flowers and wind. There would have been no real reason for her to wait for him to come back from the Moon, either. But now, with the project on indefinite hold, he would find time for Ramona.

With his morning coffee, John walked around in the house. He liked the house, an old bungalow in the city of Cape Canaveral. He would never have managed to make the place this habitable on his own. Ramona had intermingled his books and his pictures of rockets and radio telescopes with her Amerindian art and shells and feathers. Plants clustered around the windows. The house was not roboticized. The two of them opened windows, cooked, set alarm clocks and watered the plants by hand.

John unfolded a bulky printout from yesterday. Plants, walls and all faded, supplanted in his imagination by the array of radio dishes on the plain on the Moon's far side. Seven great dishes, mobile on miles of track, aimed at a point between the distant visible stars: a radio galaxy. Each dish took in a slightly unique trace of data. A supercomputer meshed the data; it limned the lobes of bright matter spewing out of the radio galaxy's black-hole heart.

But the whole business existed only as plans. The Array was as ephemeral as the equations and cost estimates that described it, and as easy to alter. Or cancel.

Ramona came back from the beach. He kissed her. "Forget what I said yesterday. What happened to Argosy changes everything. We can stay together longer."

"Maybe," she said quietly.

"I'm all but sure. The L-5's going to monopolize everything this country can launch for as long as it takes to fix Argosy."

"I found this on the beach." She handed him a shard of silver metal. John turned it over in his fingers. Sharp-edged, the sea had not had it for long at all. Ramona said, "Just before it went up—I didn't like what you said. We ARE married in every sense but white men's' law!" The American Indian blood showed in Ramona's features, but only if you knew what to look for. "Did you think it was a generous offer to legalize me if I'd go to the Moon with you?"

Warily John said, "That's just how the rules work. You have to be legally married to go with someone off Earth. Farside Moonbase would welcome a good technician like you, I know."

"You just assumed I'd go. But it's not like following you to Arecibo or even Pacifica. It's the Moon."

"It's not as dangerous as Arecibo," he joked weakly. "No Independence revolutionaries."

"That's not it at all! I thought about this all morning. The Moon is not our home. We don't belong there!"

"What?" His head hurt, crammed with equations, angles, figures, costs. Somewhat shortly, John said, "That makes as much sense as saying God would have given us wings if he'd meant for us to fly!"

"God," she said stiffly, "the Creator, put us on this Earth with the living land, the plants and animals and birds, and the seas."

He recognized Ramona's Indian oscillation. Her Indian identity peaked when white society in general or he in particular bothered her. When and if Indians bothered her she would go the other way. She had been raised in Oakland, California, mixed blood and mixed-up identity. "Honey," John said, "be reasonable. Your work helps keep the Spaceplane flying, and you're very proud of it!"

"It goes and it comes back. The Moon is—maybe it's different for white people," she said sternly. "For white men! You've always been cut off from nature, from the land, leaving Europe where your ancestors lived and died, and then moving in on us over here—and wasting the environment!"

He objected. "Don't blame me for that!"

"Land—you see, it's holy. Where you live, and who you live with, like the ecosystem. The Moon is alien land. It's lifeless. It can't be related to."

"Look," John said in exasperation, "The Moon is beside the point. The project is grounded!"

"Not if you can help it!" She gestured at the pocketcomputer. It perched beside his breakfast plate on the table, working, tiny icons flashing. "I know you. I thought you knew me, who I am. You even read the books I asked you to. Can't you see that moving to the Moon isn't an Indian thing to do?"

He could have cited the Mohawk construction workers on the girders of the L-5 base, or the Navajo slated to go to Mars. Then the phone beeped urgently. He did not need the Indian Oscillation, not TODAY. He snapped, "You're not really an Indian," and turned toward the phone.

John found Phil Taylor's craggy face on the screen. "Schropfer comes in on the Frigatebird at two and you're the welcoming committee."

Ramona heard that. So John left without saying anything more.

Puffy, thundery, showery clouds dotted the sky now. More flyable than old Shuttle, the spaceplane weaved between the clouds, heavy and graceful. A sonic boom rolled across the coast. The clouds and the sky and the plane made a striking scene and John automatically wished for Ramona to see it too. Then he remembered that he had left the house on a damnably bad note.

Touching down, the spaceplane screeched to a halt. Attendant mechanics rushed to it. John waited. After a while Schropfer emerged, staggering under the impact of the gravity of Earth. The robot shuttlevan whisked them to the main conference building. By then a cool downdraft whipped across the mall. Schropfer paused. Owlishly he contemplated the thunderheads in the wide sky. "One misses weather."

They got as far as the main auditorium before Schropfer had to sit down. Karl still presided, more disheveled than yesterday. He addressed the fresh footage of the search operation on the monitor. The divers had found a booster rocket engine, very interestingly mangled. "Engine in cold water," Schropfer grunted. "Contractor in hot. Help me up, I seem to have sat down in a gravity well!"

They found the small out-of-the-way conference room, and the rest of the executive committee of the Space Radio Astronomy Consortium waiting there, with one exception. Baltazar had managed to miss his flight from Ithaca. Two members had flown in from Green Bank. The last two attended in the form of faces on visiphone screens. Their research had taken them to VLBA Pacifica.

With something of the air of a physician arrived at the hospital waiting room to talk to the anxious relatives of an accident victim, Schropfer said, "Six months to troubleshoot the vehicle. Six more to fix it. Another one point five years to get the L-5 backlog out of the way. Add six months for nonspecific snags and bad luck. There's my guess. And I guess good." With that, Schropfer tottered to a chair and collapsed into it.

His prognosis precipitated a round of ventilation.

The Very Large Array in New Mexico lay in ruins for lack of funding. Ancient Arecibo was still creaking along. A few other ground-located radio telescopes retained some degree of viability, most notably the several Very Long Baseline Arrays strung across the most uninhabited quarters of the globe. But radio-frequency communications and noise saturated the Earth nowadays, a miasma that meant the extinction of ground-based radio astronomy. The science had to move to space. Promises to that effect had been made by the government.

"Think of government promises as paper currency," said Schropfer. "Worth as much, or as little, as the government decides in its infinite lack of wisdom. Space installations will happen. Not as soon as we planned. Jen, Zhuxai. I overheard a resounding thud last night. It was Tiger Lily hitting the bottom of the priority list."

"Damn it all!" Jennifer exclaimed. "How many delays have there been already?" Her Chinese colleage looked glum.

The Chinese had been launching satellites for long-wavelength radio astronomy: the Spider Lily series, bundles of wire that bloomed into receivers for the radio waves meters long. Simple instruments, but effective, as very low frequency radio astronomy had never been doable on Earth at all. Long radio waves from the cosmos bounced off the Earth's ionosphere. After the Spider Lilies the next projected step had been a vast deepspace antenna, a cooperative venture of American and Chinese scientific interests, to be constructed within the next five years. It would have been called Tiger Lily. On the verge of crying, Jen said, "I don't want to read about it in the |Astrophysical Journal~ when I'm eighty years old!"

Standing by the window and watching a thundershower in progress, John brooded. He kept himself physically fit. But he had been thirteen for Apollo 11 and thirty for Challenger and had now passed fifty. If the Lunar Array slid many more years, John would develop heart disease like Phil Taylor, or some other infirmity of advancing age, and be grounded too.

Schropfer finally said, "It's the L-5 station, meaning industry and glamor, versus little science 'uns like us. Any bets as to who'll fall out the back end of the wagon? No? OK." He fidgeted, seemingly finding the chair too hard on a backside that had gotten used to the Space Station's low gravity. "Now, we happen to have that one thing going for us. We're small. We might manage to leapfrog AHEAD of the L-5 parts and parcels. Which is why I came right down without benefit of reacclimitization in the centrifuge upstairs." He jerked at his shirt collar, loosening it. "They probably shouldn't let fat middle-aged bureaucrats shortcut the process like that," he added.

"Leapfrog how?" John asked quietly.

"Downsize to where we don't displace enough payload to bother anybody."

There were noises of consternation. "We're bare bones already!" said Phil.

"So we shake down the bones. Viz, do we really need a superconducting supercomputer? Cooling shell's too damn heavy."

"Do we need an inhabited site at all or will an automatic facility do the job. That's the ultimate reduction, isn't it?" said John. No larking on the Moon, just streams of data relayed through a lunisynchronous satellite.

"I don't like this," said Kris, from Easter Island. The connection seemed to be getting worse. The screen snowed and made her words hard to understand. "Downsizing, cutting corners, automating. Is it really necessary?"

"Damn right," said Schropfer, "While the government's commitment to radio astronomy is still worth something. There's a round of inflation coming on, mark my words. More promises meaning less."

Outside the rain had stopped. The damp green contours of the landscaping framed an oval lake. One small tern circled over the lake. At intervals the bird precipitously dived into the water and reemerged in a flash of wings, with a minnow in its bill.

For the rest of the day the tern stayed on his mind, a twisting little bundle of guilt, circling, abruptly plunging little shocks of pain into his soul. He finally got home after dark. Looking into the bedroom, he found Ramona sleeping. John leaned heavily against the side of the door.

The tangle of her long brown hair told him that she had been restless before falling asleep. The sheets were tangled around her body, too. He wanted to wake her up, make love to her. But that would be unfair—more like an act of hostility. She had to be at work at the Center by 7 AM. John left the house and headed for the beach. There he walked south toward the glittering hotels of Cocoa Beach. Over the sea, some moonlight leaked through clotted cloud cover. The Big Dipper lowered, in the west, over the lights of the city of Cape Canaveral.

He had not changed clothes. His tie dangled from the pocket into which he had stuffed it. He held his dress shoes by the fingers of one hand. Absentmindedly he strayed close enough for a wave to catch his bare feet. It got the hems of his slacks wet. Ghost crabs scuttled across the sand, as soundless and erratic as uneasy thoughts.

Ever since childhood and Apollo, he had wanted to go into space, to touch a strange other world: if not a gloryridden moon of Jupiter or Saturn, then at least the Moon of the Earth. He would have gone as readily after Challenger as before. But by then it had become clear that he would never be an astronaut. He became an astronomer instead.

The Moon hung over the sea, gibbous. The terminator, sunlight's edge, seemed to follow the contours of the craters. In that bright imperfect Moon, the past, future, his dreams and reality fused: to create a radio telescope on the far side of the Moon, shielded by the Moon itself from the radio noise of Earth. To go into space, only as far as the Moon, and all the way to the most distant radio galaxies. It was doable after all. Because it did not have to be an Array.

He went home and turned on the computer. With it, he connected to the national space science data base.

Ramona came into the study. "It's 3 AM."

"Did I disturb you?"

"No. I just woke up."

Loosely wrapped in her bathrobe, she looked worn out and vulnerable. John remembered the tern. "Ramona, I was thoughtless on Friday and inexcusably cruel today. I am sorry."

Eyes wide and dark, she answered, "But you were right. Indians belong. Somewhere. I've moved all my life, California, Minnesota, Florida. I don't belong to anywhere. A little to Europe. A little to Apacheria except it doesn't exist anymore. I mean, the only sense of home I've got, is nature, the Earth." She let him embrace her, as she said, "Don't tell me to leave!"

"I'm sorry."

"Can I ask, not tell, ask you, not to go, or maybe not forever?!"

"Maybe not forever," he said, and held her tighter. "It's something I have to do."

She sighed, he felt it, almost a shudder. "Why?"

She did not want a rational answer. He could not think of any other that would be real to her.

———

At 8 AM John returned to the Consortium's meeting room, clutching a cup of coffee. He had the bad-night, awake-by-virtue-of-caffeine shakes. No doubt many other people at the Center did too, today, only three days after the Argosy failure.

Schropfer listed downsizing measures. COMPUTER. He starred that. "No superconducting supercomputer for us!"

Phil Taylor said, "I hate to tell the able-bodied what to do. But husbands or wives on site. None."

The dryerase marker squeaked. "Plural of spouse. Appropriately." NO SPICE. Schropfer starred that one too.

"Mine won't go to the Moon anyway," said John.

Schropfer grunted. Then he wrote SPECS on the board. He handed out computer printouts. "Here's my compilation of what we discussed yesterday. Degrading the technical specifications."

John refused his copy. "No. That's what got Argosy into the water in pieces."

"What else can we do?" Schropfer shot back.

"Try no array."

"I beg your pardon?"

"What else? A ham radio?" demanded Baltazar. In rumpled and somewhat mismatched clothing, he had just made it in from Ithaca. He seemed distraught about the Argosy affair. Yet Baltazar, at thirty years of age the youngest member of the Consortium's executive committee, could wait longer than any of the rest of them, if it came to that.

"Jen, we could string wire out in several directions, on the surface of the Moon. Just by sending people out with spools. Your long wavelengths don't need an instrument more exacting than that!" John spoke rapidly.

Schropfer looked sturdier today. Schropfer looked quizzical. "You want me to tell Washington we'll build the Tiger Lily space antenna on the Moon, by hand?"

"Not around an existing base," said Jen. "I thought about something like that. But the bases all have people trouping around, prospecting geologists if not fullblown mining operations. And VIP tourists even!" She snorted.

John said, "First—Zhuxai, your backers in the People's Republic, how would they react?"

"They can relate to doing things so simply!" The Chinese astronomer nodded vigorously.

Phil Taylor looked discontented. "The Lunar Array turns into a mess of wire for low frequency studies?"

"It's better than nothing!" Jen retorted.

Baltazar groaned aloud, as if in pain. "That's just too peripheral!"

Schropfer said, "That does leave the rest of the radio spectrum!"

"No. Wait. Throw out the VLA model," John said. "Use Arecibo instead. Pick a sturdy crater. South of the Moon's equator—we'd like a good look at the galactic center. Build a dish in the crater, and a moveable feed in the dish. The gravity's so low that the feed can be more mobile than Arecibo's. Catch a bigger portion of the universe."

"Old ideas," Phil said flatly.

"Yeah." John held up a slim sheaf of papers. "At least as old as this article I dug up. Workshop proceedings. 1986."

Schropfer said, "Hells bells. Old ideas, but they're good as new. Never been used."

"Still . . . " said Phil.

"Phil. It'd be a beginning. Mapping fainter structures of the universe that we've never even seen before. Plus studying the very low frequencies on the other side of ten megahertz. We can string the wire for that near, or around, the dish, something like that, and manage not to trip over it, at least not too often. Then someday—the Array will get built."

"Hm!" Schropfer whipped out a pocketcomputer. His stylus scurried over the tiny keys. "No tracks. No six or eight separate freestanding dishes on said track. Less need for data crunching if it's not interferometric. Very low frequency studies as a bonus." The tiny computer spat out a strip of paper. Schropfer studied the figures on it, with dawning approval. "Construction phase will be shorter. Significantly!"

"But there was stuff we had planned, we need a large array," said Phil. The Lunar Radio Array had been his idea, ten years ago. "An interferometer does all a single dish does and better. The detail that an interferometer registers . . . " Kris and Elliot seemed less than thrilled. Baltazar ran his hand through his hair, which then stood on end desperately.

"The window for radio astronomy is being closed on us," said Schropfer. "Not by nature but by politics with some bad engineering mixed in." He sounded utterly serious. "We've got to get something shoved through the window fast. Remember what happened to the planetary scientists before the turn of the century? They got stuck with a thirteen-year gap between probes. But at least they had the Voyagers out there. And that turned out to be a hell of a lot better than nothing."

John and Jen and Phil nodded.

Indians did not care much for Thanksgiving, she said. They spent that day at Merritt Island National Wildlife Refuge instead. Early in the cold clear morning, he drove the car on a dirt road past ditches and marshes alive with birds, flocks and masses of them.

He had been in Houston, training, for the past two months. He had missed Ramona desperately. Today she looked much as she had when they first dated, wearing old neat jeans and a flannel shirt, and watching the world in general and birds in particular with serious attentive eyes. Years older than then, though, she had silver threads in the brown hair at her temples, and lines of character on her face.

"How long exactly?"

"Exactly two weeks," John said with difficulty, "until I fly out on the Frigatebird."

"It'll be a busy two weeks, I bet," she said quietly.

She was right. John had this last chance, this day, to make a separate peace with her. He wanted more. He wanted a viable marriage. Not exactly May-December, but June and November. Science and nature, man and woman. He did not know how to balance the equation. The tension on both sides made it hard to talk at all. "How've you been doing?"

She reflected. "OK. Work's been good to me. And people have been sympathetic—not critical of me or you either—they understand why I'm staying, and you have to go to work on the dark side of the moon. Oops. Far side."

"The far side is the dark side of the moon, as far as the radio noise of Earth is concerned."

He parked the car. They got out to walk on the trail toward the marsh observation tower. A mixed flock of ducks dabbled on a pond beside the trail. Duck tails stuck out of the water at various angles. How long had it been since they went birding together? Too long for an activity that he liked and she loved.

Together they climbed the tall, sturdy wooden tower. Enough of wind blew through it to make them shiver. On every side the land and water teemed with birds, flocking, wading, feeding, noisily pleased with life on this fall morning. Ramona scanned the marshes with her binoculars. "Ooh! Ducks and herons all over the place. And I see a wood stork."

At least he had not forgotten how to keep the company of an avid birder. Patiently, he listened to her report discoveries which, without binoculars and knowledge like hers, looked hardly less anonymous than pills on a gray/green/brown wool rug.

Distant launch towers and the venerable Vehicle Assembly Building cropped up on the otherwise featureless horizon. They were rebuilding Argosy in there. Next time around, the booster rockets, having been redesigned as they should have been made in the first place, would work right. The sky over the VAB was wide and clear, a sea of cool air.

John caught sight of a high and distant dot. It angled closer, a swift bird with backswept wings, wings that sliced the sea of air as effectively as the flukes of a dolphin in its own element. He put a hand on Ramona's shoulder. "Two o' clock high. Is that a falcon?"

"Oh—! John! It IS!" The raptor charged lower, higher, hunting breakfast. Galvanized, Ramona tracked it. John admired the falcon. He admired the curve of Ramona's back when the bird had spiraled out of sight of his unaided eyes.

They returned to the car. "Only my third peregrine!" Ramona sighed happily.

"It's a good sign." Starting the car, John activated the heater. Mentally he began to organize words. He hoped that premeditation would not invalidate what he intended to say.

The nude bathing season was decisively over, the beach, at this hour, thinly populated with well-clad walkers like themselves. The underlying tension of the day propelled them all the way to the local landmark, what remained of a wooden barge. It had wrecked years ago. Broken, sea-worn and barnacle-ridden, the artefact of transportation technology was dissolving back into nature.

Ramona attached her binoculars to a distant speck of bird over the sea. It might be a gannet, she announced. The prospect absorbed her. John scanned the shore's white curve to the south, the Cape. He studied the barge, the sands and the wrack of the sea. Finally, he took a deep breath to steady his nerves. "Do gannets migrate?"

She nodded. "They summer near Nova Scotia—in absolute droves."

"The falcon was migrating down the coast. Wasn't it?"

"Um-hm."

"Can we talk?"

Ramona took him by the hand and led him to a big chunk of driftwood. They sat there and huddled with each other against the wind from the sea.

He said, "I don't know if I'll like—even be able to stand—being there. I won't be doing my science, either. I've got to see that they get the dish built right, so the science will be doable!" He brought her hand, which felt cold, into the warmth of his jacket. "You once asked me why I had to go." Without further preamble he plunged into what he had been planning to say. "Imagine this. Sea creatures wandered onto the land and breathed air. They learned to walk and run and regulate body temperature. Then they ventured into the air. They flew. And mastered the air. Became the falcon."

She listened.

The surf broke around the remains of the old barge, billowed through a hole in the wood, sparkling in the sun. John wondered if dolphins had seen the old wreck happen. "Dolphins too. One kind of airbreather went back to the sea again. And there they wander and wonder still . . . . You're right: they know what launches mean."

Ramona nodded. They were on the same wavelength today. That had not been the case for months.

"Even plants peregrinate. They managed to colonize the land when it was barren as the Moon! Maybe we, men, Europeans, don't always wander because we're apart from nature. Sometimes it's because we're a part of it!"

He had moved close to her world now, as near to her reality as he had ever found himself. Then he briefly stepped into it. "Maybe it's even more primeval than that. The Creator made us all wanderers."

That statement, coming from him, surprised her. Ramona sat still for a while and watched the waves. "Then it's holy."

As lightly, John stepped out of hers and back into his own view of reality. "It's—non-trivial, most definitely. I was having strange dreams in Houston. Some of 'em scared me."

"Tell me?"

He remembered tangled skeins of dreaming, about spacecraft and radio telescopes, some of it nightmarish: explosion in the blue sky, a wreath floating on green water; or narrow gray confines of a metal habitat blending into the wide gray moonscape, unrelenting gray with no reprieve of green or blue. Chromatic claustrophobia. On the other hand, he had dreamed, not unpleasantly, about the L-5 space base.

"L-5? Why so?"

"I'm going to be doing an oscillation—spending a week in L-5 for every three on the Moon—so the body doesn't forget about full Earth gravity."

Four pelicans flew over the dunes, graceful big brown birds, in the sway of Earth's gravity, but not trammeled by it.

"By the way," said John. "The setback with Argosy scared them. The line of supply to L-5 got a hellacious kink in it then. They were rationing tools and food and even air for a while. It was uncomfortable. Now they're planning to shift the base toward self-contained, autonomous ecosystem. Plants and all. —I hear somebody sent some Wandering Jew up on a Titan VII among their personal effects. The stuff survived getting flattened by 12 g's. Now it's thriving."

Ramona laughed lightly. "That kind of plant would!"

"They really are planning to ecosystematize L-5. Plants, fruits, vegetables. Aquaculture maybe—fish farming. And they may even factor in some pretty fish, and apple trees, and birds," he said. "Because people like them. It'll be something of an aquarium in space, a miniature ecosphere."

"You think people are smart enough to make it work?"

"Maybe. It's worth a try."

"You're right."

"I started dreaming about flying. Like a bird."

"Flying?"

"Sure. The L-5 structure really is big. Gravity ranges all the way from zero to Earth full. And there's recreational space in the middle. Room to fly, to somersault, to tumble. People love it. I talked to some who've been there."

"I've always had dreams like that," she said wistfully. "Flying like a bird! Dreams where it takes work to get up off the ground, but then I'm up, I'm flying over things. Even under things like clotheslines and bridges."

"I remember, you told me about your flying dreams once. When I woke up from mine—I thought you'd like doing that. Would you?"

She looked at him, sharply. "That outfit is going to be impossible to get into unless you know somebody AND are extremely qualified!"

"You do," he said dryly. "And you are. They need good technicians. And people with green thumbs."

"Are you serious?"

"As serious as I've ever been in my life! In Houston, I developed some connections. You can come to L-5. I would be with you for one week out of four, at least. Maybe more when the project goes well. From L-5 you could see the Earth, as well as the Moon and the stars."

Ramona blinked. "But—what about the house?"

"Jen's niece just landed a job at the Center and needs a place to live. She'd be happy to rent our house. Very nice, responsible young woman. An engineer."

"Oh my, you've thought of everything."

"I tried. But I'm not telling you what to do. I'm asking. Please come to space with me."

She watched the sea. She pointed out three small shorebirds, busy on their toothpick legs, with white bellies and a marbling of gray at the throat. Turnstones, whose fragile wings had brought them from the Alaskan Arctic for the winter. "You're right about the Creator's wanderers, although I'm not sure that you believe what you said. Yet. Anyway it's true." Then Ramona said, "But the dolphins came back to the sea. So did these birds."

John's free hand was curled in a jacket pocket, together with something damp and sandy. He pulled it out. "I found this on the beach—while you were watching the gannet." He offered her a calico scallop shell, unbroken, white shell with purple tracery. "I, or if you go too, we, will come back. I promise you that."

Her hand folded around his fingers and the shell. She smiled. Then she tilted his hand to look at his wristwatch. "Can we watch a Frigatebird now?"

They turned to face the Cape to the south, and waited.

"Hmm. Maybe it's running late."

"My Bird never runs late," she said firmly. "At least not for technical reasons."

"OK. My watch is fast."

It made a dramatic appearance. The big, dark, flat plane charged out over the sea. Ponderous but capable, it climbed into the sky. A wave of sound, the roar of the ramjet-engines, broke over the beach,

Laughing, Ramona decided. She hugged and kissed him. "I will go too!"

Sharing her binoculars, they succeeded in seeing the rocket flare when the scramjet came on. It traced a thin bright arc in the sky. Riding fire, the Spaceplane angled up toward the margin of the ocean of air.

THE LISTENING-GLASS

This story was first published in the February 1991 issue of *Analog Science Fiction and Fact*. It's a sequel to the preceding story, "Wanderers," and like that one, it is now alternate history. But not by as much!

Because I'm not an astronomer myself, I did a great deal of research in writing The Listening-Glass. Even more important, I posed questions to scientist friends. These included Marc R. Hairston and Sedge L. Simons, both of whom have Ph.D.'s in Space Physics from Rice University. And both of whom have great imaginations.

My most invaluable consultant was Dr. Linda Dressel, then on the faculty at Rice University and later with the Space Telescope Science Institute. She is a radio astronomer who has worked at the big radio dish in Arecibo, Puerto Rico.

She helped me move Arecibo to the Moon.

On the Moon as on Earth, people make mistakes, sometimes with disastrous consequences. We humans are very fallible beings. The final outcome of a mistake, though, depends on what we do next.

Acrophobia. It always hit him here, midway on the catwalk. He let his gloves slide along the guidewires. Within the bulky gloves his palms sweated profusely. Ahead of him and even higher up, the catwalk ended at the antenna suspended on the convergence of three sets of immensely long cables. There was nothing under the antenna. Nothing. Hard vacuum, underlined with a thin, curved shell of material that gleamed coldly in the downward periphery of his vision. He dared not look down. If he did he would freeze.

The antenna's present position left too much slack in the catwalk for his liking. Every step caused a ripple to propagate up the catwalk ahead of his boots. In the confines of his suit helmet, his breathing sounded too quick and ragged. He tore his eyes away from the alarming frailty of the catwalk and fixed them on the motionless horizon, the tangle of crater rims on the dark gray edge of the world. The horizon reminded him that this was the Moon. It had only one-sixth of the gravity of Earth. Fact: the catwalk was rated to carry twice the mass represented by himself plus spacesuit. Doggedly he kept going.

The antenna resembled a large leggy spider, hanging upside down on flimsy strands of web. Appearances were deceiving on the Moon. The cables could easily support the antenna plus a work crew in spacesuits. Had done so during the construction phase. Making the structure sturdy enough for Earth gravity would have been over-designing to a ludicrous extent. Nevertheless, he was acutely aware of the vertical vacuum under the antenna, exceeding the height of the towering rocket that brought the first men to the Moon five decades ago. He made a quick and rather morbid mental calculation. You could stack one and a half Saturn Fives under the antenna.

His mouth felt very dry. And he detested the scratchy inorganic tang on his tongue. He could taste the gray indifference of this world. The acrophobia had never been this bad before. But then he'd never gone up to the antenna alone. At night. Stars, unsympathetic, icily burning, filled the black sky. Starlight thousands of years old rained down, and it pooled far below his feet. He resisted the urge to look down into the vast, cold, mesmerizing shimmer of it. People could freeze up here, in such a paralytic state of fright that somebody had to come up and retrieve them. He could, and probably should, turn around, go back to the habitat, and not mention this abortive excursion. No. Take another step, another, another: he was not going to let the acrophobia get to him.

This trip up to the antenna seemed to be taking a lifetime, as if the catwalk were as long as his life span. In a way, it was.

The catwalk began in the fifth grade, to be exact, with a report card that included a glaring D in Science. Bright and bored in classes taught by mediocre teachers to pupils of average intelligence, he had been indifferent to grades. But the D stung. The class started an astronomy unit. Reports were assigned, prepared, presented. The others read silly little pages about The Moon or The Planet Jupiter—childish, inept transcriptions from the encyclopedia. But he really researched his topic, at the public library. In front of the class, he drew a line down the whole length of the chalkboard to represent the electromagnetic spectrum; he showed them the small fraction of the spectrum taken up by visible light, and the far greater span of radio. He explained how radio telescopes revealed the invisible mysteries of the universe. He showed them. The next report card featured an A-plus in Science. And he had done astronomy ever since, from the backyard telescope to the vast machine on which he treaded now.

He checked his position. Fifty feet from where the catwalk ended at the antenna. The antenna was mobile within a volume of space of some hundreds of cubic meters. And when it moved, the end of the catwalk moved with it. Of course he had put the safety switch on. Hadn't he? He should not have thought about that. He froze. The moonsuit had a radio. Maybe he should tell someone what he was up to. His throat constricted. He felt his motor muscles congealing too.

With an angry act of will, he started going again. He reached the antenna platform.

Then he let it happen, impulsively looked down, through the grate of the platform floor, and past the wide wheel with the azimuth arm hanging on it; down, into the crater full of radio telescope. The edge of it marked an immense circle like an inverse horizon. Triumphant and vertiginous, he clung to the platform's guard rail. The last steps were the hardest. It was just that simple.

There had been dreary years of delay, constipation of funds, and design compromise. And then the last and hardest part. Construction. The fact that the site was on the far side of the Moon had amplified every difficulty, every mistake, by at least an order of magnitude. But now it was finished, real, and ready to be tested, first thing tomorrow. He had come up here tonight to make sure that one last detail was put right before the big day. As a manager, people said, he was too detail-oriented.

In the center of the platform stood a dog-house sized metal box which housed the equipment, which contained the detail that he was after. Making himself let go of the rail, he strode toward the housing. There was nothing to hold onto between the guardrail and the equipment housing.

Then he noticed the lights on the corners of the platform. They flashed a red warning strobe. *The antenna was being repositioned.* Shocked, he stared. It wasn't supposed to happen with someone up here! But the structure slewed under his feet. He made a panic lunge, launched himself toward the equipment housing.

Colliding with the housing, he failed to secure a handhold on the slick box, and ricocheted off. The platform dropped underneath him. He could not find stopping traction as he skidded toward the far edge of the platform. Desperately he grabbed at the guardrail, with the full force of his Earth-powered muscles, misdirected. He reached too high and jackknifed over the rail. He flailed. Then he started falling.

The azimuth arm wheeled around. It went by at the limits of his desperate reach; his glove brushed the metal frame. The arm moved away. He tumbled. Across his sight swung the azimuth arm's wheel, stars, the silver chasm of dish.

He fell slowly and realized it. A hammer and a feather have the same acceleration on the Moon and so does a man falling to his death. He had time to think. Not necessarily death. If the dish stopped him cold, it would definitely kill him. If the dish broke instantly, it would barely slow him down, and hitting the crater floor would kill him. But if the dish broke slowly it might actually break his fall.

The sides of the dish rose up with the ominous leisure of a mounting tidal wave. Just before the wave broke, he tried to fold the bulky spacesuit, cannonball, as though he were falling into a net.

His swaddled shoulder took the impact. The shocked dish gave way, slowly. Then it tore, letting him drop to the crater floor. He hit the floor bone-bruisingly hard, bounced, and finally sprawled on his back.

To his surprise, he was not dead. But he had the wind knocked out of him. He gasped for air. From the jagged hole in the dish above him, fragments drifted down, tumbling. He couldn't breathe. Darkness with red veins closed in on him. Faintly he heard a clamor in his suit radio. "John! John!!" Somebody sounded hysterical. He tried to answer. All he could get out was a broken wheeze.

The ongoing clamor in his ears bothered John. Garbled words. Verbal static. Finally, something intelligible. "ETA twenty minutes. Keep the victim immobile."

"Roger, Yuegong Base, hurry!"

He took inventory of his body. Dull pain here and there. He rolled over with a pained grunt.

A young man jumped in front of John and he recognized Edward. The computer engineer. Edward waved his hands. "Don't move!"

There was a woman whirling away from the radio station where she had been standing. He knew her too. Jennifer said, "Good Lord!"

"Good morning," he said thickly. "Tell 'em to turn back. I'm all right." With an effort, John sat up.

Edward pleaded, "Please don't move!"

John tried an exaggerated shrug, then rolled his head. Didn't feel too bad, considering. If this had been Earth and Earth's weighty gravity, he would have been dead.

Jennifer hurried over. "Lie back down! You're hurt even if you don't have enough sense to know it!"

"I want to know who moved the antenna," he said.

"I'm terribly sorry!" Edward blurted. "Your colleague sent a message saying that it was very important to look at the supernova right away without even waiting for tomorrow morning, so I entered the coordinates, I didn't know you were up there!!"

"What colleague?"

"Baltazar," said Jennifer. "Just what were you doing up there?"

"What supernova?" John asked.

"You forgot to put the safety on."

John frowned. "I put it on."

"The antenna won't move with the safety on."

"I put it on! Edward, check the safety switch!"

"Yes sir." Edward scuttled to the control panel. He called back, "It's on!" A very young, very honest man, he went on to say, "This is my fault too—I never once thought to test the safety switch circuit!"

"Not your job," John said.

"Oh, but I should have—"

"No, not you." Jennifer shook her head. "So it's faulty. What a way to find out."

Vindicated, John swung his feet around. They had deposited him on the overnight cot here in the control room. His moonsuit lay in the corner, sadly dirty and disassembled. Jennifer's Chinese colleague, Zheng, crouched there, staring at the suit. The drift of his thoughts was easy to guess. Scuffs and scrapes marred the moonsuit's outer fabric. The cranium of the helmet had a terrible dent in it. John felt a strange internal quiver that must have been a shudder. Anxiously he inventoried his body once more. All dull pains, except one tiny sharp one needling the base of his head. "I'm OK," he said shakily. "You can all go to bed or whatever."

"Not after having the living daylights scared out of us like this!"

Jen retorted, and she added, "This isn't some hotel to go sauntering around alone at night, you old fool!"

That wasn't fair. He hadn't been sauntering. And she had as many gray hairs as he did.

She refused to tell the medical rescue team from Yuegong Base to turn back.

The team, two men, thundered in through the airlock with a medivac cocoon, ready to stuff an unconscious victim into it and bundle him away. John pointed out that he could move all of his limbs and digits and felt basically intact.

The doctor, with the red cross on the arm of his coverall, frowned. "Internal injuries are very deceptive under conditions of low gravity. You need to be examined in the hospital."

"Take him!" Jennifer said emphatically.

At least they let him sit up, belted into a cramped seat behind the pilot. Moondust sprayed past the porthole at his shoulder as the moonhopper took off. The dust cleared as the hopper gained altitude. Then he could see Sand Lake with its rim wall around a wide pale plain. There lay a patch of silver threads, an incongruous cross-stitch on the hoop of lunar plain: the Lunar Far-Side Very Low Frequency Array, LFSVLFA, Jennifer's project.

The hopper looped around to its intended course. John glimpsed the radio dish, filling the crater Bolton on the edge of Sand Lake. He ought to have been inspecting the damage instead of going to the hospital at Yuegong Base.

Sure he was sick. Sick of Sand Lake, sick of the hardscrabble living conditions here. Sick of the Bolton dish. It had been a mistake on his part move up into management. A big mistake to take over the project manager's job when Phil Taylor was disqualified by a heart condition. If it had been Phil today, taking that heart-stopping fall, the hopper would be ferrying a corpse back to Yuegong Base.

Less busy now, the pilot called back, hospitably, "Anybody want a Lifesaver?"

"Bad for your teeth," the doctor disapproved.

"Good for the dustmouth," the pilot rejoined, amiably.

"Thanks." Carefully John extracted one piece from the battered roll. Cherry. He welcomed it to mask the bitter tang of failure in his mouth.

The giant crater Schrödinger rolled under the moonhopper. Sand Lake was a detail in the rough rim of Schrödinger, just as Bolton pocked the edge of Sand Lake. The far side of the Moon: big holes have little ones cratered in to blight them, little ones have lesser ones, and so ad infinitum. A short while later, the hopper passed the unmistakable ringed plain Humboldt. Something flashed in Humboldt like pale green heat lightning. A moonflash, lunar rock that sparked as it cooled off after the long hot day.

Below and ahead of the hopper, the terminator, the edge of the day, threw the moonscape into vivid relief, craters dark, rims bright. The crawling terminator would take four weeks to make it around the Moon back to this place. The hopper easily overtook and left it behind. The sun glared in John's porthole. He pulled down the sun filter. In the hopper's wide cockpit window, the airless sky was black as ever over the sunlit horizon. The arc of horizon featured a wide shallow depression, the profile of the Sea of Crises.

"There she blows!" the pilot sang out. And then the Earth rose out of Crisium. The edge of night bowed from pole to pole; day was a crescent of brilliant, glazed blue. The home planet hung on the Moon's stars as lightly as a Christmas ornament in a tree. John started to cry.

The other two men had fallen silent. Fingers pressed to the corners of his eyes, John squelched the tears. He heard a pen scratching on paper. The doctor. Making notes.

The pilot took it upon himself to dispel the awkward silence. "Ever read the book *Voyager*? About the first plane to fly around the world?"

"As a matter of fact, yes," John managed to answer in an even tone.

"That's my all-time favorite book," said the pilot. They were traversing the Sea of Crises now, with the beautiful blue globe of Earth ascendant in the cockpit window. "I always think about that when I see the Earth up there. They flew around the world—around that!" The pilot waved a hand at the Earth. "Nine days, one tank of gas, no stopping, right by one typhoon and over the mountains of Africa, and everything.—I see a typhoon up there now."

The hopper skirted Serenity, and then began the final approach to its destination. Skillfully the pilot swooped over the rill and the mountain both named Hadley. A glint of sunlight marked the Apollo 15 Memorial. It was a very long way down. Fear of falling clenched John's stomach with a vengeance.

The radio crackled on with the information that a squad of paramedics would meet the hopper at the port. What was the status of the victim?

"Not to worry," the pilot replied. "There's nothing really wrong with him that a few days of Earthshine won't cure."

"They want my opinion, not yours," said the doctor, icily.

"Hey, I know what I'm talking about. I been on the Moon for two years and you just got here!" said the pilot, and nodded to John. "See ya around."

The doctor ordered a complete physical examination. John felt tired. He just wanted to rest. Instead he was stripped and prodded and sampled, while his examiners talked in grave undertones about multiple contusions. Meaning bruises.

John had to argue for permission to make a call out. This is like jail, he thought grimly, one phone call if you insist. Finally they let him use the hospital uplink. He got a connection to Washington, DC, USA, Earth, with the bill for it to be sent to the Space Radio Astronomy Consortium. SPARAC's budget was tight, and the call would have to be held to a few minutes, no more. No problem. What he had to tell the Consortium's executive director was short and not sweet.

"I don't believe this!" was Schropfer's initial reaction. "There's only one manmade structure on the Moon more than three hundred feet high, and you fall off it?!"

"I didn't expect the antenna to move under me!"

"Why didn't you just hang on?"

"I panicked," John grated. "What's this crap about a supernova, anyway?"

"There's a brand new one in the Magellanic clouds. Baltazar was beside himself with curiosity, and it occurred to him to try the Bolton dish on it."

John swore.

"He had my approval," Schropfer said mildly. "Would have been good PR, a nice headline. NEW LUNAR RADIO TELESCOPE STUDIES SUPERNOVA."

"What for?" John asked coldly.

"Good question. Baltazar prevailed upon VLBA America to take a look. But at a declination of minus 73 degrees, only the dishes in Hawaii and the Virgin Islands could pick it up at all, just over their southern horizon. The data was noisy.

"The Australia Telescope happens to be committed to a configuration incompatible with investigating the supernova. And VLBA Pacifica is all buttoned up because of a typhoon bearing down on Easter Island. That leaves Bolton. Which is in just the right place and ready for its first trial run."

"I'd like a full report on all this."

"I take it you haven't checked your email," said Schropfer.

"They won't let me out of the hospital tonight! They're wasting my time and theirs, because I feel fine—"

"A 591-foot fall is not trivial, my friend. Not even on the Moon."

"The dish absorbed most of the impact."

With a delay of two and a half seconds, the signal traveled to Earth and Schropfer's reply came back. Schropfer seemed to pause longer than that, though, before John finally heard him say, "That's too bad."

Being in the hospital offered one single advantage: hot showers. John rubbed a clear spot in the fogged bathroom mirror and inspected his contusions. Dark bruises blotched his back, with smaller and more painful yellow spots.

It was well past midnight, Moon Mean Time. That left just enough night for it to be a very bad one. He dozed off, felt himself falling, and jerked awake in a sweat, his heart fluttering. With a loud scuff of shoe soles on a floor with a high coefficient of friction, the nurse walked in to check on him. Finally, in the last hour or two, he slept. He dreamed about moon-gray dust spattered with the vivid red of blood.

In the morning they let him go. Still wearing the despicable plastic bracelet on his wrist, he left the hospital building. The skylight over Dave Scott Plaza framed the crescent Earth. He paused to admire Earth, and another pedestrian, presumably late and rushing to work, promptly ran into him. Suddenly John wondered whether his idiotic fall had been publicized. Did people here in Yuegong Base know all about it? The prospect mortified him. Breaking into a hot sweat, he hurried toward his office.

The office was an out-of-the-way cube of space shared with the staff of the Yuegong Sino-American Observatory. None of them had arrived for the day yet. He checked the clock. 8:13 A.M. Typical, he thought: astronomers tend not to exist at that hour of the morning. He found the report from Schropfer in his email inbox, and a video file from Ramona. Remembering one last roll of wintergreen candy, somewhere in his desk, he rummaged to find it. Then he viewed the video. He sat down and sucked on a piece of candy as watched his wife's image.

Her backdrop was recognizable girderwork, the bolted-together but unfinished interior of the big space station under construction at

Earth-Moon Lagrange Point Five. "Hi. I'm in the center of L-5 Station." She placed a pen in the air in front of her. It hovered with a slight slow drift. "No gravity. So I'm not going to be saying anything too serious!" She smiled, not with her lips but rather with her brown eyes. She had secured her long brown hair in Apache braids. Very much his Ramona. She retrieved the pen before it drifted away. "I have a friend I want to introduce you to. He's very nice."

Instantly, John felt a pang of jealousy.

Ramona whistled softly, "C'mere, sweetie!" Something fluttered into the picture. A bunch of highly active feathers. It attached itself to Ramona's proffered finger, and resolved into a parakeet, perched upside down relative to her. "This is my little friend Admiral. Admiral Bird!" Ramona declared. So much for jealousy. The bird wasn't even green, it was blue. Ramona gently turned her hand and the parakeet upright. "People thought birds would freak out in zero gravity. Not Admiral! He's learned how to fly here." The bird preened the feathers of one wing. "Humans can fly in zero g too. . . ." She finished with a shy glance and a curl of a smile.

He understood, and he longed for her. The last time he visited Ramona in L-5, she had taken him to a special corridor of the space station. Not finished or furnished, the management intended it to be a weightless art gallery at a future date. It had a picture window full of stars and Moon and shining Earth. Quite unofficially, it served the inhabitants of L-5 as Lover's Lane in zero g. Where, as Ramona put it, you could make love like the birds called white-throated swifts, which mate in the air, tumbling together as they fly in the canyons of the West.

She ended the video by saying, "I wish it wasn't three more weeks before you come to L-5 again. I love you and honor what you're doing. Make it work."

It was very quiet in the office. The resident astronomers had yet to appear. Odd. Enjoying the privacy, he read the report on the supernova.

Right ascension one hour, six minutes; declination minus seventy-three degrees. That put the supernova in the Small Magellanic Cloud and closer than any supernova since the 1987 event in the Large Magellanic Cloud. OK. An interesting object. But supernovas weren't great radio sources, not until well after the catastrophic fact.

In the case of SN 1987A (appended) the neutrino blast came first, then ultraviolet. Then the balefire blaze of visible light. Satellite observatories picked up x-radiation six months later and gamma rays right after that. Eleven years later came the first whisper of synchrotron radio emission, and the first radiograph of the supernova remnant was produced by the VLA, a blurry image of the clotted shell of matter thrown into space when the giant blue star exploded.

The detection of a pulsar had been announced in 1989. And retracted in 1990. The "pulsar" turned out to have been a fluke in the observing equipment at Cerro Tololo. The real thing had yet to be confirmed: thirty years and still no pulsar, though theory predicted that the supernova should have left one to mark its place.

Baltazar knew all of this, yet hadn't been able to wait even a day to have a look at this newest supernova!

The VLBA data was interesting in a Rorschach way—the human brain could imagine something significant in it. Much less imaginative, the VLBA supercomputer had not managed to massage the data into anything recognizable. Schropfer had been in management, fund-raising, begging for bucks, so long that he couldn't even make a sound scientific judgment anymore, John thought disgustedly. He rubbed his neck. There was a nagging twinge, a crick in his neck. It bothered him more than the soreness and stiffness of the remainder of his body.

Dec -73. Solidly in the Bolton reflector's observing swath on the celestial sphere. And RA 0106. The supernova had appeared near Bolton's zenith. Ironic: right now Bolton was in a great position to register the radio data that might take months and years to show up.

John called Schropfer again. "For what it's worth to look at the supernova, we can repair the dish," he said, without preamble. "Some segments fell out. But we have spares in case of micrometeorite hits."

Schropfer shook his head grimly. "Jen did a damage assessment, which I just got. It's worse than a hole. Two of the support pylons are buckled and the whole dish is sagging. As in, out of round. As in, inoperable!"

"Oh, no!"

"What did you expect? You're two hundred pounds on Earth, the suit's just about that much more, and I'm too upset right now to convert to newtons of force that hit the dish! How in the name of perdition am I going to meet the cost of replacing pylons?!"

In shock, John shook his head. The Space Radio Consortium subsisted on whatever money its member universities could spare. Plus funding that Schropfer elicited from government and the private sector. Building the Bolton dish had blown the seams of SPARAC's budget and, furthermore, had put SPARAC embarrassingly in debt to the SETI Society. Schropfer continued, "Yuegong Hospital sent me a report on you, too. I conclude that the worst damage to you is your ego. Too bad. It would have been cheaper to fix your bones than the bones of the dish!"

Thanks for the sympathy, John thought, you little son-of-a-bitch! He signed off curtly. The pain in the neck had a name now. Schropfer.

John's workstation chimed. There was Jen's report, just in. Twelve lines long. She didn't specify what did the damage. As if God or the impersonal universe had flicked something into the dish. She was very specific, though, about the extent of the damage. And the result. To function, the reflector had to have a perfect spherical curve. And now it didn't. It sagged. He felt sick.

John left the office. Rapidly he walked through the service tunnel toward Yuegong's moonport. Residual moon dust rasped underfoot. Half-formed in his mind was the idea of quitting. Just like that. Give up and walk away. And let Schropfer have the whole mess.

First he had to find out when the next shuttle to L-5 would be leaving Yuegong Base.

He happened to see the Port Director's administrative assistant before she saw him. He disliked her: brightly blonde and polished, she always smiled too much, insincerely and in the context of explaining why it would not be possible for the Port to meet some need on the part of the Sand Lake project immediately, or according the original schedule, or at all. He ducked into a hangar. Watching the woman walk by, he compared her to Ramona, very unfavorably.

A casually uniformed man approached, wiping his hands with a towel. "May we help you?"

"I'm—looking for one of the pilots." John remembered the name stenciled on the blue jumpsuit. "Cantu."

"Over there in the moonhopper. Bang on the side."

John went that way, vaguely framing his inquiry about transportation to L-5. It ought to sound casual, he thought. A sharp smell of hot glue permeated the hangar. As he walked on the floor he felt traces of something underfoot, not gray moon grit, but slick plastic powder. The moonhopper had every service hatch and access panel wide open, and parts were lined up on the floor. When John banged as directed, Cantu popped out of a hatch. "Hi! Doin' better? Did you know you almost had tons of company back at Sand Lake?"

"We did?"

"The observatory astronomers here. They went nuts. They would have gone right over to Sand Lake. Except it seems you don't have room for them yet, or the power supply, or the connections for their instruments."

"Not until Phase II," John murmured.

"So they hauled out to L-5."

Mired in Earth's tidal forces, always facing Earth, rotating on its own axis only once a month, it would take the Moon days to turn far enough for the supernova to be seen from Yuegong Base. That accounted for the lack of life in the observatory office.

Cantu asked, "Ready to go back to study the supernova?

Going to L-5 meant running away from his work and bumping

into other astronomers who had rushed to L-5 to follow theirs. So going to L-5 was not an option. Dislocated from the idea that brought him to the port, his thoughts tumbled.

"In case you're wondering, this vehicle isn't deceased, just having preventative maintenance!" Cantu affectionately whacked the hull of the hopper.

John registered the hollow thump. "That's not metal," he said. "Come to think of it, metal doesn't predominate in any of your space-craft and vehicles. Composite materials do."

"Huh? Oh, heck yeah. Fiber, resin, glass and glue is where it's at. The Rutan *Voyager* was the first aircraft," Cantu enthused, "to really exploit composite construction—otherwise no way they could have done it. Now everything in aerospace is like that."

Thinking hard, John spoke slowly. "I've got a problem. My radio telescope was damaged yesterday. It's not made of metal—here, that was neither necessary nor desirable. The understructure is a species of L-glass/thermoplastic composite."

"Sounds familiar."

"I've got to get it fixed right away, and I have an idea, involving glue, but I need a professional opinion."

"In that case, you were talking to the right guy in the first place!" Cantu whistled loudly. "Hey, Rod! That's Sylvester Rodriquez. A master mechanic. Don't call him grease monkey, more like glue! Come into the break room and I'll put on some coffee for us."

Later that afternoon, he made a call to Ramona. She was unavailable, at work in the white room where she was a senior technician. So he left a message. He felt awkward. The accident had left a bruise on his chin, somehow banged against the helmet. "Hi, love," he began. "I'm looking forward to meeting Admiral Bird. I'm in Yuegong Base right now because we had a problem with the dish yesterday. Right now— it's Friday 3 P.M.—I'm on my way back to Sand Lake. I will make the dish work." The last sentence came out with a vehemence that surprised him. Lamely he added, "I took a bit of a fall yesterday and —well, never mind, just a bruise or two. Have a good weekend up there. Bye." He wanted to say more. But not to the L-5 Technical Support Division's message machine.

Heavily laden this time, the moonhopper pitched up on the blast of its altitude jets. This time John rode shotgun, beside Cantu. He had a vertiginously good view of the lunar Apennine Mountains: a mosaic of intensely bright and dark shapes, geological chiaroscuro. Cantu flicked the jet controls. The hopper zoomed away toward the far side of the Moon.

Since yesterday, the terminator had moved further west, further from Sand Lake. Good. Temperatures would have settled down now, all cooled off, improving the chances of fixing the dish. "I really appreciate this," he said aloud. "I'm sure you guys could find a more entertaining way to spend your weekend, even in Yuegong Base."

Cantu laughed. "Supernovas don't happen all the time, and everybody in Yuegong's got the itch to see it. No way I'd pass up the chance to hear it." These men weren't European, Castilian, like Baltazar. Indian blood darkened their skin—reminding John of Ramona—and they had the kind of practical outlook that he had met in Mexican-American men before. "This job goes on my resume," said Rodriguez, from the back seat.

The hopper made the transit from sunlight to night. Glaring gray moonscape turned to silver, a soft bluish silver: Earthlight graced the maria and the crater rims. Magnificent desolation, Aldrin had said. That was true, but only in the light of Earth. And the Earth was sinking into the horizon behind the hopper.

John thought about the *Voyager* and its long thin wings that flexed in flight. The two pilots had used biological metaphors to describe the experience. The plane porpoised. It felt like riding on the back of a pterodactyl. It flew like a great flapping seagull—around the Earth. Dick Rutan and Jeanna Yeager endured danger and discomfort, breaking-point emotional strain, nightmarish problems. He was no pilot, no derring-doer like those two. Like them, though, he had a machine made out of exotic materials, a dream, a dream machine that could frame a nightmare. Rutan and Yeager never gave up. He wasn't going to either. And if the attempt to fix the dish failed, damaged it worse than ever, if everything hit the fan . . . he was not going to quit even then. Schropfer would have to fire him. His neck hurt. He ignored it.

Below the hopper was the far side of the Moon, alien land lit only by the cold white stars. "I gather that you radio astronomers prefer a quiet neighborhood," Cantu commented. "But what do you do for fun?"

"The habitat is pretty basic. Most of it tucked into a lava tube, inhabited outbuildings radiation-shielded with bagged lunar regolith. No amenities. We read a lot. I work with an old hen who reads murder mysteries, and when I ran out of my own books I started on hers." Did her penchant for mysteries point to a dark psychological angle—something about suppressed hostility in Jen's character? Maybe it was just that too many hard weeks of being cooped up in the habitat, too closely with too few people, promoted homicidal fantasies. He had enjoyed the murder mysteries.

"That's the only way I came to read *War and Peace*," Cantu answered breezily. "Cause this guy in my bunkroom had it."

Rodriguez was a different type, a slight and quiet man, all business. "That it down there?"

John replied, "That's the Lunar Far-Side Very Low Frequency Array in the Sanduleak walled plain. Which was named for a twentieth-century astronomer and promptly if disrespectfully corrupted to Sand Lake. Look on the far edge of Sanduleak. See the bright dimple? That's Bolton. And the reflector."

"How does it work?"

"It sits there. It's a photon bucket. The bucket reflects incident radiation to the center, where the antenna is. The antenna is what moves. There's an older dish of this kind in Arecibo, Puerto Rico—a real workhorse in my field." Reflectively, he added, "Bolton is to Arecibo as Voyager is to, oh, maybe a Cessna. Principles the same, materials radically new and different. Composite construction makes

Bolton flexible—and fragile. Arecibo stood up to a major hurricane once, in 1989. Earth gravity alone would flatten Bolton."

The reflector was eggshell-thin but not rigid, the pylons stiff yet resilient, the whole structure nonmetal-like, quirky to the extent that it was hard to know what to expect of the exotic materials. John did know. He had parsed the quirks of the machine for all of the months of its construction. A kibitzer like Schropfer could have Bolton's specs strewn all over his desk, and still not know what to expect of the structure.

The hopper swerved over the shore of Sand Lake, braked and began a slow hovering descent toward Bolton. The habitat was tucked into crater Bell, right on the edge of Bolton. Little craters have lesser ones. . . . John radioed. "Anybody home?" Home sweet home, he thought. Cold showers and gritty floors. Close quarters in which your colleagues' harmless traits got on your nerves. Jen's chocolates, shedding oily brown particles on the pages of technical reports as well as murder mysteries. Zheng's bad breath. And Edward's mild-mannered, rational, relentless pessimism.

Jen's voice replied. "Welcome back. Whatever is that load on top of the hopper?"

"Popsicle sticks," said John. "And duct tape." Rodriguez grinned briefly.

"Cantu, set us down close to the crater edge. Don't worry, it's reinforced, and will not crumble. There's a crane down there that can hand the cargo under the dish. X marks the ideal spot."

"Can do," said the pilot, winking at the pun on his name. He put the hopper down neatly on the landing field's X by the brink of Bolton.

John invited them into the control room. Jennifer seemed as shocked as a hausfrau that he had brought guests home unannounced.

The guests seemed genuinely interested in the instruments and computers, and the radio contour map tacked up on the wall. "I thought your instrument wasn't working," said Rodriguez.

"We have two radio telescopes at this facility," Jen explained. "The

Very Low Frequency Array has been operational for three months now." Clicking into professor mode, she explained how her VLF Array was mapping the magnetosphere of Jupiter.

"Most stars are not single," she was saying. "Binary systems are the norm. Our Sun was very nearly a double star, the other one being Jupiter, if Jupiter had been somewhat bigger. Jupiter is nearly a star, and it generates its own heat and an immense magnetic field. . ."

John glanced at his workstation's inbox. There was a message for him, from Ramona, datelined Friday 5:14 P.M. YOU'RE IN PAIN AND I AM WORRIED! He stared at the message, unconsciously rubbing his neck.

"She's right," said Jennifer, behind him.

"None of your business," he said brusquely.

Rodriquez had disappeared into the restroom, and Cantu was being introduced to the observatory's main computer by Edward. Jennifer asked, "Why did you bring these people here?"

"They're going to help us fix the dish."

Her eyebrows shot up. "As easy as that?"

"Maybe not. It's a long shot. An idea."

"When?"

He shrugged past the crick in his neck. "No time like the present."

From this side, the dish was the dim convex canopy of a forest of pylons. Anchored in the crater floor, the slim pylons rose up to branch at the top. The branches terminated in twigs, each attached to one segment of the dish. The position of each dish segment could be adjusted by the control computer. Sensors told the computer the precise position of every segment. Adding everything up, the computer had found the dish sagging. The human eye could not detect the sag, at least not now, with artificial lights shredding the lunar night under the dish.

It was the Moon's slow midnight. But human affairs adhered to the twenty-four-hour artifice of Moon Mean Time. They had spent Friday night unloading the cargo from the hopper and getting ready. John had, again, slept badly. This time his neck hurt all night. And he was troubled by the kind of garish bad dreams that he had been having in recent weeks, the color-pandemonium with which his brain attempted to be compensate for the monochromatic tedium of waking life on the Moon. Now it was Saturday morning, still early, 9 A.M. John circled around the site with an impatient mixture of gliding and skipping steps. He wanted to get this over with.

Floodlights illuminated one of the pylons. Twenty feet above the crater floor, it bent at an angle of some fifteen degrees. The hollow-cored pylon had buckled like a soda straw. Now a long cable descended from the crown of the pylon. The cable ended at a winch anchored on the crater floor, as far away from the pylon as possible.

Two ropes, shorter than the winch cable, dangled from the top of the pylon. John called, "Jennifer, you and Zheng on this one. You'll back off and hold it taut. Out that way—right angles to the cable. Don't actively pull unless you get the word." Jen rapidly translated that into Chinese for Zheng. John continued, "You all know how hard it is to get good traction. So use the anchor posts. Cantu, you and me on the other rope. Edward operates the winch, and Rodriguez spots. He'll tell us if the pylon sways one way or another."

Rodriguez signaled assent.

The bulky moonsuited form of Edward fussed over the winch. Edward said, "This procedure still strikes me as illogical. The basic notion is to *lift*. Right?"

"Ever been to Easter Island?" John asked, "That's how they got the stone heads up. A bunch of people on the ground, pulling on the longest ropes they had."

"I hardly think that qualifies as a reliable precedent. And what about the stress on the points of attachment?"

"For the record," said John, "I'm not 100 percent sure that this will work. I *am* sure it's the thing to try. Ready, everybody? Let's do it."

Moonsuited forms shuffled to their places. At a signal from Rodriguez, Edward turned on the winch. It whirred soundlessly in the airlessness here. The cable oscillated, went taut.

Fifteen hundred feet across, the dim down side of the dish stretched away to the ends of the crater. John felt a sudden conviction of futility. Edward was right. They might as well have been insects, busy but ridiculous ants, trying to reshape this vast thing.

Rodriguez said rapidly, "Pylon's starting to straighten out. Going true. Still true. It's trying to lean to the right!" he waved an arm. "Left rope, pull!" Jennifer and Zheng pulled. The Chinese man had a foot propped on an anchor post and pulled mightily.

"Let up! Left, let up! Right side pull!"

John pulled. His feet slipped and he skidded. Cantu stumbled. They got anchored again, then, and with their combined mass under the rope, pulled. John felt the rope come to them. Over their heads, the pylon and with it the filmy acres of dish had actually responded to their puny effort.

"That's it! That's it! Ropes, stop pulling! Just hold steady there. Slow the winch—that's about right—Left! Pull, but not too hard! Good! Ease off that winch—anchor the side ropes—put the winch brake on. Not like that!" Rodriguez headed toward the winch with loping strides of a moon veteran making haste. "That's not how the brake works!"

"Oh," said Edward.

Now the pylon looked straight. Only, like a bent soda straw, it had one terribly weak point. Without the winch cable holding it, the pylon would keel back over.

Climbing into the driver's seat, Rodriguez started the crane. It was a light, long-necked, mobile piece of machinery on treads. Using the crane, Rodriguez hoisted one end of a moonglass beam. The inside of the beam was reamed out to match the curvature of the pylon and coated with glue. With some help from the ground he placed the beam up against the pylon. Glued, it stuck. Then he positioned another beam on the other side of the pylon. "Popsicle sticks in place," Rodriguez commented. With adroit operation of the crane and helpers scrambling on the crater floor, he wrapped the splinted pylon with a ninety-yard length of plastic fabric, stretching and wrapping it.

The glue had to cure. It was time for lunch anyway, though not as simple as knocking off and grabbing a sandwich on the spot: taking off the moonsuits was a chore in itself. After lunch, Rodriguez took a nap. Cantu helped himself to a murder mystery.

———

According to the computer, the dish sagged less now. So far, so good. John rubbed his neck, inflamed by the morning's exertion in the spacesuit. The more damaged pylon was yet to come.

Jennifer came into the control room to check the accumulating data from her LFSVLFA. She asked, "How did you get that material? I didn't know we had that much credit with the Yuegong warehouse."

"We don't. I faked an appropriation authorization that said something about a state of scientific emergency. And a facsimile of a fund transfer writ. The check'll bounce Monday morning."

She rolled her eyes. "Oh, Lord! This had better work!"

He shrugged around the pain in his neck. "My responsibility alone. I didn't tell our two friends that I was fleecing the Port. Cantu probably has an idea, but he can plead innocence. If this fails, it's my funeral."

"Don't say that! We didn't tell you Thursday night—but one of the air valves in your suit jammed when you fell. If we hadn't found you and taken the risk of moving you right away—!" She left the outcome unspoken. "It was the sound of your breathing. I was sure you couldn't get enough air. I was right. When we took off the helmet you were turning purple!"

Not knowing quite what to say, John said, "Thank you."

"I was overjoyed when you sat up and talked." Jennifer added, quietly, "It haunts me. I could have lost a good colleague and a good friend."

It went both ways, he thought, with or without chocolate crumbs. "You're that for me too, and you have been for years," he said. "I'm not handling everything so well. I'm sorry."

"It's half fixed," she said briskly. "You brought good help. If we had the facilities, I'd bake cookies for those guys. Very handy people. —Unlike somebody else we know of Spanish ancestry!"

John nodded ruefully. "Murphy's Law and Baltazar's Rule."

She spelled out that old joke of theirs. "The better the theoretician, the more things go wrong when he lays his hands on the instruments. Lord, if he'd been here this morning the dish probably would have fallen down around our ears."

They grinned at each other.

Rodriguez announced that the glue was 97 percent as hard as it was going to get. Cantu stretched and groaned. "Is this gonna be worth it?" He levered his feet into his spacesuit.

Struggling to squeeze into her own suit, Jennifer puffed, "Good question." She used to be skinny as a rail. But since moving to the Moon and being form-fitted with a moonsuit, she had put on weight —enough to make it hard for her to don the suit. She decided to pause for a lecture. "Normally, radio astronomers don't scramble to observe a supernova. Optical astronomers do."

"Especially when they find themselves on the wrong side of the Moon." Like an eel, Cantu wriggled into the top half of his own suit.

"It's a truly cataclysmic event, a giant star dying, blowing most of its mass out in gusts of ionized matter. I would expect radio thermal emission, though not quite this soon. Heat noise. In science," she continued, "it's also important to check for that which one does not expect to detect, or not yet."

"What's that?" Cantu asked, carefully sealing his waist seam.

John said, "The corpse, spinning in its grave."

"Doin' *what?*"

Jennifer chuckled. "He means a neutron star. The core of the supernova radically collapses into a mass of neutrons, a neutron star, with all of the angular momentum—the rotating force—of the original star compressed into a much smaller package. So the neutron star spins rapidly. Several revolutions per second."

"How do you know?" All suited up, Rodriguez waited, leaning against the airlock with his helmet tucked under one arm.

"It also has a strong magnetic field inherited from the original star. This generates powerful beams of radiation which rotate as fast as the neutron star spins. Like the beam of a lighthouse. Our Solar System may or may not be in the path of the beam. If it is, we identify the source as a pulsar, and it can be quite a lovely radio object," said Jen. "The pulsar takes time to crystallize, though." John pushed down on the shoulders of her suit. The suit settled and her head emerged from the neckhole. "Thanks. No, right now—unless all of our theories are wrong—the neutron star at the core of that supernova is buried in fire and fury. It isn't a pulsar yet."

John checked his air supply. Zheng had fixed the jammed valve, Jen said. It seemed to function perfectly. He took a deep breath. They had in-suit air for six to eight hours. Enough time for the rest of the repair job to make it or break it.

This pylon was more bent than the first one because John had hit the dish closer to it. Rodriguez made a close inspection. Everybody else stood there and watched passively. They were all tired.

Pieces of dish lay on the crater floor. John picked one up. He turned the shard over in his glove. Thin, light glass manufactured from the lunar regolith, it had a shiny metallic coating on one side. With a chill, he remembered falling toward the shiny dish, expecting to die. He would have died, had not the flexing pylons absorbed the impact; had not the matrix of glass segments sagged like a safety net before breaking under him. Looking up, he saw stars through the jagged hole in the dish.

"I'm concerned," said Edward, "that our efforts will damage the dish. It would be very unfortunate if we overstressed the points of attachment of the pylon to the dish. Look, the angle of the bent portion is more extreme than the other one was. The branches are sharply counter-bent. Can they take the strain?"

"I think so," John said shortly.

"The pylon might even break there where it's bent," Edward persisted. "Of course, the opportunity to study the supernova may be worth taking considerable risk, scientifically speaking. I don't know about that."

Jennifer put her helmet against John's, using sound conduction to speak privately. "I do know."

"I want to fix it," he said.

"You're doing this just because you're a stubborn coot who's got his back up. And the rest of us like you enough to work our tails off for you."

Like winter rain, Edward did not let up. "Shouldn't you run this by the project engineers, or possibly Mr. Schropfer, before attempting—"

On the in-suit radio, Jennifer snapped, "Edward, your point is valid but your timing stinks. Go to that winch and get ready."

Rodriguez had an announcement to make. At least five-sixths of the pylon's branches were still securely attached to the dish. "Good enough for government work!" The bent section of pylon was unlikely to break and fall off. If it did, he'd holler. And everybody should run like hell.

The winch pulled. The kink in the pylon straightened out by degrees. John imagined what he would have heard if there had been air to carry the sounds: the groan of the pylon material and squeaks from the mosaic of glass segments. Maybe reports of glass breaking. Not that, he hoped to God.

With one alarm when it keeled to the left, and those on the right side had to scrape and haul, the pylon was jacked upright, the winch cable braked. Then Rodriguez and his helpers swarmed around the pylon to put on the glue, the splints and the cloth. Edward vanished into the control room.

John piled up the broken dish segments, then swept the crater floor clean of glass fragments. You make a mess, you clean it up. He probably cut a funny figure, a spacesuit pushing a broom.

Edward radioed from the control room. "It's better, but not quite better enough. However, with some reprogramming the computer may be able to compensate for that by adjusting individual segments. I can't promise anything, of course, but I'll do my best."

"How about breaks in the dish?" John asked quickly. He had sweat that needed wiping off his brow. Not possible with a spacesuit on. "Stress fractures—?"

"Not indicated, though the computer isn't really programmed to detect stress fractures of the kind that might have been caused by today's activities. It's geared to analyze micrometeorite impact damage."

"Never mind. It sounds good enough to go with."

Within an hour, exhausted snores could be heard in the habitat. It was Sunday now. 12:17 A.M.

Past mere exhaustion, John felt morbidly sleepless. Sitting in bed, he read the supernova report again. Then somebody knocked on the door. "Come in," he said peevishly.

Without preamble, Jennifer told him, "It looked to me like you had a sore neck all day,"

"Yeah. A crick or something."

"How is the crick tonight?"

"It's in fine fettle," he said sourly. "A really great crick."

She probed his neck with her fingers.

"Ouch!"

"Let's try this on it. It's my arthritis liniment."

"I didn't know you had arthritis."

"That is my darkest little secret," she replied.

The liniment went on cool with a wintergreen reek. Then it started to feel warm. Jennifer massaged the neck. To his gratification, the knot of muscles loosened up under her fingertips. Satisfied, Jennifer told him to call it a night, and she departed. He intended to read for a while longer. But he fell asleep with the pages of the report scattered over his bunk.

And dreamed about falling toward the dish.

This time he did not jerk awake. He crashed through the dish, with bright glass panes of it spinning away. Then the dreamer lightly landed in a forest—a tropical forest, improbably situated below the Bolton dish. Color surrounded him, but not the lurid colors of his bad dreams. Lush greens, blossoming bold reds, wild purples and pinks, colors of Puerto Rico. In Technicolor. The dreamer was pleased with himself.

A glossy black toucan perched on a branch, bobbing its head with the great yellow bill. Then he saw the hummingbird. Green as a June bug, it hovered near him. The tiny bird hummed. A beam of golden light illuminated the humming bird. The dreamer looked up. The sky was a convex blue dome with a hole in it. Golden light spilled in through the hole.

The reading light was shining into his upturned face. 7:03 AM Sunday morning, by the clock, and he had slept, not long, but well.

Out of force of habit, John checked his email. The doctor in Yuegong Hospital crisply pointed out that he had NOT given John Clay permission to return to work. Two news services and an internet tabloid wanted to interview Dr. Clay about his death-defying fall from a telescope on the Moon. Finally, Schropfer had messaged, RECEIVED CONFIRMATION OF APPROPRIATION REQUEST FILLED. **WHAT** REQUEST?

John erased all of the messages.

Another habit, instilled over almost a year of being project manager here, was that of counting noses. Could everybody be accounted for—was anybody missing, out in the lunar environment, in trouble? So he immediately noticed the absence of Rodriguez from the group.

"Checking the repair job," Cantu informed him.

"The shape of the dish is just inside the acceptable parameters," said Edward, proudly, "now that the computer has made more than six hundred coordinated adjustments to the segments." Disheveled, Edward appeared to have fussed over the computer most of the night, maybe sacked out on the control room cot for a bare hour or two.

"We're ready," said Jennifer, significantly.

John shook his head. "I just remembered something," he said. "A problem up in the equipment house. That's why I went up in the first place."

Instantly Edward volunteered to go up the catwalk and attend to whatever it was. But Jennifer said, "No. He needs to get back up on the horse."

This time he was trembling inside the spacesuit, probably pale as a piece of chalk, glad that the suit concealed those facts so well. "You're three-fourths of the way up!" Jennifer encouraged over the radio. He glanced back toward the gaggle of spacesuits at the base of the catwalk. Jen and Edward and Cantu and Zheng—the last all encouraging waves in the absence of knowing what to say in English. John waved back. Without looking down, he registered the gleam of the dish, photons reflected toward where he was going now.

When he stepped onto the antenna platform, his knees buckled. He sat down with an undignified little bounce.

"That's it!" Jen cheered. "Take a breather! Look up," she suggested.

"Where is it?" asked Cantu.

"There, in the Small Magellanic Cloud, but the supernova is still too faint to see with the naked eye," Jennifer answered. "Bear in mind that the Cloud is a galaxy of stars. A few weeks from now the supernova will be outshining the rest of that galaxy."

Incalescent—one hundred and sixty thousand years ago and away—SN 2019C was the signal flare of a vast cataclysm, in which a giant star blew up hot as hell. No: it was hot, all right, but not infernal. Hot as heaven, hot as the forges of heaven. Heavy elements were being created in the supernova, iron and gold, carbon and oxygen, the atoms of which Moons and moonsuits, future Earths and living things were made.

He picked his own personal collection of atoms up and walked to the equipment housing. Carefully he lifted the broad aluminum lid and locked it into open position.

Jennifer asked, "What *is* the problem?"

Thumb to forefinger, he plucked sheets of clear plastic off the circuitry. "The contractors left the protective sheathing on."

Jennifer transmitted an unladylike curse having to do with the contractors, and what else they might have been capable of forgetting to do.

"Oh, my," said Edward, "I don't think those gentlemen would forget *that*."

John had removed all of the plastic, and the equipment looked sharp and clean, solid-state of the art. He glanced at the gleam beneath the grated floor. "Rodriguez?" he radioed. "You down there?"

"I take it you won't be dropping in."

"Not today. How's it look?"

"The job'll hold for a few years, minimum."

"By that time, it'll be time for the Phase II enhancements," John said, with satisfaction. He closed the lid and, returning to the catwalk, hurried down to *Luna firma*. When he reached the bottom, the other spacesuits clapped for him. "It's ready now," John said.

"But is your photon bucket going to work with a hole in it?" asked Cantu.

"Sure. Remember *Voyager's* takeoff? The plane flew OK anyway. Something like that." Cantu might not have been born yet then, but John remembered watching it on TV, in December of 1986, the end of the year that began, disastrously, with *Challenger*. The experimental plane rolled down the California runway, loaded to the gills with fuel, and its long, fuel-laden wings flexed down, scraping the ground. The *Voyager* took off with wires hanging out of ragged wingtips where winglets had been scraped off. And the plane did not touch Earth again before it had circled the planet. It had not really needed the winglets.

Bolton did not really need the few segments that had been knocked out of it. John felt a stirring of euphoria, the old anticipation of having a dream machine to work with. It had been a long time since he last felt that way: for months, he had stared at the diggings in the crater, thinking how little it all resembled the first grand idea. Now, Bolton was ready to meet the ancient voyage of radio waves from the universe.

Edward said, "I haven't finished checking out the computer and its interactivity with the rest of the system." Edward had a fresh contribution of rain for the parade. "I can't guarantee that there aren't any bugs lurking, and in fact by departing from the trial timetable—"

"Forget it!" John said shortly. "The time to try is now." And he started down the path to the control room, stirring up puffs of moondust.

"A radio interferometer—a chain of dishes strung across a continent, or an ocean, or even from Earth across space—can resolve finer detail. None have this aperture." He opened the window shutters. The control room was perched on the rim of Bolton, below one of the cable towers. He let his eyes follow the cables out over the expanse of the dish. Fifty acres. The antenna hung over the dish like a spider on a tricornered web fifteen hundred feet across. Behind the other two cable towers, the Sanduleak plain stretched away for gray miles. Starlight faintly reflected from LFSVLFA like a metallic hint of waves in Sand Lake.

"Human activities on Earth generate an incredible amount of radio noise, swamping the faint signals from the universe. Located here, the dish and the Very Low Frequency Array are shielded from the radio noise of Earth, by the bulk of the Moon. I might add that the Moon itself is dead quiet apart from very rare rock electric discharges. No weather—no lightning, no seismic activity. For radio astronomy, there is no better place than this. Here goes." Displacing Edward from the controls, John entered a right ascension and declination.

The red lights flashed at the corners of the distant antenna platform. John flashed back to being there, to the panicked realization that the platform was slewing out from under him. Arms crossed, John watched the antenna move. Unlike Arecibo, there was no whir and vibration from the machine. This one repositioned silently.

"First off, not the supernova," John explained. "Instead we'll scan something called Centaurus A. It's a radio galaxy, a blazing strong source in the radio sky. This is to verify that the receiver's working. Like making sure your new home stereo can pick up the local pop-around-the-clock music station before you go for the university radio station, the one with a weak and unreliable transmitter located ten miles away." He had an afterthought. "Edward, can you convert the signal to sound?"

"Whatever for?" Jen said.

"Show and tell for our company." John explained, "Radio astronomers never listen to the stars. It's not informative for scientific purposes."

Methodically, Edward made the arrangements, hitching this circuit to that.

The antenna slid slowly now, smooth as silk on glass, gliding past the point where the radio waves from Centarus A were focused by the reflector, for a drift scan. On the display screen, the signal came in with what looked like the lift of a bell curve. Converted by Edward's arrangements to sound waves, the signal hissed.

"Static," Cantu remarked.

"Sweetest static I've ever heard!" John replied fervently. The hiss crescendoed as the bell curve tipped over on the display screen. "Jen, just look at that curve! It's classic." The computer brain of the observatory, buried deep under the lunar ground, analyzed the signal. Data windows lined the top and bottom of the display screen. He tapped a window, opened it to read out the red shift of the radio galaxy. "This is great. This is instant gratification. The machine works! Jen, let's break out the champagne!"

"Coming!" She opened the locker with a cheerful rattle.

Then John entered the coordinates of SN 2019C and changed the control settings. "This time, no drifting. The signal, if any, will be too faint to catch unless we sit on it. We'll be looking for thermal radio emissions at a likely wavelength, six centimeters. Don't be surprised if we register, and hear, nothing."

"Cannot be much yet!" Zheng said. "But is good this working!"

"Absolutely, and we're going to celebrate. Champagne, anyone?"

Outside, the antenna slewed to its new position. Sitting in the master chair, John ran a hand lightly over the controls. User-friendly, he thought with approval, lucid, thanks in part to design changes that he had insisted on. "We're in position. We'll give it some settle-down time."

Poured into plastic glasses, the champagne fizzed. The sound conversion hissed just as faintly, pale noise that originated in the circuitry.

"Nada," remarked Cantu, not too worried. Champagne in one hand, he accepted a piece of the chocolate that Jen was offering around in the other.

John thumbed through the supernova report. Thirty hours old, SN 2013C should be brightening rapidly as it began to expand, on the verge of blowing its outer layers off, but still, in fact, intact. Realistically, there was no radio signal to be expected yet. At least not from 2013C.

"This machine has state-of-the art timing," John said. "Routinely, the receiver averages out any fluctuations in the signal. But a signal can be too faint to detect when it's averaged like that. So I'm going to delete the averaging, in order to search for a coherent, pulsed signal with a period of one to ten milliseconds between pulses."

Jennifer raised an eyebrow.

"Do you still want it converted to sound?" Edward asked.

"Yes. If we get anything."

"What's going on?" asked Cantu. "Making sure the corpse isn't spinning in its grave yet?"

"Actually, we don't have the resolution to distinguish a pulsar at the exact location of SN 2013C from one in the vicinity." John watched the bubbles in his glass. They rose slowly, just as things on the Moon fell slowly, giving you time to think. "Most stars aren't solitary. There's no reason for the supernova not to be in a binary star system—with a pulsar left over from a supernova ages ago, maybe even a millisecond pulsar."

"Unlikely," Jennifer commented.

"But very desirable," he countered. "Millisecond pulsars are the most accurate clocks in all creation. If we had one in the vicinity of a supernova in progress, we could observe what happened to the timing as the pulsar got hit by gravity waves, radiation, maybe plasma from the supernova. Also, the amount of mass lost in the supernova —and whether or not it breaks up into more than one body—that would register in the signal from a pulsar in the right location. And Bolton is better equipped to read such a signal than any other facility on the Earth or off it. Right, Jen?"

"Yes, but a pulsar is still darn unlikely to be there," said Jennifer. "Has the champagne gone to your head already?"

"Serendipity happens," John pointed out.

* * *

Under the rim of the crater, the big dish gleamed in the faint rain of photons. The receiving instruments caught a unique radio thread; the computer teased it out of the background circuit noise. Edward promptly converted and amplified the signal. It came out as a conversation-stopping loud hum. Echoing from the bare walls, the hum sounded startlingly pure, and made Jennifer leap up, spilling some champagne. "Edward! Make sure that's not our equipment!" she gasped.

"High C!" Cantu guessed. "Are you sure that's not little green men?!"

John said rapidly, "It's consistent with a millisecond pulsar." With a glance, he verified that the display screen was representing the signal as a series of spikes. Data windows lined up under the running spikes. John opened one window and read the period of the signal:

two point one thousandths of a second. "I think we've made a very timely discovery, thanks to you guys helping us fix the dish."

"Hot damn!" Grinning from ear to ear, Cantu pumped Rodriguez's hand, then Zheng's.

Jennifer was too surprised to be jubilant. She asked, "Whatever made you look for it right away?"

"I read over the previous data last night, and slept on it." John smiled. "And then I dreamed about a hummingbird. It was humming, just like this." He turned both palms up in the bright flurry of sound echoing around the room.

"I'll be darned!"

John laughed.

Edward solemnly announced, "I can't be *absolutely* sure it's not the equipment, but it seems unlikely," whereupon Jennifer bounded over and kissed Edward. Then she said, "Let's let Schropfer know!"

John nodded. "And Ramona."

"Of course."

Ramona would want to hear about the hummingbird dream—she would be delighted. But that was a gift to save until he saw her in person again. "She knows enough astronomical nomenclature to understand this." He sent the same brief message on its way to the L-5 space station as well as to Washington, DC, Earth. The photons of his message traveled to L-5 and to Earth at the same speed of light with which the pulsar's signal had crossed intergalactic space to meet the radio telescope on the Moon.

PSR 0106-73

IT WORKS

TRINITY BAY

This story was inspired by a real Trinity River flood some years ago. With friends (and a throng of other tourists), I watched the flood overwhelming a reservoir's dam. The flood had such power, I thought, and such possibilities.

Being a sailplane pilot myself gave me the raw material to write the flight that unfolds in this story, but inspiration came from other members of the Soaring Club of Houston. And Barry Dunning, a SCOH instructor and pilot as well as Physics and Astronomy professor at Rice University, helped me figure how just how it could unfold.

An unnatural disaster threatens the Gulf of Mexico and one intrepid pilot has a skybird seat to watch it happen.

He sailed the ocean of air in a slender ship of glass.

Balancing on a thermal, flying an airplane without an engine, he circled tightly, and the warm rising air carried him skyward. The sailplane's long, thin carbonglass wings flexed as it soared like a huge white hawk. He felt at one with the sailplane—finally, after a steep learning curve in which the Zofia had seemed too fast and sleek for him to handle—finally, Evan Gage felt at home at the Zofia's controls. His wings embraced the sky.

He'd almost forgotten the other sailplane pilots; the radio startled him. "Seven Zulu, Victor Twenty-Three, Pretty Quick, where are you guys?" The reedy voice belonged to Adam Sorrentino. Sortie flew an old racing sailplane, 22T, that fit his veteran skills like a suede glove.

"Pretty Quick is over Navasota," Beth Torres answered from PQ. No call came in from Trent Young in V23. Trent, otherwise known as the Silent Racer, was practicing for a national contest and couldn't be bothered with small radio talk.

"Seven Zulu is near New Waverly," Evan radioed. "I'm working east today."

"'East' is a four-letter word!" Sortie cackled.

"I'm in lift at 5,000 feet," Evan pointed out.

"Go ahead, be a nonconformist. The rest of us are heading west. Cloud bases are near 7,000 on the other side of Brenham. Two to Tango, out and away."

Radio reception was crystal clear. The Zofia had avionics as sophisticated as its aerodynamics, with everything wired into the flight computer. It seemed less like a sailplane with a collection of instruments than a single entity, one with a mysterious intelligence inversely proportional to its vocabulary. The variometer chirped brightly. *Up-up-up-up....* The vario sounded like a contralto cricket.

Lifted by the solar-heated air rising off a plowed field, Evan spiraled up to the gray base of a powderpuff cumulus cloud. Cool cloudbase air flowed onto his face through the canopy vent. With a flick of the side-arm control stick, he pointed the ship's nose east.

The Sam Houston National Forest spread out below the Zofia like a ragged, woolly rug. In the old days, thermals over the national forest were weak and unreliable this early in the year and it would have been smarter to fly westward, over fields and pastures and toasty asphalt. But this May was as hot and clear as the Junes of Evan's youth. Greenhouse Texas was a good place for sailplanes. To be able to fly a sky like this, in a sailplane like the Zofia—state of the art, and wondrous art it was—made Evan glad to be living now, though he wondered what kind of world his grandchildren, ages five and three, were scampering toward.

In the distance the green rug of trees gleamed where a large amount of water had been spilled on it. Torrential rains in North Texas were flooding down the Trinity River—a vast, turbid slug of water crawling toward the Gulf of Mexico. Evan marveled at the flood, and the translucency of the Zofia's canopy, as he worked his way toward bloated Lake Livingston.

A few circles in the thermals (*up-up-up!*) under widely scattered cumulous clouds regained the slight altitude lost between them. Thermals were sun-warmed air rising, crowned by clouds: solar energy kept him in the sky, Evan reflected. Of course, aviation gasoline put him in the sky in the first place. About an hour ago, the sturdy tow plane had pulled the Zofia up to 2,000 feet. Then Evan had pulled the release and gone on his way while the tow plane spiraled back down for the next customer. But avgas was solar energy too, packed in plant matter and stored in the Earth for eons as oil. Then pumped up and piped to refineries, politicked and fought over, for a century and a half since that black gold first gushed out of a hole in the ground in Pennsylvania.

Now the world's energy options were fractured. Oil coexisted with other alternatives, in a technological and political flux that sorted careers, companies and nations into the quick and the dead. Evan's own company, which specialized in energy project initiation, belonged to the former category: the quick. He'd been successful because he kept the company small, sharp-edged, and flexible, like a dagger.

On a summer Sunday, though, he enjoyed the simplicity of riding solar-heated air. He danced amid the cogs of the world's greatest engine, the atmosphere.

Evan's attention snapped fully back to flying when he noticed the watery glint around the trees below him. In stable air the Zofia could easily glide miles forward for a single mile of altitude lost. Evan wouldn't find much lift in the sodden landscape adjacent to the flood. But thanks to the Zofia's performance he could do plenty of sight-seeing before turning back to dry ground. With altitude to spare, Evan angled across the foot of Lake Livingston toward the dam.

The Lake Livingston dam was a spectacle. Full to the brim and then some, the lake overflowed the dam in a huge white fantail of water. The parking lot beside the dam, partially inundated, contained dozens of toy cars parked in rows, and clumps of animated dots by the water's edge—sightseers. Evan circled, taking in the scene from his lofty front-row seat.

Up.... Up....

Up??

With a few control inputs, Evan centered the glider in the lift and turned tight circles. *Up, up, up* the Zofia chirped approvingly, high above the roiling water at the dam's foot, where no self-respecting thermal ought to exist.

Sometimes there was no accounting for the vagaries of the air. Moreover, the superbly designed Zofia could ride the most tenuous of thermals. She could practically gain altitude on the hot air of a campaign speech. With a mental shrug, Evan accepted the serendipitous altitude.

At 5,000 feet high in the blue—no cloud overhead—he turned the sailplane out over the swollen Trinity River. *Dow—wn, dow—wn.* The sink tone was a drunken cricket with a slurred chirp. Sink was what Evan expected here, relatively cool air settling Earthward. What goes up must come back down, even if it's air. He found it weirdly reassuring to hear the vario confirm that. Assuming moderate sink everywhere above the floodwaters, he had thirty miles of leeway before he got uncomfortably low.

Evan noted drowned fields stippled with the topmost parts of crops, and cattle huddled on islands that were hills in dryer times. It all looked deceptively peaceful, considering it was a watery purgatory, anticipated and awful nonetheless, to the people who lived there. All but a few stubborn holdouts had been evacuated. He was a lucky man to sail above those troubles in a new Zofia.

Up, the Zofia suggested. *Up.*

Puzzled, Evan automatically pulled the Zofia into a circle.

Up, up!

Evan was shocked. He shouldn't get lift over water. It violated a rule bored into the bones of sailplane pilots: *Get too low over a body of water and you'll have to swim the rest of the way back to solid ground!* Yet six miles downstream from the dam, out in the middle of the flood, the Zofia balanced on a bubble of warm air like an ant on a cork. The sailplane gained altitude, chirping contentedly.

The Silent Racer had a tale about a soaring competition in France in which he got lift from a nuclear reactor's cooling pond. But reactor ponds were a *very* special case.

"How's it going, Seven Zulu?" radioed Sortie.

"I'm above the Trinity flood."

"That's right, rub it in. That hot new ship of yours can glide from there to Kingdom Come."

"Hey guys, I'm in four-knot lift going through 8,000 feet." Beth Torres sounded happy.

"Turning Giddens for Cameron," said the Silent Racer on the radio, to point out that he intended go further, faster than anybody else, as usual.

The Zofia's altimeter read 4,700 feet. Almost one mile high over a drowned landscape and climbing. Beyond doubt, Evan had found a hot spot in the flood, or at any rate a warm spot: it might not have to be more than 20 degrees warmer than the surrounding water to kick off a thermal. Evan had never heard of a warm spot in a lake. Maybe he was over some drowned hamlet—Romayor, perhaps—not cold-soaked by immersion yet?

But Evan had won his own contests in life by making it a habit to think outside of convenient boxes. Pursing his lips, he mentally reviewed what lay upstream along the Trinity River. An unremarkable expanse of central Texas terrain. A handful of common-garden-variety towns now bailing water. And Dallas. Ground zero of the great flood of 2020.

"Ev?" Sortie on the radio again. "You anywhere near Liberty?"

"Uh—" Evan distractedly checked the flight computer's graphical map. Very little on the map resembled the ground at present, with myriads of distinguishing features being under water. "Well north. Why?"

"My wife just radioed up from the ground and said there's a disaster in progress at Liberty, on top of the flood. The news media can't agree on whether it's a major pollution spill or the town's on fire. You see anything?"

Evan scanned the sky. "No, no smoke plume or—" His voice caught in his throat as pattern recognition kicked in. *Cloud street.* A line of evenly spaced cumulus clouds swerved southeastward, clouds with fluffy white tops and flat gray bottoms, like cottony paving stones in the sky. The cloud street followed the main channel of the Trinity River, but ran east of it. It was as though the clouds had developed directly over the river and were offset by the wind, which was from the west.

A cloud street should not exist perpendicular to the wind direction. Normal cloud streets formed parallel to the wind!

Warm spots laced the flood, kicking off thermals that rose invisibly to cumulate in the innocuous-looking clouds. The telltale line of clouds pointed south, like an omen written on the sky by the finger of fate.

"Say again, Seven Zulu?" Sortie prompted.

"I've got enough altitude to fly to Liberty," said Evan.

"Ev, be careful!" That was Beth's voice.

"I will." The paving-stone-gray undersides of the clouds in the street told Evan that there was probably lift under them. If not, the Zofia could easily glide to dry land. The prospect of being safe in a danger zone exhilarated Evan. So did mentally prying at the situation, trying to read the meaning written on the sky in clouds.

In the beginning was Silicon Valley. Then Silicon Prairie—the high tech environs of Austin. After the turn of the twenty-first century, Nanotech Prairie evolved around Houston with its ambitious research universities. Last, around Dallas and along the Trinity River, came what some pundits called Nanoplasm Paradise.

What if something washed into the Trinity River from the labs in Paradise? A half dozen military-industrial and corporate labs existed inside multiple veils of national security and proprietary secrecy. If a nanoplasm escaped into the Trinity flood and multiplied wildly, what would happen? Evan didn't know. The ecosystem-rights advocates who conducted protests in Nanoplasm Paradise didn't know either. If government and corporate scientists knew, they didn't publicly say. But the predicted signature of runaway nanotechnology—either robotic or cyborganic, replicating out of control—was *heat.*

Evan leaned forward and repositioned the bright red marker-bug on the rim of the altimeter, so the bug pointed at 3,000. If he couldn't stay above that altitude, he would immediately point the sailplane's nose toward safe ground, he resolved, no matter how exciting it might be to investigate the Liberty disaster. He glanced at the GPS map on the flight computer, verifying that Liberty County had several airports in range. He only had to select one and the computer would instantly give him the direction and distance to it.

If runaway colonies of nanoplasm were multiplying in the Trinity River in puddles of heat, they were destroying organic molecules, reassembling carbon and other atoms into replicas of themselves. Evan was more titillated by the prospect of runaway nanotechnology than convinced of it. Still, he had no intention of ditching in the flood, a man made of protoplasm in a carbonglass glider, to run even an unlikely risk of being remade into microscopic monsters.

Still circling in the improbable thermal he'd found in the middle of the flood, wanting to gain as much altitude as possible, Evan glanced up through the crystal-clear canopy to see a shining white wisp above him. He had already entered the strange cloud street! A cloud was only now condensing atop this thermal.

Finding himself already in the unnatural cloud street made it easy to squelch the alarmed little voice of caution in the back of his mind. He pointed the Zofia's nose toward Liberty.

Hell, Evan thought, oh hell! Liberty, Texas, was melting. And it was melting *UP*.

Liberty should have been a collection of nondescript buildings with floodwater around their knees. But the structures sagged, amid pale bubbles and spikes that had nothing to do with the architecture of houses and gas stations. A strange sheen surrounded the city in the floodwater, a glassy, purple-gray cast, like a bacterial colony gifted with rich food—on a scale that boggled the mind.

Up. Up. Circling 3,900 feet high, under a cloud in the street, Evan believed he was safe, though his heart raced from apprehension. Everything he had read and heard about nanoplasms concurred that the tiny cyborgs were too heavy to be carried into the atmosphere as aerosols and too fragile to survive outside of an aqueous environment.

Below his altitude, a couple of power aircraft quartered back and forth over the stricken town. The authorities, Evan guessed. That they flew at a lower altitude than his, not staying upwind, reassured him. Nothing on Earth could have convinced Evan to touch the glassy water around Liberty, though. He gaped at the ruined town, suffocated in spikes and bubbles of pale stuff taller than the roofs and trees. Holy Mother of God, what *was* the stuff?

Nobody had yet invented nanoscale robotic assemblers that could run away in the wild. Assembler technology required just the right atoms available to assemble, thus an exactingly designed feedstock. Nanoplasm was more potentially ecophagous—as the Life's Rights protesters pointed out.

Liberty was melting—up!—and yet the roofs of farmhouses and barns out in the country looked unaffected. The forest appeared perfectly normal. Flooded corn and soybeans still looked like the top parts of corn and soybeans. What did Liberty have that the forest and fields lacked? Azaleas? Brick? Gas stations. . . ? Evan now recalled that Liberty had a gasoline storage facility, serried ranks of tanks, brim full of solar energy in the form of liquid petroleum. Partial comprehension dawned on him and he cursed out loud.

Evan belatedly noticed more airplanes. Five shared the sky over Liberty with him. Startled, he reached toward the flight computer to turn on collision-avoidance color. But his hand froze while his mind raced.

The airplanes were all light twins, with two engines each, for insurance: if one conked out it was possible to limp away from the flood with the remaining engine. Stodgy, turn-of-the-century lines and bland paint jobs suggested government issue. Evan guessed that the airplanes carried officials and scientists trying to make sense of what had happened to Liberty. If they saw him, he'd be herded away immediately and might have questions to answer later.

Instead of collision-avoidance paint, Evan told the flight computer to camouflage the Zofia's skin.

Race competitors sometimes opted for camouflage so nobody could follow them to the choicest thermals. Flying a sailplane for simple recreation, Evan normally wanted to be visible. Now, though, a cloud-dappled blue sheen spread over the wings and fuselage. He could discern the long wing edges, but from a distance the Zofia would melt into the sky.

That programmable paint was spectacularly effective. He had damn well better watch out for those airplanes. He was invisible as water vapor to them.

A flashy, non-government-issue-looking aircraft caught his full attention by passing within 1,000 feet of where he circled. His finger darted toward the function key that would have turned the Zofia international orange even as he realized that collision was not imminent. He read the bold N-number on the other aircraft's tail: NRGY3. Then he recognized the teal-silver-red paint job. "Well, well, look who's here," said Evan.

The flashy twin, which continued a long sweep around Liberty, was a corporate plane belonging to N-ergy of Dallas.

N-ergy: Nanotechnology for the Energy Industry. The company had billion-dollar dealings, but compared to oil, gas, wind, sun, and fuel cells, the nanoscale novelties that N-ergy wheeled and dealed with struck most people in the industry as being too damn close to imaginary. It didn't help the trust factor that N-ergy was secretive, allowing almost no external review.

Evan's reflexes tingled. By seeing Liberty, he had placed himself in a risky situation. But in his life—admittedly he'd led a charmed life so far—risk always came with potential reward. Always. He knew enough now, and it was time to go.

East and west, the Trinity flood spread far and wide. The river's ominous cloud street, though, which had given him plenty of lift all the way to Liberty, continued south, toward the sea. And far off in the distance, onshore winds had created a sea breeze front with clouds that looked like whipped cream spattered in a line across the horizon between sea and sky.

Evan felt an electric jolt of anticipation as a plan condensed in his mind. He'd had nearly six decades of a good, even charmed life; his children were grown and competent parents of their own children. Flying south meant both predictable and incalculable dangers. But in the Zofia, Evan had a tool and a companion beyond the dreams of the generations of men before him.

Something huge and dangerous stalked toward the Gulf of Mexico, with puffs of cloud to mark its invisible but crushing footfalls. And Evan tracked the invisible monster like a hunter on wings of wind.

It felt profoundly unnatural to fly a sailplane toward the sea, and his nerves chorused tension.

The cloud street dwindled. Its gray-bottomed cumulus clouds became widely spaced cottonpuffs without any cool cloud shadow. Thirsty, he downed the contents of his water bottle and regretted not bringing a second bottle. His backside ached to announce that it wanted out of the form-fitting seat.

In the green countryside northwest of Houston, his fellow club members would be landing at the gliderport, hangaring sailplanes, relaxing on the deck of the clubhouse to regale each other with tales of the day's soaring, popping cold sodas and beers. Only the Silent Racer would stay up much longer—conditioning himself for long contest days. Meanwhile, Evan Gage ran toward the Gulf of Mexico, with fraying mental concentration and no spare water, in a weakening cloud street.

He felt like a quixotic fool but he pressed on.

North of Trinity Bay, the cloud street petered out completely. Had he outrun the monster?

Had he imagined it—? Irritated with himself, Evan shook his head to shake out that weak and indecisive doubt.

Did salt water stop the nanoplasm? Maybe. But Trinity Bay wasn't saline anymore, given the vast amount of fresh water dumped into it by the flood.

The Zofia drifted down through 3,000 feet above sea level, chirping dully. With the help of the flight computer, Evan calculated the best speed to fly. Even a Zofia sank fast if she flew much below *or* above the right speed for the conditions. If he miscalculated, he'd have to ditch in Trinity Bay, with the invisible monster stalking *him*. Evan gritted his teeth and double-checked the best speed to fly.

Evan had an excruciating excess of time in which to observe Trinity Bay expand as he inexorably lost altitude. Subtly textured, like damask fabric, the water looked dun-colored, only shading to blue beyond the haze of distance. The Bay's most striking feature was a big oil platform. Several helicopters hovered near the platform like bees around a rosebush.

Finally, the sea breeze front stretched across the sky above Evan, a tangled belt of crisp white clouds. "Okay, lady. We climb or else!"

Air masses collided at the front—cooler sea air meeting a warmer, continental air mass—creating the belt of clouds and, on the inland edge of the clouds, strong lift that booted the Zofia up bodily. *UP-UP-UP!* The empty water bottle skidded out of his lap. He stuffed it back in the storage webbing one-handed.

At cloudbase, Evan deeply breathed the cool air flowing in

through the vent. His fingers cramped from holding the control stick too tightly, so he flexed his hand as he surveyed his vastly improved options.

Chambers County lay to the east, its airport too close to Trinity Bay for comfort. Westward beyond the water, Baytown bristled with the silver architecture of refineries. He would shun refineries today! Better to go as far toward undiluted salt water as he could fly and still land on dry ground.

He could glide to deserted, undeveloped Bolivar Island from here. Or, by following the sea breeze front south and west, he could position himself to jump to Galveston Island—on the rim of the salty Gulf and inside the pale of civilization.

Evan looked back to the north. The monster hadn't reached Trinity Bay. Yet.

He dug the cellphone out of his shirt pocket and speed-dialed a number.

"Hello!" Leo Redwine, the Vice President for Advanced Technologies of Oceaneering International, sounded tense, as well he might.

"Leo, this is Evan Gage. Are they evacuating Painted Horse?"

Leo cursed. "We got word that the flood is bringing toxic pollution into the bay. So yes, they're abandoning the platform—helicopters shuttling workers ashore. Our techs are in the next load up to go, and they've got all of the software. I hope. God knows if we'll be able to decontaminate our equipment and how far back this'll set the project!"

"Listen, Leo. Keep your telops working. Transfer control to shore. Keep the telemetry up—the environmental monitoring, the SEANTS, in situ analysis, everything. You're going to want to know what happens to Painted Horse."

Birds chirped behind Leo's silence. The Trinity Bay crisis had evidently caught him at his weekly game of golf. "Okay." Leo hung up.

Evan felt grim satisfaction. It said something about his influence in the energy industry that the Oceaneering VP would act on his cryptic advice.

The cogs of the Earth's atmospheric engine gently meshed along the sea breeze front, and the Zofia was a carbonglass butterfly skittering through the meshing winds. Evan stayed in the lift on the inland edge of the front, flying south and west.

In a gray cloudbase haze at 2,000 feet—clouds near the coast formed less than half as high up as clouds further inland—Evan calculated a final glide to Galveston Island. He triple-checked the results, as the profuse sweat on his body chilled in the cloud-base coolness.

He hesitated.

The Zofia was a dangerously hot glider for a tired pilot. He'd been making beginner's mistakes, pushing too hard on the rudder pedals for his control stick movements, uncoordinated, as though the nerveways between his hands and feet were clogged with the metabolic debris of fatigue. And he still had to land somewhere. And the Zofia's long, supple wings made landing anywhere except on a runway tricky.

Trent Young could have handled this situation. Old Sortie, who'd flown 22T so long that the sailplane was his second skin, would have managed a safe landout in 22T in Evan's place. Beth Torres flew a trusty little glider that could land on a postage-stamp of a field if necessary. And Beth was young and resilient. "Evan, you may be too old for this to be a lark," he admitted to himself.

But the sea breeze front was moving north. He could delay, and have no choice but to to land on Smith Point in a ragged cow pasture, or he could set out across Galveston bay *now*.

Once and for all, he flicked the control stick toward the ocean-blue southern horizon.

Under the seaward edge of the frontal clouds, heavy sink threatened to plunge the Zofia into the bay. Evan instantly aimed the nose down and she arrowed through the sink, going downward fast, but forward, out of the plummeting cooled air, even faster.

They didn't make sea breeze fronts like they used to, Evan thought in sharp dismay. The front's sink was stronger than any he remembered from his younger days. It had robbed him of irreplaceable altitude. The air behind the sea breeze front was stable and devoid of lift.

Holding the Zofia's nose steady, aiming for the ribbonlike barrier island in the distance, Evan discovered the cellphone still clutched in his left hand. So he called his wife.

"Evan!" she exclaimed. "I got a call from the gliderport! Mr. Sorrentino was worried that you might have landed out in—"

"No, I'm in *Nigdzie*," Evan interrupted. They'd adopted that code word—Polish for "nowhere"—almost two decades ago. Evan had been in Saudi Arabia when the oil fields became killing fields and American specialists escaped through the byways of the Middle East, with not everybody making it out alive. *Nigdzie* meant somewhere better left unnamed when unfriendly ears might overhear.

"Oh, no!" Malgorzata said. "Evan, be careful!"

"Always, Maggie. Always. *Ja cię kocham*," he added, *I love you,* in her native Polish.

The Zofia might kill him.

He wouldn't be the first middle-aged sailplane pilot to die when his performance curve dropped below that of his glider near the end of a flight. That would be viciously ironic and unfair to Maggie. Her father had designed the Zofia, the old aeronautical engineer's crowning achievement in sailplane design.

Do-wn, do-wn, do-wn, the vario repeated, like a dismal metronome. Evan swallowed around a dry throat. He was dehydrated. And low. He'd reach Galveston Island with few options left The first time Evan had landed a single-place sailplane, faster and more sensitive than anything he'd ever flown and without a back seat for the instructor to rehearse landing with him before he did it on his own, a thunderstorm developed near the gliderport while he played in the sky; when it came time to land and it dawned on him that he had unpredictable wind to contend with, he'd been scared spitless. Like now.

The last card up his sleeve was the Zofia's almost magically high lift-over-drag ratio. Sixty to one, and not just with the leading edges clean of bugs and every other parameter impossibly perfect too. Her glide ratio was a reliable, stake-your-life-on-it, sixty to one. *60:1, 60:1.* His brain recited the ratio like an incantation.

Evan scanned the east end of Galveston Island, looking for enough unobstructed real estate to put the Zofia down on. Soggy salt marsh fringed the bayward side of the island. The roads all had light poles hemming the asphalt in. The beach on the far side of the island looked landable, but sand dunes flanked the beach. If he didn't clear the dunes, and one of the Zofia's wings struck, she'd cartwheel, and he would be a dead man.

He crossed the water's edge low enough to see the cordgrass heaving on the bay's foamy wavelets.

Up, the Zofia whispered.

The sandy, hot dunes were generating weak lift. Evan seized it. Circling, he inched upward with the intense patience of a man extricating himself from doom.

A great dark bird slanted toward him. For a few moments it soared with him, cocking its head, as if puzzled at the huge cloud-blue fellow bird. It had long slender wings, sculpted by evolution to ride the air just above the swells of the ocean, skimming the sea.

Evan only had a few glimpses of the frigatebird before it veered away, but that was enough. It left him with hope. He was in possession of the closest thing mankind had created to wings like the frigatebird's.

With a thin cushion of altitude, Evan set off along Galveston Island. It had been a hot day on the Island. Wisps of lift from the dunes, and hot air percolating off the wide asphalt length of Sea Wall Boulevard, were just enough to keep the Zofia aloft. The Zofia skimmed westward less than 800 feet above the heads of oblivious tourists.

By circling above the sun-baked parking lot of a Wal-Mart, Evan gained 150 feet of altitude—a jackpot reward under the tight circumstances.

Evan's cellphone chimed. To his surprise, it wasn't a worried Maggie. It was Leo Redwine. "Okay, Ev, I got the ball rolling. Now you tell me—what's going to happen to Painted Horse?"

"God only knows," Evan said. "Just get your best people in position to follow the telemetry from the SEANTS."

Evan's brain sparkled with inspiration, possibly a final surge of neurotransmitters before fatigue shut his neurons down. "Contact Zhenyang Chen at the Center for Biological and Environmental Nanotechnology at Rice University. He goes by Zeno. Get Zeno Chen into the loop."

"What the hell do I say to this guy?"

"Tell him I said this is the opportunity of a lifetime for him." Even remembered attending the Tenth Nano-Vivo Summit at Rice where Chen had opened his eyes to the possibilities of biological nanotechnology. Evan subsequently sought Chen out. They talked at length. He knew what Zeno and Zeno's field could do. "Leo, this is the opportunity of a lifetime for us too," Evan added. "Meet me at my office first thing tomorrow morning."

"I'll do that," said Leo.

Through a sea haze, Evan discerned the glass pyramids of Moody Gardens, which let him locate the criss-cross concrete lines of Galveston's airport. Overjoyed, he radioed, "Scholes Tower, this is glider Four Seven Seven Zulu, three miles east."

"Scholes?" the Silent Racer radioed back. "Gage, are you approaching *Scholes Field!?*"

"Sorry, I'm on the wrong frequency!" Evan hastily changed frequencies and repeated the call.

"Aircraft calling Scholes, say your type again?" replied the control tower.

"I'm a glider descending through 500 feet. I'll land straight in on the closed runway near Flights and Sights."

"Okay," said the tower controller, who couldn't very well order a low and engineless glider to fly a regulation landing pattern. "Cleared to land runway One Six. Be advised of heavy helicopter traffic in the area."

They were evacuating oil platforms in the Gulf, Evan guessed. As well they might. He veered toward the back side of the Island rather than venture between the busy helicopter base and the sea. Moments later, he was glad he'd changed course: a burly chopper churned by off his left wingtip, oblivious to him.

Gradually losing altitude over blocks of tract houses adjacent to Scholes Field, Evan smelled barbecue smoke. He crossed the airport perimeter and lined up with the closed runway with his heart racing. He pulled the airbrake handle. Twin red panels rotated up out of the wings, and the Zofia dove to Earth like an angel on company business.

Argk! Argk! blared the gear-up warning. Evan yanked the landing-gear lever just in time to lower the main wheel and touch down with a tire-rubber bounce rather than a shriek of shredding carbonglass. He rolled along the concrete, jolting on grassy cracks, and came a stop near the FLIGHTS AND SIGHTS sign. Last of all the Zofia's left wing delicately tipped onto the pavement.

"We did it, lady," Evan sighed, with his head in his hands. "We did it."

Evan opened the canopy and climbed out with effort. Dizzy with relief, stiff and sore, he felt more like seventy-nine years old than fifty-nine. He staggered into the bungalow that housed Flights and Sights.

Inside the air-conditioned main room, a small excited crowd clustered around a flatwall television showing a map of the lower Texas coast. Ominous red lines outlined the extent of the Trinity flood. The red-lined zone included the refineries of Baytown.

Evan went to the restroom. He washed his face. He drank six cups of water while the newscast showed incredulous newscasters and flummoxed local officials. A strained University of Houston researcher tried to say something accurate but not definitive about runaway nanotechnology. It was clear that the authorities weren't explaining much, but the news media were busy adding two and two.

Conspicuously absent was footage of Liberty's meltup. Evan knew he hadn't been seeing things when he gaped at that transmogrified town. The talk at Flights and Sights was of the gasoline storage facility near Liberty catching fire. But no one had seen images of the fire on any news channel or Internet site. Evan suspected a news blackout, the meltup of Liberty being kept secret while N-ergy and the government tried to make sense of it behind the red curtain of the restricted zone.

The President of the United States was reported to be en route to Houston, together with the Energy Secretary.

Evan felt better now—not a day over sixty-nine. He left the air-conditioned bungalow to go back outdoors into the warm sea air. The setting sun blazed in a sky-wide pool of light, a glorious greenhouse-world sunset.

The Zofia rested with her left wing down, the slim right wing angled up into the sky, and her cloud camouflage still on. Blue and cloud-silver shadows ghosted across her skin. Two line boys, whose job it was to promptly secure visiting airplanes, hovered, fascinated and unsure what do to with the Zofia.

Evan pulled the Zofia off the runway himself and tied the wings securely to the ground while he explained programmable aircraft paint to the line boys. Meanwhile he mentally kicked himself. Dehy-drated and distracted, he'd forgotten about the camouflage. Lucky the Zofia hadn't been turned into glass confetti by colliding with that helicopter!

Finally Evan opened the canopy to turn off the master electrical switch. Then he remembered the startled radio call from the Silent Racer: *Scholes?!*

He'd flown from the gliderport to Lake Livingston to Scholes Field. According to the flight computer, which had dutifully kept track and only needed to be asked to produce the number, he flew 206 miles today, the longest soaring flight of his life. More than 100 miles of it had been above water and below 5,000 feet of altitude. That probably qualified him for a record in the annals of the Soaring Society of America, provided, of course, that life for the SSA and the world would ever be normal again. While he flew, the world under his ship's cloudy wings had tilted on its axis and gone spinning toward an unexpected future.

Evan had adult children younger than the cushions he borrowed from Flights and Sights' ancient couch. But it beat resting on bare asphalt. He lined the cushions up in the Zofia's dark shadow under a glaring security light and stretched out on the cushions. Stars twinkled in the humid sky. The steady sea breeze kept mosquitoes—and perhaps other, invisible, unnatural bugs—at bay.

In the thrill of the chase, it had been easy to believe that nanoplasms were too fragile and too heavy to spread in aerosol form. In retrospect, it was easy to doubt. When Evan dozed off, he dreamed about plastic twisting like a pinwheel in his lungs. He woke up with an unpleasant catch in his side.

The sound of an approaching vehicle and headlights splashing the Zofia brought Evan to his feet. The car stopped with the muffled rattle of a safety chain, and behind it the Zofia's own long white trailer gleamed in the night.

Beth Torres hopped out of the car. "I went by Rice University, like you wanted, and got these people. And their equipment."

Three young males emerged from the car. Two were Zeno Chen's graduate students, the third a post-doctoral researcher whose name was Jeremy. Soon they were helping Evan take the Zofia apart. All three wore thick plastic gloves.

"The wing is secured by a very snug pin," Evan explained. "I can pull it out, if you raise that wing tip there —now jiggle it—"

"Ugmff!" said the grad student at the wing base when the wing came free he took its weight. "This is heavy!"

"Which edges are important?" Jeremy asked.

"The front edges catch bugs in flight." Evan pointed out the leading edges of the wings.

His helpers inexpertly but successfully manhandled both wings into the trailer, upright in the wing cradles. Then all three Rice researchers disappeared into the trailer with the wings. Clinking and whirring noises came out of the trailer along with quiet, purposeful voices.

Beth had watched the proceedings. She looked at Evan with large dark eyes. "Nice of them to clean your leading edges for you."

"They're cleaning the leading edges like they've never been cleaned before," said Evan.

"I'm glad you have a connection like this. The government doesn't know what to do."

"These guys do." Evan put a reassuring, and well-washed, hand on the young woman's shoulder.

The grad students emerged from the trailer, Jeremy gestured, and Evan took their place in the trailer. He crouched between the wings as Jeremy ran a small vacuum cleaning device over his clothes. In the darkness, Evan could make out a label on the vacuum cleaner. It said CBEN CHEN LAB.

"Should I worry?" Evan asked Jeremy in a voice barely audible over the vacuum cleaner.

The post-doc shook his head. "If one of these things was alive when it landed on your mucous membranes, your immune system would dismantle it immediately. Just shower when you get home. You won't shed anything alive into the sewer system—except your usual microbes." Jeremy methodically vacuumed Evan's hair, which stood up under the nozzle. His scalp tingled. "The real danger is to the world energy infrastructure."

Evan's shoulder rested against the Zofia's wing. He put his hand on the leading edge to stroke the slick carbonglass. He felt found no grit, no sticky dead insects, no holes where a nanoplasm had attacked his sailplane. "So the issue is containment."

"Containment is the great big burning issue," Jeremy agreed. "Whatever we find on the cleaning cloths and filters, it's going to be powerful evidence. Zeno said you had some kind of graphical track too?" Jeremy snapped the vacuum cleaner off.

Evan downloaded his track from the Zofia's flight computer to Jeremy's notebook. "The loops in the track are where the water was warm. The densest looping was Liberty."

"What did it look like?" Jeremy asked in a murmur.

"Like nothing I've ever seen," Evan answered. "Like a plastic riot."

Evan stood at his office window, which he'd switched to transparent mode for the twenty-seventh floor view. Sunrise light bathed the shiny flanks of neighboring skyscrapers. Gazing east, Evan half expected to see a distant, glassy eruption, which would mean that the nanoplasm had reached the refineries beside Galveston Bay, and it was the end of his world.

"Your visitors are here," said David, his sleek and competent administrative assistant.

Evan turned to greet them. After yesterday's marathon flight, he felt horribly tired. But he could hide physical and emotional wear and tear. The gabardine armor of a dark business suit helped greatly.

Well aware that the visitors were key players in the energy industry, David served coffee with practiced nonintrusiveness.

"Everybody else in downtown Houston is gaping at the news or trying to hack past the security firewalls to get the real facts," said Ann Cohan. "Or making contingency plans in case the city has to be evacuated in spite of the reassurances of the President. So why are we meeting with you?"

Evan answered, "N-ergy made the little bug that caused this big trouble."

Ann gave him a sharp, gray-eyed look. "How do you know?"

"I have a friend in a high place." Her picture hung on the wall near his desk: his Zofia when she was brand new outside the factory in Poland. David, standing behind the visitors, got the joke and flashed a grin. "N-ergy created a nanoplasm that metabolizes oil. It's going to transform our business."

Ann Cohan was a major oil company executive. Every strand of her silver hair reflected a critical decision in a rough, unforgiving business. "I don't need you to tell me the game's over if a plague destroys oil," she said sourly.

"It doesn't do that. David, please go gape at the news for us. Interrupt if there are any new developments. Ann, the nanoplasm doesn't so much destroy oil as it transforms petroleum into other stuff. Stuff that may be useful."

"Just how do you know?"

Evan gestured toward his other visitor. "This is Leo Redwine of Oceaneering, International. Oceaneering had an experimental research project operating from the Painted Horse platform in Trinity Bay."

Leo looked rumpled from lack of sleep, but ecstatic. "Deep sea ANTS. We deployed the first swarm at Painted Horse, in shallow water, to test them, just last week."

"ANTS means Autonomous Nanotechnology Swarm," Evan told Ann. "Small mobile robots designed for space missions, or in this case undersea missions—SEANTS. Each unit has sensing or analyzing instruments. They operate far away from human controllers, to intelligently explore the unexpected."

Leo cracked a grin. "The SEANTS are even better than the designers claimed when they were sober. We got a good picture of the whole nanoplasm event. We think we even sampled the nanoplasm itself. In-situ analysis results have been coming in since midnight."

The three of them pored over the results that Leo showed on his laptop. Ann looked faintly stunned as she viewed pictures of the superstructure of Painted Horse. The platform's framework sagged amid pale, iridescent shapes that looked like giant soap bubbles, carelessly pitched cellophane tents, and huge pinwheels made out of plastic wrap.

Leo scrolled through a set of sketchy diagrams on his laptop screen. "That guy from Rice—Chen—is a ball of fire. Brilliant scientist. He took data coming back from the SEANTS and figured out what was happening. The nanoplasm converts crude oil by a kind of catalytic processing. It's like metabolic activity and like chemical plant processing. The result is a complicated set of polymers that link into macrocopic structures."

"The petroleum reservoir is turning into useless plastic?" Ann threw up her hands. Her company had a large stake in the shallow water oil field in the region.

David briefly reappeared to report, "Petroleum pipelines are being shut down all around Galveston Bay! That's to stop the nanoplasm from spreading through the pipelines!"

"If it's out of control, it doesn't matter how useful it might be," Ann grated.

"Containment is the great big burning question," Evan agreed. His wristwatch read 9:03. He activated the Webwall with a virtual address at Rice University. The wallpaper—David had cleverly selected an Oriental pattern of clouds and cranes for today—shimmered and faded to reveal Zeno Chen in his own office, sitting behind his desk with an expectant air. They had agreed to touch base at 9 a.m. After introducing Chen to Ann Cohen, Evan said, "We where just speaking about containment. What can you tell us?"

"Salt is a hostile environment for the nanoplasm," Chen said. "It won't survive farther into the Gulf than Trinity Bay and that's only while the bay is flooded and the salinity is abnormally low."

Chen didn't bother to code his words. There were first-rate security protocols on both ends of this webcall. And today the communications lines in Houston would be clogged with references to the catastrophe. A data miner didn't stand a chance of sifting this particular conversation out of the haystack of hysteria.

"Will it choke the reservoir under Painted Horse?" Evan asked.

Chen steepled his hands. Beside his elbow, the workstation displayed what looked like a child's multicolored doodling, but it was the Zofia's path in the sea of air yesterday, recorded by the flight computer. "When we overlaid your path on the drainage basin of the river, your warm spots were all places where water and oil coexisted —such as a pipeline with a leak, a flooded service station."

Leo raised a bushy eyebrow, evidently starting to comprehend what Evan had been doing yesterday.

"Oxygenated water was present in those places, whereas the oil reservoir is anaerobic. I don't think the nanoplasm will proliferate there—but it is too early to tell for certain."

"Let's consider what we do know with certainty," said Evan. He made a deliberate, summing-up gesture with his hands. "It changes oil, or rather, changes some or all of the various fractions of petroleum, such as gasoline—into materials with polymer properties.

"Once the nanoplasm runs away, it consumes conventional structural materials. The painted Horse platform will never be the same again. Liberty either! But it's less than the all-consuming plague everyone fears. It might be a way to convert oil into polymeric materials with less environmental costs than the conventional process. Less pollution and heat. Less monetary cost than having stringent heat and pollution controls in a refinery. Less impact on an overheated, overpolluted world." Evan paused for dramatic effect. "Everyone else is still riveted on containment and control. No one else is thinking about exploitation yet."

"The nanobug must be patented to the max," Leo pointed out.

"Perhaps a nanoplasm with this talent escaped from N-ergy," said Chen, "but possibly it came into being as nanobiotechnological entities mingled with pollutants in oxygenated flood waters."

Evan remembered the roiling water below the Lake Livingston dam, where he had found the first hot spot.

"Hold on just a minute!" said Ann. "Dust from China and viruses from Africa show up in North America. How can we be sure this thing won't spread by air?"

Evan's fingers tightened on the pen in his hand. He realized he was holding the pen with the same severe grip with which he had held the control stick yesterday. "What did they find?" he asked Chen.

"Nothing," the man on the wall said. "Nothing. Some interesting DNA fragments but nothing alive. It will not travel that way." Zeno smiled faintly. "Jeremy has not been able to create any riotous plastic here in the lab, none at all."

Evan hadn't realized how his spine had been a knotted rope of tension, until he felt some of the knots loosen.

"The best models lead us to believe it won't survive in the air," Chen told the others. "And so does a serendipitous test yesterday, a hard one."

"Test?" said Ann.

Leo pointed to the Zofia's picture. Ann uttered an expletive more often heard in the oilfield than in the boardroom. But she got her feet back under her quickly. "Now what?"

"Ann, your company owns oil leases in Trinity Bay, and has the universal profitability and environmental problems with oil. Your company, Leo, is the best player in the underwater marine research and robotics business, bar none. Zeno, this problem is squarely in your ball park."

Evan sipped coffee that David had made the way he liked it, pungent with cardamon, a taste he'd acquired, along with a taste for danger, on the Arabian Peninsula. This was the most volatile opportunity of his entire career. Unlike his actual and virtual guests, did not have the engines of a corporation or a university driving his endeavors. Only the great engine of fate itself.

"Natural oil seeps exist on the bottom of Trinity Bay. And now the nanoplasm is introduced. Before the salinity returns to normal, it'll be a garden of Eden down there, for the nanoplasm. A week or ten days is a long time for microbial evolution."

Zeno nodded, telegraphing agreement.

"Since Ann's company owns the leases on the affected seabed, and is understandably concerned about the integrity of the wells, nobody has a better right to go in and assess the situation. We can see how this microbial garden flourishes. We can observe evolution diversifying it. And take advantage of it."

"Behind the government's back?" asked Ann.

"The United States government can't bed down with your corporation, Ann, or with Leo's. But my company can be a discreet go-between," Evan assured her.

"Is Rice aboard?"

"Not exactly," said Zeno Chen. "I am aboard. And thanks to Mr. Gage, I have a head start on every other researcher who will be attracted or assigned to this problem."

Ann nodded. Delighted, Evan let the corners of his mouth lift in a smile. He knew he had Ann on board now. He had all three of them.

"It's a risky proposition," said Ann, "but it might be very rewarding."

"It's exciting as all hell," said Leo.

"There is potential for terrible destruction, as well as terrific discovery," Zeno said slowly.

Evan nodded. He felt it. Fate's own lift going *UP*. Strong lift meant strong sink. This business would be as risky as it was rewarding, with discovery and destruction equally likely and some conceivable outcomes straight out of hell. It frightened him and exhilarated him. And there was nowhere he had ever wanted to be more than here, now. "All of you are right. This is a lot like a certain day in 1945. That was in the New Mexico desert. This time it's in the Gulf of Mexico. This is the day after another Trinity."

A PILLAR OF STARS BY NIGHT

Originally three *Analog* stories, together these tales form a short novel
—a novella—which was published by Avendis Press in 2014.

---

*By the late 21ˢᵗ Century, Earth's ecosystem may be damaged beyond
repair. Two young life scientists struggle with the decision whether or not
to join an exodus to a new world on the other side of the stars. Their skills
will be critical in creating a new ecosystem on a barren colony world. But
no one knows whether such an undertaking is even possible. To try and
fail would mean the death of every hope and every hopeful colonist—
unless something utterly unexpected changes the odds.*

1

THE FALL

Thin red clouds fringed the southern edge of the early sky, shreds of pollution that had drifted from sources hundreds of miles away. Such clouds promised yet another hot dry day Outside. Mark Willson glared at them through the glass and gray lattice of the dome, then left the observation deck and went to the mess hall, two levels down.

Will Diaz was having breakfast. Mark took a seat at the table next to the Chief Engineer. "Did you look out at the sky?" Mark asked.

"What was it?"

"Herring sky."

Will groaned. Then he asked Cookie for a second cup of coffee. The ration was one cup per day, but she poured him another without comment. Breakfast was eggs scrambled with diced prickly pear cactus, hot sauce, and cornbread.

Mark asked Cookie for peppermint tea instead of coffee this morning.

"What's on school for you today?" Will asked.

"Saturn's great white storm," Mark answered.

Will flashed a grin. "Now that's cool weather for you. I saw the one in '50, from outsystem. That was when I was serving on the *Jovian Explorer*. Saturn looked—"

Aggie Robbins, the agronomist, chose that moment to interrupt, leaning over Mark's shoulder to address Will. "My tomato plants can't take another 100° high," said Aggie, flatly.

"I've got worn-out, broken-down, duct-taped-together air conditioners," the Chief Engineer growled back. "So sit on your tomatoes."

"Well, I hope we all like eggplant. That may be all that bears through this summer." She departed in a huff.

"Cluck, cluck, old hen," Will muttered. Pushing his empty plate away, he left to go to the air conditioning plant.

Mark spent the morning on Netschool. Today's meteorology seminar was based at Cornell University. With classmates from all over the inner Solar System, Mark studied the equations that described the great white ammonia storm on Saturn. Mark wished that the seminar had been scheduled for this afternoon, not this morning. Too important to miss, it was making him put off his chores until the heat of the day.

After school, Mark reluctantly left the relatively cool classroom in the Mission Control Center. The Center's screen door slammed behind him. He scuffed along the well-worn path that marked the ecological boundary between the glass-domed veldt and the miniature sea, the horizon of which was a curtain of glass a hundred yards away.

The wave machine hidden in the water made the little sea surge against its little shore. Mark remembered that he had dreamed—a recurring dream that he had had before—about running across mountains and valleys, all the way to a real sea. Maybe it was the prehistoric sea that had once covered this land. It had no name in the dream, just vastness and blueness and cool wind. Wind, he thought, must be like standing in front of the air conditioning vents, only wider.

While he stood here daydreaming, the day was getting hotter. And he had to get today's chores, formally known as the individual work list, done today, because there would be more to do tomorrow.

The path took Mark to Mander Creek. He waded across. The water felt pleasantly tepid to his bare feet.

People getting their chores done had been wading back and forth all morning and splashing water from the creek onto the path. Mark found butterflies on the wet dirt, two Blues and one Sulphur. Slowly and quietly Mark crouched beside them. He rubbed a finger across his sweaty brow, then extended the finger toward the nearest Blue. The butterfly obligingly climbed onto Mark's finger. When its tickly little hind feet touched his skin, the butterfly discovered that Mark tasted like the salt it craved to supplement its nectar diet. The butterfly uncurled the long coil of its proboscis to sip the perspiration. With a finger of his other hand Mark collected the other Blue the same way. He transferred it to his equally sweaty and tasty nose and crossed his eyes to look at it. It flexed its wings, a brown blur with a lavender sheen.

Butterflies loved the endless bright and humid days. Mark didn't, but he had work to do. He gently placed the butterflies on a spot of nice mud.

A glass pyramid six stories high housed the rainforest. It included a miniature mountain with the cascading waterfall that was the source of Mander Creek. Mark felt rather than heard the water pumps, a subsonic presence, as he skirted the mountain. The rainforest floor was flowery green shadows heavily laced with organic smells that were cloying in this heat and humidity. Mark passed a few other Ecos. They nodded. He nodded. You didn't chat at people in the wilderness biomes, because they might want the solitude that was not available in the Domicile.

At the end of the rainforest, the glass pyramid slanted down to the ground, thwarting the trees. There the Ecos had their garden: papaya, coffee and huge stalky banana trees that pressed against the glass; lesser plants, the chilies and tomatoes, corn with beans twining up the stalks, and cotton plants crowned with white bolls. Millet grew where the glass met the ground.

The millet was mixed in with numerous green blades that were not millet. Grasses and little trees from all over the Ecosphere had made their way here. Mark knelt to pluck the aliens one by one. He sorted them by species, putting the sprigs into a sorting tray. He would return each green sliver to its proper biome. That was the problem with compressing a world into eighteen acres: most plants and animals could travel that far. Chickens from the agricultural biome had been found nesting everywhere from the rainforest to the Mission Control Center. Where the chickens, potbellied pigs, water lines, and air conditioning vents went, plant seeds followed. Keeping all of the biota sorted out took incessant work. Homo sapiens occupied the entire Ecosphere in the ecological niche of predator cum caretaker.

His sweat attracted gnats and small flies. He thought about Will Diaz, in the air conditioning plant, where it was hotter than this, with grease and grime to get on a person's skin. As daily temperatures soared in the desert Outside, the air Inside expanded as it heated up. The hot air would have blown out the sealed glass walls if not for the variable volume chambers, gigantic bellows designed to soak up the expanded hot air—Lung One and Lung Two. "The lungs are mechanically simple," Will had told Mark a few days ago. "No danger of 'em breaking down. But we need AC too. One of the units is on its last legs, and right now I can't take it out of service long enough to rebuild it again!" Will had added, "After I die and they compost my body, don't look for my soul in purgatory. I've done my time in the AC plant in Ecosphere!"

Mark had been pulling little green sprouts all summer, which was less purgatorial than Will's job, but he was sick of sprouts. He looked out through the glass, across the desert and toward the blunt spine of the Davis Mountains.

Green things die in the desert, and in the cities, Mark's mother always said, and there's not much Outside that isn't one or the other. The Net brought a seemingly endless supply of images of pretty green cities and parks, elsewhere on Earth. "Edited!" his mother said vehemently. "They crop out the pollution and the ugliness. And then they fill up the blanks with artificial prettiness!"

Mother had walked into Ecosphere twenty years ago and let the airlock seal behind her. She and the others were scientists, participants in the largest and longest lab in biospherics the world had ever seen. Mother and Will and Aggie and Cookie and thirty of their colleagues. They had stayed in Ecosphere tending it and learning from it for two decades. And now they understood biospherics pretty well. They, with the planetary scientists, meteorologists who had studied Venus and Titan and Saturn, and the restoration ecologists, knew enough to save the world. But it hadn't made much of a difference in civilization's priorities.

Even around the Ecosphere, the Ecos had seen the landscape around Ecosphere get drier and grayer over the years while they labored Inside. The red herring skies started ten years ago. In a kind of response to the evils Outside, the Ecos had let the airlock vestibule turn into the Junkyard, full of scraps and old parts and a few nesting hens.

Mark shivered. The landscape on the other side of the glass was no computer generation, it was real, and, in the hot midday, midsummer light, fiercely desolate and pale. Smudges of moving dust—dust devils—stalked the gray hills. Suddenly Mark felt sick and weirdly cold. Maybe it was the heat, maybe even heatstroke coming on. Wiping the sweat out of his eyes, Mark backed up into the spindly shade of a coffee tree and sat down to rest.

A butterfly flew by on huge wings shimmering like twin scraps of blue silk. Mark knew the Latin names for every butterfly species in Ecosphere, and all of their sexual dimorphisms, and this one was his favorite: a male Morpho Amathonte.

Not even the Morpho made Mark feel better today. Its home rainforests, shredded by logging operations in the previous century, were dying now, even as the trees tried to propagate northward to escape the desertification that pressed upon them from the south; but there were huge polluted cities blocking the way north of the Central American rainforests. Morpho was a refugee. The butterfly was blissfully unaware of its situation, only knowing its duty to patrol its territory and at intervals revisit the dun female who rested under a branch nearby. Going on about its butterfly business, Morpho went away, its blazing blue instantly extinguished when it flapped into the deep shadow of the forest.

Mark went back to Eco business, the millet. Outside, waves of heat rippled over the tawny desert, like a sea of visible high temperature.

Something creaked over Mark's head. It wasn't a croak, a tree frog. It was a creak. High up on the glass wall of the pyramid. The wall creaked again. Mark frowned at the lattice framework and the glass up there. It was the south wall, the one subject to the most heat stress for decades. Once white, the lattice had been weathered gray, scoured by sandy Outside winds and etched by acid rains. Maybe the framework, like Will's air conditioning machinery, had become brittle, or even misaligned. Squinting up at slightly imperfect triangles around stressed panes of glass, Mark could imagine the frames expanding in the ferocious heat of this day.

With a third creak, a jagged and branching crack appeared in a section of glass high up on the wall of the pyramid. Stunned, Mark stared. The hot expanded air inside Ecosphere wanted out. The air pushed pieces of glass out into the Outside. The rush of outgassing atmosphere stirred the banana leaves near the breach. Shards of glass trickled down the outside of the pyramid wall, like raindrops, but brighter.

Mark screamed for help.

There was a makeshift scaffold made of pipes and parts snatched out of the machine room under the mountain. Will Diaz's assistant, Joya, climbed up the scaffold armed with a big container of glue. "Give me the plexi!" she ordered.

The Ecos on the ground handed up the big sheet of Plexiglas from the Junkyard.

Mark remembered things that the outplaneters at Netschool had told him. How the death of airlessness or, on Titan, poisonous air, hovered over their sealed domes, and what happened if an accident or an act of sabotage cracked a dome; the panic, the quick action when the dome cracked; the slim hope of averting total disaster. Here nobody would die. The disaster would be the end of a twenty-year scientific experiment and of Mark's world.

"Damn!" Joya struggled with the plexi, which was too heavy for her to lift easily.

Will Diaz grabbed Mark's shoulder. "Go up there and help her!" Will boosted him onto the scaffold. It would not hold much more weight than his and Joya's and that of the Plexiglas—if it did as much. The scaffolding quivered under them. The Ecos on the ground made ready to catch whomever or whatever fell.

Joya slathered glue on the Plexiglas. The pyramid glass slanted over their heads, so they were in an awkward position as they tried to place the plexi up against it. Worse, the lattice was in their way, interior struts making it impossible to position the piece of Plexiglas. Every time Mark or Joya shifted their feet, the rickety scaffold shook.

"Put it outside!" Will Diaz ordered in a loud voice.

"What do you mean?" Joya asked over her shoulder.

"Tilt the plexi through the hole longways, then it'll lie on the outside!"

"It will slip off the pyramid!" she yelled back at him.

"Not if it's propped on that horizontal bar!"

Right under the broken pane, the pyramid's framework wasn't flush with the glass. A main structural bar was there and it protruded, making a small ledge, wide enough to prop the Plexiglas on. "We could too easily drop it!" Joya objected.

Captain Fleming arrived at a run, announcing, "We're not contaminated yet, the positive pressure's kept outside air from coming in! If we can seal this up, people, we're still in business!"

"Fix it!" Will Diaz bellowed up the scaffold.

Mark grabbed a banana tree that jammed up against the glass. With the help of it he started to lever himself through the jagged hole in the glass. Air still escaping from Ecosphere drafted past him.

"What are you doing?" Joya hissed.

"If you're in and I'm out," he answered, "we can stand the plexi on the bar. Then I'll come back in and we slide the plexi over the hole."

"Don't!"

But Mark was already out. A yell went up from the Ecos on the ground, Will Diaz audible above the rest of them. "Don't fall!!"

Mark found a toehold on the ledge. There was a wind out here. He felt it blow on him and he breathed it. If this had been Titan, Mark would have been breathing poison. But the wind descended from the oxygen blue sky of Earth. Dry, it cooled his flushed skin. He swiveled and leaned against the pyramid, his hip resting against the vertical frame between the broken glass section and the unbroken one next to it.

In the west, the sun was setting in a butter-golden brightness such as Mark had never seen in his life. He made the mistake of glancing directly at the solar disc. It left one small intense green spot of after-image on his retinas. Dazzled, he groped for the end of the Plexiglas that Joya handed him, and they started to maneuver it out.

The frame he was leaning on produced a grinding sound. Alarmed, Mark blinked down to the ground. A twenty-foot drop, but not vertical, rather a glass slide. "Joya, more of the glass up here is loosening! Maintenance had better go over all the seals."

"Tell Will later. Take it!"

He had most of the weight and most of the control of the Plexiglas now and struggled to stand it on the bar. But the wind exerted a force on the plexi that Mark hadn't expected. Suddenly he realized that he was either going to lose the plexi, or his balance, or both. Mark threw his weight against the plexi, pushing it up where it needed to be against the breach in the glass. Then Mark fell, skidding down the glass wall to land on dirt and cactus. He rolled off the cactus. Inside, the Ecos were screaming and waving, all except Will. Will was pointing away from the rest of Ecosphere, emphatically gesturing toward the east.

Mark looked that way.

The sky unfurled over his head, vast and vivid and intolerable.

Mark ran. He stumbled on the loose stones of the ground and

kept going, running his breath out, until he dimly realized that the sky had mostly gone away. Wheezing and shaking, he collapsed. He was in the Southaways gulch and out of sight of Ecosphere.

Mark's heart fluttered. He was Outside. Outside for good. He could not go back into Ecosphere, could not ask them to open the airlock, break the seal, admit him and the dust and microbes he had picked up, particulate Outsideness clinging to him. Shuddering, he thought he might be sick. Then he stopped himself. Not only was he out, he was out in a cruel desert, and vomiting would make him lose body water. He would dry up like a fish out of water and die.

Mark licked his lips, which felt parched already. He was thirsty. Mander Creek would have been wonderful right now. It would have felt so good to drink and to bathe his feet. They hurt. His soles were calloused because he never wore shoes at home, but the wild desert surface was rougher and hotter than any ground in Ecosphere. He huddled on the warm dirt in the gulch, glad for the stony walls that let him see not too much of the terrible wide open sky.

Something pricked at the palm of his hand, so he moved it. There were scrubby grasses poking up out of dry, stony, but living dirt. Grasses growing not because someone had planted and tended them, but because it was the way of grass in nature to grow in open places. Mother was wrong. Things did live in the desert. Unfortunately Mark Willson was not a xerophyte. He would die in the desert.

Will had been pointing east, the direction of Mount Locke, with broad emphatic gestures. Suddenly Mark understood why. He limped toward the end of the gulch to peer out. There was a road. It looked terrifyingly endless and empty. The colors of the sky overhead—blue to red—were more vivid than he had known, much brighter than the herring sky he had seen this morning. He realized that the glass of Ecosphere had been dirty. Over him now was the untrammeled and plain truth of sky, and it intimidated him. He craved retreat, staying, hiding in the gulch. But there was no water there.

A shaggy bird with a long tail ran out onto the road. It was one of the Outside birds known as roadrunners; Will called them by a Spanish name, paisano. Will used to call Mark "Paisano" when he was a little boy, so small that Ecosphere seemed enormous, because he had loved to run all over the place. Braking to a sudden halt, the roadrunner twitched its long tail and considered Mark with one eye; then it dashed off down the road, disappearing around a curve.

In the shades of sunset, Mark painfully stepped onto the road, old, with cracked asphalt. It was too hot to stand still on. He walked, fast, after the roadrunner had gone. Behind him the road began at Fort Davis. On the other end of the road, east, lay the top of Mount Locke and the Ecosphere's nearest neighbors. He thought he saw the domes on the mountaintop, turned into pink pearls by the sunset. The pink pearls were a long way away and a long way up from here. They looked too close to the awesome sky.

He tried imagining that glass was still up above him—like the wide span over the veldt and ocean biomes. Higher, cleaner but still sheltering glass. Suddenly he realized that it was true. The Earth's atmosphere was like greenhouse glass, and not all that clean, either: sunsets and sunrises were red because of pollution in the air.

The reddened sun set. The glass of air turned transparent and planets and the brightest stars appeared in the sky above Mount Locke. A cool wind cut through the loose homespun fabric of his clothes. His feet hurt. So did his backside, where he had landed in the cactus. So did the cut on his right forearm, a long curving scratch where the broken glass of the pyramid had grazed him in getting out. Mark forced his physical discomfort out of his mind. Life in Ecosphere had made him good at that. What had to be done had to be done. He trudged on. At least the road bed was mostly flat and easy on his feet, warm, though slightly sticky. Or else the stickiness was blood on his feet.

From the direction of the Mount Locke, he heard a mechanical sound, correlated it with a cloud of dust. A car sped down the winding road toward him. It occurred to Mark to get out of the way, and he jumped off the road just as the car's headlights flashed over him. But the car braked. The driver leaned out. "Are you Mark Willson? From Ecosphere?"

Mark was barefoot and wearing Ecosphere homespun. He must

be either somebody from Ecosphere or a revenant peasant from the 13th century. He nodded warily.

"I'm Edwin Ferris from the Observatory. Your Captain Fleming called us, said you'd been shut out by accident, and could we try to find you! He asked us to take you in for the night. Definitely! We'll be home in no time. Hop in!"

From the Net, Mark knew about cars. Mark was pretty sure that this one was an electric-powered, all-terrain vehicle, a Sand Rover. But he had never traveled in a car or any other mechanical conveyance. Gingerly he put himself in the seat indicated. "Th-th-thank you very m-much." His teeth chattered.

Edwin Ferris turned the car around. The motion made Mark clutch at the seat. "Had to charge up first, because I just got back from a supply run to Marfa. I'll turn on the heater."

The first curve took Mark by surprise, centrifugal force nearly throwing him into Ed Ferris' lap. Ferris laughed. "You don't have to compliment my driving. Nobody else does! Just buckle up the belt." Abruptly, Ferris sobered. "Your Captain Fleming said you've never been out of Ecosphere. Makes sense if it's been sealed for twenty years. So you've never been in a car before, have you?" Ferris slowed down. "I don't want to traumatize you!"

Ferris had wispy gray hair. He looked older than anyone in Ecosphere. But he sounded like any of the old men, professors, scientists and parents of Ecos, that Mark had met on the Net. "Are you an astronomer, sir?" This time Mark suppressed all but one chatter of the teeth.

"Oh, we do some astronometry, Earth-Moon distance measurements to the centimeter—it changes, you know—and parallaxes for the nearest stars. That's really important. We have to know exactly where and how far away they are, before we send starships!

"But serious astronomy is done in space these days. We're just a teaching facility. And a meeting ground for astrophiles—people who love to look at the stars. Most professional astronomers don't, you know, look at the stars with their eyes. Machines find asteroids and comets. But at MacDonald Observatory you can still see the stars for yourself."

"Can you see the storm on Saturn?"

Edwin Ferris beamed toward his passenger. "If you're interested, I can show you that tonight! Even from Earth, it's quite a sight." In his enthusiasm, Ferris speeded up. Then slowed down again. "Sorry!" He turned on the Sand Rover's heater.

Warmth flowed onto Mark's feet. His shivering subsided. He watched the rock layers of a road cut seeming to flow by. The car was going uphill in looping curves. He felt like a dreamer again, running with effortless grand gestures over a strange landscape, fearfully exhilarated. He could have explained that feeling to an Eco, but not to a stranger, though this one seemed friendly and good. He said, "I like riding in your car."

2

CHRYSALIS

A hurricane saved Ecosphere. One of this century's monster storms, the hurricane battered the Gulf coast, but by the time it got to the Davis Mountains it was all rain. Cooling the land and the air, the remnants of the storm took the load off Will's ruined air conditioning unit.

The rains brought cacti to life. Mark could see the faint colors of cactus blooms in the gray dusk before dawn as the Sand Rover zoomed down the flank of Mount Locke. The last two weeks seemed like the same kind of variegated and thorny blur, as he thought back over living at the Observatory. As promised, he had been taken in. Ed had shown Mark Saturn, with its blaze of white. and star fields, the glories and the depth of the stars. The nearest stars parallaxed as the Earth orbited; those were stars near enough for starships from Earth to reach, said Ed. To Ed's surprise and delight, Mark had quickly begun to learn how to find stars by celestial coordinates, to point the telescopes and operate the other instruments.

Helping Ed had been interesting and far easier than interacting with the rest of the staff at the Observatory. He felt as though he had been blundering into social thorns the whole time. Especially when it came to the women—an astronomer and a technician. They made him nervous. And his nervousness made him quiet and skittish around them. Once, soon after he came to the Observatory, Mark had heard the two women, who had underestimated his hearing, agree that he was socially retarded. That overheard remark had hurt. Remembering it still hurt.

"Your Ecos must be real morning lovers," Ed grumbled. Ed hated sunup in any other context than as an astronomer's bedtime.

"Contractors are diurnal too," Mark pointed out.

"But why do you have to get there before the contractors so much as open a tool bag?"

"I'm not sure," Mark answered. "Will said he wanted me to look over the contractors' shoulders while they do the work. It was the Captain who asked me to come at 0600 hours. I guess he wants to brief me."

Or, he thought, drum me out officially, in person, over the inter-communication system. Captain Fleming must have figured out that Mark didn't fall off the pyramid entirely by accident. Falling had been accidental—the wind's fault—but Mark had not had to put himself out there, in imminent danger of just that. Deep down, he had wanted out, just like the hot air, just like the banana trees crammed against the glass walls. He remembered the old running dream. It had been a symptom of his agoraphilia. The Captain must know that. The Captain of Ecosphere had always known everything. Mark's stomach knotted around the bagel and chocolate milk he'd had for breakfast.

Ed slowed the Sand Rover to look for the turnoff to Ecosphere. "Twenty years and they still want to keep the experiment going and stay in? All of them?"

"There's a girl near my age. Her name is Nessie and her dad is the physician, Doctor Tu. I think she wants to go to medical school. For the grown-ups, though, the scientists like my mother, there's so much to learn that all they want to do is stay and keep the experiment going."

He had talked to his mother on the Net. She was happy that he was safe. And something else: she had seemed relieved. She had never really wanted to be a mother. She had given birth to Mark for the sake of the biological model which postulated a certain number of children. That was the kind of secret that wasn't much of a secret in the confines of Ecosphere. On the Net, Mother had talked to him like an adult, and enthusiastically filled him in on the operations of Ecosphere in his absence.

"What about your fa—Diaz?"

"He's older than most of them. Almost sixty, so he had half a life outside of there. He's content as long as it's doable to keep the machinery running."

Ed found the turn and drove into the gulch. "But you weren't."

Mark gave him a shocked look.

"Wanderlust," said Ed. "Characteristic of the young males of the species."

The track was rough. Ed had to hold the Sand Rover's speed down to not much faster than Mark had run, two weeks ago. He had shoes now, machine-made shirt and pants, and a sweater, loaned out of the kindness and the pity of the people at the Observatory. Mark desperately wanted to ask Ed if he could make a life for himself in the outside world. The question tied itself into a tangle of hope and fear, unaskable. Ed wasn't a stranger now, really. But Mark was.

A twisting turn, clambering over a rise, and the end of the gulch revealed it, a quarter of a mile away, the Ecosphere: the barrel vaults of the Ag biomes, the long glass hall of wilderness, and the rainforest under the high tower of glass on the east end. Inside lights were already on—to give the Ecos extra day while it was still cool enough to work. The lights silhouetted the twenty years' worth of rainforest that pressed against the pyramid of glass. Ed whistled softly. "There are a lot of trees packed in there."

"Part of the plan was to grow a rainforest." To Mark's eyes, Ecosphere was astonishingly small and frail and full. "It looks like a chrysalis." He had never thought so when he had lived Inside and it had seemed like a palace. "Have you ever seen one, Ed? A chrysalis that's ready to break open, and it's transparent, so you can see the butterfly inside?"

"At the Cockrell Butterfly Center in Houston," Ed grunted. "Contractors aren't even here yet! Go report to your Captain. I'll catch some more sleep."

Mark got out of the car where Ed had parked it in an ancient and barely discernable parking lot. Nearby was the old communication station under its weather hood. Mark stared at the dusty equipment. He had talked to the Captain on the Net, to his mother, to Will, and to half of the other people in Ecosphere since he left. This was different. Mark keyed in Captain Fleming's private number. Maybe the intercom wouldn't work. But it did.

Fleming answered at once. "Saw you coming." Behind him, Mark recognized the walls of Fleming's office in the Mission Control Center. "Mark, it's too bad you're out. But it turned out to have been the best thing that could have happened. You are responsible for the Genesis Foundation taking an interest in Ecosphere!"

Mark let out a long inaudible sigh of relief.

From the Observatory, Mark had talked to Will Diaz, whose dark mood had been brightened by learning that Mark was safe. Ed Ferris had gravitated into the conversation. It had turned out that Ed remembered the long-ago *Jovian Explorer* mission and was pleased to meet one of the former crew members. Learning of the mechanical crisis in Ecosphere, Ed suggested that the Ecos contact something called the Genesis Foundation. Ed was on the Board of Advisors. A day later Captain Fleming had been talking directly to the Genesis Foundation.

And now the Foundation was going to replace Ecosphere's air conditioning units.

"Is that Ferris yonder?"

Mark had sighed out all of his breath, and struggled to get enough of it back to make an audible voice. "Yes, sir. He's resting. He usually works all night and goes to sleep at sunup. It was good of him to drive me here."

Fleming laughed dryly. "He'll have his reward! The Foundation's Executive Director is coming. Kalpana Warren. Make sure you roust him in time to meet his heroine." Mark nodded. Captain Fleming continued, "You'll be Will's eyes on the outside during the contract work—you already knew that. For me, you're my proxy. As such I want you to understand the whole picture. The consortium that built us in the first place is no longer viable. The universities have expressed a sudden lack of interest on the grounds that it's less than a perfect experiment in biospherics now. That means they can't spare the kind of money it would take to make the repairs we need.

"The government, meanwhile, has realized that biospherics is hard work, and they have elected to go with the kind of space habitats into which you throw a steady stream of resources to keep them going. But the Genesis Foundation is keenly interested in Ecosphere even as is, with mechanical damage and our blowout the other day. The ultimate goal of Genesis isn't pure biospheric isolation, but modules on an Earthlike but barren world. Terraforming modules." Fleming cleared his throat. "I think their shrinks are interested in us too. Why, I don't know."

Mark could guess. The staff at the Observatory had been shocked to hear that the Ecosphere had a three-to-five male-female ratio. Only a couple of the astronometers nodded with tentative understanding when Mark explained the biological rationale. The others seemed scandalized that he had no full brothers or sisters but two-and-one-on-the-way half-siblings. The Observatory people seemed to think that the Ecosphere people had gone strange being physically isolated from the rest of the world for so many years. The Genesis Foundation probably wanted to know what to expect of human psychology in a small, sealed and isolated terraforming station on an inhospitable world.

"Never mind. The important thing is saving Ecosphere! I gather that it may have been Warren's decision, personally. Her party will arrive by 0700 hours. That's Dr. Warren, mind you. I don't want her getting the idea that we're a bunch of beggar biologists in here. So try to tell her things about Ecosphere that'll impress her!"

"Yes, sir."

The Captain gave him a little semi-salute, and signed off.

Strangely enough, instead of feeling better, Mark felt worse now.

He wasn't sure that he was up to the job that the Captain had given him. Captain's proxy—to a powerful Outsider woman? Chilly nervousness crept down his spine, into his legs, making them ache.

Agitated, Mark had to move. He began to circle around the Ecosphere. Inside, Ecos were hard at work. They appeared as blurry, blank shapes behind the glass, which was colder than the humid air and heavily fogged. None of the Ecos Inside had rubbed a hole in the condensation to look out and see the new day.

Mark had talked to almost everyone on the Net. But he wanted them to look out and see him now. He had always looked out from the observation deck on the roof of the Domicile and from the gardens on the ground by the glass. He had watched clouds and dust devils and road runners and tumbleweeds. Maybe he had been the only one interested in the land Outside.

His legs definitely ached. His throat felt scratchy. Maybe he was coming down with something, he thought. Almost two weeks since he bolted from Ecosphere: just about time enough for the new germs he had met at the Observatory to incubate into a cold or the flu. And if he got sick, he wouldn't be where Doctor Tu could take care of him with a cool stethoscope and soothing words in Chinese. And he wouldn't get any of Cookie's chicken soup.

Mark craved the warmth and security, the familiarity of Inside. Tears oozed out of his eyes, drying quickly in the desert air.

He passed the desert biome, gentler and foggier than the continent's-interior badlands out here. He paused by the agricultural biome. He recognized the skinny, bustling form of Aggie Robbins, the Chief Agronomist. Nearer to the glass stooped the bulky shape of Davy Annson, hard at work weeding. Davy was Aggie's right hand, better than most Ecos at the simple, manual work that Ecosphere required so much of, valued for his productivity and for his pleasant temperament too. Outside Davy would have been a pathetic misfit: he was mentally retarded.

Mark swallowed hard. His throat definitely hurt.

Kicking rocks, Mark cut across the bay between the Ag Biome and the rain forest. The bay traced the edge of the veldt, the thick pelt of the grassland visible Inside. On this side a smattering of scrubbier grasses fringed the glass, huddled against it like children outside a candy store window. Runoff during rains made the glass edge of Ecosphere more hospitable than the desert at large.

Mark located the plexi-patched glass on the rainforest wall. Under the patched glass was a clump of prickly pear with some broken pads and stems—the cacti he'd landed in. Absently, Mark rubbed his backside, remembering how the pricklies had retaliated. These prickly pear looked stringier than the ones which flourished in the desert biome and had to be eaten back, turned into nopales and pear jelly. Cookie would have thrown up her hands at these specimens and said, *That's not coming through my kitchen, feed 'em to the chickens!*

Yes, there was life in the lands outside of Ecosphere. But the world was in a great die-off. The future would belong to cactus, insects, and small weeds that traveled where great trees could not. Cactus and cockroaches and crabgrass would inherit the Earth.

In the cloudy green garden under the bevel of the pyramid, Mark distinguished a person, a girl. It took him a few moments to recognize Nessie picking papayas. Unnoticed—she paid no attention to the desert Outside either—he watched her. Smart and skinny and assertive ever since Mark could remember, Nessie was a year younger than he. Once on the playground when they were small she had slugged him and knocked him flat. In the last couple of years the two of them had teamed up for Netgames, placing as high as fourth in solar-system wide competitions.

The woman technician at the Observatory, Kalyn, had been surprised that Mark had never kissed a girl, receiving the information with a startled glance of her blue eyes and a gesture brushing her long blonde bangs back from her face. But it made sense. Forty original Ecos from all over the Earth had loved and quarrel with each other and, in any event, had children. The population was now about fifty, a good match for the carrying capacity of Ecosphere. But fifty was too small a group to grow up in and marry someone. Fifty was a human natal band. The adults might as well have been his aunts and uncles. Nessie might as well have been his sister.

Through the glass, Mark realized that Nessie was not really skinny anymore. And she had another name, he remembered. Vanessa. Vanessa, the lithe shape, was making him feel very much like Kalyn did, even though Kalyn curved more dramatically. The difference in shape didn't matter as much as the similarity. Mark felt attracted, confused and socially retarded.

He hurried the rest of the way around Ecosphere and turned back toward the car. Finally, over his shoulder, he saw two misty little kids Inside, stooped over the backwater of Mander Creek, probably intent on counting salamanders.

Mark checked the time. It had taken twenty minutes to walk around Ecosphere on the Outside. It took longer than that just to walk from MacDonald Observatory down to the mailbox on the main road!

The early sun gleamed golden highlights onto the vaults of Ecosphere. The morning was cloudless and the sun would not be mild for very long. Thanks to Will Diaz, Mark had a fair amount of melanin in his skin, but it was no match for the ultraviolet that streamed through the Earth's ozone-depleted atmosphere. He sat down in the Sand Rover and reached for the sunblock stashed in the glove compartment.

Rumpled and sprawled in the front seat, Ed opened his eyes and said, "A chrysalis. Yeah, Monarch butterflies, right? The ones that migrate so far. The caterpillar bundles itself into a chrysalis, and the chrysalis finally turns into a transparent thing with the butterfly's wings and legs and feelers packed inside. Then it breaks open and the butterfly crawls out limp as a wet dishrag, and it hangs onto a nice safe twig while its wings dry. More wing than you'd imagine could've fit into that tiny shell. I have seen Monarchs, by the way, on goldenrod plants, years ago, when I used to have a place in the country outside of Austin. The wings look like orange and gold stained glass." Ed's face was flushed with enthusiasm and early sunlight. He waved his hand toward Ecosphere. "A chrysalis! The life of Earth, packed into a glass shell. Ready to break out and fly. To the stars." Then Ed asked, "Is the Captain going to let you back in?"

"No."

"Did he say why not?"

No. He hadn't had to. Outside is Outside. "I've— for one thing, I encountered a lot of microorganisms since I got out, that might change the whole microflora of Ecosphere."

"I'm sure you encountered some of Kalyn's last Saturday night," Ed said mildly.

Mark felt his face flame with embarrassment under the sunblock.

When the rain was followed by cleared skies, the observatory staff had thrown a party. They called it a Star Party, with candy sweeter than Cookie's syrup corn balls, liquor stronger than Ecosphere home-brew, and music.

Mark had listened to the silences under the conversations at the party. There were almost none of the subtexts of tension, attraction, grudges and other unfinished business, the unspoken but perceptible dialogues under the audible ones, that he had been used to in Ecosphere. He felt lonelier here yet freer. As he sampled candies from bowls placed in the corners of the recreation room, Mark had felt a breeze through the open window.

Drier than the airs of Ecosphere, fresher than the drafts from the air conditioners, the wind had intrigued him. He went outside onto the telescope plaza.

He still wasn't used to the vista under the plaza. It made his head spin and his adrenalin rush. Miles of low gray land lay in the gloom of twilight. Nearer, the ragged crowns of lesser mountains than Locke glowed in the late sun. Unlike the barren plains, the mountains were flecked with green. Mount Locke itself harbored cacti and various bushes and sloped into canyons with juniper trees and oaks. The mountain was a high island to which many species had retreated out of the desert drought. Locke was like Ecosphere, an oasis.

The wind smelled green. It reminded Mark of the smell of Ecosphere, though a thinner and more elusive green. Mark had an urge to run with the wind across the mountain. But his feet, blistered, bruised and cut when he ran away from Ecosphere, had not completely healed.

To Mark's dismay, Kalyn had trailed him onto the plaza. She had asked how old he was.

Mark answered, "Sixteen."

"Oh, then you're an under-socialized overachiever who just looks younger than he is! I thought you might be a fourteen-year-old genius," said Kalyn.

"I'm sorry," he said, cautiously.

"Oh, I'm not!" Before he quite realized what was happening, she was teaching him how to kiss. She tasted sweet too. Preoccupied while the sun set and the stars came out, they didn't notice Ed wandering across the plaza, admiring the Milky Way, cutting close around the corner of the telescope housing, until he almost tripped over them.

Now, Ed smiled at him. "Kay's a nice girl. I approve, in case you were wondering." Ed changed the subject back. "So the Captain can't let you back in. His loss will be my gain, I hope. I can offer you a job at the Observatory. Technical apprentice."

"Thank you—but—"

"But what?"

Mark confessed, "I'm not sure I'd be happy at the Observatory, either, forever."

"I'm not hoping for forever, just more than the three months we had our last sharp technician! Normally we get two kinds of app tech: the terminally lazy and the up and coming who up and go somewhere more prestigious. Stay a couple of years. You can save up money for college. And practice your social skills, too. Sound good to you?" Ed raised a bushy white eyebrow at Mark, winsomely.

Mark nodded. And then he sneezed.

"Bless you."

Through the window of the Sand Rover, Mark heard a distant noise. "Ed, they're coming. Kalpana Warren is supposed to be with them."

"What?!" Ed started straightening his rumpled shirt and fumbling for a comb.

Mark jumped out of the Sand Rover. Leading the way toward the vehicles in the lot, Mark sneezed again.

Suddenly he felt good. Even with this cold coming on. Even though he knew how much the Outside could hurt, even though today he had seen the cozy green goodness of the Inside, unattainable, for him, forever. He felt good anyway. He had a job and a safe place to stay while he learned about the Outside world, how to live there and—he softly gasped, adding it all up for the first time—how to love. Kaylyn had been inquiring about the state of his feet for days. Yesterday she had said—offhandedly, but with an interested blue gleam of her eyes: "When your feet are all healed up, we can hike over to Juniper Canyon. There won't be anybody else there, especially not old guys walking around stargazing!"

Mark made himself stop thinking about the future. He had work to do right now. Kalpana Warren must be the gray-haired woman in a bush jacket and safari hat, energetically climbing out of the jeep. It occurred to Mark that she might be receptive to a walking tour around Ecosphere. She was dressed appropriately. And it would only take twenty minutes.

Ed had really liked the chrysalis idea. Maybe Dr. Warren would, too. Mark quickly planned how to say it, tell her that the Ecosphere was packed full of Earth's life, but not just that, knowledge too. Ecosphere held twenty years and fifty lives' worth of discovery about what makes a world work. Mark would evoke the image of a Monarch butterfly in its chrysalis, ready to emerge and unfurl the beauty of its wings and fly a great distance. Here was a potential emergence as glorious as that, destined to fly the greatest of all distances: to the stars.

3

THE FOUNDATION

Dozing in his sleeping bag, Mark Willson heard a shrill, faint and unwelcome whine. Culex as well as Saltmarsh and the Asian Tiger mosquitoes thrived here, so he pulled the bag's mosquito hood around his head. Just before he slid back into sleep, he vaguely realized that the sound was not a mosquito at all. It had an unpleasant metallic edge. Later, a meadowlark singing woke Mark up for good. With a yawn, he turned his mind to the day ahead of him. He had work to do on his doctoral dissertation in ecology: "Restoration of a Coastal Tallgrass Prairie." This morning he would do a species count in the J-3 plot of his grid of string laid across the grass. Writing up notes and analyzing data could wait for the heat of the afternoon.

His notebook trilled at him. The message window said *Call Ecol Office.*

Not yet, Mark thought.

URGENT

But it had said *URGENT* two days ago, when the new department secretary wanted to know where the *Lepidoptera* reference disk should be filed. He would call back later.

Mark walked out onto the porch of the study hut. Not to start work quite yet—he still had to eat breakfast and find his hat, essential under Earth's frayed ozone layer. A pool of coral glowed in the eastern sky, the sun rising on the little piece of prairie, silhouetting the warehouses in the large industrial district that started where the prairie grass stopped. A mile to the west, the Clear Lake City rail station gleamed in the early sunlight. Mark breathed deeply of air that smelled damp and green, like a healthy greenhouse. He loved spending the night in the study hut, waking up to mornings in this oasis of hope for life on Earth.

Sunflowers flanked the porch, taller than Mark although he had the advantage of standing on the porch floor. *Helianthus giganteus*, huge and hairy stalks festooned with sunburst blooms. They were volunteers: unlike most of the flowering grasses, they hadn't been reintroduced here by ecologists, but showed up on their own. They were a resilient species. Even if the world grew still hotter and ecozones climbed to higher latitudes, with the sea flooding behind, *H. giganteus* would stalk northward along with its preferred climate.

Inconspicuous in a melee of sunflower leaves, a coffee cup belonging to Annetine van Leeuwen rested on the porch rail. The cup was genuine porcelain with a thin gold rim and a quaint Asian butterfly design. Mark smiled. Anna must have forgotten it before she left for Amsterdam to visit her relatives this summer. An entomologist, Anna had reintroduced butterflies, beetles and other insects to this scrap of prairie. Mark found an accumulation of coffee-tinted rainwater in Anna's cup. He crouched to empty the water onto the bright blue dayflowers by the porch steps.

A shrill whine, like the mosquito he had thought he heard before he got up, pierced the air. Mark jerked his head up. That definitely was not a mosquito. It was machinery, and closer than the warehouses, hidden from his view by the tall grasses and sunflowers.

Mark ran along the cross-prairie trail toward the strident sound. Grasses whipped his legs.

A huge, orange, hydraulic monster was scything down the grass on the far edge of the prairie. The machine hit a stump and emitted another whine.

Mark dashed to the machine. He stepped in front of it.

The operator stopped it with a thunk and shouted at Mark in Spanglish. *Man, are you crazy?!*

Mark understood the Spanish-English pidgin. Racking his brain for usable words, Mark explained the situation in Spanglish. *This place belongs to the University, for to study flowers and birds and all! Don't hurt the grass!*

The machine operator explained in turn. *The tide is high in Galveston, and she is red.* Red tide, the toxic bloom of microorganisms in the sea that had occurred more and more in the Gulf of Mexico as the Earth's climate warmed. And melting polar ice made high tide on Galveston Island very high indeed. *The streets fill with dead fish and things. Stinking germs come in the houses of the people. People will get sick there. So they come here.*

Mark recoiled in horror, realizing that the prairie had been designated as a refugee camp for people fleeing from a disease-ridden fish kill on Galveston Island.

Two uniformed men approached Mark over the carnage of mown grasses. Their uniforms were those of security contractors. "What are you doing here?" demanded one.

Mark fumbled for his identity card. "I work here. This is a University study area, and—"

"Not any more, it isn't. Maybe you didn't get the word. This real estate's been appropriated for a refugee camp."

Mark protested. "It already is a refugee camp for the plants and animals here! The University—"

Running Mark's identity license through his pocket computer, the security guard laughed. He flipped Mark's license back at him. "People come first. And you're an unauthorized civilian. Leave it, kid."

"*Why here?*" Mark screamed.

"It's the only piece of empty clean real estate in a hundred miles!" the other, older guard retorted. "You're educated—don't you know anything about politics?"

The machine operator shrugged at Mark, impassive.

Mark could collect his gear if he did so in five minutes. In ten,

Mark stood on a buckled asphalt road outside of the fence around the prairie. Yellow tape strung along the fence said RESTRICTED DO NOT ENTER. Mark clutched a flimsy printout, a trespass warning. If he tried to reenter the area he would be arrested. His hand, holding the printout, shook.

Mark turned away, stumbling on the road's cracks and potholes. Weeds grew in the broken edges of the asphalt. Dandelions. Ragweed. Peppergrass. In front of a particularly big and ugly warehouse, the roadside weeds were brown, treated with herbicide, dead, fringing a ditch filled with chalky water. There would be no frogs in the ditch. Frogs breathe with their whole skin, and when their world is poisoned, they die, and the ecosystem falls apart where the frogs should be.

Mark felt unfriendly eyes on him: guards at the front gate of the warehouse, sizing him up as undesirable. Mark avoided their gaze and their gate.

A red tide rose inside of him, echoing the sickness of the sea. It was his blood, and he heard it pounding in his ears. Tears, salty and hot, hurt the skin of his face, already sunburned because he had forgotten to put on his hat.

The Clear Lake railstation was busier and noisier than usual when Mark lugged his gear up the high stairs to the platform. Unloading a train of machinery and supplies in yellow wrappings, workers and a few peremptory officials crowded waiting passengers to the edges of the platform. The morning wind came up. It blew from the south, from the sick sea, and it stank.

The high-speed train took Mark north. The wide, smog-smeared city of Houston, with a beveled crown of an arcology that reared above the smog, flared on the horizon. Houston swelled and swallowed the train.

Mark got off at the South Main railstation and shuffled toward his home. When he reached the security gate of the graduate student apartment building and thumbed himself in, Mark realized that the red tide inside had receded. He didn't feel angry any more. Instead, he felt like a beach littered with dead hopes and dreams.

His roommate was seated in an armchair in the living room, contemplating the antique picture on the wall. He waved a hand at the sound of Mark's entrance without looking Mark's way. Ev—who was, as of a few months ago when he had successfully defended his own doctoral dissertation in molecular biology, Dr. Evan Reynolds— seemed preoccupied.

Wretched and dirty, Mark intended to creep wordlessly to his bedroom. But Ev snapped out of his reverie and looked around. "Wait a minute—what are you doing back? And your face is burned! What happened?"

Mark mumbled an explanation.

"Oh, no!" Ev leaped out of the armchair. "It's probably been in the news, which I have not been watching. I would have called and warned you! Damn it, your department should have!"

"Never mind." Mark veered toward the kitchen to make the coffee that he never had this morning. His head ached. He fumbled with Ev's coffeemaker. Following Mark into the kitchen, Ev hovered behind him offering sunburn ointment.

Clumsy and distracted, Mark knocked the coffeemaker over. Wet grounds spilled out of the gold filter cone onto the counter. Mark stared at the mess. It was hard to breathe and harder to speak. "Remember Samantha Berry's last lecture? The new world?"

Ev leaned against the counter. "Ecology 401. Midway through the semester. 'A new world'," Ev quoted Samantha Berry. "'Not just a bubble on a moon. And not an inferno like Venus or a frigid, desiccated desert like Mars. A green new world, if human colonists are smart and diligent enough to terraform it properly'."

That lecture had been Professor Berry's way of announcing her resignation. Six weeks later a starship had departed, with ten thousand colonists in cryostasis, to be revived hundreds of years in the future at an Earthlike world near a Sunlike star. Berry was one of the colonists. Her colleague Annetine van Leeuwen took over teaching Ecol 401.

"There's going to be another terraforming starship," Mark said. "It's being built now."

"I know," said Ev. "A family friend is the principal contractor, operating out of Luna Prime."

"This one's sponsored by the Genesis Foundation. They've asked me to go or at least serve as a consultant in the planning process. What they want to do they're calling creation ecology, and it's a lot like restoration ecology. I've made up my mind to do what I can to help them. And maybe when the ship leaves, I'll go with it."

Ev stared at him. "I don't believe I just heard you say that. It's the stress of the morning, isn't it?"

At that moment, a roach crawled out of a cranny in the kitchen counter and ventured toward the spilled coffee grounds, feelers twitching. Mark's stomach turned at the roach.

The land here had been coastal tallgrass prairie, with a delicate web of naturally evolved species. But prairie was supplanted by the city and the opportunistic species which exploded in that kind of ecological vacuum anywhere in the world. Pigeons, crabgrass, rats, gnats. And roaches. The city teemed with roaches, even in the better neighborhoods in spite of pest control and fastidious housekeeping. In the poorest areas they were a crawling, chitinous plague. The delicate web of species had been blasted. And he, Mark Willson, could not restore it. He slammed a first down on the counter. The roach scuttled back into its crack. "I can't stay here and watch the Earth die!" he yelled.

Ev said slowly, "I was thinking about the stars just before you came in." He gestured toward the framed picture hanging on the living room wall.

The antique print depicted the star cluster called Pleiades shining across the night sky of a distant world. The print was pretty and precious.

Ev would never go to see any distant stars with his own eyes. Ev had everything he wanted here on Earth. And if that wasn't enough,

Ev was a citizen of the Solar System, cosmopolitan and comfortable with the offworld lifestyle in habitats and colonies. Ev said, "I always thought you were the last man on Earth who'd talk about leaving for the stars."

"I'm not," Mark said. "You are."

Ev smiled. The smile traced the lines of his grin, without any humor in his eyes, which made his expression seem like a rictus. "I know. Don't I have a lucrative job with the number-one genetic engineering corporation in the world? And I'm good at what I do. I can get blood out of a turnip. Blood and money. Out of turnips and mice and butterflies."

Mark recoiled. He gritted out the words, "You'll get used to your job."

"Should I? You help green things grow. But what I do—should I get used to it?"

Mark could not handle Ev's problems and, if that was what this was, Ev's guilt. Not now. Mark turned away.

"I am the taskmaster, living chromosomes are my slaves! Should I get used to that?" Ev insisted, following Mark back into the living room.

"What else?" Mark grated.

"It wasn't just has-beens like Berry. Thousands of the best and brightest people went on that starship too. Such as Joseph Devreze. As in Devreze dogs, Devreze sprites, Devreze twists. He was the best theoretical molecular biologist of this century. But he went to the stars."

The Pleiades print, Mark belatedly noticed, had been shifted to a new spot higher on the wall, and Ev's side-table moved beneath it, with a model of a spaceship and crystal vase on the table and fresh flowers in the vase. The arrangement looked incongruously like a shrine. "I think I need to go to the stars too," said Ev.

No, Mark thought. Ev would never do that. Not bright-eyed, mercurial Ev. "You don't mean it."

"Well, do *you*?"

"I said I'm thinking about going. And I am," Mark said. His own voice sounded bleak.

I n the middle of the following night, Mark had a nightmare. He woke up in a sweat with his heart fluttering, his limbs semi-paralyzed, his sunburned face hot and hurting.

His small bedroom was full of plants. In the faint nightcity light from the window, the plants had dim, gray and somehow dreadful shapes. Mark groped for the switch to throw lamplight onto the plants and make them return to green normalcy.

It was the Pleiades. Ev's picture had gotten to him.

Ev had found the print at an exclusive gallery Uptown a couple of years earlier, fallen in love with it, and purchased it on the spot with his father's credit and his own good-sporting grin, while Mark boggled at the price. Mark had thought that he had gotten used to it, respecting the fact that it was classic space art though not to his own taste. It had a nice name. "Ladies of the Lake." But the picture had finally unnerved him.

He had dreamed about that world with no living green, only ice mountains ringing a blue sea of nitrogen, bitterly cold to all eternity, beneath a night sky radiant with blue starshine. The cold burned. The stars' irradiance would destroy the delicate molecules of any Earthlike life. "Ladies of the Lake" told him what the stars were like, the reality of space outside of the sheltering fold of the Earth.

Too tired to be fully awake, too disturbed to be fully asleep, Mark twisted in his bed, hagridden by seven sapphire stars.

E v admired both views. This was a good table by an extraordinary window, beyond which the bright, benighted city of Houston stretched into the distance. The air swarmed with the firefly lights of the aircraft that, in this century, had replaced ground-going automobiles for the travel needs of people wealthy enough to own their private transportation. The other and more immediate view which presented itself to him was that of Dr. Miraly Fiorenza, seated across the table. She had a thoughtful expression on an intelligent face, and a sapphire-blue blouse cut attractively low.

Miraly seemed interested in his account of disaster on the prairie and the decisions that ensued from it. "That was a year ago? Why aren't you selling your possessions and living like a monk?"

Bingo, Ev thought. She really was interested. And not just in the story. He felt a pleasant erotic thrill, and answered, "The Ship won't leave for another two years."

"*Carpe diem*?"

A dark-clad waiter materialized. This, the Houston Club, was the apex of the arcology that crowned the city. The club was the jewel in the crown and the haunt of the rich and powerful, and fraught with unwritten rules. One rule was that everyone in the party must order a drink. Another rule was that the drink must be something classic. In mid-twenty-first-century America, wealth and power donned the trappings of earlier ages. Ev ordered two Old Fashioneds, and thus obeyed that rule with conscious irony. With a satisfied twitch of expression, the waiter glided away.

"There are more important things to do than curl up and wait for the trip," Ev told Miraly.

"Such as?"

"Mark is supplying seeds to the Genesis Foundation for the terraforming project. And I'm working hard, and learning all I can, at Pennington Genetech. We may need new organisms in the new world. Organisms that somebody like me can tailor from normal species."

The waiter returned with the drinks. Ev sipped his. It was perfect, a fine balance of the bitter and sweet and citrus on the base of alcohol. He waved his glass in a circle meant to include the ambiance, the view, and Miraly. "In the meantime—*carpe diem*."

Her lips on her glass curled in amusement. "I absolutely cannot imagine you on a frontier world."

"Oh?"

She made a circular wave to imitate his. "I know a fish in its water when I see one."

"I grew up on Titan. Dad's an executive with the Lunar Mining Company, trans-Martian division." Ev was gratified to see her react with surprise. "Frontier worlds are nothing new for me."

"Well, well. You don't seem nearly hardscrabble enough to be an outplaneter."

"The company pays Dad handsomely. While I was growing up, we vacationed on Mars, Luna, and Earth, first class all the way. I also spent five years at an exclusive boarding school."

"Thus the polish," she mused. "But you, digging in the dirt to make tomatoes grow on a colony world? I still don't buy it."

"When the Ship finds a new world, the plan is to have Ship as an orbiting city while the world is terraformed. The first generations downside will live in domes. Only people like Mark will be digging in the dirt."

"He sounds sweet."

From her tone, Ev realized that he must have described Mark in terms that appealed to Miraly. Did that mean she would prefer a man like Mark to one like Ev? Not necessarily: maybe she liked lost kittens and sad-eyed puppies. And maybe she would accept an invitation to go home with Ev just a bit more readily if it involved the occasion to meet and sympathize with sweet Mark. Ev filed the thought in the back of his mind. "He's not cut out for modern life. Doesn't quite realize that Earth is like one of those plants of his. Goes to seed and dies."

"Is it that easy to for you think of Earth dying?"

There was a barb in her words. The black-haired rose had a few thorns, Ev thought, intrigued. "Have you observed Earth from space?" he countered. "What with the smog and desertification visible from orbit during the day, and huge splotches of urban light on the night side, it's obvious that Earth is going to seed."

"But it's not natural for Earth to die, like it would be for one of Mark's plants. It's things like pollution, war, overpopulation, politics."

Ev sighed. "I won't argue that. Pennington reeks with the kind of politics that promote the unfettered exploitation of resources, environment or sustainability be damned. Genetic resources are the big issue—and cash cow—at Pennington, but the top dogs support the politics that keep the outplanet colonies dependent and feeding Earth minerals and helium-three for industry. I have not breathed a word about my future plans around Pennington. If the corporate climate is one that doesn't favor independent solar system colonies, it abhors the idea of a starship that leaves and sends nothing back."

There was a Netnode on table, discreetly metal-toned so as to blend in with the general decor. Miraly activated it. The node had a small, jewellike screen and audio muted so as not to disturb other guests here. Ev could barely hear the locator beeps and buzzes as Miraly pulled up a map of the world.

More eager to watch her than the little screen, Ev admired the graceful lines of her body draped by the blue blouse. Tapping the screen with a fingernail, she linked to a region in Brazil, then a medical update indicated by a caduceus icon. A window in the screen showed a ball-and-stick sketch which Ev recognized as a virus of some kind. "This is a disease of cattle," she said crisply. "Somehow a section of its DNA crossed into a human respiratory virus. The result is called KAV, and it's infected hundreds of people in Amazonia."

For the first time during the whole date, Ev remembered that she was a doctor and professor at the medical school in Galveston; her specialty was virology. He had met her at a genetics conference the week before.

She went on. "Pennington Genetech has invented an antivirus, and patented it. And is waiting for the World Health Organization to come up with hundreds of millions of dollars for it. Until then, Pennington won't release the antiviral gene sequence to the public health authorities. The death toll stands at—" She fished for the figure, and displayed it. "One hundred fifty-two as of today. It will rise rapidly. But Pennington's chief executives seem to share the belief that seems all too common today—that the answer to overpopulation is disease. As if the suffering doesn't matter."

"I know." Ev studied the screen and her intent face, more hard-edged than it had been just minutes before. He said slowly, "Is this why you accepted a date with me?"

"Did you know there's a joke in the medical community about researchers who work with Pennington? They are a specially genetically engineered strain of human being without the heart. I wanted to find out if you were a typical Pennington clone. And you aren't."

"Glad to hear that," Ev murmured.

"Who do you know at Pennington?"

"Not top people who could spring the virus sequence," Ev answered, suddenly impatient. "Does this mean you won't see me again?"

Her wide, elegant lips turned in an ironic smile that surprised him. "No, as a matter of fact, I think I'd like to see more of you."

Maybe the Old Fashioned was going to Ev's head. But he knew Eros to be as psychoactive for him as alcohol. Ideas were mixing in his brain, crossing over from one domain to another, dangerously recombinant. "I have an idea. The Genesis Foundation hinted at channels for under-the-table contributions to the gene library. The Foundation thinks the same kind of politics that Pennington exemplifies are going to weigh against free access to biological specimens for the Starship. Therefore I'm playing with ways to make contributions from Pennington's gene banks to the Starship's library—without Pennington's knowledge. I think I could smuggle the virus sequence out. Probably within a week."

Surprise and dismay flashed across Miraly's features. She hastily put down the glass. "That would be faster than official deals ever could be—but it's—I'm not asking for that. Are you sure you don't know somebody who can make it happen above board?"

"Absolutely. I don't," Ev said soberly.

"But you could get into serious trouble."

"If I do it for the Ship, which I probably will, I'll run the same risk."

"It's a game to you, isn't it?" she said quietly. "Plotting to go to the stars, and if there's a bit of opposition to outwit, so much the better. What will you do when it's time to cash the chips and either leave forever or stay?"

"I'm planning to go."

"I bet you stay. That you don't get caught if you do smuggle genes out of Pennington, but you stay anyway."

"Maybe." Ev kept his tone noncommittal.

Women didn't usually affect him the way this one did. But then, in his experience, matrons doted on him, while younger ones fawned or flirted. Miraly did neither. Ev felt the way he had when he first saw "Ladies of the Lake" and met brilliant, hard-edged beauty that he could not live without.

He had two years to persuade her to come along to the stars.

I n the three years since the disaster of the prairie. Mark's life had been, to all outward appearances, normal. He was now a junior faculty member with papers to publish and classes to teach. In secret, he harbored a purpose and a dread that gave him broken sleep and bad dreams. The single worst and most compelling nightmare happened one evening as he napped after dinner. In the dream, Mark beheld a cosmic wake, the Earth in a tattered, dull green death shroud, and passing comets with the wings and the faces of archangels, mourning. Later that same night, he went through the motions of teaching a seminar in a stunned daze.

With his perpetual ache of insomniac fatigue, the afternoon class in introductory ecology was the most difficult part of the day for him. But he prepared methodically, presented thoughtfully, and struggled to get the importance of the subject across to disinterested young minds.

Early in the semester, Mark had issued each student in Intro Ecol a glass ball and the task of filling the ball with water and a balanced population of algae, brine shrimp and micro-organisms. The balls were then sealed. By now, mid-semester, a variety of initial mistakes in the composition of the microecologies were apparent, in the form of sick and cloudy or dead and slimy contents in the glass ecospheres.

"The Earth is an ecosphere too." Mark meant to make one more, conclusive point before the hour was over. "That is, a system closed except for energy, receiving from the Sun a fairly constant amount of electromagnetic radiation. Energy from the outside was necessary but not sufficient for life on Earth; life also had to organize itself into a dynamic yet stable balance."

"It's not materially closed any more," objected a student named Pol—one of the Mark's least favorite students. "We've got space resources now."

"True. But Earth always had space resources in the form of meteorite and comet impacts, and cosmic rays and dust." To decisively regain the upper hand, he threw out a testable packet of information. "Life on Earth may have originated with organic compounds formed in interstellar dust clouds. In the early days of the solar system, there was a continual rain of interstellar dust, some of which contained hydrocarbons, including molecules that may be considered the precursors of amino acids. Thus the dust from interstellar space seeded Earth with the potential for life, if the Cosmic Genesis hypothesis is correct."

Pol slouched.

"With or without closure of the planetary ecosystem, it's vital that populations of organisms be in balance, constituting a dynamic, yet stable, system. If an ecosystem is destabilized, you get a runaway degradation of the environment—as in some of your ecospheres. In other words, a partial or total die-off."

Pol interrupted Mark again. "But space resources mean we can live under domes on Earth even if nature dies."

"Don't count on it," said Ev, who, to Mark's complete surprise, had appeared in the classroom doorway, startlingly out of place in an expensive business suit. "The out-planets could decide to keep their resources instead of throwing them down into a gravity well."

Mark introduced Ev to the class. "This is Dr. Evan Reynolds. A research scientist with Pennington Genetech, who grew up on Titan." Mark wondered with alarm why Ev was here. It had to be Ship business.

Without asking permission, Ev picked up Pol's ecosphere and walked away to the window's light, examining it. Then he said, "You botched this one. And no fair opening it to fix it up. So you might as well throw it away." Ev tossed the ecosphere back to Pol, who bristled as he caught it.

Mark hastily dismissed the class. Pol left muttering. Some of the departing female students giggled and whispered among themselves with backward glances. Resplendent in the business suit, Ev radiated a sardonic intensity which blew the last of the students out of the classroom, including those who might have lingered to ask questions.

With the room cleared, Ev turned to Mark. "Today the Supreme Court upheld the Alaska law. No exports of wild biomatter. Interpretation extended to seeds and other germ plasm."

Mark felt a surge of consternation, with a sharp and unsettling undertone of relief. He collected his thoughts out of the mishmash of feelings. "It's ridiculous! The law in Alaska was meant to prevent wild places from being dug up wholesale. Seeds, and germ plasm, which the Starship needs, are different! What are a few seeds?"

"They're seeds of an idea, and the idea is a new world," Ev said forcefully. "Listen. The Genesis Foundation expected this. The Ship leaves *tonight*."

"What!" Mark sagged against a counter.

"Everybody won't make it before the launch, so there'll be a whole fleet of rocket planes and Clippers coming up from Earth to meet the Ship tonight and in the next few days. It'll be a mad scramble. The Ship will add passengers from the colonies and outworlds all the way to the end of the Solar System. But they've asked some of us on Earth—such as biological scientists—to come tonight to maximize the chances of us making it out unhindered."

"Unhindered?" Mark stammered. "What does that mean?"

"Mark, the court's decision is going to be a signal flag. It will encourage protestors, corporations, and the government itself to undertake God only knows what actions against people trying to join the Ship and against the Ship itself. It's a good bet that the President of the U.S. will declare martial law at midnight tonight."

Mark's nerves jangled. "Wait. Wait! The Ship can't possibly have absolutely everything it needs yet for terraforming—"

"The more genes the better," Ev agreed. "We ought to grab extra seeds on the way out."

Automatically, Mark led the way toward the reference collection. Mark thought about the little dead ecospheres. Wrong initial conditions. In some cases, only slightly wrong. End result, the slime of decay. He felt hot and prickly. "They're sure they've got everything to make ecosystems?"

"The planetary ecologists have been running computer models continuously with the species actually in the Ship's freezers. The more diversity and redundancy the better. So, now that the chips are down, the Foundation is grabbing everything it can, be it animal, vegetable, or virus."

"The Foundation is *stealing* biota?"

"All over the world."

Astounded, Mark asked no more questions.

"We have to go by Anna's office, don't we?" Ev asked. The Ecology Department occupied one floor of the ancient Biology building. The reference collection was located just down the dusty and crowded corridor from the office of Annetine van Leeuwen. "Does she know you've been planning to go?"

"She guesses," Mark said tersely. He did not elaborate on Anna's sharp glances, the frosty nod of her head when he asked for specimens for fictive research needs, intending to send them to the Foundation for the Ship. For years, Anna van Leeuwen had been outspoken in her criticism of Samantha Berry's decision to leave on the earlier starship. Anna had complained bitterly about having inherited the department chairmanship from Berry. Before the Starship, the two middle-aged women had been friends and department allies.

Ev said, "She may have heard about today's court decision. It's headlining the news. If she sees the two of us she'll either talk our ears off or call the campus police."

But Anna wasn't in. The door of her office hung ajar, giving Mark a glimpse of the usual clutter within, and her desk, for once, unaccountably, clean.

Knowing that Anna might be no farther away than the women's restroom, Mark and Ev hurried by. A few minutes later, Mark reached into the freezer for small vials marked with his own neat handwriting.

In her valedictory lecture, Professor Berry had described Starship stasis, the cold storage for plant seeds, germ cells, bacterial spores, and people. In a few months Mark would be in the freezer, and in a few hundred years, on the other side of the stars, being pulled out, insensate but alive—if he was lucky. His hand shook.

"Don't make it too obvious," Ev advised.

Mark selected Little Bluestem seeds—a keystone species in its native grasslands—then five more vials at random. On impulse, Mark also seized a vial that contained the fat seeds of *Helianthus giganteus*, the stalking wild sunflowers. He rearranged the vials to obliterate incriminating gaps. Ev leaned casually against the doorjamb to watch the hallway. "Not a sight or sound of her yet. Let's get out of here."

When they were well away from the reference collection, Ev said, "I have to run next door and pick up something of mine that they've been keeping for me. And drop off a letter to Burch, my old advisor. Explaining everything. It's OK—he's out of the country and he won't get back to open the letter until next month."

Mark should have left a note for Anna. He owed her that much, at least. Too late now. They exited the Biology building into the breezeway outside.

The day was gray and muggy, typical of this climate zone of greenhouse Earth. Some of the ancient bricks in the walls of the Biology breezeway were molded with intaglio designs, biological ones—stylized scorpion, jellyfish, moth, protozoan, annelid. The intaglios had crumbled at the edges from decades of exposure to the acid air.

The breezeway led to the Biosciences building, where some of the bricks were intaglioed with a double helix. "I'll be back in a minute." Ev bounded through the main doors.

The Rice University campus was old, some of its brick buildings dating from the twentieth century. Huge and slowly dying oaks lined the sidewalks. There seemed to be an unreal calm here today, like the Jurassic fern swamps on the eve of the great Cretaceous extinction. Mark wondered what obscure plants and animals would inherit the Earth this time.

Ev emerged from Biosciences holding a small animal carrier labeled LIVE MICE HANDLE WITH CARE.

"Patented mice?" Mark asked. "You think the new world will need them?"

"You never know," Ev said vaguely.

It was Ev's ego showing, Mark thought. He couldn't take his prized possessions to the stars, but he'd bring something he invented. They crossed the campus together in silence.

Waiting for the train at the South Main Rail Station, Mark started to say "Bluestem—" but stopped himself. People milled around the station, University types whom he vaguely recognized, and others whom he did not know. The Genesis Foundation definitely would not want its plans overheard, today of all days. Mark took his notebook out of his pocket. He urgently pecked out the words *One grass won't save the new world.* After showing the statement on the little screen to Ev, he erased it.

Ev shrugged.

What if the models are wrong?

Ev took the notebook to enter the words, *we'll make it work. i'll make it work. are you coming or not?*

It was hubris enough to attempt restoration ecology on Earth, to mend the gashes that humanity had torn in the planet's living fabric. But to plan to terraform a whole, strange, undiscovered world—on the basis of hurried models based on familiarity with no living world besides Earth—this went past hubris into the realm of collective, suicidal insanity. On the train, Mark slumped in his seat.

Ev had the notebook. He handed it back to Mark. *you still haven't decided, have you*, it accused.

The monorail took them toward the center of the city, first through the highrise residential district with frequent stops, among them the one that Ev would have taken to go to the place he shared with his girlfriend. Thoughts churning, Mark asked, "What about Miraly?"

Ev grimaced. "She understands everything all too well. But she still won't come."

Mark was startled. Ev had been so sure that Miraly would go with him to the stars in the end.

"I left everything with her. Including 'Ladies of the Lake'." Ev settled back in his seat, profoundly pensive.

Mark could not understand how Ev could leave Miraly. Mark loved the Earth. And he did not know whether, loving Earth as he did, he could bear to desert it.

Over the city loomed the shape of the Uptown arcology, a pyramid supported by three pillars—each pillar a skyscraper in its own right, but dwarfed by the pyramid. Mark blinked. Today everything seemed unfamiliar, in the dreadful light of leaving forever, unreal. Uptown reminded him of an ancient motion picture about an invasion of huge long-legged machines from Mars.

Entering the Wards, with no stops for the poor and crowded people who lived there, the train accelerated. Hurtling along its elevated rack, the train arrowed under the skirt of the pyramid, decelerating. When it halted, they exited onto a platform.

Another train would soon come to take them to the airport. Ev had bought tickets for both of them on a commercial flight to Star Field.

The platform stood high enough above the ground to activate Mark's uneasy fascination with heights. He peered over the guardrail into the dirty and dismal neighborhood below the rail track. Neighborhoods like this stretched for miles in the innermost part of the city, the enormous area called the Wards, crammed with the underclass which was truly, physically under—relegated to the ground beneath the shining bulk of Uptown, in its shadow.

Garish words, both Spanglish and the semi-literate English called Manglish, were scrawled on every wall and sidewalk in sight. A rotten smell drifted up from the Wards, lofted by the heat of the day. It was not the reek of a living compost heap; it was truly foul.

"I see somebody I know," Ev said. He nudged Mark's shoulder, indicating a middle-aged man, face obscured by large dark Virtuality glasses, who disembarked from the train farther down the platform. "Pennington company man. I do believe he was lurking around the South Main rail station, and now he's getting out here. He may be following me. So let's visit Uptown."

Mark was appalled—less so than if Ev had suggested an excursion into the Wards, but not much less. "No!" he hissed. "I do not want to spend any of my last minutes on Earth in Uptown!"

"Pennington doesn't like the police becoming involved in its affairs. The company might take rather forceful action on its own, without stopping to consult the police, if it should realize what I've done." Ev pointedly did not indicate the mouse carrier under his arm, draped with his concealing suit jacket. "I don't want my colleague over there to know where I'm going or guess why. We can lose him in Uptown. Come on."

Mark followed with great reluctance. Even when he had occasion to go there briefly and in the best of moods, Uptown always made him feel like a gasping fish out of water.

Ev was an amphibian. And he led them to the Uptown escalator at a brisk stroll. Ev leaned against the escalator's handrail as he turned to talk to Mark, on the next lower step. "This is a world-class Highcity, you know."

"As a matter of fact, I wouldn't know," Mark replied, glum. "I don't patronize them like you do."

Ev swept the escalator and the sidewalks below with his gaze. He said cheerily, "It's in the same league as LA High, the Tower of London and Luna Prime. With a better unifying environmental motif." Mark snorted in disgust. Ev turned to take a well-timed step off the escalator into the shopping district.

As he followed suit, Mark looked over his shoulder. He thought he saw the Pennington man, the thick black Virtuality glasses bobbing among the other heads of people being conveyed up by the escalator. But Ev led Mark away quickly. Mark lost sight of the glasses in the crowds that filled the lowest, mall level of Uptown.

Throngs of people, the City's professionals leaving work and its affluent and leisured class coming for entertainment, surged through the pyramid's thoroughfares in waves, much like corpuscles pumped through broad arteries and narrow capillaries. Except that Uptown had no heart.

The upper levels of Uptown levels were full of offices. An artificial stream descended from the pyramid's apex to its base in spectacular indoor waterfalls. Between descents, the cascade flowed through pools and fountains on each level. Lush, well-groomed vegetation fringed the stream. "They did a particularly nice job with that fall," Ev remarked, wandering toward the pool at the foot of the waterfall that tumbled down to mall level.

Mark glowered back. He loathed the stream. It pretended to be the soul of a forest. Clear and lifeless, a zombie imitation of something natural, it was an only an elaborate exercise in plumbing.

Ev stepped onto the stone path that led behind the falling water. Directly behind the waterfall, its sound absorbed his words. Only Mark heard him. "Mark, *have* you decided? It's not a game anymore, not even for me. If we get stopped before the Ship leaves, it could be unpleasant for us. You can back out now without having lost much more than a good many nights' sleep."

The liquid curtain blurred the crowds and the stores and bright lights of Uptown into a patternless watercolor. But the sharp edges of Uptown's artificial color in fresh sharp memory, pained Mark as did the foul reek of the Wards, Uptown's malignant shadow. And the whining sound of a bulldozer hitting a stump still rang in his ears even now, years later. "I want to go to Star Field."

"For sightseeing, or for a further trip?" Ev asked drily.

"I'm still thinking."

Ev sighed. "Follow me." He plunged back into the shopping district.

Minutes later, to Mark's surprise, they stepped out into daylight high on the pyramid's side, at the skyport. Ev said, "Interested parties could find out about the airline reservations I made for us, but not that I parked my dad's jet here. I used an alias."

A valet wheeled the Merlin out, its silver skin and blue stripes gleaming, freshly washed. Under its forward-swept wings, the two big ducted fans were locked into position for a vertical takeoff. Ev preflighted the Merlin. He cycled its control surfaces and checked the fuel. Mark steeled himself and climbed in, buckling himself into the copilot/passenger's seat.

Ev peered into the cockpit at Mark. "Usually you say something about how *little* it looks, and you pace around looking unhappy until time to take off. I guess you mean what you say about going as far as Star Field."

Grim and impatient, Mark watched Ev, now in the pilot's seat, finish the preflight checklist, using a string of icons on the glass instrument panel. The jet engines spooled up with a rising whine. "Here we go," said Ev, commanding takeoff thrust. The ducted fans lifted the Merlin almost straight up from the pyramid into the gray air. The ascent tweaked Mark's stomach. High over the city, the Merlin's fans rotated into position for horizontal flight. The Merlin surged forward and merged into the interstate air traffic stream.

4
_____

FLIGHT

The little jet tilted toward its final course, westward. Mark stared out at the horizon that was bloodied by the tag end of sunset. The live animal carrier rested on Mark's lap. One of the mice inside squeaked.

"Hey, thanks for holding that," said Ev. "The trip would jolt them more if the carrier was just strapped in the baggage rack, and they're gentle and insecure by nature. Nice mice."

Mark glanced at Ev. Tonight—maybe because of the red sky's light tinting his blond hair weirdly pink—Ev looked strange to Mark. Mark remembered the Reynolds family nickname for their son. From an early age his parents had called him Bem, short for Bright-Eyed Monster.

Ev informed him, "That's San Antonio off to the right, and the Edwards Plateau, where the land stops being coastal plains and develops wrinkles—see? I can get us an even better view if drop a wing." Ev's hand rested on the slender sidearm control stick. He twisted his wrist.

The earth below lazily tilted. Mark closed his eyes. "Ev, you know how sometimes I don't tolerate heights too well? Today's one of those times."

"Oh. Sorry!" Leveling the jet, Ev asked, "I don't suppose you've thought about how we're getting up to space?"

"As little as possible," Mark replied grimly.

Ev flew in silence for a few minutes. Then, "Since this is the last flight—I'm going off the Air Net to do my own flying. OK with you?"

Mark nodded.

"I may even take the scenic route, since we have time to spare. Thanks to Dad," Ev added, giving credit where credit was due and where the line of credit was extensive: the jet belonged to Ev's father. "Some private jets can't get off the Net at all. Dad calls 'em overgrown model airplanes. If you're feeling vertigo, keep your eyes on the horizon. Hey, look at the sunset, that's quite a sight! Have you ever seen a sea of red like that? The orange-brown streak at the bottom of the sky, though, that looks a lot like Titan. And for the same reason. Hydrocarbon smog."

From Titan, Earth was just a blue star beside a brighter white one, the Sun. That must have made it easier for a Titanian like Ev to think about leaving forever. Ev did not seem unhappy, just excited.

Mark hoped that Ev would fly in a straight line with minimal sightseeing. Instead, the Merlin banked again. Mark felt his stomach quiver. "Why'd you do that?" he asked crossly.

"I didn't," said Ev.

The Merlin had an elegant instrument panel with dark, blank spaces for everything not in use. Ev tapped the panel with one finger. More of the dark places lit up: gray-green screens contrasted with the spidery graphics traced across them. Small bright icons flashed. The Merlin had more numerous and informative, instruments than did a typical personal jet. Scanning the instrument readings, Ev said, "Aha!"

"What?"

"We're back on the Air Net and San Antonio control is attempting to fly us in their direction. They can do that if a pilot is drunk or disabled." Ev quickly touched a keypad set in the instrument panel. "To regain control from their override requires a complicated response sequence, demonstrating that I am not incapacitated." The Merlin's slow curving turn stopped, the jet's nose swerving back toward the sunset. Ev looked over at Mark, and his face was somber. "I wonder who persuaded San Antonio control to do that."

The instrument panel flashed an eye-catching, bright red icon. Ev interpreted. "Traffic at four o'clock. No response to my computer's request that they identify themselves. Move your head so I can see past you." He studied the night sky beyond the back end of the cockpit's bubble canopy.

"Is it going the same way we are for the same reason?"

"Maybe, maybe not. He's bigger than us. Mark, this might be somebody trying to stop us from reaching the starship."

Mark broke out in a sour sweat. The idea of leaving Earth had given Mark nightmares in plenty, but not even the worst one had included a scenario like this.

An instrument beeped shrilly. Ev muttered, "And that's a signal from somewhere." Ev cross-checked the strange signal. "Somebody's feeding us a false navigational signal. I think it's our anonymous friend. Well, the Merlin's smart enough not to buy it." Ev patted the instrument panel affectionately.

A moment later, the jet dived. Mark clutched the mouse carrier, from which came alarmed squeaks.

Ev cursed. "They're trying to force-land us!"

"Can they??" Mark almost shouted.

"Get the hell out of my fly wires!" Ev punched in a reprogramming sequence.

Desperately Mark wondered if being forced to land in San Antonio would be so bad. It would mean not having to leave his world after all, and a final end to nightmares and frantic plans, and getting out of the sickening air.

The Merlin leveled off. A radio transmission must have come to Ev through the slender headset he wore. His face looked startled as he listened to whatever was coming through the earphone. With abrupt motions of his hand, Ev changed the radio receiver to a different frequency. "It's a Pennington corporate jet," he said to Mark.

"I thought we got away from that company spy before we took off. Apparently not."

Ev sent the Merlin into a climb, a steep one. In their carrier, the hapless mice lost their footing and slid across the carrier's floor, scrabbling for footing.

"Are you important enough that they'd send a company jet after you?"

"Yes," Ev said curtly. "So are the mice."

"What can he do to us?"

"I don't know and I don't want to find out. Sit tight. I'm going into afterburner."

The climbing Merlin's nose already pointed toward a star above the red horizon. The engines screamed and the jet leaped toward the star. Its rocketing ascent pushed a load of gravity on Mark. He sank deep into his seat.

Ev grunted, "*Ha*! Can't catch us now!"

Mark felt his face sag on its bones.

"Pushover!" Ev's jet dipped its nose back toward the horizon. Mark's stomach tried to somersault. A distressed noise escaped from him.

"Swallow to get your innards back on line," Ev said. "*Damn*! He's coming after us—let's see you do *this*, you bastard!" Ev twitched the sidearm control stick.

Urgently wanting to follow what was happening, Mark looked out the window to his right. He was shocked to see the whole, wide purple sky in that direction. The jet was pivoting on its left wing.

The Merlin bolted toward the southwest. Mark's stomach settled, squashed, into the wrong internal place. He clamped his teeth against retching. Levelling off, the jet streaked across darkening land with its nose pointed just south of the setting sun.

"I outmaneuvered him!" Ev crowed. He looked at Mark. "Feeling OK?"

Sweating profusely, Mark snapped, "No! Them either," Mark added, meaning the mice. "I think they're dead."

Ev took the mouse carrier and peered into it. "They're OK. They just fainted, the climb in addition to the low cabin pressure got to them. Poor mice," he crooned over them. "If I'd meant you to fly, I'd have given you wings."

Making a last-ditch fight against airsickness, Mark stared at the horizon with its brilliant puddle of sun. Shades of red stretched from horizon to zenith, flaming ocher to vermillion to maroon. Mark saw the spectacular sunset as a barrier, forbidding and insurmountable.

The Merlin was a very expensive and capable private jet, but not orbital. They might reach Star Field. But they would never make it past the red sea of air that was the sky.

M ark looked pale but relieved, leaning back with his eyes closed. Ev concluded that Mark was through being sick. "Since I wasn't replying to him, and since I outmaneuvered him, the Pennington jet gave up and flew back to San Antonio," Ev told Mark. "We're approaching the Mexican border now. I don't think we'll have any more trouble in the air. That was what pilots used to call 'yank and bank'! It's not recommended for this jet, but she turned the trick beautifully, didn't she?"

"I still don't like flying with you," said Mark. It was his first complete sentence in the last fifteen minutes.

"I had to evade that guy. I'm sorry." Ev was aware that he did not sound sorry. Exuberance had leaked into his tone. In flying, Ev was very much at home. People on Titan rarely traversed the nitrogen ice fields on the surface of that world, but flew everywhere instead, using blunt-winged craft to ply Titan's dense atmosphere. Ev clapped a solicitous hand on Mark's shoulder. "Feel better now?"

"At least we made it to Mexico," Mark muttered.

"So we did. But since the Desesperacion, the government of Mexico is for most intents and purposes a puppet of the U.S. The U.S. government pulls the strings and makes things happen in Mexico. I won't be surprised if there's trouble of some kind later today."

Mark groaned.

"Don't worry. The Foundation won't be surprised either," said Ev. "We're more prepared than you realize."

Below them now was the dammed Rio Grande, a trickle finding its way from one jagged drying lake to the next. Ahead, the setting sun glared on the Mexican desert. "God damn it all," said Mark suddenly. "I remember the first starship, when we were kids. Videos of the Ship under construction and the crew in training, blue uniforms and all. Everything was grand and heroic. Just before they left there was that ceremony, broadcast to the whole Solar System. Flags and music and holo-convocation and all. When Berry left, on the second starship, there were some critics, one political party disapproved of it, but there was still a ceremony. Why do *we* have to scheme and steal and run away at night?"

Ev pulled a sheaf of papers out of the personal-effects pocket beside the pilot's seat. He extended to Mark the flimsy Netnode printout pages from *The Wall Street Journal*. "Scan that editorial."

STARSHIP BRAIN DRAIN said the headline.

Mark grunted. "No wonder you printed it out. It's about your hero, Devreze."

"Read on." Ev had practically memorized the article. It held that Devreze's departure on the last starship had constituted an unacceptable loss to science and civilization. Devreze exemplified the young scientists who had deserted the Earth for the stars—some of the brightest, best-educated, and most highly motivated minds of their generation. The tap had been left open and irreplaceable brainpower had drained away. This time, the *Journal* declared, it was the responsibility of government, industry, and citizens to firmly close the tap. The Starship should be stopped, the departure of Earth's best minds prevented. By whatever means necessary.

"I'm no Joe Devreze," Ev said, when Mark seemed to have reached the bottom of the page. "But I'm good at what I do. You're a very good ecologist. Read the part about disease."

Mark read aloud. "'If a sudden new disease selectively struck down a comparable fraction of the first-rate talents and first-born achievers in the upcoming generation, an outcry would be raised around the world, and there would be an urgent search for amelioration and cure'."

"Harsh metaphor, isn't it?" Ev sighed.

Encountering clear-air turbulence, the jet bounced. With slight movements of the control stick, Ev shepherded the jet through the bumps in the air, into smoother air. Beside him, Mark held on to the carrier with its precious mice, buffering the bounces for them.

Clouds flecked the land below, small ones, as round as dry cotton balls. Few people still lived in the barren land under the cotton clouds. Half the population of Mexico had pressed into the slightly greener plains of North America, an unstoppable surge of desperate humanity that had been named the Desesperacion.

Mark watched the wasted land unfurl under the jet's gleaming canard. "Why the hell are we going to look for a world across the stars to try to terraform it? We could restore this one, more easily. There's so much here to work with even now. We can clean up the pollution and rebuild degraded ecosystems. Why not?"

"Politics, religion, war, and overpopulation," Ev said patiently. After all, the two of them had had this discussion before, with each other and with Miraly. "The mindless horsemen of environmental apocalypse. In my opinion, the worst of them is politics. Or, I should say, politicians to whom their own power and prestige is their first concern, all else be damned."

Through gritted teeth, Mark said, "I hate politics."

"I don't blame you," Ev said, remembering the disaster of the prairie.

"Did you see the way the editorial concludes?"

"Yes."

Mark read it aloud anyway, his tone shocked. "'Mr. Kristeller, the Director of the Genesis Foundation, should return to Mars. There he can contribute to the expansion of Earth's resource and economic base, rather than organizing the modern-day equivalent of the Children's Crusade'."

"Harsh," said Ev.

"Do you really trust Kristeller?"

"Yes."

"But he's a Martian."

Ev twitched the corner of his mouth disapprovingly. Evidently, Mark was upset enough not to remember—or not to care—that his present company was Titanian. "Actually, Kristeller is a biologist who got blacklisted in the industry here and took a job on Mars four decades ago. I guarantee you he knows how hard terraforming is—and that Mars isn't the right place for it. He says it would go faster on an Earthlike world, and he ought to know. You're right in a way, though. Kristeller is a naturalized outworlder. Living away from Earth makes a person develop a certain perspective." Ev added, "And I'm a Titanian. Compressible tentacles concealed under the suit, remember?" Ev wiggled one eyebrow, a little trick that Ev had discovered when he was the small boy called Bem.

"Compressible wings, maybe," suggested Mark, with a wan smile. "I'm sorry. I forgot."

The sun seemed to move up in the sky. Flying faster than night-fall, the Merlin was catching up with the day. The land below folded up into a mountain range, brown and deeply shadowed. Ragged peaks exceeded the altitude of the jet as it angled through a pass between the peaks. Ev could have flown higher, maybe should have, to conserve fuel; but he did not want to invite radar detection quite so blatantly.

On the other side of the mountains, the jet soared with a lift in altitude. "Updraft," said Ev, "the wind from the sea hits this range and rises. The Gulf of California is in sight, and so is something else." Squinting, Ev pointed to a thin dark line above the shining arc of water on the horizon. Perfectly straight and vertical, the line bisected an otherwise irregular, fractal panorama of hills and cloud-studded sky. It was Star Tower, and it went past the top of the sky, all the way to the Starship. Ev's heart beat faster.

"Oh, God, it's tall." Mark's voice sounded strangled.

Ev gave a surreptitious glance toward where the used air-sickness bag had been stowed. "Think of it as a giant beanstalk."

"No," Mark objected. "Remember how the fairy tale ended?"

Ev laughed. "It won't fall down. Not yet."

But as he flew on toward the Tower, Ev sobered. This wasn't a fairy tale. It was less like a fairy tale than he had ever expected. The back seat of the Merlin was empty. No Miraly.

Ev scanned his instrument panel in a pilot's crosscheck, an active pattern to avoid instrument fixation. He felt empty inside, like the Merlin's back seat, with an aching void behind the busyness of flying and planning. He could not ever remember feeling this way before. Was this how Mark had felt when they killed the prairie? No wonder Mark had been so distracted and unhappy since then. Emptiness where the heart should be was like a black hole, an ache that bent your fabric of thought and feeling around it.

Now, with his destination in sight, in the lull between the uncertainty of getting this far and the *terra incognita* that was the future, Ev's mind returned to last night. His last night with Miraly. And he hadn't known that was what it was until the end of it.

M iraly had been at work in her hospital all day yesterday, and well into the evening. In the private peace of the home he shared with her, Ev had put on his Virtuality visor and gloves and became a spider on the world's web.

Lurking in the Netnews-casts, he saw protestors and their angry hand-lettered signs, listened to learned commentators discuss the impending Supreme Court decision on the law against removal of wild matter from natural areas. He checked the Ship's tome, and saw that the announced departure date was unchanged, two months away. He also found the clue that told him, and anyone else who knew what to look for, that was untrue.

The Ship had been christened. Its name was *Primordium*. The naming of it meant that it would leave tomorrow. Tonight would be Ev's last on Earth.

Knowing that, Ev followed the web to his favorite places, Paris, Rio, and Ares City. He gorged himself on the sights of the Seine River and Carnival and the dour red walls of Valles Marineris, heard the woodwind music in the Brazilian streets and the thin Martian wind in the solar arrays of Mars One, and talked to people he knew and did not know, wishing them *bon jour, buenos dias,* and on Mars with its long year marked by the imperceptibly slow circuit of the Sun in the pale sky, "Bright Day!" Then he signed off the Netnode.

Web-decompression always took a while: readjusting to sights and sounds that were given, not chosen, and basically static, not in the polysensory flux of the Web. He focused for a while on the subtle blue colors in "Ladies of the Lake." Then he went to the kitchen to inhale the lingering aroma of coffee from this morning and chicken cacciatore from last night.

The technology they were taking to the stars was old, Ev reflected. Old and reliable. Space was a terrible place to have a sophisticated black box that might stop working. At the distant star that was their destination, they'd have computers all right, but not universal, ubiquitous, polysensory access to the Web of so complicated a world as this. Mark would be right at home. Ev would miss the excitement.

Miraly came home from the hospital late due to an emergency. Ev presented her with chocolates—her favorite kind, Swiss confections with hard shells and creamy centers. He began kissing her while her lips still tasted of chocolate. They made love. As much or more than ever before, he thrilled to the feel of her warm breath and cool skin.

At last, she looked at the clock. 4 AM. "It's today, isn't it?" Her voice was low and serious.

For the first time in his life, Ev was at a loss for something eloquent to say. He tried and finally failed to think of something better than, "It's your last chance to leave."

"No, not mine. Ours. To go or stay together."

"You're still staying?" he whispered.

"Yes. And you're going." It wasn't a question.

Realization shot through Ev, and left a sudden shaft of hot emptiness in his soul, like the scalded air left behind by a bolt of lightning. "Why?!" he shouted.

"I've told you many times!!"

ALEXIS GLYNN LATNER

"I don't understand!"

"Don't yell at me!"

Ev clenched his teeth to silence himself. As long as he had deluded himself that Miraly would come with him, it had been easy to plan to go to the stars. Now it was a gaping, awful prospect that he wanted to rail against.

Miraly said, "Listen to me. Forever after this, Earth will know there are other worlds with intelligence on them." Her voice sounded solemn and almost ceremonial, resonating in the room's semi-darkness as though it were a theater, rather than a bedroom. "Finally, there will be no doubt that there is other intelligent, civilized life in the universe. Not under our control. I think it will change the politics, the ideas, the whole way civilization is headed. I can tell by how hard they're fighting it."

Ev shook his head. "Fighting hard and dirty. I can't see any sense in staying through that."

Miraly sighed. "Dear sweet Mark works on grasses, and you work on genes. Neither of you have a lot to do with generations."

"You're being about as clear as the atmosphere of Venus," he said, with a pained grin which there was just enough soft light for her to see.

"Oak trees generate new oaks. People have children who grow up, and neither oaks nor people are like century plants that grow for a long time, go to seed, and keel over dead. Earth is more like an oak or a human."

He groaned. "For God's sake stop being so Venusian—what do you mean?"

"Some people hoped the outplanet colonies could be like children of Earth who grow up. But the Moon and Mars and Titan never will be full-grown worlds like Earth. Yours will. Ev, people do sometimes try to hang onto their children forever. But having full-grown children who leave you and live out there, apart from you, maybe stronger and wiser than you, makes a difference in how you live. Knowing that other civilizations exist out there will make a difference for the Earth."

"And that's why you can stand to stay?"

She nodded. Strands of her dark hair loosely framed her fine-boned face, and made Ev's heart pound at her beauty.

"You never explained it like that."

"I've been thinking very, very hard these last few weeks."

Ev groaned again. "I understand what you mean now, but I can't buy it. I can't accept it."

"The reason I can, is because I'm not going. You are. You have to have your own truth, and it has to be about the new world, not the old one. Ev, what is it?"

"What?"

"I mean exactly what I asked," she said crisply. "Why are you going?"

Ev got out of bed, threw on his silk pajama bottoms, and paced in a hot sweat. He was Ev Reynolds, first the boy and later the man could always say something plausible. Not tonight. Tonight, what he said had to be not just plausible, but true.

Mark wanted to husband a new world; he also needed a simpler world than this Earth, even if a harder one. Ev respected Mark's motivations. Certain other people were not attached to much in this Solar System, and were out for sheer adventure or a clean slate in life—motives that had gotten a great many strange lands explored in the history of human life on Earth, but not Ev's motives. Then there were the people who gave Ev the general impression of rats leaving a sinking ship. It had to be a better thing than that for him.

"It stopped being a game for you a while back," said Miraly. "I realized you'd go. But I still don't know why. I'd really like to know." She paused. "Ev. I wasn't going to tell you this. But I think it's the only way to make you tell me why you're doing this. And maybe tell yourself. I haven't used birth control for weeks. And I'm pregnant."

Stunned, Ev halted his pacing. He couldn't keep his voice from rising to a near-shout. "To make me stay??"

"No, so that your father and I have part of you to remember you after you're gone!" She put her arms around herself, not him, and the gesture tore at Ev like a bandage coming off a wound. It was the first motion of her pulling away from him.

In pain, he asked, "What do you want me to do?"

Of all women, only she could have said what she did next with no acid in her tone, just level honesty. "Tell me, what am I going to tell your child?"

Ev could not reply. They held each other in silence for the slender remainder of the night, tightly. In the morning she left for work in the hospital in Galveston. Ev waited for the call from the Genesis Foundation.

Visiting the bathroom, Ev stared at himself in the mirror. He looked haggard. And this morning, of all mornings, he saw the first faint wrinkles of age in his skin.

Ev had always overlooked wrinkles in women, and disparaged them in other men. *What you get for living too close to the Sun. Gravity's calling card.* But today young wrinkles stood in his own face to tell him that the irresponsible kid he had been was no more. He had to do something with his life, something more permanent than his physical being.

I know I have to go. But how can I explain to her? And to myself? Waiting, he stared at the "Ladies of the Lake" as if to ask the painted stars: *what is my why?*

It was a large picture, and a compelling one. Ev let himself slide into it, imagining the scene as if he were the first man to explore that nameless world with new stars in its sky reflected in the nitrogen lake: starry Sisters in their swaddling nebulosity, and the other stars, red and blue and yellow, that belonged to the same young open cluster.

Lost in the painting, Ev imagined climbing one of the sharp islands that ringed the nitrogen lake. He chose the island or peninsula in the left edge of the picture that had a low saddle-back profile, climbable in the world's relatively low gravity with easy, careful strides. He wore a cold-moon spacesuit. There was the inhalation and exhalation of his own breathing in his ears, and static—the soft radio hiss of atoms of gas in the Pleiades' nebula.

Since this was imagination anyway, he let his boots make footprints in the nitrogen frost. The footprints were dark and graphic—the frost was thin; under that layer, the mountain was sooty with stardust, grains with embedded glassy traces, primitive organic compounds, everything that had been swept out of space by the radiation of the new Pleiades and clotted on the skin of this planet.

At the top of the ridge, Ev turned his face up to the shining skein of stars stretched across the black sky like the bright banner of creation itself. Thus it was, like this, when my own Sun formed, Ev thought. In its day it was one of a cluster of stars. They condensed out of thick dust and gas that had been blown into the Universe when the most massive of the First Stars turned into novas and supernovas.

I started in the stars. I am atoms forged when supernovas died. I am Earth distilled from the dust between the stars. "For you are dust and to dust you shall return."

Startled so much that his imagination fell back out of the Pleiades print, Ev took a deep breath. His mind, strained with lack of sleep, gingerly cradled the new, sharp idea that it wasn't exile but homecoming that he was poised on the brink of, return to the once and future glory of the stars.

Then the Netnode trilled, and the contoured tone told him that it was the Foundation calling. His return to the stars had begun.

The Gulf of California flashed beneath the wings, a narrow sea of glare. Mark hardly noticed. His eyes were glued on the base of the gigantic tower that was the axis of Star Field, Baja California.

The Star Tower had been constructed here in case it fell down in whole or in part: it was better for it to fall into shallow sea than onto possibly inhabited land. Mark's heart fluttered. It hadn't fallen yet, he reminded himself. It had already launched the two earlier starships on their journeys.

Runways described a geometric pattern around the foot of the tower, buzzing with arriving traffic. Some of the aircraft landed the old-fashioned way, rolling to a stop. Newer types landed vertically, touching down like dragonflies in a whirl of delicate wings.

Listening to his headset, Ev frowned. "Control wants us to hold off while they figure out where to let us land. I'd really like to ask for a close-in vector around the Tower, instead of the regular hold, so I can get an eyeful of the thing."

"Go ahead. I don't have any lunch left to lose."

Receiving the vector he wanted, Ev banked the jet around Star Tower. "Reminds me of flying around Titan station, but this is a bigger machine—much, much bigger—in a deeper gravity well. In fact, it shows you just how deep Earth's gravity well really is."

Ev tipped the jet's starboard wing down. Mark looked into the ravines of the tower's vast buttresses.

With a flip of the wing, Mark's stricken gaze traveled up—and up —and up. Star Tower lifted past fluffy cumulus clouds toward the edge of the atmosphere.

Swinging away from Star Tower, the jet soared out over the Gulf of California. Green salt water extended far to the south. Shallow, with pale sand underneath, crinkled with waves, the water resembled a celadon glaze. Mark longed to be down there. To glide across the warm shallow sea under his own paddle power, wavelets lapping the prow of his kayak in quick succession.

The long dark shadow of Star Tower lay across the water.

Near the edge of the Gulf, some small ships and barges were conspicuous, dark spots on the bright sea. They clustered around the mouth of a narrow channel cut into the desert in the direction of Star Field. With shiny, curly wakes, some of the ships seemed to be circling aimlessly. "Now, what's all that?" Wary, Ev did not take the jet down to look more closely. He snapped on the jet's Netnode, quickly asking it for a search *of headline news re travel, international, interplanetary, interstellar.*

Ev paged through the headlines. "Here, 'Supreme court rules against removing plants, animals'—that we knew about," he murmured. "And, 'Genesis Foundation to Appeal'. Sure. *In absentia.*" Then Ev said, "Damn!"

US President denounces Genesis Foundation.

Through clenched teeth, Ev muttered, "He hates us. He's an old, powerful politician. He wants to keep the world and the future in his control." Ev quickly paged on.

The news-node in San Diego, California, reported enormous traffic jams at the U.S.-Mexican border. Mexican customs had initiated vehicle and cargo inspections on an unprecedented scale.

Ev said, "I see. The President leaned sufficiently hard on Mexico to ensure its cooperation in hindering us. That must be the Mexican Coast Guard down there, having words with ships trying to reach the Star Field canal. Trying to delay them."

The opposite shore of the Gulf was clearly visible, low brown ridges of dry land. Before they went that far, Ev sent the jet into a high, wide turn to head back toward Star Field.

The Netnode beeped shrilly. *Breaking News: Space Launcher Misfires.*

The La Jolla Launcher had misfired today. The Earth-to-orbit payload launched by the long electromagnetic gun streaked into space on the wrong trajectory, accidentally aimed too low and too far south. The errant payload crossed the restricted space above Star Tower, missing the Starship by some seven kilometers.

"That was no accident," Ev growled. "More like a warning shot across our bow." He turned off the news and increased the Merlin's airspeed.

Now the sun was setting in their eyes, again. The Tower loomed, dark and endlessly high, against the red sea of sky. Strobe lights raced up the Tower's beveled flank toward its heights to warn aircraft against collision.

Ev said, "Damn it, they still can't give me clearance to land on the field. Too much traffic in line ahead of me. But I'm running out of fuel. The afterburner ate a lot." Ev fumed. "I could declare an emergency and beg for a slot, but I don't want to."

"So land on the desert," Mark replied.

"Too much loose sand. Landing on it would sandblast the jet and Dad would kill me."

Mark scanned the terrain. Roads and railways spidered away into the dim dusty distance of the peninsula. There were empty spaces in the interstices between roads and rails. "See that high spot by that dry wash? It's the closest flat ground that isn't a storage yard or a runway."

"And Dad isn't going to have the chance to kill me, is he?" Ev murmured. He conferred with approach control. Then he said, "They agree. Here goes."

The Merlin hovered down toward the landing place. Mark noticed a jagged outcrop and urgently pointed it out to Ev. Ev made the jet skate to one side to avoid the rocks then lowered the jet toward the ground. The jet wobbled unsettlingly in the air. "Lot of convection currents," Ev said, his words terse. Sand sprayed up past the canopy.

Ev cursed vehemently just as the Merlin settled down with a thump.

"What happened?" Mark demanded. "Did we almost crash?"

Ev snatched off his headset and glared at it. "I was just informed there's a one-week customs embargo for plants and animals being taken into Star Tower! My mice are OK. They're patented. Your stuff —I don't know. They'll probably take your seeds away."

Mark sat still. After the flight, the silence seemed sudden and extreme.

Mark thought, *No*. The new world should have a chance. The bluestem and *Helianthus* would help that chance. Opening up the mouse box, Mark poured the seeds into the feeder. The mice squeaked uneasily. "I can tell the seeds apart later," said Mark.

"Even if they've passed through the mice?"

"Mice never digest all the seeds they eat."

"Good idea."

Mark stuffed the labeled vials under his seat. Ev hopped out to inspect the Merlin's sandblasted underside.

The hot desert air smelled sharp, sandy with fine particles raised by the jet's landing. They had landed a good two miles away from the

Tower: it stood on the other side of a wide dry wash and a storage yard full of cargo containers. According to the Tower control, a land rover would come to get them. As soon as one could be spared.

Mark felt better, less queasy and more decisive. "We've got to hurry," he said. "We can walk."

"And leave the Merlin?"

"We were going to anyway," Mark pointed out.

Mark's legs wavered under him. He made them work, aiming himself toward the distant tower. Cacti and stringy succulents studded the barren ground. The sky overhead was not the greenhouse overcast it had been over Uptown Houston. Orange and red flooded the western half of this desert's sky. To the east, several stars punctured the cloudless purple. Mark imagined a star world with even less ozone than the Earth had now, a climate with more severe extremes, a desert qualitatively different from this one: never and nowhere softened by life.

The dry wash lay across their route to Star Tower. "That looks rough." Ev sounded reluctant.

"It is." Mark picked out a trail to the bottom, down a bank sharp with stones. Ev exclaimed in dismay as the stony ground shredded the edges of his expensive shoes. Mark's light hiking boots, his chosen everyday footwear, fared better. The last few yards were an uncontrolled scramble.

Mark gathered himself up from the sandy floor of the wash. Ev slapped sand from his suit.

A dry wash: but not always dry, and that made all the difference in the world to the organisms here. Glancing around, Mark noted mesquites and acacias on the wash banks, the serrated blades of agave, and small grasses. Lizard and rabbit tracks crisscrossed the rippled sand floor. Plants grew in the wash with its occasional water; animals lived and foraged here on account of the water, the plants and the shade. This dry wash was a lifeline in the desert.

Go to a new world. No jungles yet, no prairies, no forests. Just empty seas and hot, dry continents, infrequent rains that flash away in floodwaters unchecked by vegetated ground. Find a watercourse.

Introduce living things like these. The ecology might creep down the watercourse, and from the watercourse, the green blush of life might spread out into the barren land. With luck and work, terraforming might succeed.

For the first time, Mark felt hope. Halfway across the wash, Mark picked up a stone, water-worn smooth, a pleasing dull green color. On impulse, he put it into his pocket for a talisman, a last touch of Earth. A negligible, maybe-fifteen-gram addition to his personal effects.

Mark enjoyed using his leg muscles on the way up and out of the arroyo, and moved fast. Behind him, Ev commented, "I can tell you're feeling more like yourself now."

Mark always felt like himself when he had the chance to walk somewhere. A woman professor—Samantha Berry? No, Anna, of course, in that strident Dutch-accented tone of hers—had once joked that Mark would walk to Mars if there were a way. He now found himself walking to the stars.

5

EXODUS

Mark had seen pictures of the Star Gate before. Pictures had not prepared him for the reality of the foreboding arch in the immense tower.

Graffiti marred the stone-sheathed wall of Star Gate, including, ABANDON ALL EARTH YE WHO ENTER HERE.

"Charming," said Ev. His collar was open and he looked wilted.

Inside the tower were crowds of people, a din of activity, jarring after the quiet of the desert. Ev made sense of it all before Mark did. Ev muttered, "Looks like Mexican Customs gets to screen what's going through their country to the stars."

Hundreds of would-be star travelers had arrived by air, land and sea only to find themselves in the bottleneck of Customs. The travelers were angry and agitated. Mexican Customs seemed unsure as to why it was necessary to confiscate and embargo biota, or just how to define "biota," but had decided to seize live animal carriers and containers labeled as animals or plants. An alarming pile of such containers occupied the back corner of the screening area: living things wanted—needed—by the starship.

Some men and women in plain clothes stood behind the Customs agents on the other side of the checkpoints. Anglo-Saxons or blacks, they wore a uniform air of grim efficiency, and seemed to have a dangerously good idea of what they were supposed to look for and why. Ev let his breath out between his front teeth in a hiss of dismay. "There's no velvet glove on the iron fist today. No consideration for the illusion of Mexican sovereignty. Those are the President's men— federal marshals. Whatever happens, remember—the marshals' authority has limits, at least until martial law is declared, which it hasn't been yet. They can't arrest us because we haven't broken any laws."

Ev shouldered his way to the front of the line like an eel, towing Mark, who stepped on toes and bumped into elbows. Ev showed the harassed Mexican Customs agents his mice and the patent documents to prove the mice belonged to him. He offhandedly identified the grass and sunflower seeds as premium mouse chow. Cheerfully he turned his tailored pockets inside out to demonstrate their emptiness. Customs waved him through, mice and all.

But the Customs agents checked Mark's identity license with harrowing interest. One of the ominous suits, the marshals, gravitated over for a look at the license and at Mark. The marshal gruffly told Customs to take Mark aside.

Mark's stomach knotted. Directed to the back corner of the customs area, he had to wait while the crowd filtered through customs and dwindled. He seethed, but felt no more free to run away than were the confiscated small animals in their cages around him. Then he was escorted to a small featureless room. Oddly, it was not the marshal who interviewed him; the marshal guarded the exit, silent and intimidating. A Customs agent directed Mark to empty his pockets onto a table. The agent examined his belongings. "What is this?"

"My notebook," Mark answered, voice choked with tension. The marshal's eyes bored into his back.

"And this?" The agent picked up the green stone. "An egg?"

"*No.*" Mark could not keep disgust out of his voice. The customs agent met his eyes with a mild glance that slid over Mark's shoulder to the marshal.

Despite what Ev had said, Mark expected the marshal to arrest him, to handcuff him. Yet the marshal said nothing.

Mark never wore a watch. He relied on excellent time sense instead. A clock on the wall was conspicuously placed. It was also wrong, at least half an hour slow. Mark suddenly realized that the marshals might have decided that certain kinds of scientists were worth the effort of delaying until they missed the Ship. With no legitimate authority to detain him, the President's men had resorted to trickery.

Mark turned to confront the marshal. The big, hard-featured man glared at Mark. "Your clock's slow," Mark announced. "I'm leaving now. You can't legally keep me here." His voice shook. "You can keep the things I had in my pockets. Except for this." He picked up the green pebble on the table. "Which is just a stone. There's not even any moss on it."

The marshal scowled. Mark's insides clenched, but he shoved past the marshal anyway. The marshal shoved back, sent him bumping hard into the doorjamb. Mark ricocheted out into the deserted corridor, and the marshal did not pursue him. Mark hurried toward the heart of the tower.

At the far end of the corridor, Ev paced. Behind him was a large portal. Jerking his thumb into the doorway, Ev yelled, "It's about to leave!"

Mark sprinted. The two of them scrambled inside just before the doors closed. Ev turned around and flung an arm around Mark's shoulders. "*Touchdown!*"

Mark wiped sweat off his brow. Unlike his hot, sick sweat earlier, it felt cool, more like the breaking of a fever.

Buoyantly Ev led the way up an escalator to a spacious room, appointed like a hotel lobby and laid out around a huge column with twelve blank sides. Twelve outer walls echoed the central column. Each wall had a large window.

"Welcome to the televator. This is the observation deck," Ev explained. "You don't have to look out if you don't want to." Presently there was nothing to observe beyond the windows, just the walls of the tower. Avid to see the sights of the trip up, Ev made a beeline for a soft, deep armchair beside one of the picture windows. He offered Mark the chair. "You'll be better off sitting down for the ride."

Mark sat. Once again the mouse box rested importantly in Mark's lap. Scratching noises came out of it, and Mark peered into the box. "All three are eating."

"I did a good job with them. They function normally."

It wasn't that hard to genetically engineer mice that had one or several altered traits, but otherwise were normal. Ev always said mice were easy. "They're not just patented fancy mice, are they?"

"No." Ev spoke in an undertone, still secretive, conscious of the increasing crowd of people in the observation deck. "Their chromosomes are artificial, containing a complete set of mouse genes, plus a great deal of surplus DNA and, of course, genes which specify that the surplus remain unexpressed. The unexpressed DNA happens to be that of other species from the company's gene banks."

"You mean you stole genes?"

Arms crossed, Ev radiated self-satisfaction. "It's amazing how much DNA can fit into the chromosomes of a mouse's cell. I filched the genetic code for several hundred assorted species."

Mark felt a gentle surge of inertia that pushed him into the plush seat. The walls of the tower blurred, making the vertical rows of lights turn into beaded strands. Ev settled onto the generously wide arm of Mark's chair, the better to see out.

The deck had filled up. There was conversation in the background, sporadic exclamations louder than the general conversational buzz.

"We're the last off the pad," Ev said, "Look up through the skylight. You can see the next to last."

Another televator was going up too, higher than their own and on the opposite side of the tower. The televator was a torus with a twelve-sided hole in the middle of it, through which ran a barely visible, vertical wisp of smoke. There were other smoke streams in the tower, a dozen in all. Ev explained, "It's a vacuum here inside the Tower. Those particle streams are ionized molecules. To be exact,

Carbon-60, buckminsterfullerene. The streams flow up to lift the televators or cushion them on the return. The streams also keep the Ship up. It's riding on the particle turnaround—on top of the whole thing."

Looking up, Mark could see no other televators but the one just above their own, apart from that only the tower walls, dwindling to an apparent point of closure. It was a horribly long way up, he thought, with more televators and a starship out of sight in the vertical distance.

Ev reflected. "C60. Stardust. We are being lifted up by the same kind of soot that exists in cold dust clouds between the stars. It was also the ion propellant for the Athena series of star probes around 2040. Appropriate, isn't it?"

That other televator rotated. So did their own. Theirs too was a torus in midair, slowly circling around a thin stream of soot. That was why this observation deck was centered on a column with twelve blank walls: a particle stream went through the middle of the whole televator, and all three stories of it was being lifted up by insubstantiality, up, and up. Little spiders of panic danced along Mark's spine. "Ev," Mark choked. "Are we safe?"

"I think so. The President can't do anything as crude as turning off the particle streams. Or shooting down the Ship. It was chartered as an international effort. More likely, he'll send the Space Force up from the White Sands and Cascade bases. That is, he'll so decide and so order, but I don't think we have to worry about it."

"No??"

"No." Smiling slightly, Ev made a hand motion which Mark interpreted as, *wait and see.*

Ascending at an already terrifying speed while rotating, the televators were still accelerating. The beaded strands of lights on the wall of the tower twisted into helixes. To Mark's alarmed fascination, the top of the tower was now close enough to appear as a definite circle full of stars.

Ev followed Mark's gaze. "Ever hear the one about being able to see the stars from a deep enough well?"

The televator rocketed out of the top of the tower. Mark instantly recalled that the Star Tower terminated above the thickest layer of Earth's atmosphere. The Tower was a rift of vacuum in the ocean of air. The particle streams, however, kept going. So did whatever they carried. From here on up, this machine was called the Space Fountain.

Below but not quite below them, the edge of the planet glowed crimson with the Sun disappearing behind it, the red rim of the sea of air that they had crossed. They had made it to space.

And now that they were out in the open, somebody could turn the Fountain off. Or shoot the televator down with the La Jolla Launcher. Or—"Ev! Why's the televator still spinning? It is under control, isn't it?"

"As far as I know, the rotation is just for the view, which is magnificent. Relax and enjoy it. If were you, though, I wouldn't look up," Ev added, by which time Mark already had.

Above, in unbounded, black, starry space, a square platform hung, suspended. The flanks of the starship *Primordium* bowed past the platform's edges. In an inverted bowl under the platform, the Star Tower's particle streams were magnetically turned around. Only the thrust of the turnaround, only the turning soot, kept the platform up. And ominously, like a loose falling object, the platform and ship parked on it rotated.

It was the televator rotating, Mark reminded himself, trying to clamp down his jolted nerves.

"Don't look up. Look outward," Ev reminded him.

But gazing out stirred up feeling deeper than simple phobia, and more painful. Space was black, with stars, like night. It was eternal night out here. Mark had left blue sky behind, with white clouds, celadon salt waters, and the rosy morning and evening colors of the Earth's horizons—all behind him, in his past and irretrievable. His chest tightened, making it hard to breathe.

Rotating, the televator swung them away from their destination and back over the face of the Earth. Sunlight brightened Asia, but night had fallen over North America. The continent was feverish.

Cities showed up as yellow splotches, connected by glowing trails of electricity like the tracks of a cancer's metastasis.

Talk in the observation deck quieted. People were clustered by the windows, watching. Some cried, sniffling sounds audible in the absence of chatter.

With thumb and forefinger Mark squeezed the inside corners of his eyes to hold in tears. He whispered, "Life is down there. Green land. Blue sky. Only there. And it's dying. And, oh, God, everything else is dark. Cold. Lifeless. Ev, we've got an impossible job to do. To try to give a world like that back to the universe."

Silent, Ev processed what Mark had said. Earth slipped across the window. In the background, conversation built up again, with people pointing out favorite landmarks on the home planet to each other, voices low, as if in attendance at a wake. The televator inexorably rotated back toward the cold bright stars.

Ev said quietly, "The Genesis Foundation was prepared for what happened today. We're coming away with a tremendous quantity and variety of seeds and animal germ cells. We'll—"

"And bug eggs," said a voice behind them, loud enough to be startling and even more so because it was a very familiar voice. "Ef'ry one forgets to mention much less thank God for the insects!"

Ev whirled toward the thin, middle-aged woman with surprise written on his face.

She said, "I saw you perched here like a fine-feathered songbird, and I thought to myself, so! Such a surprise to see *him*!"

"The surprise is mutual, Professor van Leeuwen," said Ev. Mark did not recover as smoothly. "Anna!" he gasped. "You?"

She answered simply, "I have finally decided Samantha was not such a fool to go to the stars."

"Did you bring beetles and butterflies or did Customs get them?" asked Mark.

"I did not decide to come just today, so already many of my species are up there. Good ones." She added, "I smuggled more butterfly eggs through customs just a little while ago. My precious butterfly eggs, disguised as makeup in my purse. To be exact, eyeshadow."

"You don't ever wear eyeshadow," said Mark.

"The Customs agent knew that, I think. There he was, a nice-looking gentleman with hair gray around the edges, and I, a forty-eight-year-old lady with some gray hair too, am explaining to him my blue and mauve, some green, and bright yellow eyeshadow. He let me through and said not a word to those people in the suits which were the ones to watch out for. So they did not confiscate the eggs." Anna saddened. "Oh, Mark. Remember the poor restoration prairie?" Tears leaked onto Anna's cheeks.

It was a memory etched with the acids of shame and anger. Mark put his arms around Anna's bony shoulders. In Mark's own eyes, tears blurred the Earth as it slid by behind Anna with all its burned forests, polluted seas, and blasted prairies. "We'll try it again," he managed to say.

"That we will," said Annetine. Sniffling, Anna turned to Ev. "Here are we two being so emotional, and not you, eh?"

"It won't hit me until we pass the orbit of Saturn," said Ev.

"So." Anna sat down. She fished a tissue out of her handbag and blew her nose. Mark and Ev sat on either armrest of the chair beside her. "Mark Willson, you I suspected maybe to meet on this trip. For months you have been asking for specimens for this and that flimsy reason. And looking every day gloomier than the day before. I have been thinking to myself, maybe Mark is going to the stars. But Dr. Evan Reynolds, *you* surprise me!" She regarded Ev with blue eyes that were red-rimmed, yet piercing.

Mark said, "He surprised me too. Not to mention Pennington Genetech."

"I would imagine, if today he quit from that high-paying job."

"I did more than just quit at Pennington." Ev indicated the mouse carrier. He grinned brilliantly. "Madam, I robbed the Pennington gene bank."

Annetine laughed, her characteristic, ringing laughter that could splinter the quiet in a small room. It sounded wonderful to Mark. "So how long have we until the docking?"

Ev gestured upward. "The ship is accelerating too. We're playing catch-up."

"We're already on our way?" Mark discovered that his battered stomach had one more flipflop left in it.

"Yes. Ship, televators and all, we're ascending, on the grounds that the authorities will throw everything they have at us if they realize how much genetic material we've stolen and how many good scientists are going with us."

Anna nodded.

Images appeared on the twelve walls of the middle of the deck. One flat video screen showed the Genesis Foundation's Director, Kristeller, in an interview; on another screen appeared the President of the United States, in a news conference. There was sound, the words of the two men, but muted and from here audible only as a murmur. While the cold night of stars wheeled by the windows, Mark watched the other videos—pictures and diagrams of the Ship. There was a depiction of the vaults of stasis, ready to receive and freeze thousands of colonists. Mark's eyes shied away to another screen, showing the greenhouse that would grow for centuries while people stayed in stasis. The greenhouse was crammed with young plants and seedling trees. Mark imagined the trees patiently growing for a century and more, a tangled green heart within the traveling starship.

The televator wheeled around. Below the wide window, Earth receded with the speed of ascent. Sunset, faded to maroon, rimmed the western edge of the planet. Closer and darker was the bulk of North America, detailed by the lights of the power grid. "We've got friends in low places," Ev announced. He pointed down. "Look at the western seaboard."

The power distribution grid was fading, like a sudden, visible cooling of the continent's fever. Umbra within penumbra, the center of the brownout was black. The blackout radiated from Star Field.

"The lights are going out down there. And so are the machines," said Ev. Elsewhere in the observation deck, puzzled voices were raised as others noticed the same thing.

Mark jumped up. "Are they shutting the Fountain down?"

"Just the opposite," Ev announced. "It was risky—interfering with the computer that controls the continental power grid. But a top executive in the power consortium was in on the plan. Look. You can see it happening. Power is being diverted to the Space Fountain, on an unprecedented scale. From which we get one hell of a boost."

"The executive," asked Anna, "has he gotten away with us?"

"No. He's over the upper age limit. He stayed, and he'll probably be in prison for the rest of his life."

"Just for giving us a head start?" Anna asked in dismay.

"And for destroying the Space Fountain." Ev smiled thinly at Anna, who gaped at him. "The energy surge will burn out the power plant and disperse the particle streams. So nobody can use the Fountain to come after us. And the North American launchers and spaceports that the authorities might have aimed against us are dropping out of service. The west coast Space Force bases are blacking out." Triumph edged Ev's voice. "Nothing on Earth can stop us now."

Mark sat down again on his arm of the chair. He felt dizzy.

On one video screen, the President of the United States appeared in a new mood. He was furious. He knew of the blackout. And he was telling the nation and the world that the blackout had caused a high-speed train accident in Nevada, and in California, a mid-air collision of two planes because the Air Net had been out of operation before emergency power came on. Five people had died. "Innocent blood," Anna murmured, shaking her head. Ev just stared at the floor. The President's words were easily audible to the shocked, soundless audience in the observation deck. Anyone responsible for the blackout could be charged with terrorism. They would face the death penalty.

The televator turned back toward the stars. This time, Mark recognized the thickest congregation of stars as the Milky Way. He had seen it from lands and seas on Earth, the glowing path across the sky; here it was vertical with respect to the view from the observation deck window.

Apart from the video screens, there were no lights on the observation deck. The Earth below had fallen under the pall of a night without the yellow glow of electricity, and Mark's eyes had adjusted to the darkened world. The Milky Way seemed like a solid mass of brilliance, a glittering column of bright stars and dust standing over the dark limb of Earth.

Ev said, "Mark, you're wrong."

"About something, or about everything?" Mark asked. He felt utterly drained.

"You said the stars are lifeless. They aren't. Cosmic genesis, remember? Big blue stars forge atoms—iron and oxygen and carbon. And when they turn into supernovas, they throw all the atoms of new stars and worlds and life out into space. So the Seven Sisters are our sisters. And organic molecules first formed in interstellar dust clouds. In the beginning, they rained on Earth, remember?"

"It was a hell of a long way from organic molecules to life on Earth," said Mark.

"At the start, Earth was a hard, hostile place. Life changed the water and the land, the air and the weather, slowly and surely, to make a place conducive to life. But, see, what we're doing is taking life back to the stars, where it came from. This time life will remake a hard world much more quickly." Ev smiled radiantly, not at Mark or Anna, but at the stars. "Life was exiled on Earth for four billion years. But it belongs to the stars."

Never had Mark known Ev to be much of a visionary. But what he had said sounded right. Mark nodded with a lump in his throat.

Anna laughed, though not as ringingly loudly as usual for her. Wonder softened her laughter. "That is good, Ev. Don't forget what you have told us here. When the going gets hard in the future, we will need to think that way about what we are doing."

Ev stood up and put his hand on the glass, leaning toward Earth. "I won't forget. Neither will somebody down there. When we get farther out, I'll be able to talk to Titan and Titan can send a confidential message back here, and I'll tell her."

Mark knew who Ev meant. "You can say I love her too. And that I'll always remember her no matter what happens."

Anna reached up to squeeze Mark's shoulder. "My dear boy, don't worry. He's right. It's meant to be, that we will reach a good new world."

Mark thought about an unseen world, starstruck and barren. He felt his life point that way like a compass needle that stopped whirling and found its orientation. Mark looked up. *Primordium* still hung above their heads, and not so far above as before. Now it did not seem altogether like a threat to him. It was a promise, an immense and unbreakable one, the promise he was making to world he loved: to implant its living soul, its ecosystem, in the soil of a new planet with his own hands.

<hr />

One by one, the speeding televators caught up with the Starship. Surface-to-orbit spacecraft, shuttles and space-planes, came too and made their made rendezvous with the Ship, bringing everyone else who had gotten away from Earth, with more of the stolen treasures of living things and seeds, genes and germ cells.

The Space Fountain poured out its final and fullest power, damaging the machinery irreparably. The Fountain pushed the star-ship to geosynchronous orbit and past that point, cast the starship on its course. The huge engines blazed to life. *Primordium* hurled itself into the desolation of interstellar space. And in front of the starship, the bright Milky Way stood out in the endless night, marking the direction of the journey that had just begun.

THE LIFE-BLOOD OF THE LAND

E arth had been a greenhouse, wrapped in dirty air that made dawn long and rosy. Not so this planet. Here, in the early morning, the home dome's skylight let Mark see a square piece of pale, cloudless, bluish-green sky.

The new day highlighted the wrinkles on Evan Reynolds' face and hands. Ev cleared his throat. "Mark, you and your people are doing a good greening job here. But about this wild water chase of yours. Isn't it time to give up?"

"No. It's there, just deeper than we thought." Reckless, Mark added, "I dreamed about it last night."

A pained expression crossed Ev's aged features. "You always were a dreamer."

"So were you!"

"Not any more," Ev said. "I've got the whole godforsaken ecosphere to think about."

When they left Earth, they had been the same age. Not any more. Ev had been revived forty years ago, while Mark remained in the cold zone of the Starship, undreaming, unknowing and, for most practical purposes, dead. Ev had thrown himself into the work of the new world and climbed as far up as the ladder went. Ev became the World Director of Ecogenesis. And old. And unfamiliar.

Mark fumbled for a reasonably clean mug, which he filled with water. He put the mug into the microwave oven, antique but sturdy technology that worked well for its intended purpose.

"Rainwater runs off too fast," said Mark, facing the oven instead of the old man who had once been his best friend. "The soil needs to be conditioned so it can hold water. Drygrass and associated microorganisms accomplish that. Lusher vegetation, more organisms, would do it faster. If we can find groundwater, bring it up and fix it in biomass—"

"But you haven't found any."

Mark opened the oven. Hot water vapor emerged, carrying a chemical stench. Behind him, Ev demanded, "What the hell was cooked in there last?"

"Drilling mud. They're trying to adjust the additives for downhole conditions such as heat."

"Is the mud made with water from your cisterns? Convince me your stinking mud isn't a waste of water."

Mark placed the mug beside the jar of instant coffee on the table in front of Ev. "The geologist thinks water migrated deep into the rocks in ages past and got trapped there."

Stirring the coffee, Ev's spoon rattled in the mug. "She probably just wants to get her hands on a long core sample." He was a tired and decisive old man. It still unsettled Mark that Ev's hair, the little left of it, had turned yellowish white, the remains of what had once been a blond mane.

Mark turned away from Ev to take a fly out of the mesh box in the refrigerator. He lifted the lid of the terrarium on the kitchen counter and dropped in the chilled fly. The golden garden spider in the terrarium waved its forelegs attentively, hungrily. Mark selected another fly. Today, two flies, not just one, for the glorious and hungry spider.

Ev asked, "Pet?"

"Our mascot. What we're trying to do is weave the web of life across the land, strand by strand."

"How deep is your hole in the ground now?"

"A couple of miles. The water will be under pressure." Vividly dreaming in the dim earliest hours of this morning, that was what Mark had seen. "The water will spurt up out of the ground like a geyser and fall on the ground like rain out of a clear sky."

"I can't sell dreams to the Creation Council," Ev retorted. "There are more promising places to drill for water. And a limited supply of drilling equipment."

Thawed out, the flies buzzed in the terrarium, about to blunder into the orb-woven design of their destiny. The sound irritated Mark's already strung-out nerves. He said tersely, "We've hit hard rock. Impermeable enough to trap water underneath. Hard stuff."

"Let me guess. You need another drill bit."

"A bit with diamond teeth," Mark said softly.

"What! Damn your monomania! Mister, I don't play favorites. You have gotten what you asked for, so far, because you've been doing good work out here in the blasted interior. Don't blow it on a pipe dream!"

A sleep-rumpled resident of the dome started to enter the kitchen. Finding the Director of Ecogenesis sitting in there and vehement, he backed out. Mark was sure that interested ears would now be stretched toward the kitchen from the safety of the hallway. Mark felt himself flushing, hot and probably brick red. "Listen. Your job is the toughest in this world. You have to cover land with grass and forests. But where water should be easy to find, it isn't. Or you get too much water too fast, like that hurricane that went inland and ruined the manioc plantations. There've been stupid decisions—mostly not yours—on top of good bets going bad, and the greening isn't going so good."

"Says who?" Ev asked curtly.

"I'm an ecologist. I can read the handwriting on the wall." Mark wasn't going to spell it out aloud—not with his people listening in the hallway. But he knew the truth. The Ship had been incredibly lucky, finding a planet where life already existed. Evolution here had gone as far as marine microorganisms. The shallow seas were full of plankton that had changed a primeval atmosphere to breathable air comprised of oxygen and nitrogen. All that lacked was to green the land. But that alone was harder than the children of gentle Earth had anticipated. The human and biological resources that the Ship had brought from Earth were finite and dwindling. The greening of this world was failing.

"Try a bad bet for once." Mark listened to himself with a strange sense of detachment, as if his words were more real than his body. "Give me a diamond drill bit."

Ev's face contorted. It darkly fascinated Mark, how anger looked so ugly on that aged face.

Slowly, incredibly, the anger resolved into a grin, weirdly familiar, the grin of the bright-eyed kid on the other side of the stars. Ev said, "Hell, Mark, maybe you're right. Maybe I have been hedging my bets too much for too long. Let me think about this. I might just give you what you want."

In the achingly cold gray hour before sunrise, Mark watched an acre of grass burn. Fire spread like a puddle, exploring combustion possibilities in the sparse dry vegetation. Mark held a shovel poised to beat back the edge of the fire if it started moving too fast. Ten others, greeners who worked in his outfit, formed an arc of vigilance downwind from the fire. The heat felt good at this chilly time of day.

Beside Mark, the biologist Chang beat out a forked tongue of flame. "Watch it, boss," Chang said. "If it gets out of control, and we have to call down the fire squad from the Ship, there'll be the devil to pay."

Mark evaluated the extent of the burn. Summer's drought would soon end in fierce storms with lightning falling thicker than rain. The lightning never found the tinder to start a real conflagration, only small fires that puddled ahead of the prevailing wind. The firebreak was now big enough to thwart one like that. If worse came to worse, there were concrete cisterns buried in the ground, water saved from the last time the creek ran wet with storm runoff, with which to damp a wildfire. "Let's put it out." With his shovel, he threw dirt onto the flames. The greeners followed suit. Having smothered the fire, they sifted the ground for embers, mashing those they found to harmless bits of ash.

Somebody shouted, "Zeppelin!"

Like a pink pearl in the dawn-lit sky, the supply zeppelin approached from the distance, floating down toward its pier.

A sweating and sooty Chang materialized at Mark's shoulder. "When he visited us last week, were you able to persuade the Director to give you soil polymer?"

"I didn't ask."

Chang frowned. "We need soil polymer in the Canyon."

"No more than other outfits need it for their special places. There's never enough to go around."

Chang held his tongue, as usual. Mark thought, *What we really need is an artesian well.* Throwing his shovel on the pile with the others, to be cleaned and returned to the tool shed, Mark turned away from Chang and walked toward the zeppelin.

On the zeppelin pier lay a heap of goods fresh out of the cargo bay. Mark's assistant and the zep pilot haggled over minor additions and subtractions to the supply list. But they had already dispatched a high-priority package to the drilling derrick.

Mark wanted to run, made himself walk so as to appear more calm than he felt. His destination, the derrick, pointed toward a morning sky of ceramic blue. Grass covered the hills beyond it. But the green was fragile—a mere sketch on the pale ground, too easy to erase. He needed water to make the green deeper and more durable.

On the derrick's platform, the drillers in gray coveralls and

Tinaja, the tall blonde geologist, clustered around the new bit, which they had lifted from its bed of packing material. It looked like a sea serpent's head. Tight plates of metal, edged with dark industrial diamonds, ringed a hollow maw.

Tinaja handed Mark a small piece of paper. Mark unfolded it to read a few words in Ev's graceful but age-shivered handwriting. *This is it. No more.* Mark crumpled and stuffed the paper into his pocket. "Let's use it today."

The foreman attached the diamond bit to the drillpipe. Everyone waited, tense, until he announced that the connection was right and tight. Then the crew lowered the drill stem into the ground. Lengths of pipe, lifted from the stack and locked on one after another, followed the bit into the deep hole.

"It'll take a while to get it down there, won't it?" Mark asked Tinaja. "I need to do something in Creek Canyon."

"Go right ahead. This'll take most of the morning."

Mark headed for the gulch between the hills. Out of sight from the rig, he stopped to pant. This world's atmosphere was high-mountain thin here in the interior.

The gulch opened up onto a canyon, the floor of which was a wet-weather creek, a ribbon of rounded stones. Mesquite fringed the creek. The stringy little trees had long roots that reached deep in the ground, finding moisture from the last rains months ago. Tiny, tough green leaves fringed the mesquite's twigs like tatted lace.

Mark crossed the stony creek bed. On a patch of soft sand under the canyon wall, the fanned footprint of sporadic rain runoff, he discovered the zigzag trail of a small snake—a wondrous trace of animal life in this once-desolate place. Creek Canyon was Chang's territory. Chang did good work.

Mark had told Tinaja he needed to do something in the canyon. True in a way. He needed to think.

A planet wears life like a green skin, he thought, the patterned skin of a snake. Like a snake, the Earth had changed its skin many times in geological history at one transforming catastrophe or another, most recently the environmental disaster constituted by *Homo sapiens*. It had never mattered much to planet Earth if, while its continents collided and split wide open above the simmering cauldron of its mantle, its green skin largely died and sloughed off every so often. The death of a snake's, or a planet's, skin only matters to the skin itself.

Humans had been part of a thin, fragile and impermanent skein of life on Earth. Even more so here. If the greening of the continents failed, this planet would endure, uncaring. But the human colony would be forced to live beside the shallow seas, in domes like surf bubbles that shimmer for a little while then pop and vanish.

No. This raw land had to become a place for mesquite and snakes and people to exist under the wide blue sky.

With a groan, Mark stretched out on the sand in the shade of the canyon wall. Overhead, the zeppelin floated away with a mechanical purr that barely distorted the silence. In the canyon, a grasshopper trilled. One of the grasshoppers of the admirable Chang.

Mark woke up in full hot sunlight. In the distance, he heard the derrick with its signature clangs and bangs. He broke into a sweat, remembering Ev's note. *No more.*

Mark returned to the derrick at high noon. Unbuffered sunlight blazed down. Near the derrick, the field of boxy solar energy collectors threw off dazzling reflections. Heat shimmered over the roof of the powerhouse from which electrical cables snaked away to the home dome, the shop and the derrick.

They had stopped drilling. The crew languished on the platform, sitting or lying down under tarps hung up for shade. Only Tinaja seemed alert and unwilted as she picked rock chips out of the sieve.

Mark ran up to join her on the platform. "Can the diamond bit cut the caprock?" he asked.

"Does good," she answered. "Want some lunch?"

Knees weak with relief, he sat down. "Yes, thanks."

Tinaja handed him a metal plate. To his surprise, beside the pile of cooked prickly pear cactus on the plate lay several little chips of rock, clean and moist. Drill chips right out of the sieve. "Tinna, why are you serving me rocks?"

"That shiny bit broke through the caprock an hour ago," said Tinaja. "Into soft old limestone." She pointed at the rocks in his plate and grinned at him. "There was a sea down there once, and may just be some of it left! Will salty water be OK?"

Salt water would be wonderful, Mark muttered in his sleep that night. Salt water would be wonderful. Residual adrenalin smoldered in his nerves like embers in ash. Finally Mark snapped wide awake in a cold sweat. Pulling on his clothes, he left the dome.

The wind outside blew as cold now as it had been searing hot at midday. Overhead the sky was clear, strewn with scintillating stars.

Near zenith was a thin, ragged ring of pale nebulosity. The astronomers said the ring marked the death of a giant blue star so near that it would have washed out all of the other stars in the dark night sky. But it evolved rapidly and exploded, supernova, tens of thousands of years ago, a cosmic catastrophe in geological time, leaving a nebula around a neutron star.

Yellow light shone in the window of Tinaja's lab in the shop shack. Mark had meant to start one of the nocturnal walks for which he was notorious; he changed his mind. At the door of Tinaja's lab, he knocked before letting himself in.

Tinaja was engrossed in her work. She had a computer running, its screen split four ways, textdisks and printouts strewn about the table, and cylinders of stone in front of her, plus rocks and sands in at least ten piles, and a microscope. Wisps of honey-colored hair had escaped from her ponytail.

"I took a core sample," Tinaja announced. "This is the supernova layer. There are isotopes aplenty. This planet was cosmically irradiated, all right, but good."

"That's great! That you found geological evidence of that, I mean."

Tinaja made a wry face. "Look in the microscope."

The magnified shapes, though worn and fuzzy, were insistently reminiscent of regular geometry. Mark saw spirals, cones, fluted spars and tiny boxes. "Microscopic marine shells."

Tinaja said flatly, "Right. This is, after all, limestone. But the variety of the shells is phenomenal, compared to the species that exist in the seas now."

"From the Near Supernova layer?" Mark's skin crawled. "There must have been a die-off. One that the world hasn't recovered from."

"Look." She held out a curved, rough cone about an inch long. "Found this in the core sample. It was sheer accident that the whole thing was inside the core."

"Worm shell?" Mark guessed.

Her face was intense. "I don't think so. Granted, this is an alien world. Who knows how evolution goes here? But Mark, I think it's a tooth. Look—see how it's worn flat, here? Predators' teeth get wear patterns like that. Worm shells don't."

Sheer shock made Mark feel cold and numb.

"Mark, what would have happened if this world had an extensive ecosystem?" she whispered. "What if it had been like Earth?"

Appalled, Mark forced himself to marshal his education in life sciences and answer her. "The atmosphere must have been partly stripped away and the oceans boiled off to shallow seas. Enough marine microorganisms survived to recolonize the seas. But on land, judging from what we found when we got here, there was nothing left. The continents must have been sterilized. It was as though the evolutionary clock were set back." He swallowed with difficulty, his throat constricted. "Almost to zero."

Three hours before dawn, the foreman flipped the main breaker at the powerhouse. The drilling rig's lights came on. The crew checked their equipment. There was little of the usual banter and horseplay this morning. Two miles down, hole heating up and pipe supply dwindling, today looked like the last day, one way or another.

The foreman replaced the corer, a hollow sharp-rimmed cylinder, with the diamond drill bit. Then the crew lowered the bit into the ground. Joints of pipe followed it, each attached swiftly but securely. Time passed, metered by the clank of pipe being joined to pipe.

Mark felt nearly sick. He'd had too many broken nights and too much work, and now there was a fossil tooth—evidence of sudden death on a planetary scale. Visible through the thickness of the atmosphere near the western horizon, the shredded supernova ring shimmered like the winking of an eye, a vast lidless eye with a tiny, implacable pupil.

The plunging pipe changed its tune, decelerating. Tinaja called out in a clear voice, "We're here."

A small crowd of greeners had come out of the home dome to watch. Somebody slapped Mark on the back and blurted something about luck. Whether they believed in Mark's dream or not—opinion was distinctly divided—the greeners wanted water.

Mark joined Tinaja on the platform. The drill bit met solid limestone far below their boots. The foreman sent the helper, a boy named Dusty, up the derrick to mind the moving parts at the top.

Two miles long in a hot narrow hole, the pipe behaved like a wet noodle. It took several turns at the top to get any rotation at the bottom to cut the rock. The mud pumps ran at full throttle, forcing cool mud down the throat of the pipe. The mud came back up the hole outside of the pipe, carrying rock chips and heat with it. A fat hose took the mud back to the tank, dumped it in through the mechanized sieve called a shaker. The shaker rattled mindlessly. Thick and grayish-brown, the mud cooled in the open tank. An automatic stirrer made swishing sounds.

Tinaja paced between the rotary table and the shaker. She scraped chips of rock out of the shaker and examined them. She patted the pipe. "Down some more, baby, down some more."

Machinery rattled and clanged, and the pipe turned tirelessly. Mark saw the knife edge of dawn, a thin rim of light on the eastern horizon. Directly overhead, a bright point of light traversed the dark sky. It was the Starship in polar orbit.

"Pay attention, skygazer!" Tinaja said sharply. "The mud's changed!" She crouched beside her shaker, watching the mud stream through it, heedless of the spatters. "Frothy."

"Watery?" Mark asked instantly.

"Maybe."

Mark stared at the twisting snake of pipe. A scar on the metal revolved with it and slowly moved down.

Some mud bubbled up over the rotary table. The foreman watched it inundate his boots. Over his head the returning mud hose suddenly twitched. "Is the planet fartin' at us?" asked the foreman.

"I don't think that's possible," Tinaja replied in an uneven voice.

With a loud burp, mud spurted high out of the hole in the middle of the table. On his perch up in the derrick, Dusty ducked. "It's throwing mud at us!" he sang out.

"You're not safe up there," the foreman decided. "Come down."

A minute later, a brief gout of mud came out of the hole. Mud, with rocks in it, rained down on the platform. "I drilled up water on Earth but I but never seen the likes of this." The foreman sounded uneasy.

Dusty scurried over to peer into the mud tank. "It's making bubbles and the mud's higher in the tank than it was!" he reported breathlessly from the edge of the platform by the tank.

"Mixed with water?" Mark demanded.

"Nosir, it's just really foamy."

Another gout of mud, a hard one, shook the pipe.

In a sharp voice, Tinaja told the foreman, "We can't have any sparks. If this is some kind of natural gas, then it could be flammable."

The foreman nodded, then grimly started checking around for moving parts that might strike sparks, or loose electrical connections that could arc.

To Mark, Tinaja muttered, "Natural gas is not supposed to exist on this world—but neither are teeth. Maybe there is a kind of natural gas down there. It might or might not be associated with water." She cursed briefly and vehemently. "I never studied this in Ship school!"

The scar on the pipe turned around and around without going down. Mark approached it, leaning as close to the pipe as he could, heedless of the mud piling out onto on the table. He asked, "Why have you halted the downward motion of pipe?"

"I haven't," said the foreman.

"But it's—"

The pipe slithered upward in front of Mark's face.

Swearing in surprise, the foreman tried to clamp the pipe. The upward thrust of it tore the clamp apart. Accelerating, the pipe broke something high on the derrick. A piece of metal fell clanging down. Tinaja yelled, "Can't you stop it?"

The foreman bellowed back, "No! There's godawful pressure under it!"

The platform shook spasmodically. Dusty lost his balance. Letting out a terrified yell, he slipped into the mud tank with a thick splash.

Closer to the tank than the others, Mark shouted, "I'll get him!" Holding a jittering railing, Mark reached for Dusty. The boy's muddy hand slipped out of Mark's.

The pipe thrusting itself up out of the ground muttered and moaned, noises that vibrated through the platform. Mark heard a shriek from strained metal at the top of the derrick. Tinaja screamed, "It's breaking the rig apart! Run!"

With shouts and curses the drillers and Tinaja leaped off the platform and scattered. On his third frantic try Mark got a handful of Dusty's shirt. Dusty scrabbled to get some leverage for himself on the slippery side of the tank.

The hole roared. The platform rocked. Mark almost fell into the mud tank himself. Then he hauled Dusty out while mud and rocks and metal parts rained on them. Dusty shrilled, "It's shooting into the sky!!"

Dusty meant the pipe. Drillpipe arched high in the air over the derrick. It was being thrown up out of the hole—lofted by gas escaping from underground. The platform quaked. Glowing light bulbs swung wildly on their cords. Any moment now, one of them would smash into shards and sparks.

Mark threw Dusty off the platform and the boy hit the ground running like a jackrabbit. Mark jumped down and angled away from the platform as he raced toward the powerhouse. In the corner of his eye he saw hundreds of feet of noodle-soft pipe still shooting up into the air.

Gravity overtook the airborne pipe. A loop of it hit the ground in front of Mark. Thundering, it broke up, thirty-foot lengths bouncing wildly. Mark cowered. But he had to reach the powerhouse. He jumped over a steaming length of pipe to get there.

Tinaja reached the powerhouse just ahead of him. He nearly collided with her. She grabbed the derrick main breaker and threw her whole weight to turn it off. Then she looked past Mark and gasped. *"Too late!"*

Mark turned, his stomach knotted with dread.

Fire flared above the derrick. Heat from it struck Mark's face.

The hole under the derrick threw up another gout of mud. Choked, the fire shrank dramatically.

"Now what?" Mark asked hoarsely. Tinaja just shook her head.

They stood closer to the derrick than anybody else. Spectators and drilling crew had fled to the nearest hill with the last of the pipe crashing to the ground at their heels. His eyes transfixed on the damaged derrick, Mark moved in front of Tinaja, for the little protection that he might give her.

The derrick coughed. Then it threw up thick globs of fire. Mark groaned in dismay. His dream had come true, the right image in terrible wrong colors, like a demonic photographic negative. What should have been pale and cool burned instead: a geyser, not of water but of fire. Black smoke coiled into the sky. The derrick howled and shook. Ropes of orange fire coiled up into the air and fell back to the ground, splashing flame. Tinaja let out a shrill cry of dismay. "It's oil! Oil burning!"

Around the derrick, clumps of dry grass caught fire. The wind blew up a swirl of thin brown smoke, and the smoke pointed toward Chang's Creek Canyon.

Mark shook off the mesmerization of the flames. He took Tinaja by the shoulders. "Run to the dome, raise the alarm and radio the Ship for help!"

Without a word she sprinted away.

Mark charged uphill, toward the greeners and drillers, waving his hands. "Wildfire! Equipment to the Creek!" He panted. "Sand plan!"

Shovels and buckets were cached near the dry creek. Greeners and drillers broke out the tools and frantically shoveled sand over the cacti to protect the plants' roots. Disturbed grasshoppers jumped and flew short distances.

The firebreak executed so carefully, just yesterday, to guard the canyon, utterly failed. Mark knew that it would. Spurred by the hellfire of burning oil spewing out of the ground, the grass fire rapidly sidled around the firebreak in the gulch. The front edge of the fire penetrated Chang's Creek Canyon. Burning bits of vegetation flew through the air.

"Fall back—across the creek bed!" Mark waved everyone across the stony bed of the dry creek that might halt the fire and help them save this, the shadier and greener side of the canyon.

Mark flung the lid off the nearest flood cistern. He plunged a bucket into the warm water. Drillers and greeners threw water on the vegetated ground and splashed the mesquite trees in desperate haste.

An isolated fire flared up in the bushes under the canyon wall. Side by side, Mark and Chang beat it out. Chang had no words of recrimination to spare for Mark. Not yet.

A sudden and startling mechanical noise reverberated in the canyon. Mark looked up, stricken by hope.

An airplane thundered overhead. It banked. On the second pass, the plane dumped a dense streamer of orange powder onto the fire in the gulch.

Coughing, Mark recognized the harsh chemical. *Deus ex machina*, the firefighting squadron had descended from the Starship in a shuttleplane loaded with fire-suppressing chemical. The plane circled back to release another load. Then it banked toward the column of black smoke in the sky beyond the gulch.

Mark told Chang, "Check around for hot spots and put 'em out."

Chang nodded, expressionless.

Mark recrossed the stony creek bed. The mesquite trees on the bank, leaves singed off, bore orange powder like a dusting of weird snow.

The chemical had taken the fight out of grass fire. Only a few patches smoldered sullenly. Mark emerged from the bitter smoke in the gulch just in time to see the fire squad's plane making a brave pass at the fiery fountain spewing out of the drilling rig. The plane tossed an orange plume of chemical at the rig.

The oil inferno barely flickered.

Mark felt detached, like a spectator at a grand and tragic show. He watched the derrick collapse, its metal girders melted, inside the flames.

Something new flew down out of the sky. Not another lumbering shuttleplane: this was a screaming splinter of a jet. The jet charged toward the towering fire. Then the jet pulled up, releasing a dull gray object to tumble down and explode in the midst of the fire.

The bomb's shock wave flattened and extinguished the flames. Mark cheered wildly.

Wreckage and dirt fell over the drill hole. But black oil still came out of the ground. Not ablaze anymore, the oil spurted like blood from a cut artery.

The jet arched and returned. This time it hurtled low over the singed landscape. It dropped a second bomb directly onto the hole in the ground. The cratering blast shattered the rock, stopped up the hole. Only a little more oil oozed out. The jet screamed away.

Mark's ears rang from the two explosions. He did not know how long he had been standing here watching the attack on the fire. It seemed to be nearly noon now.

Mark gave the black, oily bomb crater a wide berth. Yet he found a blob of oil in his way, flung far by the bombing, sticky and smelly, the ancient dark blood of the planet.

The wildfire had run through the field of solar energy collectors next to the derrick. The structures drooped over the charred grass. In the distance, the green grass sketch on the hills had turned ugly, charcoal splotched with lurid orange.

The home dome seemed deserted. It was not flammable, so no one had stayed there to worry about it. Mark fed the spider her overdue breakfast. She was important. A symbol of the web of life. Of which the most vital strand, for the life of continents, was grass. Mark sat down at the kitchen table. Hard hot daylight beat down on him through the skylight, since no one had closed the shutters. Shaking, he folded his arms, buried his head in them, and cried.

Someone shook him by the shoulders. "Mark! Are you hurt?"

Mark flexed his hands. Under a crust of sooty dirt, his raw skin oozed blood and blister water. He shuddered. He looked up at Evan Reynolds. "How come you're here?"

"I was watching from orbit," said Ev. Behind him stood Tinaja, disheveled, her face pale under streaks of soot.

Ev went on, "I watched the terminator sweep toward your part of the planet. Then I saw the flare. It was incredible—there shouldn't have been that much fuel on the entire continent. My people analyzed the flare immediately. Then they did a data base search for how to fix an oil well blowout, which is what that kind of thing is called. I came down with the fire squadron."

Tinaja pulled Mark over to the counter sink. She started cleaning his blistery burns with soap and water from the kitchen reservoir. Mark's fingers and palms hurt fiercely. The pain seemed irrelevant. Through a scratchy, aching throat, he said, "I opened up the gates of hell. It burned up the grass." Mark felt a quiver in his insides. Maybe he was going to be sick. Or sickeningly sad.

"Mark. Where does soil polymer come from?" Ev asked.

"Garbage. Our conversion rate is up to thirty-seven point six percent," Mark said defensively. "It's the best I could—"

"You've done fine recycling around here," Ev soothed. "Polymer comes from garbage after you process it, more or less turning garbage into petroleum. We've been making all of our petrochemicals that way."

Tinaja gasped. "*Petrochems!* I studied that in Ship school. We examined precious little samples—plastics, solvents, fertilizers." She pulled a wrinkled tube of burn ointment out of her pocket. "Medicine."

"Petroleum is the most useful stuff in creation," said Ev. "We had no idea that it existed on this planet—that there'd ever been plant and animal life in such abundance as to turn into reserves of oil—except for one round of speculation years ago. Too far-fetched to waste resources looking into, I thought." Ev sighed deeply.

Tinaja smeared burn ointment on Mark's hands. Mark leaned on the counter. He felt dizzied, as new ideas surged and glittered in his mind. Star-burned ecosystem. Petrochemicals. Soil polymer. Holding up his dripping hands, he blurted, "Now we can green the land!"

"What?" Tinaja asked. "How?"

"Let me demonstrate." Ev produced a vial from his coat pocket and poured a small pile of substance on the counter. "Soil polymer." He sprinkled water onto the polymer. It absorbed the water like a sponge. He dripped more water onto the polymer, which kept sucking it up, swelling. The scant handful of plastic sand turned into a gelatinous mass.

Tinaja poked the swollen polymer. It quivered brightly.

Mark straightened. His back ached, but the weight of the world had just rolled off his shoulders.

Ev explained, "This material absorbs four hundred times its weight in water. Mixed in the soil, it does wonders for water retention. With enough of it, Mark's outfit can turn this land green as grass. Not in my lifetime, but in yours."

Tinaja let out a joyful cry and flung her arms around Mark. She exclaimed, "The oil can't be just here—there must reserves all over the planet!"

Mark's heart lurched at hearing another and even brighter hope than he'd expected, like the sun rising after the first flush of dawn. "Then we'll use it to make the whole world green again." He returned Tinaja's embrace as Ev beamed at him over her shoulder. "Not in our lifetimes," Mark added. "But someday."

QUICKFEATHERS

Originally a short sequel to my science fiction novel *Hurricane Moon,* subsequently this story was integrated into my novel *Downfall Tide.*

The verdant world called Green poses many geological and ecological puzzles for a new colony from Earth. But the most perplexing and painful puzzles are those in the human heart.

Planet Green is a geological puzzle wrapped in an ecological enigma, inside a planetological mystery. The geological puzzle is this: a planet that's had vegetation for billions of years should be oozing with petroleum. But we can't find it. Not in the places Earth-trained geologists know to look. The landscape west of Unity Base gets a lot of their attention anyway, because the geologists are convinced that the underlying rock formations will yield oil, if we can just figure out the rules of the geological game here.

I'm not convinced that we need to play this game. Green has other sources of energy—sun, wind, and above all, tides. Yes, oil is wonderful stuff that yields fuel and petrochemicals, plastics and medicines, but none of that will solve the crisis facing us now. Our compulsion to seek oil strikes me as a superstitious reflex; it's like resorting to black magic. It's because in all of our hearts, there's a cold core of fear that there may not be a human future on Planet Green.

My role in resource exploration is aerial survey. I fly a motorglider equipped with scanning and mapping instruments. The motorglider's engines run on biofuel produced from plant matter, but most of the time—more and more, as I learn my way around the sky—the motor stays off. I take advantage of atmospheric thermals, which are abundant in the long days here, and I work ridge lift when there's wind. So I usually don't need the engines to keep us aloft. By "us" I mean myself and my observer. It's dangerous to be out alone on Planet Green. The danger has less to do with the environment than with what's between our ears—how we react to an environment we didn't evolve in—but that doesn't make the danger any less real. The buddy system is Standard Operating Procedure for everyone in the field.

Given the cross-training we've all had, my aerial observer could be anybody from a mechanic to a medical technician to a stray scientist. My favorite observer happens to be a theoretical molecular biologist. His name is Joe Toronto. After the long starflight from Earth, depending on how optimistic you felt about this new world—or how much trouble you were in on the old world—some of us changed our last name to honor our city of origin. Joe came from Toronto. I grew up on a farm near Brightwood, Tennessee. I chose to keep my family name, and I'm still Rebecca Fisher, but I named the motorglider *Tennessee Kite.*

Joe works long hours in Unity Base, and it's hard, risky work. He's repairing the human genome, damaged by our starflight taking hundreds of years too long. Every so often he likes to get away and ride with me in *Kite.* He is the most imaginative scientist I've ever met, which makes a surprising difference: he's better than anyone else at seeing what none of us expect here.

The long days of Planet Green give thermals plenty of time to develop. And overdevelop. One day Joe and I found the sky getting crowded with clouds that had roiling gray roots and icy crowns. I diverted to one of my emergency runways, a stretch of rough limestone ridgetop marked by an orange emergency supply barrel anchoring a wind sock. With a rainstorm bearing down on us, we jumped out of the motorglider, tied down the wings and tail, and ran for more substantial cover. Where the ragged ridge abutted a slightly higher hill there was enough of an undercut to provide a shelter from the storm.

We ducked into the undercut with a cursory look around for hazards like loose rocks that could turn an ankle. We knew we wouldn't meet anything alive that was particularly dangerous. Animal life on Green tends to be small, slow and soft. No dinosaurs, no birds, no herds of herbivores with carnivores stalking them. The most conspicuous life form on the ridge was a frilly blue lichen with chartreuse fruiting bodies. Planet Green is big on lichens.

At the back of the undercut I noticed a narrow gap with deep shadow behind it: a cave. I turned on my pocket flashlight to investigate the cave. At first I found nothing but stone, sand, and silence. Then I noticed a black substance coating the roof. I touched the black stuff with a gloved finger. It wasn't mold. It also wasn't sticky asphalt, but looked enough like some form of carbon to make my interest level spike very high.

"Back up," Joe said. The sharp edge on his voice told me he was either excited or alarmed. I backpedaled until I bumped into him. "Look down." He pointed past my shoulder at the floor of the cave, a fine-grained gray stone with sand drifted over it. The sand almost covered a long, shallow, curved depression. "Look at the whole floor. What do you see?"

The depression extended almost the fourteen-foot width of the cave floor, and it had an unmistakable shape. I yelped, "Wings!"

Rain lashed the ridgetop outside. The cave stayed dry and quiet.

We brushed sand off the shape in the stone. Under my fingers there appeared a stony tracery of feathers at the edge of a wing. I was astounded.

Planet Green seems primitive, quasi-Devonian, yet life on Green is older than Earth itself. That's the ecological enigma. After peaking in complexity eons ago, the ecosystem on Green devolved from more apparent complexity to less. Lichens and ferns are ubiquitous, while we haven't found anything flower-like. What Joe and I had discovered in the cave was far more momentous than flowers. We were looking at the fossil of an extinct Green-bird. It had lain in fine-grained, water-saturated sediments, undisturbed, as its flesh dissolved and its form turned into slaty stone.

I've seen pictures of the Archaeopteryx fossils on Earth. Even the most intact of them looked like a run-over, smashed chicken. The creature on the cave floor was very different. With its wings outstretched in a lifelike way, crested head turned to one side, tail fanned out, it looked at peace. Entranced, I was only half-aware of Joe prowling around the rim of the cave until I heard him take in a sharp surprised breath. He said, "Remember cuneiform—the first writing —marks pressed into clay with a stick to count sheep and vases of olive oil?"

Joe's flights of mind could leave me way behind. "What about it?" I looked up. My eyes had adjusted to the dim light, and I saw markings on the cave wall. Rows of marks spiraled from the ceiling of the cave to the bottom of the wall, where the marks were obscured by drifted sand.

Joe stood there smiling at the marks. "Anybody who can count can think."

As what he meant sank in, it made the hair on the nape of my neck rise. "The black stuff on the ceiling," I said. "It's soot from ancient fires."

There's one possibly sentient species on Green that we know of, and they don't even live on land. The species in question is something like a cross between seals and sea cucumbers with some salmon thrown in. We call them Green-seals. Every springtime they migrate out of the sea and swim upriver to reproduce by giving birth to live young, who then spend an undetermined amount of time living on land as what we call zucchini slugs. Joe is convinced that the Green-seals devolved down from beings much like us. "They discovered fire, worshipped a bird god and wrote in the cave, and later returned to the sea," he says. Everybody else thinks the seals are boring, smell bad, and have unattractive offspring. The truth may lie in the Green-seals' DNA, but it's not Earth DNA, and it'll be a long time until Joe can read it.

Green is a geological puzzle wrapped in an ecological enigma inside a planetological mystery.

The planetological mystery is Planet Blue: a moon as big as Green, but covered with oceans and rotating so rapidly that hurricanes ceaselessly spin across its face. A large moon is a very good thing for an earthlike planet to have. It stabilizes the planet's axis of rotation, providing seasonal change within a climate that doesn't vary wildly. It generates tides, making the interface between land and sea procreative. Earth's own moon had a lot to do with Earth's evolutionary success. Planet Blue, though, doesn't make scientific sense. No ecosystem as old as Green's should have a moon as close as Blue. Over billions of years, the two worlds would spiral away from each other, spin down, and end up phase-locked with each other, having the same period of rotation. Planet Green's leisurely day is 52 hours long. Fast-spinning Planet Blue's day is 8 hours. That can't be, not unless there's been major interference with nature.

In the early days of the colony, we sent an unmanned exploration drone down through the hurricanes to sample one of the islands on Planet Blue. The drone came back with a chip of rock that turned out to be an artificial material. The island chains in the worldwide sea of Blue are artificial stuff. For reasons unknown, somebody long ago changed Planet Blue on purpose. It was remodeled on a mind-boggling scale, nudged back in from maybe ten times as far away as it is now, and spun up.

Blue's artificial islands show two hundred million years of weathering. Tens of millions of years is a long, long time for sentient beings. That long ago on Earth, there weren't even any mammals yet. Whoever the movers of Blue were, they're nowhere in evidence and are probably extinct. Could they have been the ones who wrote in the cave? That seems like the most unlikely hypothesis of all—that beings capable of moving a world would worship birds.

With all of us busy founding a colony, trying to understand ancient cave-writing rates as a sideshow, a hobby to be pursued in spare time, of which we have very little. Our brand new civilization will soon need to tap into Green's natural resources. Metals, diamonds and corundum, uranium, and, if you insist, petroleum. We won't repeat the chain of events that sent Earth's ecosystems to hell in a handbasket. Resource extraction on Planet Green will proceed delicately and deliberately. The first step is simply to map what's here and understand why various resources are where they are—to learn the rules of the geological game.

Everybody out in the field, though, keeps an eye open for the fine-grained, alluvial sedimentary rocks that can present bird fossils. Now that we know to look, we're finding lots of them. Most resemble the first one, fossilized bone, beak, and all, with wings fanned out. We've also found rock shelters, grottoes and additional caves with writing on the walls. Some of the sites have been exposed to the elements for millions of years, and everything is weathered down to wisps. But a few of the caves seem to have been sealed off until relatively recent, minor seismic activity cracked them open. In those sites everything is well preserved, even the pictures scratched into soft stone or painted in colored pigments on the walls. Pictures of birds galore, trees, and quadrupeds and snakelike things—the kinds of creatures you'd expect to see on a world with plants, but we've never found here. But no pictures of anything with hands and tools.

Maybe this cave-writing race had a taboo about depicting itself?

Some of the writing did turn out to be tallies of numbers. But most of it was far more complex than enumeration. Even with the help of the Starship's artificial Intelligence, the meaning of the writing proved elusive. Meanwhile the tally of worshipfully fossilized bird fossils increased. There were three different species. The first kind had long, tapering wings with a span averaging twelve feet. There was an even bigger species with long, blunt wings. A third kind of bird was much smaller, with relatively short wings.

Occam's Razor says you shouldn't multiply bird gods without a good reason.

One day I was thermalling in *Kite*, turning ascending circles on a bubble of warm air, not far from Story Bird Cave and over the same ridgy limestone landscape. The engine was off. *Kite* was functioning as a pure sailplane, and I imagined my own shoulders extending into the long white wings. I could feel the wingtips dip and lift, reading the textures of the air. Sailplane wings look deceptively plain—just long curves and smooth skin with faint stripes—but are as sophisticated as anything ever made by human hands. The ghostly stripes in *Kite's* wings are Sinha-Blazek deturbulator strips.

I only wished there'd been an Earth-hawk, or even just a turkey vulture, sharing the thermal with me that day. On Earth, the only thing better than flying and feeling the wings of a sailplane as an extension of myself was doing so in the company of a hawk. It was something about Green that always made me a little sad—that the sky is devoid of feathers, flight and song. So I imagined thermalling with a Green-bird. Happily climbing the sky with my imaginary bird-friend, I remembered the marks in the cave, and the realization hit me like a bolt in the blue: though the marks could have been made by pointed sticks, talons could do it do. Then I knew the key to translating the cave writing. It was simple.

Assume the cave writers are birds.

With that breakthrough, the Ship's Intelligence began to be able to translate the writing that spiraled down from the apex of Story Bird Cave. This is how it started:

The People were beset by dragons, but the People were brave and swift of wing, and the dragons didn't eat too many People.

Dragons is a highly questionable translation. The Ship's Intelligence is working on more urgent problems, and for an Artificial Intelligence, it may be distracted. Or it may be eccentric in its old age. The journey here took a thousand years of relativistic time, with astronauts and colonists stored in cold stasis while the Intelligence guided the Ship. There's no other computer that old, except maybe on Earth, which is impossibly distant in space and time. Furthermore, Earth was wracked by war and ecodisaster when we left. I wouldn't bet on much remaining of civilization there, much less a computer of the same vintage as the Ship's Intelligence.

Elderly and eccentric as it is, the Intelligence decided that it was dealing with a mythological history involving unearthly beings. When it translated Story Bird Cave, it upped and used supernatural terminology.

Between the deep sea and the high Hinge of the All, the world was long and rich. In warm marshes that teemed with fish-fingerlings, young People practiced how to be hunters of fish in the open sea. Dangerous monsters infested the sea but the People were strong and maneuverable, and the brave-winged hunters always found fish to bring home. Except for the marauding dragons, the People were happy.

Then one day a great blue pearl appeared in the sky. It deranged the sea.

That bit stopped the translation in its tracks. Finally, Joe—at work in the lab in Unity Base, with our doctor, Catharin, who's his wife and my best friend—suddenly laughed. "The pearl in the sky was Planet Blue."

Catharin isn't fazed by Joe's fugues of imagination. She countered, "Why call it a pearl?"

"Their universe was a bivalve. Sea in the bottom half, sky in the top half. The Hinge of the All was a high mountain range beside a long, narrow coastline. And their homeland—the coast between the mountains and the sea—was the meat in the cosmic shell."

I heard about Joe's guesswork that night at supper in Unity Base.

"Story Bird Cave could be a historical record," I said.

"That would depend on how the rest of the story goes," Catharin answered.

The sea rose. Waves climbed onto the land and snatched at the People's nests. The sea flooded the nursery marshes, and sea monsters swam up into the marshes. The old People said: that sky pearl has deranged the sea. The sea is climbing out of its nest. Soon we will be caught between hungry dragons swooping down from the air and many-toothed monsters swimming up out of the sea, with nowhere safe for our young. The world is ending.

It's a mistake to think of anything on Planet Green in Earth terms, but I can't resist imagining a Cretaceous sea full of toothy plesiosaurs. Then the big blue moon gets shoved in *close*—as near to Green as Luna was to Earth, but six times the apparent size in the sky, and twenty times as bright. It twanged Planet Green hard—probably set off earthquakes and volcanoes, possibly induced global warming and rising sea levels, and certainly created tides like nothing the Bird People had seen before.

There was a bold young fish-hunter named Wander. Now Wander said: I have watched the sky. Not all clouds blow against the Hinge of the All and stop. The highest clouds freely go back and forth. Maybe there is another world on the other side of the Hinge of the All. I am brave and strong and [unclear]. I will go look.

The she-People, brooding eggs saved from the waves of the sea, clacked their bills in anger. They said: You should stay here guarding our nests!

But he set out anyway.

Clear as a bell, except for one word. In the phonetic notation we're using, the unclear word is /a*a/. It consists of the most common vowel sound in the language flanking a rasp or rattle from a bird's throat. /A*a/ probably means "smart," because next comes this passage:

*Wander was very /a*a/. He remembered what the old People said about* *dragons. He waited for a windless day and set out early in the morning because he knew that the dragons couldn't climb the sky then. Without a strong wind, dragons can only fly down.*

I visualize the story's dragons as pterosaurs. A survey team out in the field recently found a fossil like that. It looks mangled, as if it died by accident. Like pterosaurs, it would have been too big to get airborne without a headwind, too heavy to stay airborne without ridge lift or midday thermals to keep it up.

A dragon leaped from a cliff, its greedy beak gaping. But Wander had /a*a/ feathers. He outflew the dragon. Unscathed, he soared into the high chasms of the Hinge of the All.

That /a*a/ word perplexed me for weeks. Meanwhile, I carried geologists and their instruments all over local creation searching for crude oil. Green is very old, and has been vegetated longer than Earth has existed. Plenty of organic matter should have accumulated underwater and been buried by silt and sand, heated and compressed and cooked into oil. The geologists have identified ancient basins, the ghosts of long-dead seas, and deep beds of shale and sand. Places where oil should seep and puddle and pool under the planet's skin. Except geology on Green apparently didn't work that way. On some of my flights I imagined my Green-bird friend again because the imaginary bird was better company than the frustrated geologist sitting in *Kite's* passenger seat. I pondered how a Green-bird might feel about flying. I wondered what /a*a/ could mean. I've never seen a feather that's *smart*.

When I found a little spare bandwidth in the uplink to the Ship, I talked it over with the Intelligence. We decided on the word "quick." Wander was brave, strong and quick. As a child he was a quick study. His feathers were quick in the sense of aerodynamic. An imperfect translation, but it'll do for now.

Wander expected it to be hot in the Hinge of the All. Did the Sun not alight on the Hinge at the end of every day? Instead it was bitter cold. Frigid winds blew in Wander's face, tossed him to and fro, and tried to fling him against raw stone.

It took humans more than a century to learn how to fly up close and personal with mountains. Sailplane wreckage in the Alps and Andes and other mountain ranges attested to the danger of the learning curve. In that environment, hang-gliders have some advantages over sailplanes and airplanes. A hang-glider in a bad patch of wind may be able to put his feet down and land. Which is what Wander did.

He took shelter in the lee of a boulder. Even there the wind disheveled his feathers. Cold and hungry, he longed for the nursery marsh of the People, the warm water full of sweet crabs and minnows. Then he heard a voice. It said: Hello!

A witch hovered in the air.

Witch? The Intelligence's peculiar linguistic sensibilities are showing again.

Of the three kinds of Green-birds that were interred in watery sediments, the smallest kind has opposable claws at the main bend of their wing. They were sometimes buried with artifacts, including polished stones and sticks just the right size for their opposable claws to grasp. Using sticks might have seemed witchy to Bird People like Wander who talked, but didn't use tools. Instead of "witch" I'll use the word "raven."

When I mentioned this to Joe, he shook his head. "No organism here is what we knew on Earth. Green-birds aren't birds. Green-seals aren't seals. Green-genes are deoxyribonucleic acid, but with coding utterly alien to ours."

Joe may have been the smartest human being in the Twenty-First Century. He was a genetic inventor, creating genetic tools and marvels and a few monstrosities that never should have seen the light of day. Finally he made an enemy so powerful and so vengeful that Joe's only escape route was the Starship. In *his* spare time, Joe tries to understand Green-DNA.

I conceded his point about Green-life. But convergent evolution happens. On Earth, both bats and birds had wings. A penguin's wing had the same cross-section as a fish's body to move efficiently in water. For my own paraphrase of an ancient story written by birds, I'm going to call the Green-birds with short wings and opposable digits "Ravens." Not "Green-ravens." Microanalysis of fossil feathers found evidence of color; their plumage was purple.

Now the Ravens were smaller than People and lived in all the nooks and crannies of the world, eating every kind of small thing with fur or scales or feathers. That included nestlings, so she-People on the nest spread their wings and clacked their bills whenever Ravens came near. The People's sentinels at the nursery marsh chased Ravens away. But in the bleak Hinge of the All, even a Raven was better company than wind and snow and rock. Wander moved over and the Raven deftly landed beside him. The Raven carried a magic stick under his wing. Leaning on his magic stick for balance in the wind, the Raven asked Wander: What brings you here?

Wander answered: The world is ending. I want to fly over the Hinge of the All and look for another world.

The Raven cocked his head and said: You have long wings and quick feathers, but you don't know the ways of the wind in the mountains. I do. Let me ride on your back and let us go together. I'd like to see another world, but own wings are too weak to make it over that.

The Raven pointed with his staff. In the distance the highest part of the Hinge of the All stretched like a bleached sea monster's bony spine from one end of the sky to the other. Dismayed at the sight of it, Wander asked: Do you think there's a world on the other side?

The Raven answered: When I pry at stones or roots or leaves or ice, there's always something interesting to find. We should pry at the edge of the world and see what's there.

Never before had any of the People had a Raven for a companion. But the world had never been about to end either. Wander said: Hop on.

The best guess from the Intelligence is that the consonant in /a*a/ was a trill. Nice to know, though it would be nicer to know what the word means. It comes up again and again.

Now the Raven's name was Quickclaw. He preened his feathers smooth and perched between Wander's shoulders. Hunching low as he clung to Wander's feathers, he taught Wander how to ride the wild tangled winds. They threaded their way through the Hinge of the All until they saw a pale green plain among the mountains. Quickclaw shouted: We need to rest and eat. Fly down, but be careful because Sky-Spiders live there. They go back and forth to the sky on strings, and they have many shiny things and pry even more than Ravens do.

God Almighty. Does "back and forth to the sky on strings" mean contrails? Could this be the intelligent race that moved Blue, and they had a space base on an altiplano on Green? Story Bird Cave might contain historical clues to the ultimate mystery of Planet Green—the huge blue moon. By pointing that out, I got the priority of translating Story Bird Cave upped.

The Ship's Intelligence soon produced this:

Wander spiraled down to a quick stream in the high plain. They thirstily drank. It was very cold that night, but Quickclaw found a hot vent in the ground. Snails clustered around the vent. They gorged on snails and stayed out sight of the Sky-Spiders. After two days they saw strange flat clouds overhead. Quickclaw climbed on Wander's back and said: Fly high!

Wander flew up and up. Quickclaw urged him on: Fly higher!

Wander beat his wings and climbed higher into the sky than he had ever flown before. The breath sawed in and out of Wander's lungs until he thought his chest would burst from exertion. Then a strong wind seized him and lifted him up, higher than the Hinge of the All. The tallest mountain bore a smoking black crater on its peak. It was the Perch of the Sun, scorched from the Sun sitting there.

Quickclaw spotted lenticular clouds, a sign of mountain wave. Wander flew up into the wave and it carried them over the highest mountain in the range, which was a live volcano. I wanted more about Sky-Spiders, and didn't get it, but I did get evidence that this story is reliable. It describes mountain flying realistically. People with wings would know.

The cold air was too thin to feed Wander's blood. He dizzily panted. The edges of his vision faded. Staring ahead, he saw the Sun gliding away from its Perch. Wander stretched out his aching wings and followed the Sun. Quickclaw shouted: Look! Under the Sun!

Below the Sun a green land stretched away into distant haze. Wander glided down into good thick air. Then he laughed. The Raven on his back chortled and cheered.

The Starship's Intelligence really is eccentric. Stubborn. It doesn't like to speculate about what comes next until it's sorted out what it already has. I think its linguistic expertise was based on a professor who kept her cards up her sleeve until her conclusions were ironclad enough to publish. The next line of the story came out as *Beyond the Hinge of the All, they found many cathedrals.* The Intelligence couldn't explain why it used that word. Then it wouldn't give me any more translation of the story. I wished we could bring a linguist-colonist out of stasis, but there was no way to justify that, for an incredibly ancient linguistic puzzle, when our colony's future had just hit an utterly unexpected roadblock.

Not only was there no crude oil in the sedimentary rocks, waiting for us to find it, but there were no diamonds in igneous rock formations. No copper or iron ores anywhere. No bauxite. No uranium. We came up empty-handed for every mineral resource on our shopping list. More people were awake now, revived from stasis, including the core of the Colonial Government. And the boneheadedness of our leaders was astonishing. They weren't interested in developing the resources that we had in abundance: sand, sun, sea, and tides.

When I fumed about the Colonial Government's stupidity, Catharin shook her head. "It's not simple stupidity. They're afraid, and they haven't yet faced it."

She knows about facing fear. As the Starship's Physician and chief medical researcher, she'd realized early what stasis that lasted a thousand years had done to us. It wrecked molecules, triggered autoimmune disorders and cancer, and, in insidious ways, damaged the human genome. She's battled biomolecular catastrophe ever since. To help her, she enlisted Joe, who had been no humanitarian on Earth. His unflagging genetic repair work represented a major change of heart, after he faced his own psychological demons soon after we got here.

Cat and Joe both knew that all of our original colony plans were dead on arrival at Planet Green, and for there to be a human future on Green, we'll have to invent new plans. When I advocated alternate resources, they backed me up. Meanwhile there was endless discussion about the puzzle of geology so deficient in metals, oil, diamonds, etc.

I had my own guess about that, but I only confided in Cat and Joe. I told them, "If Green was the cradle of a civilization powerful enough to move the blue moon, then on the way up they mined this world out. There won't be much left for us to find."

"The ground rules are different from Earth," Joe said ironically. "We knew that."

"Yes, but we can't comprehend what it means," Catharin pointed out

In the end, the cathedrals riddle solved itself in the very next line of the story: *They saw no people in the branches.* Oh. To birds a *tree* can be a cathedral.

The rest of the Bird literature uses images even more poetic than that. There's one cave so large and with so many scratches on the walls that it might be a library. It's mostly untranslatable. The Bird People seem to have had a mystical Dreamtime concept, somewhat like that of the Australian Aborigines. The Green-Dreamtime inspired reams of otherworldly poetry.

Story Bird Cave is a simpler type of literature. It has the earmarks of being ancient oral tradition that crystallized into writing soon after writing itself was invented. The original events were carried in the Bird People's unwritten memory for a long time, and turned and cut and polished like gemstones. Whoever finally wrote it down added their own rudimentary literary sensibilities. But it's understandable. Mostly.

They glided down to a small river. Wander saw the riffle that gave away a fish. He swooped to seize the fish in his talons. Wander ate the fish and it was very good. In the grass beside the water, Quickclaw snatched up a fat little no-legs. It quicked and he ate it with relish. Right now I don't like my translation of /a*a/ as "quick." The context makes the word seem to mean "twitch." Language is based on metaphors, and this particular metaphor isn't obvious to hominids like myself. Especially not in the next line. *Quickclaw said: This is a good world with plenty of quicking meat!* Evidently, /a*a/ can mean "delectable." Maybe food so fresh that it's still twitching as it goes down qualifies as really tasty....

At the end of the day the Sun fluffed its fiery feathers and settled into its nest at the end of the sky. Wander said: This is a good world. My people could live here.

Cleaning his bill, Quickclaw said: I would like for my mate to see this.

As far as we've decoded the Green-Bird literature, there's nothing about Wander's people having mates. Maybe they were never monogamous. Or they always were. Either way, it wasn't a detail worth singling out. On the other hand, there's a lot in the literature about mated Ravens. Ravens in love, Ravens making babies, Ravens fooling around with Ravens other than their mates. Ravens in off-and-on mating situations which seem to resemble my relationship with our colony's chief helicopter pilot, Dom Cady. Humans are a lot like the Ravens.

We know where the Hinge of the All is. Once it was a coastal range of high mountains, but eons of weather and the tidal assault of the sea eroded it down. On the seaward side, after the new blue moon's tides scoured away the Bird People's homeland, erosion rebuilt a wide sloping shelf of land. Salt marshes grew back again.

Inland from the mountains, a wide shallow basin filled in and heaved up into the ridgy limestone plateau that's there now. Finally we arrived and picked this time-worn mountain range to bear the first human footprints on Planet Green. Unity Mountain, with our base on its top, is an unimpressive mountain now. Two hundred million years ago it was the volcano called the Perch of the Sun.

At midday the Sun bypassed its Perch on its way to its nest at the end of the sky. At night the great blue pearl raced across the dark sky. The stars in the blue pearl's path dimmed, hiding from it. Wander said: At home in the old world, the blue sky pearl is driving the sea crazy. My People are in danger. I must go back to them.

Quickclaw said: We should pry at the valleys on this side of the mountains. We might find passes that will be easier going than flying over the mountains into the wind.

Now Wander had been thinking about the cleverness of Ravens and how, being much smaller than the People, the Ravens ate different things. Wander said: When we get home, let's invite your mate and your relatives to help my People fly the mountain winds, so People and Ravens together can come here to live. Ravens would all enjoy living here. Ravens could pry for a thousand years and not find all of the new things in this new world.

Liking the idea, Quickclaw chortled.

Wander flew homeward with Quickclaw on his back. They picked their way through windy, barren passes in the Hinge of the All. Finally they reached Quickclaw's home territory. They soon found Quickclaw's mate. When she heard what Quickclaw had to say, and saw how glossy his feathers looked from the nutritious food in the New World, she flew to tell her friends and relatives the news. But when Wander saw the old world again, he knew that he didn't have much time. The deranged sea was chewing on it. The world looked like a ragged blade of grass. The sight wrenched his heart.

I know how Wander felt.

Like Wander, after I grew up I journeyed far away from home. Farmers, including my parents, tend to want descendants who stay on the farm *and* an offspring or two who go find success in the wider world; belt *and* suspenders. I had three brothers, all hardworking farmers. I was the kid who left the farm. I became an engineer and an astronaut with missions to the Moon and asteroids under my belt.

But when I came home for my first visit in ten years, I saw that we were in big trouble. Earth's oceans rising in the Twenty-First Century had triggered huge population shifts when people living in coastal areas were flooded out. Sunbelt Cities like Chattanooga and Atlanta, burgeoning at the end of the Twentieth Century, grew even more wildly. That meant a lot of farm land paved over. It also meant family farm economics trumped by high-output factory farming. Factory farms bred not only livestock and crops, but pesticide-resistant weeds, anthelmintic-resistant internal parasites, and antibiotic-resistant diseases. Every one of those problems threatened the Fisher farm.

To top it all off, Earth's destabilized climate brought calamitous rains to the hills of Tennessee. Where the rains washed raw gullies in the hills, the land looked like it had been raked by monstrous claws. We Fishers, like everybody else in the county, had lost most of our crops. We were just lucky that the house and barns hadn't been in the way of a flood avalanche.

My parents called a family meeting about what to do. In truth, the question was where to go. American farmers had been moving to Central or South America for decades. But it had become almost impossible to find a country that wasn't aflame with violent civil unrest, and arable land not overrun by desperate people displaced by the rising sea. My mother threw up her hands. "Where else in the world can we go?" We were sitting at the table of our rambling old farm house around a still-sturdy, century-and-a-half-old oak dining room table.

My father looked across the table at me. He said, "It may have to be to another world."

Until that instant, I'd been following the work of the Aeon Foundation with detached fascination. The Aeon Foundation intended to privately fund a starship to colonize a new world. It was a fascinating endeavor, but I knew I could never leave Earth for good, forever leaving behind the farm and the family I came from, the land I grew up on.

But the land was dying. And my family decided to go to the stars.

In his sorrow for the ruin of the world, and because he had spent days in a dragon-free place, Wander forgot to look up. A dragon plummeted down at him and he barely dodged its gaping beak. He smelled its foul breath. But suddenly the air filled with Ravens, Quickclaw's mate and many others, all darting at the dragon's eyes and tail. The dragon swatted at the Ravens, but they were small and nimble. Wander wheeled close and raked the dragon with his talons. The dragon turned tail and flapped away.

Wander returned to the People with a flock of Ravens in his wake. He told the People: I've seen the world beyond the Hinge of the All. And the Ravens are now my friends, and they will teach us all to fly in the Hinge's winds. Let's go.

But the She-people slicked their feathers down angrily. They said: Few enough eggs hatched this year and our young are just beginning to fly. Do you expect us to leave our young behind? Or let these Ravens eat them?

Wander said: Show the Ravens where to find fibrous marsh grass and stringy seaweed. The Ravens will weave nest-bags to carry everyone too young to fly to the New World.

Are we to carry burdens like that and fight off dragons too? demanded the suspicious She-People. Are you planning for us to carry snacks to the dragons?

He answered: I have a better idea.

With Quickclaw, he flew south to the land of the trolls.

For trolls, read huge carrion-eating birds with gray feathers. A better translation than "trolls" might be "teratorns"—the enormous Ice Age vultures of Earth.

The Intelligence's persistence in translating the words for additional intelligent bird species as supernatural beings is very interesting. When you think about it, coexisting with an equally intelligent species was a situation we never had as humans on Earth. Or if we did, it was in the Paleolithic, when Cro-Magnons shared part of Europe with Neanderthals. By the Neolithic, the Cro-Magnons had the continent all to themselves.

As I write this today, it's Green Year Twelve, the twelfth year since Starfall. My personal account of the Story Bird Cave translation was always a pick-up-and-put-down, spare time kind of amateur history, but the last time I touched it was six years ago. A lot has happened since them. Some things were good and hopeful. Other things were ominous or bad.

Earth crops in our pilot projects didn't grow as readily as we expected. The probable reason was microbe disconnect. Earth had an invisible world of microbes that the visible plants evolved to coexist with. The microbes of Green are alien. Until we get this figured out, until crops grow reliably, we won't revive many farmers from stasis. I may not see the rest of my family for a while.

Without mineral resources and Terrestrial crops, what we have to work with on Green is sand, sun, sea, and tides. A certain amount of plastic and paints can be made out of native plant matter, and buildings out of concrete and glass. What we need more than anything else is energy. I went back to my original profession, being a structural engineer, and I designed a tide machine to straddle the river near Unity Base.

Building the tide machine has taken politics and persuasion, blood, sweat, and tears, and engineering that's never done before. It's also cost me one of my best friends in the universe. The river is how the Green-seals come inland to give birth to their sluglike young. Joe got upset because the tide machine might kill migrating seals.

I said, "Look, Joe, for humans to live, something has to die. It may be cows or catfish or pole beans, but that's always the cost of keeping people fed, clothed and housed. Something has to die, even if it's just the weeds on a fallow field when you plow it to plant a crop." I didn't say out loud what I thought about the worldview of city people. For city boys like Joe, food is something that just appears. It costs only money. The universe doesn't work that way.

Joe said, "The Green-seals aren't weeds."

"No, they aren't, and they can learn to stay out of the tide machine." I was so upset that I raised my voice, almost shouting at him. "I don't want to hurt the seals! I don't think the machine will hurt or kill many of them before they learn to avoid the machine."

He scowled. "Killing any of them is too many."

And then he relentlessly opposed the tide machine. His opposition fractured the colony. Some who took Joe's side were people I cared deeply about. Some on my side were careless young visionaries and others were politicians I don't trust. Catharin adamantly refused to take sides. She stayed on cordial terms with me, but I could no longer confide in her. For a long time I didn't have the heart to go back to translating Story Bird Cave.

On my 44th birthday, celebrated with a small group of friends not including Catharin and Joe, I picked the story up again where the bird heroes went to talk to the big gray vultures.

The Teratorns lived on a plain of grass between the Hinge of the All and the sea. Herds of four-legs lived and died on the plain, and the Teratorns ate dead ones. Wander and Quickclaw arrived at the end of the day as the Teratorns returned to their roost on a ridge swept by the wind from the sea. Wander said: We flew over the Hinge of the All and saw another world. It has many four-legged grass-grazers, alive and dead, so there is plenty of carrion, as well as food for Ravens and my People. If we join forces, we can all get past the dragons and the mountains and reach a safer world. Rise as much as it will, the sea will never get over the mountains.

Most of the Teratorns laughed. But one she-Teratorn said: I can see with my own eyes how the sea surges higher with every tide. When it inundates the grass plain, we will have sea on one side and stone on the other, with the four-legs all swept into the water for sea monsters to feast on. Then we will starve. I see no reason to perch here while the world drowns. My clan will go to the new world.

Now the she-Teratorn's name was Sees-Far-From-On-High.

Another way to render her name is Descry. But it makes sense for vultures to have a long-winded language with many-syllabled names. Their lunch won't run away while they take their time saying things.

Quickclaw's relatives made nest bags, just like they made for their own young, but larger. Wander, Quickclaw and Sees-Far-From-On-High decided that the middle of the day was the time to set out. Into the nest bags went the People's young and the Oldest who could no longer fly far. Then the People climbed into the sky with Quickclaw and his mate and relatives, and the Teratorn clan carried nest bags full of the very young and very Old People. Young Teratorns clung to the backs of their parents.

In the foothills the air swarmed with hungry dragons.

Not all stories have happy endings. I don't know how happily the story of our colony on Green will end, much less the story of my own life. I feel a need to find out how the Bird People's adventure ended. I'm guessing that it turned out pretty well. Even though it doesn't look that way now.

Ravens darted around the dragons, pecking at the thin skin of the dragon's bellies. The most daring of the Ravens pelted the dragons' eyes with sharp rocks. The People raked the dragons' throats with their talons. Dragon blood watered the wind. The she-People were the fiercest fighters of the People, keeping the dragons away from the Teratorns.

The Teratorns were almost as big as the dragons, but could turn smaller circles, Stretching out their wings in the air that swirled up from the Sun-warmed foothills, the Teratorns climbed the sky faster than the dragons.

Two young People fell out of their nest bag. A dragon snapped up one of them. The other one fluttered to land on a Teratorn's back. The Teratorn said: hang on!

Teratorns with their burdens circled tightly and soared high while the Ravens and the People fought the dragons. Blood and feathers scattered in the air.

Everyone who was still alive soared after the Teratorns and escaped toward the safety of the mountain passes. Behind them the dragons hissed in fury. Wander was the last of all the People, and the dragons almost caught him. But his feathers quickened and he escaped.

In the mountains, the Peoples regrouped and flew on, with Ravens teaching People how to fly the quick winds. The Teratorns were able to stay higher, in smoother air.

Deep in the mountains lay the high plain with its grass and snails. The People wanted to stop there. The Ravens warned them about the Sky Spiders. Then Sees-Far-From-On-High called out to her clan: Don't stop, stay high. I see Spiders getting in and out of shells with wings. And the Spiders have stretched their threads far and wide. They are cutting holes in these mountains, melting the mountains' hearts like ice, and bleeding the mountain hearts away. We are too big to hide from those Sky-Spiders, and we should have nothing to do with them.

Did a giant vulture just describe resource extraction? I think she did. We've been exploring the land westward of Unity Mountain for resources, but it looks like the Sky-Spiders got there first and plundered the land. Surprise.

A new world wouldn't be new without some surprises—not always nice ones.

The Peoples found flat clouds and lifting winds and flew over the smoking Perch of the Sun. The new world unfolded under their wings. The People told Wander: truly it is a new world with rivers full of fish. Sees-Far-From-On-High said: there's more. Far to the west, between here and the Sun's nest, I see an inland sea, and it has many fish in it and many four-legs in the grass around it. This is a very rich new world. But in the air over the inland sea, I see dragons even bigger than the ones we left behind.

Oh, hell. The story started at the apex of the cave ceiling, where the lines of marks were obscured by soot when we first found it. Now the story is down to where the marks were half-hidden behind sand at the bottom of the cave, they've got dragons in their new world, and the word /a*a/ is conspicuous by its presence in the last line of writing around the cave.

A couple of days ago, I shared the sky with cloud-dragons: cumulonimbus clouds with lightning claws. I used gliding speed to dodge them, pushing *Kite* to the limits of its performance, and *Kite* outran the clouds. The Sinha-Blazek deturbulator strips on Kite's left wing caught my attention. In the striped areas, the wing skin shimmered.

The technically advanced materials on the wing were vibrating at just the right frequency to damp down the beginnings of the turbulent separation of the air stream from the wing. Deturbulator strips let *Kite* fly better in more attitudes, open up the corners of *Kite*'s performance box.

Just like that line from Story Bird Cave about how Wander got away from the dragons. *His feathers quickened.*

It had been under my eyes every time I flew *Kite.* Nature got there before Sinha and Blazek did. The feathers of raptors can vibrate in a highly specific way, deturbulating the air stream over a bird's wings. It may feel like a pleasant shiver to the owner of said wings. For Bird People, it attracted cultural meanings. Metaphorically, the word /a*a/ can mean *quiver with wonderful consequences*—speed; intelligence; harmony; goodness.

I told Joe about it. I added that maybe my own mind isn't very quick. I've been thinking like an optimistic and ox-stubborn engineer, intent on solving a problem without fully understanding it, plowing my way to the solution of an engineering challenge with principled disregard for unintended consequences. It hurt to admit that to a brilliant scientist. But my conscience said I had to.

Then I challenged him to figure out a way for the seals and the tide machine to coexist. He thinks he can get the seals to follow a channel around the machine. And I'm holding up the machine to let him.

Maybe the Bird People were quick in a way we aren't.

At most of the fast-moving, tight-maneuvering moments of human history, we had turbulent separation. War. We've had whole civilizations clash and crash. Even on a new world on the other side of the stars, in a colony only twelve years old, we've already experienced an ugly rupture.

In the Green-Bird's whole vast literature, we can't find references to wars among Bird Peoples. Territorial tiffs, yes. Conquests, pogroms and World Wars, no, and nothing about gods and kings either; perhaps there's a connection. The Bird Peoples hyperevolved without the destructive turbulence that marked human history. What made them so quick? Green-genes? Having wings? Not having a world rich in mineral resources, because an earlier race mined everything out on their way to a level of technology high enough to move the blue moon?

Maybe all of those factors contributed, but I think the true answer is written in the last line of the story—the line that runs all around Story Bird Cave at the bottom of the wall.

Wander said: Ravens are quick of claw, the People quick of wing, and Teratorns have quick sight. We are all People, and we are quicker together than apart. Dragons or no dragons, this is the world for us.

Wander was a culture hero. For humans, a culture hero is the legendary person who discovered fire or founded a dynasty, or someone who invented a momentous machine at the dawn of history. On this new world, the dawn of history is now.

My tide machine works. It turns the river tides into energy enough for a city.

The seals are bypassing the machine in the channel that Joe devised. He figured out how to infuse the channel with water-soluble scents that mean *this is the right way,* while suffusing the tide machine's water intakes with smells that shriek *danger* to the brains of the seals. What gave Joe the motivation to devote months of his life to a side channel for Green-seals, I'll never know; I think it has to do with expiating his old scientific sins on Earth. How an arrogant primate figured out the high points of the smell language of giant aquatic slugs is even harder to understand. But he did it. The seals are using the channel and staying out of the tide machine.

Meanwhile the long, bitter rift in my friendship with Joe had the effect of mending fences between me and Dom. By the time Joe and I became friends again, Dom was firmly entrenched in the habit of being my husband. Our on-again, off-again marriage is on for good.

Dom is ferrying materials by helicopter to the site where we'll build the first human city on Green. It will be a city made of glass, with daylight and starlight streaming into it. Since you can't have a city without farming—food won't magically appear here any more than it did on Earth—we now have an all-out project to establish crop cultivation, with the intense involvement of microbiologists, and the results are starting to look good. To no one's surprise, or I should say, to no farmer's surprise, we have to have animal husbandry too. It takes cattle and sheep, their manure and their microbes, to successfully cultivate Terrestrial plants here.

Before long it will be time to revive the other Fishers. My mother and two of my brothers are agricultural engineers. As farming gets started on Planet Green, there will be Fishers' hands on the plows and mass spectrometers.

Crops and calves wouldn't matter if we couldn't have children. But thanks to Joe's inventive repair work on the human genome, there will be a human future on Green. Some of the very first children born here have grown up and had healthy babies of their own. Maybe in a thousand years, Joe and I will be culture heroes for Green-humans.

Wander, the bird-culture hero, invented the cooperation of intelligent species.

We don't know for a fact that Homo Sapiens ever had that opportunity, but it might be a test we flunked in the Paleolithic by driving the Neanderthals into extinction. If cooperating with other intelligent species is a test the universe administers, then the Bird Peoples of Green passed with flying colors. They used fire. They farmed shellfish and grains—I can't wait to inform my brothers that the first and finest farmers on Green were intelligent crows.

The Bird Peoples domesticated dragons. They adorned themselves with jewelry, sang songs, dreamed dreams, made love, wrote a vast and subtle literature, and built cities on the shore of their inland sea. They buried their dead in the silt of the deltas where rivers met the sea. Above all, they cooperated.

A decade after the first time I saw Story Bird Cave, after years of poring over digital images of the cave and the computer's repristination of the original writing, I went back in person yesterday. Joe went with me. Humans going out into the wilderness on Green still use the buddy system, especially when the big blue moon is nearly full.

I'm a first generation leader now, with a lot of leeway if I want to use it. Yesterday I used it. I gave myself permission to light a small, clean fire in Story Bird Cave. Then I sat crosslegged in front of the long-winged fossil bird in the cave floor.

"I see why you wanted the fire," said Joe. "It makes the bird look alive." Flickering firelight made the fossil impression of the bird seem to breathe. The stone feathers seemed to quiver. "What do you think? Is it him?"

I said, "I think the Bird Peoples regarded this as him, and it inspired them."

If humans flunked the test of learning how to cooperate with another intelligent species back in the Paleolithic, we may have another chance coming. So far on Planet Green, there were birds whose intelligence waxed after the waning of a civilization powerful enough to move the blue moon. That, our government assures us, was two hundred million years ago, a span of time which takes the definition of ancient history to an extreme, and we don't need to worry about the world-movers. But one thing about petroleum is that there's such a thing as young oil that forms in ten or twenty thousand years. We haven't found any of that either. I think somebody used it up or took it away, long after the Birds, who never seemed to have done much with metal, much less oil. The latest guess is that the Bird People laid eyes on the Sky Spiders very late in their long oral history, long after the lives of their early culture heroes. The Sky Spiders probably had nothing at all to do with moving the blue moon. They might have been like us: an intelligent race from across the stars, intent on colonizing this old world—or this star system—with how much ultimate success, it's so far impossible to say.

I touched the feathers impressed in the fine-grained gray stone.

My intuition insists that we'll have a second chance to figure out how to cooperate with another species. Maybe in my lifetime. It might be the Green-seals. Thanks to Joe, at least we didn't start out by setting up a machine that mangled them. Or maybe there'll be new arrivals from interstellar space. If weren't the first newcomers, we probably won't be the last either. Or maybe we'll send a mining expedition to the asteroids of this sun and find the remote descendants of the Sky Spiders.

Somewhere not far away, there are people besides us. They have something to offer us, we have something to offer them, if both sides see it that way. It never worked out on Earth. But this is a new world. When the time comes, I hope we'll be guided by a kindred spirit named Wander, and get it right.

CLOUD SKY CITY

In my science fiction future history, which stretches from the 21st Century to the 70th, and from Earth to the Sagittarius Arm of the Milky Way Galaxy, there's a wide expanse of space and time that the 70th Century knows as the Dead Zone. But a lot happened here, not all of it having to do with destruction.

―――――

A remote colony world in the distant future poses an archaeological riddle. The ruins on the planet Ende bespeak an ancient starfaring destination. In seeking to understand the riddle of the ruins, a young archaeologist finds a mystery about humanity's once and future destiny—and her own.

―――――

The rented landflyer skimmed the foothills of the Endish Range under a ceiling of featureless gray cloud. Carolinna dela Manta had a wide view of the barren landscape through the flyer's canopy. Across the lowest slopes of the mountains trailed ancient rock walls, as meandering and aimless as though, two millennia ago, they had been flung down out of the sky like so much string.

None of the sketchy ruins suggested the time-eroded foundations of a city.

Distracted, Linna almost let the landflyer brush the jagged crest of a wall wandering over a hill. She jerked the thrust lever up. The flyer grudgingly lifted itself over the obstacle. An outdated but serviceable model rented from the trading post just a few hours ago, the flyer was a perfectly adequate platform for Linna's work here. But the survey wasn't starting out the way she'd hoped.

Linna opened her notebook. "Initial aerial survey of the ruins is inconclusive," she dictated. "There's no evidence of a starport-industrial complex. Despite the central role of Cloud Sky City in the mythology of the Endish natives, it's not obvious that their ancestors constructed a city in this location in the Colonial Age."

It was of course possible that the myth of Cloud Sky City had no historical basis. The annals of archaeo-history were full of dead ends. But Ende, she silently vowed, would not be one of them.

Cold air probed the edges of Linna's cold-weather coverall. The flyer lacked cabin heating, and it was early Spring on Ende, warmer than Endish winter but frigid compared to anywhere else.

She tilted the flyer over the shoulder of a low ridge. More walls skeined away downhill. "The purpose of the extensive wall structures is unclear. They might have been field terraces to start with, but if so have been abandoned. The natives subsist by fishing and harvesting plants in a huge lake." Far away, she could see the slate-colored Lake of Ende.

Suddenly Linna flashed back to her summers as a young girl, camping beside sun-glazed blue lakes on her home world, New Catalunya. The rocks that previous generations of campers had arranged—big stones piled up into seats, ringed around camp fires, laid down to line ditches—had fascinated her. Campground stones had sparked her dream of becoming an archaeo-historian. She wanted to discover new ruins of the old Colonial age when the human race crawled away from Earth across the stars, slower than light and with hopelessly high hopes.

The Colonists settled on as many as twenty scattered worlds, and tumultuous centuries passed on Earth until the unexpected invention of fast star flight. Whereupon Earth set out to conquer the stars, in the process rediscovering its old colonies: some extinct, some flourishing, most somewhere in between, a function of how hospitable or marginal a planet the Colonists had stumbled onto in the first place.

Ende's name was an anagram of "Eden." Never had the hope of paradise on the other side of the stars been as misplaced as on Ende.

Air turbulence brought Linna back to the present with a jolt. The walls, higher in this area, blocked the wind and made it eddy and uplift.

Rough stones fitted together with no apparent mortar comprised the walls. It was primitive construction, and much the worse for centuries of weathering. Lichens laced through the stones might be doing more than their share to keep the walls standing.

The flyer's remote sensing equipment consisted of one camera. At least the crude device had a notebook connection. Linna quickly programmed the notebook to diagram the walls surveyed so far.

She frowned at the resulting image on the notebook's tiny screen. The walls traced across the mountain foothills in a very roughly semi-circular way. The walls could have been centered on something important. But the focus was empty: the only thing there was kilometers of barren slope between the walls and the slate-gray lake.

Disappointment—no less acute for being premature—grew into a lump of ice in Linna's stomach. Maybe there had never been a Colonial city here. And if not here, then nowhere on Ende. Only this region had ever been colonized.

If Cloud Sky City had never existed, it didn't matter to Ende, a world harsh enough to have shrugged off any Colonial attempt at a city. But it mattered a great deal to Linna. She'd studied at the great old University on Terra with enough distinction to be awarded a much-coveted prize, which she'd used to fund a one-woman expedition to Ende to look for Cloud Sky City. Her friends and colleagues had thought it was a breathtaking gamble. But that Linna dela Manta could pull it off if anyone could.

No matter how she altered the parameters of the map, her notebook still showed the sprawling complex of walls to be roughly centered on empty, steeply sloped, featureless land. Exasperated, Linna tossed the notebook into the luggage web. She checked the flyer's fuel gauge—it read only a third down, which was what she expected, since she was halfway through her planned flight—and continued flying her survey grid. Ende had only recently been rediscovered. No archaeo-historian had been here before her. Something undiscovered had to be here to study and learn from. And she would find it.

On a ridge of land ahead of the flyer rose a wall bigger than the rest, with an odd design etched on its face. It looked as though the wall bore a corrupted frieze. She flashed to the guess that it was a remainder of an ancient marketplace. Or, more plausible: the ruins of a religious shrine, a sanctuary. What form would religion take at the end of a long star flight to the bitter end of the attainable universe? Energized by anticipation, she briskly swooped down to land the flyer in the wind lee of the big wall, descending on a torrent of downducted engine thrust.

Linna instantly saw that her "frieze" was only a scribbled expanse of lichens. For all its height, looming a good ten meters above the flyer, the wall was just more dark gray rock work.

Mortarless.

Unstable.

Shoved by the flyer's landing wash, the wall swayed against the milky sky. Linna watched in horror as lichen threads stretched and snapped. Thrust-up to takeoff would take the old flyer twenty seconds—too long! She hurled herself at the flyer's door and jerked it open.

Harsh thundering noise assailed her. The roof of the flyer sagged. Terrified, she wriggled out of the seat and dived onto the flyer's floor. The sagging roof propped itself on the empty seat frame, which gave a shrill groan. Then the awful, hammering thunder trailed off.

The instrument panel, jammed up against the crushed seat, sizzled. A wisp of smoke curled out of it. Spilled fuel, loose wires, she thought disconnectedly. What if it caught fire?

The door was crumpled, but ajar. Frantic, Linna crawled out of the flyer, heaving fallen stones aside to escape from the machine.

Behind her heels, the flyer erupted into fuel-fed flame. Linna scurried away from the hard heat.

Notebook, she thought numbly, sitting up on her heels. Notebook? She desperately searched the pockets of the coverall. She found her survival kit and her radio, but not the invaluable notebook that contained not only her preliminary findings so far, but all of her research about Ende.

She'd tossed the notebook into the luggage web. The notebook's circuits would have been fried by the fire. She stared mesmerized at the burning flyer, incredulous at her own stupidity.

The burning flyer dimmed and dwindled to a shapeless lump of metal and plastic. Cold washed around Linna's feet, like undertow exploring someone wading on a treacherous shore. The intensifying sensation scared Linna into thinking more clearly. She picked up the radio, fumbling with the boxy little device.

A piece of it came off in her gloved hand. Unnerved by the broken bit, Linna desperately tried to activate the radio.

It didn't work. It was broken.

The radio had been stowed in a pocket on the left side of her cold-coverall. And her left hip ached ferociously. She dimly remembered the nearly crushing force of the roof of flyer. The radio had been in the wrong place, briefly but disastrously ground against her hip.

Linna stared up at the empty, milk-blue sky. Accident without immediate help was incomprehensible. On New Catalunya, the air net would have vectored help in at once. And red-and-blue parrots would have flocked to the scene to scold the careless flyer. Here there were no parrots, no people, nothing but gray desolation.

She remembered being told that the flyer's transponder-locator wasn't working. She'd idly suspected that the flyer was usually rented to shady prospectors who didn't want their whereabouts known. But she'd shrugged it off, knowing she had a survival kit and a radio

Linna started shaking. The flyer was ruined. She was stranded. In the field. On the farthest frayed end of civilization. Suddenly she couldn't swallow. She grabbed the disregarded survival kit and opened it with shaking hands to assess the contents. Food cubes. Firestarter. Water pouch. Tent.

She could survive. And she wasn't badly hurt. She could hike toward help.

The trading post lay on top of a mountain, but she wasn't sure which one. She couldn't walk back to the post without knowing where it was and how far. The opposite direction was a better bet. The natives living near the lake might help her.

She could see the great lake in the clear distance. What looked like tiny rafts of debris on the near shore were the Endish villages, too far away for people or even buildings to be distinct to Linna's eyes. Taking a deep, shaky breath, she started walking downhill.

Downhill would go to the lake. Eventually. Mentally Linna kicked herself. She'd made a series of mistakes, starting with substandard emergency equipment and ending with a careless landing. She knew better. She'd worked in the field before. But she'd let herself be distracted by the unpromising-looking locale. Linna cursed herself for letting disappointment evolve into unmitigated disaster.

Hours later, Linna was stumbling with fatigue and the lake looked no closer than before, the villages still distant and indistinct, like flecks of wood washed up by the water. She had a worsening headache—she must have hit her head on something when the wall crushed the flyer. Now every step she took jarred the bundle of pain in her head. Above, gray clouds massed in the sky, blotting out the sinking sun and its wan warmth. Without direct sun, the whole landscape faded to dreary shades of gray.

Dread clutched Linna's lungs. She could die on Ende.

She fought off panic, reminding herself that she had the kit with tent, food, and water. She could survive a night on Ende. But the emptiness and loneliness of the world appalled her. Linna ignored the headache and the pain radiating from her badly bruised hip and staggered on.

The chill breeze made her eyes tear. She was struggling ahead in a blur when someone stepped in front of her.

Linna halted in shocked surprise. He had the stocky build of Endish natives, and native clothes—leggings, a hooded parka, thick animal-skin gloves.

"Hello," she gasped. Most of the natives supposedly understood the trade-pidgin used at the trading post. And it was based on Panglish. Desperate to communicate, she blurted, "I was flying—I was looking for Cloud Sky City. A wall fell on my flyer. I need help."

He backed a step away from Linna. A short bow hung on his belt. Small dead animals dangled from a thin rope slung over his shoulder, dripping blood onto the gray ground in red spatters, the most vivid color Linna had seen on Ende. He turned away from her. Before Linna could cry out in dismay, he looked over his shoulder. "Come home."

Trade-pidgin was a skeletal language. The hunter probably meant *come to my home.* Hurt, shaken and desperate, Linna started after him.

She followed him for what felt like days but might have been only an hour or so, and he never touched her, but never got far ahead of her. He waited for her to painfully pick herself up when her foot slipped on a mossy rock and she fell. He glanced back at her often. His eyes seemed unnaturally bright, as if he had a fever.

It finally surprised Linna when he halted at a dome of dirt. She looked around dazedly. The earthen hovel was isolated, nowhere near anything else that looked like a dwelling, or anything manmade at all.

Linna felt afraid. But the natives of Ende rarely harmed outsiders.

The hunter reached out to a stiff curtain hanging in what looked like the hovel's doorway, half as tall as a person. "Come home," he said again, his eyes shining bright. Disconcerted but having no alternative, she crouched to go in.

The warmth of the hovel, relative to the bitter cold outdoors, came as a shock that swept Linna's remaining strength away. Half-conscious, Linna tumbled into a pile of furs on the hovel's floor. The furs smelled strongly, like smoke and food and life.

Every morning, the relentless grayness of Ende pushed Linna closer to the brink of despair. The afternoons were tolerable - it was Endish springtime, as warm and bright as the climate would ever get. But the headache she'd had for days was always worse early in the morning, and every day on Ende dawned as empty, gray, and chill as death. Today was no exception.

Carrying an empty water bladder and clumsy in the windless cold, Linna trudged along a faint trail on the moss-mottled ground. The trail paralleled a wall made of ragged stones. Featureless otherwise, the gray-green land stretched up to the mountains, their heights cloaked in dismal cloud.

In a stunted tree beside the wall, a drab little bird shrilly buzzed. It was a bitter antithesis of Catalun parrots, and its call pierced the aching fog in her brain like a knife. She stumbled on a loose rock, caught herself on the wall with a painful jolt, and stood paralyzed. *What would Iste think if I died? Do ghosts die in his mythology?*

A stubborn ember of hope flared in Linna's mind. Pushing herself away from the rock wall as though it were the bulk of her despair, Linna followed the trail. The water bag, made from the bladder of a giant fish, was awkward even empty, too thick to fold, too slick to grip easily with gloved hands. She wrapped it in her arms like a baby.

The bird abruptly cocked its head to peer down at something on the other side of the head-high wall. She heard a crackling scuff like something heavy moving on the moss.

Iste had gone to fish in a little boat on the great lake. She was alone. Linna's skin prickled. She approached a narrow gap where the frost-heaved wall had fallen apart. Hugging the edge of the breach, she warily peered across the spilled stones.

An enormous four-legged creature glared back at her. It lifted its shaggy head, baring fangs.

With a gasp, Linna stepped backward, then bolted toward Iste's hovel. The beast shadowed her on the other side of the wall, moss crackling under its fast-moving bulk. Linna shoved her way past the skin in the hovel's narrow doorway. She huddled inside, shivering in terror, glad the hovel had thick earthen walls.

Finally something parted the door-skin. She jumped. But it was Iste. Reeking of raw fish, he peered into the gloom in the hovel. The only light came from the smoke hole over the cold hearth. Iste saw the empty water bladder and scowled. "Bad woman!"

"There was a big animal," she stammered. She didn't know the trade-pidgin word for what she'd seen.

Iste snatched up the water bladder and left. When he returned later, with a full water bladder, he said, "Red-bear was here." His face had smoothed into the unreadable mask that was Iste. He poured water into his cooking shell. "Make fire."

With the electronic firestarter from her survival kit, Linna lit a tiny bundle of tinder on the hearth, her fingers clumsy with cold. The firestarter was good for a thousand starts. The counter said seventeen.

Every day Iste demanded a brief morning fire and a slightly longer evening fire. She'd started Iste's fires for eight days. Even the first time, when he'd demanded that she make fire and she'd resorted to the firestarter, he hadn't marveled at the device. It was her job to start the fire; whether by normal or magical means seemed immaterial to Iste.

He dropped what looked like wrinkled marbles, the root called hodo, into the water in his cooking shell. Feeding bits of peat to the little fire, Iste kept the water boiling long enough for the hodos to soften. Meanwhile he laid strips of raw fish beside the fire.

With a shiny tin ladle, Iste dipped out boiled roots and laid them together with pieces of charred fish on two shiny disks, scales from a giant fish. He gave Linna a scale loaded with food. They took turns drinking hot starchy water from the ladle.

The food and water stilled Linna's shivering and cleared her mind. Red-bear was the pidgin word for an Endish ursoid. The animal she'd seen, pony-sized, with thick legs and reddish fur, matched what she now remembered shown in the orientation holo. Red-bears could wrestle a giant fish or a lake-seal out of the water to devour on shore. They occasionally attacked a seal-sized human. With a shudder, she imagined fangs and claws shredding her flesh.

"You see red-bear where wall fall down."

"Yes, then I ran back."

"Red-bear follow. Tracks to here, unhn," he grunted. "Good woman. Run fast."

Linna felt absurdly elated. Her nerves knew she'd survived a brush with death today. Her stomach, which had been painfully slack, registered warm fullness. It was unaware of the shortcomings of Endish food. The natives subsisted on a sketchy ecosystem that lacked several nutrients essential to outsiders. The original Endish gene pool had, for some reason, been extraordinarily varied, and somewhere in those genes had been a variation that equipped the natives to live on the limited nutrition available on Ende.

"Red-bear go away," said Iste, in an almost conversational mood. "Everybody lake-by better watch out. Lining-up time make red-bear mad."

On this moonless world, the natives marked time by the positions of the sun relative to its distant, red, companion star. At this time of the year, the two stars aligned in the sky, the chip of ruby glare eclipsed by the wide weak yellow disk of Ende's sun. With Ende pulled marginally closer to its sun by the gravity of the red double, there followed what passed for spring. "Do you mean the red-bears are irritable and restless? Why? Is it their mating season?"

He scowled. "You forget too much."

"I'm not a ghost," Linna protested. "I'm from a world like this one, except warmer, with more people."

"World is world. Dead people go to Cloud Sky City and forget everything from here. Sometimes come back, though."

Unlike primitives before the Star Age, the degenerate native culture of Ende imagined heaven as a city. It was their attenuated memory of the cities on the Earth their ancestors abandoned.

She'd tried to reason with him before. It was worth trying again. "You use a new tin ladle. And steel needles. Those things came from Outworld. My firestarter isn't magic. It's just a tool, like your knife." She waved the firestarter for emphasis. "Why can't you believe I'm just an outworlder, not somebody back from the dead?!"

"Got skin like us," he replied.

True, most of the trading post personnel had darker or sallower complexions than Iste. But most of the millions on Linna's home world had light brown skin, just like hers and much like his.

"Got eyes like sky. Eyes turn blue in Cloud Sky City," Iste said with the irrefutable illogic of delusion.

Maybe this gray hell was Linna's own afterlife. Hoping to discover a forgotten city on Ende, instead she'd found hundreds of kilometers of rotten rock walls and a crazy man who thought she was his dead wife. Tears pricked her eyes. He hadn't pressured her for sex. She didn't know what she would—or could—do when he did.

"Red star in lining-up time goes behind sun where bear not see it," said Iste. "Red-bear get mad."

Every day Linna had tried to convince him to take her to the trading post. But he wouldn't budge from his mad convictions, woven from the superstitious beliefs and the cultural mores of Ende. So she'd started planning to escape from him.

At first she'd suffered from strained muscles and foot blisters from the long hike to find help. Those had healed. Even her injured hip felt pain-free yesterday, once she warmed up and moved around at midday. Her chronic headache lingered on, but it was bearable. But Iste's warm, smoky hovel seemed safer than wild Ende. She'd not tried to escape so far.

The cold truth finally came home to her, unfolding in the center of her body, crowding out her breath. From here on, her physical condition could only deteriorate, worn away by too little food and too few vital nutrients, and the daily battle against cold she wasn't adapted for. She could cower in Iste's hovel indefinitely while death, as insidious as malnutrition or as brutal as the inevitable Endish winter, waited for her just outside the door-skin. Or she could try to escape. But that had to be soon or never.

Iste was crazy. But he was cunning enough to leave her alone only when she could not escape. He went fishing in the distant lake early every gray-palled morning, while Linna woke up stiff with cold and weak with hunger, barely able to fetch water. By noon, the clouds unveiled a pale blue sky and Iste came home to mend nets in clear midday weather. Brighttime, he called it, the only part of the day with light and warmth enough to make it feasible to do handwork out of doors.

Iste fetched net-making materials from a cache nearby. Linna surreptitiously checked her own cache, a hole scraped out under the ragged rock wall. She was afraid the red-bear might have raided it. But her hoarded food lay undisturbed. Maybe the red-bear hadn't wanted hodos and two foil-wrapped nutrition cubes. The bear was, after all, a voracious carnivore.

A thin yellow flare arced across the blue sky, marking the trajectory of a distant ship in ascent toward orbit from the trading post's mountaintop landing field. Linna intently noted which peak it was: the flat-crowned, big-shouldered mountain directly opposite Iste's hovel from the distant blue-gray lake.

From here she could see distinct huts and longhouses in the nearest lake village. But with Ende's annual slight warming, ice marshes around the great lake thawed and treacherous bogs opened up. The villagers knew safe ways around the bad places, but according to Iste the bogs had already claimed a stray pony.

The land between Iste's camp and the mountaintop was rocky and raw, relentlessly cold, but solid. And the flares of ships marked the trading post. If she started out in fair weather, certain which peak she had to climb, she might reach the post, the one footprint of civilization on the planet.

As dull as Ende's sun was, compared to the radiant solar star of

Linna's home, the light nonetheless cheered her. The day's temporary warmth relaxed her. Her intractable headache had finally gone away. Linna felt almost confident. Today, she would watch for opportunity.

Iste spread out a net made out of string, the brown fiber of a weed that grew in the lake. The edge of the net secured the fiber ends in elaborate knots. In one place, the net's knotted rim was torn from a struggle with a monstrous dish-scaled fish. Iste pointed. "Make it back."

"I don't know how."

"You forget too much," he said dourly. Then he showed her how. Apart from chiding his forgetful ghost, he was patient with her fumbling fingers, demonstrating how to mend the net's border with the complicated knots that would not slip when wet.

Iste was not an old man. His tawny skin was sleek, his hands nimble in making and repairing things. He had never hurt Linna. Iste was a good man by the mores of a culture poised on the knife edge of survival, where a man had to have a wife to survive. His delusion about Linna had wrapped itself firmly around a core of realism: a man alone was an impossibility.

Ende was a terrible place for a human colony. This region, the equatorial and most habitable part of Ende, remained largely desolate even after two thousand years of settlement.

"Gotta shit," said Iste bluntly. He disappeared toward the area dedicated to excrement and fish waste, in a deep little hollow at a distance from the hovel.

Linna snatched up a coil of lakeweed fiber. Shaking with sudden determination, she knelt beside the stone that lidded her cache and scanned the landscape for any omen that this might be the wrong time for her flight.

To her astonishment, Linna saw two figures in the distance, natives making their way uphill from the lake, apparently headed directly toward Iste's camp. Linna froze. Now what? Hope these two could talk sense into Iste, or run away from all three of them?

If she ran, she would be as visible to the visitors as they were to her now. She remembered what she'd intended right after the wreck, before Iste, with his impenetrable craziness, found her: locate some natives and ask for help.

When Iste returned, he stood waiting.

One of the two visitors was a man, the other—smaller, with a skirt dyed purple over Endish leggings, and a cape decorated with embroidery and shiny fish scales—a woman. Linna had an impulse to rush to them and beg for help. She restrained herself. Native women didn't talk before being spoken to. Outworld women were advised to do likewise should they need the cooperation of the natives.

The visitors stopped a few feet away and stood as still as Iste. "*Ache, Iste,*" said the man.

Linna's lingchip, the device implanted in her brain to interpret language, promptly activated. She'd obtained an Endish patch at the trading post. *Ache,* according to the chip, was the native word for hello and goodbye.

Iste had never spoken to Linna in his own language. He insistently used trade pidgin even when she coaxed him to do otherwise. Finally she'd recalled from the notes in her lost notebook that bereaved spouses on Ende were supposed to stay silent for a full Endish year. Maybe trade pidgin didn't qualify as real speech, allowing a bending of the rule.

The male visitor regarded Linna, then turned his whole body toward Iste. "What woman is that?"

The visitor had used Endish, but Iste was sticking to pidgin. "My woman. Your sister."

The visitor's eyes went wide and his woman companion gasped audibly.

This was Iste's dead wife's brother. Linna bit her lip, making herself wait for the right time to speak to him.

Iste's brother-in-law asked, "Did she show up an eightnight ago?"

Iste grunted. Minimal affirmative.

"Well, a trader rep came to our village yesterday. He said a woman Outworlder came and got lost. He was asking people if they knew anything about it. Look, Iste, this is that woman."

Relief made Linna almost woozy. This man was perfectly sane. And somebody from the trading post was searching for her.

"No, Okarde. No." The chip didn't supply a translation for "Okarde": it must have been a personal name. Iste gestured as if cutting something with the edge of his hand. The helpful chip was audiovisual, attuned to the gestural as well as verbal parts of language; Linna abruptly understood Iste to be signaling vehement disagreement. "See color clothes? My woman make good color clothes."

Linna's rented cold-coverall was blue with yellow tunic, brighter shades than any of the native dyes.

Okarde nodded. The chip apprised Linna that a nod on Ende meant *no*. Okarde went on, "She's wearing trader clothes. Get her back to the traders or we'll all be in trouble."

Iste nodded energetically. *NO!*

"Listen, Iste, your woman could not come back. You never sent the bright wing for her."

Linna had read about an Endish funeral rite called the Bright Wing Ceremony, in which the natives called back the spirits of the dead by flying a kite, a fragile, temporary link between their bitter land and its citadel-heaven in the sky. The rite had fallen into disuse since the establishment of the trading post.

"Bunkum," said Iste, using trade slang for inferior goods. It jolted Linna that even Iste, too proud to work in the beryllium mines for the traders, still using dishes made from the scales of the monster fish he hunted, doubted his people's old ways. For cultural precepts he had substituted personal delusion. "She come back anyway."

"Listen, listen, Iste. My mother's father came back. He was a red-bear. My clan remembers."

Okarde sounded patient enough to reason with Iste, whose reason had been mangled by grief. Surely Iste would have to change his mind. Linna seized at that hope. She didn't hate Iste. She didn't want him to be completely shattered by the truth—or to turn violent, either.

Okarde went on, "Sometimes dead people come back as birds. Fur-weasels maybe. Even darkfish. But not people."

Iste snapped, "Ghost look like people."

"Ghost?" Okarde echoed. Making circling motions with his hands, he gestured futility. Iste was as impervious to Okarde's reasoning as he had been to eight days of Linna's. "Men have argued enough," said Okarde. "Yayu." With his knuckle, he gestured toward the woman who'd been silent up to now, probably his wife.

Yayu looked sadly at Iste. "She's not your woman. You know that."

Iste nodded, *no, no, NO*. He curled his gloved hands like tightening springs, like a cornered man.

"You say." Okarde pointed to Linna with his knuckle.

Linna wanted to blurt: I am an outsider! Take me away from him, away from here! But something made her swallow the words with an audible gulp. Her mind raced.

Teetering on the brink of craziness, Iste was a good man with missing linkages in his mind. As an archaeologist, Linna had been trained to think like the mute ruins. Look for the fourth wall, the center hearth. Dig where they might have been. Was Iste missing his people's spirit ceremony? Could that set him right, make him let her go voluntarily?

But why did that seem so utterly important?

The natives waited. They had hardly moved during the whole exchange. Their world did not reward wasted motion.

Linna shoved her confusion aside to sort out later. She knew what she wanted to make happen, if not why or whether it would succeed. She still held the coil of fiber she'd meant to steal. What other kite string could they use? With the coil, she gestured toward the sky. "It's not good for Iste without sending up the bright wing."

Okarde blinked. Then he grunted. "Yes."

Okarde's wife said, "Yes. Yes." She gestured with her fingers, weaving them together to mean collective agreement.

Iste shrugged. The lingchip made no comment. The shrug must have been a foreign gesture that came from the trading post together with the pidgin and trade goods that had irradiated Iste's world.

In pidgin, Okarde said, "Good. Iste and Yayu make the bright wing right. I go bring *tugapu*."

Tu, "she" plus gape, "man," literally, "she-man," the chip told Linna. It was the Endish word for shaman.

Iste seemed distracted. Forced closer to reality, he was visibly pressured. Linna felt anxious about him and exasperated with herself for feeling that way.

The woman, Yayu, looked older than Iste, with wrinkled skin and graying hair. Either age or some less obvious social factor gave Yayu the authority to direct Iste in the making of his kite. She sent him to his cache for long thin fish bones and a wide sheet of fish skin thin as parchment, along with a skein of lakeweed fiber finer than what was used for nets. He framed the kite with three bones, tied together at one end, fanned at the other, with a fourth bone tied across the frame. Yayu approved the frame. Iste then sewed a triangle of fish skin onto the bones. The resulting kite was broad as Iste's height.

A wind picked up, blowing clouds across the sky and cold air off the lake. The kite briefly slipped away from Iste's hand and skipped across the ground, eager to fly. Watching Iste catch it, Linna felt a muddled mix of pity and curiosity.

Yayu had Linna inspect Iste's skein of lakeweed fiber for weak places. Yayu herself cut out weak sections and made small, clever knots to tie the lakeweed into one thin, long kite string.

Ende's weak sun teetered on the zenith of the sky and slipped off, sliding down. Shortly thereafter, Okarde returned with a new stranger who rode a shaggy brown pony.

Yayu and Iste rose to stand waiting. So did Linna.

The shaman wore the clothes of a woman, with a skirt of dyed cloth and a cape decorated with embroidery and tiny crystals like frost. But the shaman was taller than Iste or Okarde. The age-rough voice that called, "*Ache!*" was male.

He dismounted from the pony with the stilted grace of an older woman. The shaman's strong-boned face, though, with wisps of white hair showing around the hood of his cape, was that of an old man. Linna recognized an ancient pattern, ages older than civilization, a primeval human solution to discrepancy of sex role and temperament. Every individual had a stark choice in life: to live as man or woman. The few who chose a role opposite from their sex, and showed skill at it, were holy people, visionaries or leaders.

The cross-dressing shaman regarded Linna with copper-colored eyes.

"See, Tugapu?" said Okarde.

"My woman, Tugapu," said Iste. He sounded pleading.

Tugapu said, "I see sky-eyed woman, and bright wing ready, and clouds on the wind. Good." Tugapu turned his pony loose to graze on the sparse ground. Then he ceremoniously counted those present, including Linna and himself. "A hand of person. Enough to make bright-wing work. You talk Ende?" he asked Linna.

Linna hadn't had enough money to buy a full two-way Endish program for her lingchip. "I can't speak your language, but I understand it."

He replied in Endish. His utterance struck sparks of meaning from the chip, like an iron blade up against a spinning whetstone. "And I understand yours somewhat. Good." The shaman turned half around and raised both hands toward the sky. "Ah, behold, friends and foreigner, here is a man alone, this man Iste. Where are the dead? Since our ancestors came across the stars from the Womb World to live here, there are so many generations that the top three hands of this ground is People."

The shaman faced toward the mountains, the starship-touched heights with rock walls scribbled all across their nearer foothills. Linna's attention sharpened as she listened. The litany had embedded in it some relic knowledge of the Colonization from Earth. Maybe here was what she'd sought in the first place, ruins of the early Colonial days: ruins of memory more well organized and informative than the ubiquitous rotten walls. Linna listened with the same intent curiosity with which she'd first seen the walls.

"Will the ground speak softly at night in the hogan, or make fire for this man, or spread hodos on the ground to dry so that he has food for the winter? The Endish ground brings no *** to Iste. How can a bereaved man have ***?"

Attempting to translate Tugapu's word, the lingchip generated several alternatives.

Futurition

Help

Hope, the lingchip decided.

Linna thought she understood. On Ende, a man alone was an impossibility; help was hope was the only chance to have a future. The language embodied the inescapable logic of life here.

"Hear me, a People came before us People. In this is hope. A People arose after the stars vomited out dust and iron that formed into round worlds, but long before our ancestors came out of the Womb World. The Before People came of age long ago and learned to shape the mountains and the waters of worlds like a potter shapes clay, hear me!"

Linna stifled a yelp of surprise. The shaman had just paraphrased the most mystifying archaeological puzzle of all time.

Traces of an ancient, alien interstellar civilization had been found in the stars. The relics were as cryptic as they were widely scattered. The unknown makers had been tagged Dawn Builders by the few controversial archeologists attempting to explain the incomprehensible artifacts.

But how had the idea made its way to this remotest end of starflight? The trading post wouldn't disseminate ideas about Dawn Builders along with trinkets and tin dippers!

"They left here a waymarker for the ones who would come after. It wasn't just a heap of stones for birds to nest on and lichen to creep into the cracks, but one that only people can see, only with the eyes of their minds. Stone heaps fall down. The Before People's waymarker lasts forever."

Linna felt dizzy with changed expectations. Could the shaman possibly mean what he said, or even know what he was talking about? Dawn-builder artifacts had been claimed on a dozen Colonial worlds. Such claims seemed irrefutable in perhaps four instances. But the technological principles underlying the artifacts had so far been a riddle without an answer. One otherwise reputable team of archaeologists had ventured that the alien technology might be psychic, depending on some still poorly understood synergy between mind and specific kinds of matter.

"Here in the center of the world rise the mountains they made to be a travois carrying their sign through the ages."

The Endish Range was an orographic oddity—a range of mountains arrayed in a tidy v-shape for no identifiable geological reason. Geologists had relegated it to the ranks of relatively minor planetological puzzles. Meanwhile and elsewhere, archaeologists argued about whether Dawn Builder "artifacts" included geological details on several worlds, dubious features blurred by continental drift.

But Ende was so old that it was very geologically stable. What the Dawn-builders had made would stay that way. For untold eons. Linna found herself nodding eagerly.

Tugapu stared at her. "You disagree, sky-eyed woman?"

"I'm sorry, when I nod, it means I agree. The things you say are true."

"*Spisi,*" said Iste. *Fish-shit.*

"No!" Linna insisted. "A dozen worlds have traces of the Dawn B — Before People. I studied this a little." It had been peripheral to her studies in human archaeo-history, but unforgettable as a weird and vivid dream.

"Ah," said the shaman, fixing her with those compelling copper eyes. "*Tekirte.*"

Literally, he said *he-woman,* the lingchip explained in her brain. The word denoted the female counterpart of shaman: a visionary woman chieftain.

All three of the other natives regarded her with surprise on their faces.

With a single verbal stroke, the shaman had redistributed the balance of power in this group, handing Linna a measure of authority. She guessed that she now had permission to speak out of woman's turn. But she had to be diplomatic. Or she'd lose her new credibility. She took a deep breath. "Please say on."

"My friends and foreigner, in lining-up time we can make the Before People's hinges in the sky turn, by sending up a bright wing and hunting it with our attention. Why?"

Linna sensed Tugapu posing a test of her knowledge. She had the answer he wanted. She could not possibly render it into trade-pidgin, though, at least not before they all grew weary of the clumsy attempt, so she plunged ahead in Panglish, hoping he understood well enough to get the gist of it. "Some smart thinkers who study the Before People's handiwork say it's psychic engineering. Minds make it work. Focused mental attention makes something happen. There are a couple of places where the psychic technology may be powered by the orbital symmetries, ah, by a world and small moons moving in a harmonious way that gives it power."

What about a world and two suns? What could a Dawn-artifact do if it were powered by a double star? She took a breath to steady herself. "But there's one thing more thing proposed as intrinsic to their devices, ah, important to make things work. Crystallized carbon —diamond—somehow is a catalyst. Icestone is what I mean," she added, recalling the trade-pidgin word. "It needs icestone to start what happens."

A pidgin word existed because high-grade diamonds occurred in these mountains, not in rich veins easy to mine, only in glistening rare bits found by natives on rare occasions. The traders at the post paid bounties for diamond.

The shaman interlaced his fingers, the gesture of total agreement. The small diamonds embedded in the embroidery of his cape sparkled like fresh drops of dew. "True."

Iste looked confused, like a man clinging to an overturned boat in rough water. "True?"

"It's truth," said Linna, emphatically. This was the first thing about Ende that had made archaeo-historical sense. Linna was as intent on the shaman's story as a fish-hunter who caught a glimpse of a great fish in the deep water.

The shaman took a lustrous stone from a pocket under his cloak. "Some people will sell anything for trader money. They use glass in the Bright-Wing ceremony instead of diamond. You can get big pieces of glass from the traders cheap, very pretty. It doesn't work, though." He affixed his diamond to Iste's kite.

Placing both hands on Iste's shoulder, Tugapu explained how Iste should give the kite into the arms of the wind when the time came. Iste seemed numb and slow to understand. The shaman was patient. He'd dealt with the bereaved many times before.

"Go to your brook and pray until sunset," Tugapu finally instructed Iste. Iste obediently walked away. Okarde trailed after him, vigilant in case the red-bear returned to threaten the solitary, preoccupied man.

Tugapu sat in the lee of the wall near Iste's hovel. With a gesture he invited the women to rest likewise.

Yayu said, "I hope his real wife comes back today. Then he won't mind when we take Sky-Eyed Woman to the trading post."

"Yes. That will prevent discord," Tugapu replied. He turned to Linna. "It's the Endish way. You did well."

For primitive peoples in the harshest environments, social discord was the evil of all evils. Had Linna absorbed some of that attitude from Iste, and was that why she had suggested this instead of immediate salvation?

Or had she simply submitted to her captor, let him force her to be willing to play the role of devoted ghost?

On impulse, Linna asked Tugapu, "Do you really believe in ghosts? Before I came here, I learned all I could about Ende, what Outworld visitors had said. There wasn't any mention of ghosts."

"I heard something very interesting today. The trader who came to our villages asking about a lost outsider said she is a young woman, from a new place, but she has old learning."

Surprised, Linna chose her words with care. "I studied on Earth —the Womb World. That's where all the old learning is best kept now. I've learned all I could about ancient history before our ancestors left Earth. The place where I was born is new, though." New Catalunya was a post-Colonial world, discovered on the wings of fast starflight, a thousand years after Tugapu's ancestors settled on Ende. No locale on New Catalunya could be said to have topsoil of which the top fraction consisted of molecules that had once been living humans. The dead of New Catalunya were an imperceptible trace of atoms in land and sea and wind. Beyond whimsical campground stones, could that have been what attracted her to archaeo-history—a need to connect with a deeper human past?

"I thought all Outworld people lived in new worlds, and always looked for new places with new things to buy and sell, and thought about nothing but tomorrow."

"That describes civilization all too well," she admitted.

"Here it was like a man in a hurry stepping on a thin-frozen puddle," the old shaman said quietly. "The ice cracks and gets smeared with ugly mud. The man will go on his way. Hurrying— somewhere. I think his face is turned away from his own home."

"Some thinkers say it's a need—an insatiable hunger—to find another intelligent race," Linna said. "We've never found anyone else."

"Hmmm. Anyway, that man doesn't think twice about the ice he stepped on." Tugapu, in his adult life, had seen his culture craze like ice under the impact of the trading post bringing mercenary outsiders and trade goods, taking away diamonds and beryllium. "There are no ghosts on Ende. Memories of our dead return to us as animals and plants in warmtime. Not as somebody's shadow walking around by itself! Ghosts are a trader idea. I don't believe in them."

Daylight shaded into a fainter but pinker illumination from the setting sun. Thick clouds, higher than the morning's pall, rode on a rising wind. With a piercing whistle, Tugapu summoned Iste and Okarde back.

"Tugapu—" Linna hesitated, remembering Iste's blunt impatience at too many questions. Had that been his craziness, his Endishness, or just Iste? "Do you believe in Heaven?"

"What?"

"The place where people go when they die. What Cloud Sky City is."

"Ah! You mean *****."

The lingchip offered a flurry of alternate translations for Tugapu's word.

end + beginning.

memory

remembrance

communion

Endbeginning.

The lingchip's efforts made Linna's mind reverberate like a tapped bell. Evidently, whoever had translated the Endish word as "heaven" had used a short cut for an untranslatable religious concept.

The brothers-in-law returned. Iste took up the kite, holding it poised over his head, while Tugapu held the string. The kite quivered as Iste shook with feeling trapped inside himself.

Tugapu gave a brief shout. Iste tossed the kite up and Tugapu stepped sharply back, keeping tension on the string. Filling with wind, the fish-skin parchment fluttered. The kite angled up into the sky, taking its glistening burden of diamond.

Tugapu pumped the kite string, chanting. His voice shaped the same phonemes as before, but these were not Endish words. The chip disregarded his utterance. The chanting had an almost hypnotic effect, welding Linna's attention to the kite dodging higher into the sky.

The invisible red star pulled Ende toward its primary sun. With incipient warming came atmospheric turbulence. A strong flow of wind carried clouds into the V-shaped Endish Range. Clouds had amassed between the mountains. The clouds had thick gray hearts and sunset-tinged pink fringes. Linna thought she saw a faint pulse of lightning. The points of the kite sparkled.

Linna's attention wavered as she realized that the kite string might be damp, the lakeweed fiber might have metallic content, and the kite might draw lightning down on all of them.

"Watch the kite! Our minds must be in accord!" Tugapu hissed.

The old shaman knew what he was doing. Linna returned her gaze and attention to the kite. High in its ascent, it slipped inside the grayness of clotted cloud. Lightning flared inside the clouds.

Linna felt a sudden conviction of combined effort, like being part of a team game. But this was mental, and as precise as turning a key in a lock. The hair on the nape of her neck rose.

The cloud lit up again. This time it stayed illuminated. There was a bubble in the clouds, an area empty of cloud but full of shapes outlined in clear pale light. Linna gasped.

Crisp edges and sharp angles contained smaller and even more complicated shapes, an infinite and compelling geometry. And it moved, meshing and rotating, continual change with standing waves of geometric form.

The vast structure appeared to be made of light and air, ethereal as a mirage. But it had enough solidity to divert the wind, making the blowing clouds eddy. It hovered before the rough, dull backdrop of the Endish Range.

Its brilliant complexity announced alien intelligence from the dawn of time.

Linna would have watched, mesmerized, if it had remained for a night or a year. But the geometric vision vanished like a soap bubble. Cloud poured into the place where it had been.

Okarde and Yayu looked at each other in mute amazement. Shaken, Linna sat on the ground. Now she knew why the Endish, with their dim legends of civilization, called it City. It reminded her of Earth's ancient urban cathedrals. But the most elaborate temple on Earth had been a primitive dusty toy compared to Cloud Sky City.

Her cheeks felt wet and chilled. She had been moved to tears by Cloud Sky City.

Ende breathed its own awe. A breeze coursed over the land, startlingly warm and moist, the earliest trace of Ende's spring.

Tugapu brought the kite fluttering and rattling to the ground. The air seemed clear as glass, all the way to the distant walls trailing over the low slopes of the Endish Range like aimless sketched lines.

Chirping broke the soft silence. A bird perched in the stunted tree that grew beside the wall. Illuminated by the setting sun, its feathers glowed soft blue and yellow, the plumage of spring.

"Iste!" Tugapu pointed at the bird. "See her!"

Iste stared at the bird. Then tears trickled from his eyes, frozen grief beginning to melt like winter's ice touched by the spring.

It was just a bird. A coincidence. This was spring, and time for birds to have their brief breeding plumage, and for red-bears and other creatures to migrate.

But if Iste believed that his wife had come back to him he would not have to be a man alone any more, a crazy driven man, doomed. He could live again and find another mate. Alone, his only hope had been believing in a ghost.

He looked at Linna. Their eyes met. His were wide, brown, vulnerable.

"*Ache,* Iste," Linna told him. Hello and farewell.

Okarde led the way up the mountain trail. The nighttime cold of Ende pressed around Linna, only staved off by exertion. Okarde said he knew the trail like the inside of his own kayak. Linna believed him. But she had been desperate for so long—and right now the elation of seeing Cloud Sky City was so buried by how cold and tired she was— that she half-expected more dismay.

Yayu had stayed with Iste to wash his face and feed him a meal, fulfilling the ceremony. But Tugapu rode his shaggy pony. He coaxed it close to Linna, and she felt its hot breath on her neck. "What will you tell the traders?" Tugapu asked her.

"Nothing about Cloud Sky City," she said emphatically.

"I hoped you'd feel that way," said the old shaman.

"I won't mention the Bright Wing ceremony, or your diamond, either. And they won't wonder about what I don't tell them. Traders expect archaeologists to go off looking for something that isn't there and not find anything profitable."

"Did you find what you were looking for?"

Linna had been thinking about this all the way up the mountain. She might, after all, have found something to justify the prize she'd been given by the University. But only if she made what she had seen all too public. Scholars and scientists ferreting after the mechanism of Cloud Sky City would be no better than traders and prospectors after minerals. Finally she answered, "No. I didn't know the Before People had been here. I was looking for buildings from the old days when our ancestors first struggled to the stars."

"It's easier now," the shaman said. "People in the Outworld glide across the stars as easily as fish-hunters in kayaks cross the lake."

The night was clear, the sky strewn with stars like the diamond-sprinkled embroidery into Tugapu's cloak. Star flight should have been the fulfillment of twelve thousand years of civilization. But it hadn't worked that way. Not all the rediscovered Colonial worlds nor even all the stars in the galaxy were enough. "I think fish-hunters get what they need and go home happy," Linna panted, "but Outworlders are still looking for what they need."

Okarde, gesturing toward the crest of the mountain, interrupted. "Top part too hard for talk." People and pony labored up the steep trail in silence. Tugapu soon dismounted to spare the pony. It was slow torture to keep climbing at Okarde's steady pace, with the cold intensifying, tearing at Linna's lungs like a dull knife. Her legs felt like lead weights and her toes ached.

From Iste's camp to trading post was not a great journey for natives who knew the way. Alone, though, she would not have made it this far. Help is hope.

Okarde signaled stop for a brief rest. As she wheezed, Linna could dimly see the whole mountainside, spreading out and down to the distant lake barely visible as a sheen of reflected starlight. The scene looked familiar. She'd seen this land from the same perspective once before. It had been effortless then, gliding out in the landflyer.

The ragged old walls lay under the darkness, semi-circled around empty land.

Or semi-circled around empty air.

Linna's mind lurched in sudden realization. What if not just a handful of people, like today, but thousands had all focused attentive minds on a diamond high in the sky? Cloud Sky City would have appeared to all of them, right there: where the walls silently proclaimed that something important should be.

Linna's heart raced with the thrill of understanding. Ende had been a pilgrimage site. That was why the walls were so extensive and disorganized. People numbering in thousands had camped on the mountains' skirts, building rock walls to break the wind and separate one group's small ground from another's. They'd lived in temporary structures long since obliterated by time. The pilgrims had come across the stars the hard way, in dangerous stasis that lasted for empty centuries, not to build a city, but to marvel at the apparition in the sky. Thus the extraordinary genetic diversity of Ende.

She almost tripped in distraction. End is beginning, and memory is heaven. "Tugapu—" she gasped, "Does Heaven— I mean Endbeginning—mean there's hope? For people who have died or for people who live now?"

"Ah. Both." He walking steadily up the steep trail. "The Before People knew that."

The monument of the Dawn Builders meant something infinitely greater than Iste's wife or Linna's survey. But the devastating limitations of slow star flight had strangled the wonder of Ende before civilization even knew what it had missed.

The empty hole in the heart of civilization hadn't changed since then. But everything else was different now.

A star fell out of the sky. It blazed brighter, until it touched the top of a mountain, a landing starship backlighting the blocky shapes of the trading post in front of the landing field. Yesterday it might have left a world ten stars away.

The trail abruptly leveled. Tugapu reined in his wheezing pony. The landing ship's flare illuminated his somber, aged face as he looked directly at the boot slowly shattering his people's existence. "We'll go home now. You can see your way."

Linna blurted, "Yes. I can. The Outworld is like Iste. Alone and sad and crazy. It needs to see Cloud Sky City!"

Instantly the shaman fixed her with piercingly intent eyes. "How?"

Linna felt a lump in her throat. She could imagine the terrible possibilities that might spring to Tugapu's mind: traders—or scientists—stripping Cloud Sky City's secrets out of the mountains like beryllium ore. "To do any good, it would have to be the way we did today. With minds working together. Just watching to see. I don't know that can happen. But it happened once, almost. I'll have to study old learning to find out more about that time." Buried in the rubble of the cataclysmic history the early Star Age, there must be some clues about the pilgrimage—references to the Eden that ships came across the stars not to create or possess, but just to see. Her mind flew back across the stars to Ende. "If I came back here, could you tell me the old stories of Ende?" she ventured. "Teach me about Ende?"

He answered indirectly. "What about those smart people who see other things the Before People made, and try to figure out how they work?"

Some of the Dawn Builder Hypothesis archaeologists were as egotistical as they were brilliant. At least one, by all accounts, was a different and better sort. "There's one man who studies the Dawn Builders, who has the reputation of—looking before he steps on ice and breaks it. I think I need to talk to him—but not others. Not now. Cloud Sky City isn't like a mountain to mine for beryllium. I understand that now."

Tugapu smiled. It was the rarest of Endish gestures. "It's good you're so young. You'll need a long life to accomplish everything. My own road ahead is short now, so come back soon."

Linna felt her whole life pivoting like a compass needle, swinging toward Cloud Sky City. In a daze of changed reality, she thanked Okarde for bringing her to the trading post. In reply, he held out his hands palm up—gesturing respect, the lingchip told her.

Then Tugapu raised a hand in benediction. "*Ache, Tekirte.*"

With startled wonder, Linna recalled that shamans like Tugapu might never have children. Sometimes, instead, they chose successors.

GLORYSTAR

This was my second published story, in December of 1990—but it comes from the far end of this future history: in the course of their very adventurous lives, some of the people in this story will meet some of the people in the last story in this collection, The Fair Game.

In a thousand-year war in the far future, tactical genius is like a supernova—a sudden flare of destructive creativity. The crew of the exploration starship Dragonfly want no part of it. But a brilliant military tactician puts them in unprecedented peril.
Now they face three possible outcomes: die, escape—or win.

My people have not lived on a planet for a thousand years. For star-voyagers such as we, the galaxy is a sea of suns, with spindrift of dust and nebulas. And *constellation* means something quite different from patterns of fixed stars in a world's night sky.

I was the astrogator's apprentice. I knew that starships traveled in a series of instantaneous jumps. The galaxy contained a finite number of points, between which such starflight could go, and the points of starflight constituted sets. We called the sets constellations. An astrogator could live and learn the constellations for a lifetime without mastering them: they were that complex and crucial. In my short career I had learned only a little about the constellations, and it was recent learning, not engraved very deeply in my brain and reflexes. The idea that our constellations might not be real at all—might be a veil thrown over the stark truth of starflight—did not disturb me. It only stirred my curiosity.

The ship's technician had just come up to the bridge. He opened a console and put his head and hands inside it, intent on making some miniscule repair.

"Kluge? Have you ever heard of uncertain constellations?" I asked him.

"No," he grunted. "Why?"

"Plerion was just saying—"

"Plerion has strange and downright dangerous ideas. And you, lass, are supposed to be keeping your mind on your duty!"

This was the first night of our mission. I had flown with the starship *Dragonfly* twice before. This time, finally, I had the training to qualify as crew, albeit the youngest and least experienced of the crew. As such, I got the first night's watch. I should have been utterly attentive to the constellations in the astrogator's window. Instead my attention flicked away toward the other, the mysterious uncertain ones, gone from the window now, but distractingly apparent in my imagination.

Fortunately our safety did not depend entirely on me. *Dragonfly* did its own watching. The icons of its watchfulness flashed on the astrogator's window: course, energy levels, and the presence of a deadly danger, behind us now—a black hole. *Dragonfly* flew itself, aiming for our mission's destination. Starflight registered on the constellations as a kind of chromatic ripple. A faint scrape came out of the console. Kluge had wormed in so far that that only his sandals showed. He always liked to make his inspection and repair rounds in the middle of the night. I tried to do my job better, watching the astrogator's window intently.

Something flashed in the window. A new icon, a red triangle. Unbelieving, I recognized the Dire Icon. Then another one appeared. I yelped.

Dragonfly did not wait for me to touch the red alert button. Its alarm rang through the night-lighted bridge and the corridors below it. Kluge came out of the console like a snake. The alarm sounded and resounded, a harsh triple tone, *Enemy, Enemy, Enemy!*

Captain Sinter and our astrogator Zeph came running in, with Plerion the tactician right behind them. I sprang from the astrogator's chair just before Zeph would have thrown me out of it. More Dire Icons appeared on the window. There were five—now ten. White-hot shock shot through the group of people on the bridge. "We've stumbled into a nest of them," Sinter said, grating out the words.

Evaluating the constellations in the astrogator's window with one experienced glance, Sinter named a point. Zeph immediately changed our course to make *Dragonfly* jump to that point. Sinter's pick flared bright blue. It faded as his next point flared. The constellations in the window rippled, very slightly, as Sinter extricated us from the Enemy's midst in small moves that would be almost undetectable to the Enemy. The Dire Icons did not seem to react.

Fine detail was written on the Dire Icons. Sinter peered close. "Warships, no less," he said, and ordered another slight jump.

"Holy mother Terra, save us!" gasped Kluge.

Dragonfly was not supposed to tangle with the Enemy. Not under any circumstances. It was a starexplorer, a long, thin, fast, frail starship, with a profound and subtle machine intelligence, all kinds of instruments, and no weaponry. It could outmaneuver any one of the warships—but not all of them. Not if they noticed us and decided it was worth their while to catch us.

We felt a tremor, more vibration than sound, transmitted through the structure of the ship. The voice of our engineer seemed to come out of the air over the bridge. "Five's unlocked now."

Sinter said, "Thank you."

Another jump. Sinter spaced jumping and waiting, at irregular intervals. He wanted us to look like a random fluctuation in the constellations. Wait. Jump. Waiting pulled our nerves taut and jumping snapped them. Still the Dire Icons did not react. Somebody let out a sigh, long, shaky, and premature.

Sinter stood behind Zeph in rumpled clothes that had been flung on hastily. In a level, intense voice, Sinter said, "How in the name of Malison did this happen?"

And I knew. In a fractured second, I recalled the chain of events that led to this outcome.

My knees nearly buckled with the shock of realization.

We had departed from our mother ship, *Parhelion*, some hours earlier. This was not meant to be a typical mission for *Dragonfly*. There were no scientists manning the instrument stations—no visitors wandering in the corridors—no new people settling into the living quarters. With only a skeleton crew, *Dragonfly* seemed vast and empty. After dinner the starexplorer dimmed its lights and its emptiness filled up with night.

I reported to the bridge to take my watch. The bridge was a solid structure, long, but not very wide, curved, and studded with consoles. All around this bridge—the starbridge—lay a huge sphere of visual screens: the panoply. Stars in every direction, starry space broken only slightly by the dark traceries of ship that held the screens in place. Overawed, I stopped short.

Zeph was waiting for me. A man alone on that slender bridge across the stars, the astrogator gestured to me. *Come.* The astrogator's window was a high circle of amber, crossed by a mesh of coordinate lines, with hundreds of bright constellation points and scores of icons. Zeph stood aside and I took his place in front of that window for the first time in my life. Zeph gave me a long, steady, serious look. Then he left the bridge.

Zeph was not much of a talker. Now I understood why. Being here at night, surrounded by the panoply and faced with the golden window, could squeeze the banal chatter out of a person. Tense, biting my lip, I pored over the window, trying to apply months of study to the dense field of symbols. I struggled to comprehend the changes that flashed across the window with every starflying jump that *Dragonfly* made.

Near midnight an icon on the window told me that *Dragonfly* had detected a black hole near our course. I made sure to log it. Then I turned around to look for it on the panoply. A spiral of bright light marked the black hole. The spiral's black heart was the star that had collapsed into a singularity and was destroying its binary companion star, sucking in the incandescent matter. The sight of it made me shiver.

In the very center of the panoptic sphere hovered a hologram, a model of *Dragonfly*. The holographic *Dragonfly* pointed away from the black hole. Course changes rippled across the constellations as the starexplorer gave the black hole a wide berth and then returned to its course. *Dragonfly* would have avoided the black hole even if I had never logged it. From a safe distance, *Dragonfly* analyzed the black hole system. Information scrolled across the astrogator's window.

My mind strayed still further away from the constellations. I started thinking about another peril lurking in the stars, a danger more insidious and evil than black holes. The Enemy. The language of my people had a word for the Enemy, a word out of ancient history. The word meant Nameless. It also could have been translated Shapeless or Uncreated.

I was no historian. I uncritically shared the legends of my people concerning the Nameless Ones. More than a millennium ago—so went the popular version of our history—the human race had achieved a high level of civilization, a web of culture spun across a score of colony worlds. Then out of unknown and unexplored space came the attack from an alien race—fleets of warships, covering whole worlds with flames of war and destruction—nothing less than an evil empire bent on the conquest of humanity. With great valor, humanity fought back.

My ancestors were fighters. In the end they won the war, but lost their homes. The sweeping battles of war had ruined whole worlds, leaving ecologies ruptured, cities leveled. The interstellar web of civilization was hopelessly broken. Having starships, but no homes to which to return, my ancestors wandered from star to star. Finally they left the known colonies altogether in travels that took them across a thousand years of time and thrice as many lightyears, winding their way through the galaxy in the general direction of long lost Earth. They sought the resources and the knowledge that would be needed to start civilization all over again. They never found Earth. Instead, learning how to live as star travelers, they fell in love with the wilderness of stars. It was ironic that the ancient Enemy caused my people to be. We gave the Nameless Ones that much credit, at least at the level of popular legends and proverbs.

Then, a few years before I was born, my people stumbled onto the core of the Nameless One's old empire—shrunken as a white dwarf star, and still malignant.

Now my people had ships patrolling, mapping the Enemy's extent, its fleets and nests. And *Dragonfly* was on its way to a place far away from any of the Enemy, there to practice tactics that might one day be used to our advantage in war.

Shivering, I tried to refocus my whole attention on the constellations. But my imagination kept running anywhere and everywhere else, to old legends of war and Earth, to planets, strange life forms, discoveries that my people had made over the millennium, and mysteries still undiscovered, waiting for us in the stars. I imagined that the starlight from the panoply, washing over the bridge, was palpable, cool and clean.

I did not hear Plerion coming. Quick and graceful, she appeared suddenly, as if she had materialized out of the starlight.

Quickly I stood up to make a small formal bow. "Hello, Tactician!"

"Greetings." Standing face to face with me, she sized me up. "How old are you, Cob?"

"Fifteen, Tactician."

"You're big for your age! You'll be a taller woman than I am." Even in the night, my height and the structure of the bones of my face gave me away. Plerion asked, "Can it be—are you a Guardian?"

Reluctantly I nodded.

"Then what are you doing here?"

"I want to be a ranger," I told her. "Sinter is my best friend's uncle. So he agreed to take me into *Dragonfly*."

Plerion laughed. "A Guardian who follows desire, not duty? How refreshing!" She sat down in the astrogator's chair as if she meant to stay for a while.

I pounced on this unexpected chance to ask questions—one of my specialties in life. "Tactician, what are we going to do tomorrow?"

"Practice tactics," she said.

"How, Tactician?"

"You really want to know?"

"Yes!"

"Very well." She relaxed. My family would have called her pose a slouch. She slouched like cats do—as if they have no muscles in their bodies, as if their skins are full of feathery nerves. "Are those the stars?" She gestured at the panoply.

"No, Tactician," I said promptly. "The eye can't see the universe in stardrive. So *Dragonfly* paints the picture for us. The ship's intelligence generates the image, how it ought to look. And the computer corrects the image all the time." Between jumps, the starexplorer paused in real space, and its computer reconciled the visible cosmos with what it imaged on the panoply. It did this even as we talked, I knew, but the procedure was too subtle to see.

"So. You're ahead of most people in understanding. You know that the real stars aren't what we see on the panoply. It's an illusion. What about the constellations, in the window?"

"Oh, yes!"

"Yes, what?"

"They're there. We jump from point to point. There are universal sets of points subject to local transformation—"

"I know, I know. Let me rephrase that. Are the constellations true?"

I felt confused. "Yes?"

"Are they the whole truth?"

Here I was on firmer ground. "There *are* more," I said, "if we operate at a higher energy level."

She shrugged. "Highenergy constellations. Like the faint stars that the ancients saw with telescopes, invisible to the naked eye. New stars in the same old constellations. Constellations! Useless old word. Language is so inexact—not like mathematics!"

"What else is there, Tactician?"

"Do you really want to know?"

"Yes!"

"Sinter might not like it," she said, "if I corrupt the education of his little Guardian."

That nettled me. My people called my particular family the Guardians, that being a not-always-affectionate nickname for us. My family guarded the traditions of our people with a passion and a vengeance. We were officials, admirals, judges—pillars of society such as that. But I wanted to be a star ranger. I said, "He doesn't have to know that I know."

"Good idea." She reached over to touch the astrogator's controls. The golden window went glittery. It filled up with faint flickering points of light. "Constellations," Plerion said precisely, "are just the points that are probably there, rather than the ones that probably aren't there over an interval of time. There are an infinite number of constellations. If you count these, the temporary ones—the uncertain constellations."

The window swam with them, and they flickered in and out of being. "Oh," I said. "Then can we go by them just like the regular constellations?"

Plerion laughed. A clear ringing laugh, it reached the rafters of the panoptic sphere and echoed back like the amusement of the stars. "What an unorthodox, unthinkable idea. And—true!"

The window glittered. The old constellations—now just the steadiest of all the points in the window—flickered at the limits of discernibility.

"Plerion, why are the constellations, the certain ones, flickering like that now?"

"They are a function of the uncertain ones. A concatenation of probabilities. They last for a long time. But not forever. They can cease to exist—even just when a starship constellates."

"What happens to the ship then?"

"Oh, it ceases to exist, at least in this universe. Look closely. There is a single point on the window that's absolutely steady. It, and only it, is certain to the end of space and time."

She meant the black point in a ring of flashing red. The black hole.

With a strange curl of a half-smile, Plerion asked softly, "Knowing what you do now about the old constellations, do you still feel comfortable at the thought of using them?"

"Sure," I declared.

"Then do so for me."

"Tactician?"

"Oh, for Malison's sake, I'm not that old. Call me Plerion. See that? It represents a multiple star system. White dwarf, red giant, blue giant."

"There might be moons or even planets!" I imagined worlds in orbits lacing among the three stars; strange light and shadows falling on the icescape of nameless land.

"*Dragonfly* should explore that system."

"Plerion—you want me to change *Dragonfly*'s course?"

"You're the astrogator, tonight. According to the rangers' rules, I'm not allowed to direct the ship, but you are."

She was right. I, the astrogator's apprentice, considered crew tonight, on watch, could do that. The realization thrilled me.

"Do you not know how yet?"

I knew how. And I thought that the tactician, with the blood of my people in her veins and a starship like *Dragonfly* at her disposal, wanted to see the multiple suns. Sinter often told Zeph to redirect the starexplorer, in order to visit stars and their planets. Plerion specified the new coordinates, sharply divergent from our previous course. And I redirected *Dragonfly*. Smiling, Plerion reached toward me. I thought she meant to ruffle my hair. But no such condescending gesture as that—she touched my lips. Then she touched the astrogator's window to make it return to normal. "I'll be back shortly."

Just as Plerion left was when Kluge came in to repair the console. He made a courtesy bow—the kind he always gave to military people, a bit jerky as though his backbone needed oiling, telegraphing his unspoken reservations about militarists.

I was happy. I had directed the starship.

Minutes later I realized that it was I who had directed *Dragonfly* right into a nest of the Nameless Ones.

———

The Dire Icons shifted.

"That's it, they've spotted us," said Sinter. He gestured toward Plerion. She stepped forward immediately. This had turned into a military crisis. *Dragonfly* was hers to command now. Plerion spoke for the engineer to hear. "I need maxenergy!"

In answer, *Dragonfly* vibrated, the vibration trailed away, but left a subliminal hum. The hum meant that the engines could operate at the highest possible energy level—at the price of minimized control. The engines were slightly unstable now.

Plerion called for something that only a starexplorer like *Dragonfly* could have done. *Dragonfly* stretched energy fields like wings into stardrive space. Twisting its wings of field, the ship darted into a new constellation, one at the constellation-space equivalent of right angles to the first. That would be a hard move for a warship to follow.

Kluge sent out a distress call to *Parhelion*.

"Now to reconstellate." Plerion evaluated the constellations, the possibilities accessible from this new position, points of light cascading across the astrogator's window. She decided quickly, called for a series of zagging jumps through the constellations.

"She's good at this," Zeph said, to me.

I turned my head to look at the panoply. It depicted the Enemy starships as flat as cutouts. Only one, closer than the rest, seemed three-dimensional. I leaped to the conclusion that we had shaken off all of the Enemy swarm except for one.

Zeph muttered, "Astrogators don't rubberneck. Always watch the window!"

The Dire Icons assembled themselves into a pattern.

Zeph hissed, "We're being herded into a trap!"

Kluge cried out with real fear in his voice, "They want us!"

Plerion reached between myself and Zeph. "I'll try something different!"

I heard Sinter ask, "Are we ready?"

"By now I'm sure everyone's said their prayers!"

The throb of the engines, shivering the ship's structure, told us it was a maxenergy jump. I did the wrong thing again. I looked around and saw how panoply blurred, and went blank, dark, starless. We had jumped into the uncertain constellations. And the image-generating brain of *Dragonfly* did not know what to make of it.

Then stars wavered back onto the panoply. An incomprehensible dull surface blocked out almost half of the stars. A combination of curves and angles and albedo. An enormous strange bulk no more than a *Dragonfly*-length away.

Plerion gasped. "No! Damn!"

"That's camera-visual!" screeched Kluge.

"It's a Nameless warship—get us out of here!" Sinter yelled.

"I'm lost!" Zeph said in a strangled voice.

Plerion leaned over the astrogator's console. "I'll try again, oh damn!" Her hands darted over the console. "Remax!"

Louder than ever, *Dragonfly*'s hum shook my blood. For the second time, the panoply darkened, starlight gone. The astrogator's window emitted flat golden light that turned Zeph's face to stone with hollow eyes.

The panoply filled up with stars again. The stars wavered, oozing and eddying. Nebulas crawled in different directions as *Dragonfly*'s machine intelligence tried to reconcile where it thought we should have been with what its instruments registered. Jumping through the uncertain constellations had confused *Dragonfly*. Its confusion on the panoptic sphere surrounded us like a feverish sick cosmos.

"Watch the window!" Zeph ordered me harshly.

The Dire Icons had all shifted to the far edge of the astrogator's window. Plerion slapped the console, calling up data which scrolled across the window. She crossed her arms and let her breath out sharply. "We are safe now, little thanks to this damned ship!"

Dragonfly shivered as if the engines brimmed with energy, spilling energetic bits. Sinter called out to the engineer, "Rose—end of emergency." Slowly the shivering eased.

"Not a moment too soon," came the engineer's voice. "Five slid out of place. I thought we'd have to get rid of it. Consider us limited to four until I straighten things up down here."

The panoptic sphere normalized.

"Look sharp," Sinter said to Zeph. "If the warships give chase—"

Plerion interrupted. "Reconstellate," she told Zeph. "That way." She named a series of points. "They won't chase us because they have no idea where we went. We'll proceed to a safe place to lie low for a time. There."

Sinter nodded curtly. "Where is there?" he asked Plerion.

"A good place to lie low."

"Fine. But where?" Sinter repeated.

"I don't know," Plerion admitted. "I'll have to think about it."

"Zeph?!"

"I can't tell where we are in constellation space. We're disoriented," the astrogator said unhappily.

Kluge rolled his eyes. "And we can't broadcast a come-find-me signal to *Helion*, not with a swarm of Enemy near!"

With an uncharacteristic cool correctness, Sinter said, "Plerion, do let me know when you have a good idea about where we are." Sinter folded his arms. "We've got to get back to *Helion*. The tactical mission is over. It failed."

She lashed out at him. "Your ship failed! It botched the job in an unbelievable way—it jumped directly toward the Enemy! That wasn't my intention. Your ship did that!"

Coldly, Sinter answered. "I beg your pardon. You tried an unscheduled and unprecedented tactic. This is a proven ship. The failure was in the tactic, or possibly the tactician."

"In no way!"

Sinter turned to me. "Rose needs an extra hand. Go."

But I dragged my feet. On the starbridge behind me, I heard Sinter's voice, cold as ice. "You had better figure out exactly what happened and do it in a hurry, girl."

She was furious. "I am not a girl! I have a Name and you know what it is!"

"Then conduct yourself accordingly."

The starexplorer had the oldest, simplest kind of artificial gravity. It spun around its axis. I floated along the axis with *Dragonfly* spinning around me. My nerves were still fired up with adrenalin and flinching from Dire Icons and uncertain constellations; I clumsily missed some of the handholds, my fingers skidding on the grainy wall of the axis. But the spiraling night lights had a reassuring effect on me. Plain and familiar, they glowed softly in the night.

At the well down to the refectory, I called out, "Dally? Are you down there?" No answer came out of the well.

Even though the axis was a weightless corridor, the engine ring seemed down. A long way down. Finally I swung into the last well on the axis. I descended the ladder.

Dally stood there, hugging himself against the cold of the engine ring. He gave me a strained smile. Behind him Rose was tense and busy, and I knew enough engineering to understand why. The power of starflight came from *Dragonfly*'s own black holes—singularities of much less than stellar mass—controllable, but not tame. There were four, two dyads, a stable arrangement for such things in the engines of starships. *Dragonfly* had a fifth black hole as well. Its position was adjustable. Certain configurations let the ship access the highenergy constellations at the expense of safety: the fifth black hole could slide either purposefully or by accident. In our final flight from the Enemy it had very nearly done that. Rose had managed to get Five back under control. But surges and slacks of power had gone through the control circuits. Rose touched a series of switches. They retorted, sparked at her.

The communication net all over the ship was still open. "Kluge! Help!" she called. To me, she said, "This has never happened to us before—and I certainly hope it never happens again!"

Dally said, "Poor Hiss is hiding somewhere." He meant the ship's cat.

"Dal, go sniff around the ring," Rose ordered. "Burnt smells, chemical leaks, tell me. Cob, help me open this panel." Rose tossed me an unfastener.

Kluge clattered down the ladder with his tool kit. "Where's the problem?" Rose pointed at the engine control circuits, uncovered now, and visibly melted in places. Kluge unpacked his thin spidery tools. We waited for him to render a verdict.

The daylights had not come on, nor would they. It would have taken a more serious crisis than this one to make Rose ask for daylight in her engine ring when it was supposed to be night. Day and night had been given to us by Earth, and were holy, inviolable. And we could see in the dark anyway—our eyes registered the near infrared wavelengths. Looking away from Kluge and the emergency light shining over his head, my eyes adapted. In shades of gray I could see the floor curving up in the two directions perpendicular to the axis. Massive braces like ribs jutted out at regular intervals along the ring. Centrifugally *up* from where we stood, massive plates, the engines' plating, tessellated the ring.

I sensed the black holes in their cryogenic crypts: the presence of mysterious power. Maybe it was their gravitational effect, bending the fabric of the local universe, that registered on some obscure physiological sense. Maybe it was my imagination. The power and the cold in the engine ring unnerved me even more than usual in this dangerous night. I admired Rose very much, but I could never become an engineer. The engine ring was too far from the glory of the starbridge and too close to the power of the black holes. And too cold for me. Cryogenic cold leaked out of the engines. Rose usually wore warm clothes, with a hood and a mask to cover her face below her eyes.

Kluge reported. "I can fix it."

Rose sighed relief. Then she reported to Sinter on the bridge. "We'll soon be fit to *fly*. Do we know where we are yet?"

"Yes," came Sinter's voice. "Zeph and the tactician have figured that out. I'm coming down."

Through the communication net, Rose had heard everything that happened on the bridge during the crisis. Now she turned the net off. "The tactician," she remarked, "is quite as brilliant as we were led to expect. But—like my engines—not altogether stable at her highest brain energy!"

Dally came back. He reported, "Two leaks and a fried circuit." Rose made a disgusted face.

When Sinter came, he immediately went to Rose. Husband and wife, they hugged each other. Sinter said, "Our ship almost *collided* with the Enemy!"

"Five almost got away from me," she replied quietly. "But it's back in line."

"What was it like?" Dally asked eagerly. "The tactic, I mean."

"Weird as all get-out!" Kluge said emphatically. "The panoply went *dark*."

Zeph said, "Like a dream." He had appeared at the door of the engine room. His voice sounded oddly flat. "Like dreaming of dying and going not to heaven and not to hell, but a dark place."

"Well, anyway, we got away from the Enemy, and in one piece, thanks to Rose and Plerion!" said Kluge.

Zeph said, "Yes. We do have Plerion to thank. Yes." His voice sounded flat.

Rose said, "It's time for rangers to talk in private."

Sinter nodded. "Plerion's taken the astrogator's watch. You're dismissed, Cob."

Sent away again, I felt like crying. I went back up the axis, and ducked into the well that led down to the refectory, our dining hall. The hall was long, large enough for thirty people to share a meal. High on one wall of it was drawn the Dawn Icon. The huge circle, circumscribing a square, represented a planet. It was divided in halves bright and dark, day and night, with the terminator a spindle that broke out of the bounds of the circle. Gilded, the Dawn Icon's spindle faintly glimmered.

I was hungry, famished. It had been a long time since dinner, hours ago and even further away from now in emotional space. At dinner everything had been wonderful and right.

By tradition the first meal on a ship's journey was a festive one. On this occasion *Dragonfly* had departed from *Parhelion* with a skeleton crew and only one guest. Having such a small number to feed, Dally outdid himself in culinary artistry.

Our foodstuff came from culture vats. Dally had tinted and shaped foodpaste into a reddish-brown fish, complete with scales and shiny black eyes and rippled fins. The fish posed as though swimming, on a bed of ruffled green seaweed. Our most basic, stiff, translucent sort of foodstuff Dally had carved into geometric shapes, stacked on a tray in an elaborate lattice. He had made cakes of rougher and more fibrous stuff—intensely flavored cakes, some sweet and some not. Besides the other food on the table, a peach lay in a golden dish. The peach was real. It came from a tree in the gardens of *Parhelion*. In a niche in the wall of the galley, a glass vase held roses—also from *Parhelion's* gardens.

At the low table, where we all sat on cushions, Dally put the two adult women next to each other on purpose. They were a study in contrast. Compact and dark, Rose had brown hair, brown skin and eyes, coloration like most of my people and like me. Plerion, taller and more slender, had green eyes and a rare reddish-gold shade of hair.

She had an assertive temperament to match her striking looks. In short order, we learned that Plerion was a theoretical mathematician. Analyzing the mathematical basis of the constellations, she had discovered a whole new aspect of starflight. Many experts were convinced that what her theories predicted would be feasible in practice, with the effect of revolutionizing starflight and not incidentally giving us a tactical advantage over our ancient Enemy. But the High Admiral had shown great reluctance to put Plerion's theories to the test. Only grudgingly had he agreed to send *Dragonfly* on this mission. "He thinks we first should study the ancient military texts for anything they might say about this," Plerion said acidly. "Study the books of the ancients for at least three generations of lives and brains! Not many agree—but the ones who do are the same kind of old fossil. Old and powerful."

The rangers glanced at me. The High Admiral, the leader of the starship fleet that was our whole nation, was my great-uncle. Dally passed his sweet cakes around, to a flurry of compliments, and then he changed the subject.

The meal ended when Rose sliced the peach. "Remember home," she said simply, and gave each of us a slice. She made less of a fuss over the ceremony than some people might have. It had at least as much impact that way. We did remember. Earth was the paradise that the human kind left and lost. Whenever my people departed from a safe harbor, or a mother ship, on any journey, we ate a piece of fruit in memory of Earth. Tradition called for round fruit, reminder of the roundness of a planet: peaches, oranges, apricots. I always wondered if the ceremony could be done with with a bunch of grapes.

Sinter and Plerion left, going to talk business on the starbridge. The rest of us stayed in the refectory. It was tacitly understood that Sinter would keep Plerion out of earshot for a while.

Rose spoke first after Sinter escorted Plerion out. "There," said Rose, "goes the queen of the young Turks. She has a following among the military faction—the most militant of the lot. Mark my words, both the militarists and the traditionalists are waiting to hear how *Dragonfly* performs for her. Do let's all avoid making mistakes!" Ruefully she inspected the cut on her finger. The knife had slipped as Rose sliced the peach, a minor accident from which she recovered so gracefully that it did not mar the ceremony at all. She had been inconspicuously pressing a napkin over the cut to make it stop bleeding. "She is beautiful. Those of you who like to look at women are in luck this time."

"With you here, we've never been out of luck," Kluge said loyally. "Awright, Dally, what's the inside track on the tactician?"

Dally, with his extensive social network, could find out almost everything interesting about anybody. He divulged that Plerion was a personal friend of young Prince Aurin.

"That explains a lot," Zeph said.

Kluge shook his head. "Not even Aurin could get her made tactician, if she couldn't do tactics," Kluge said. Rose nodded thoughtfully.

Dally continued. Plerion came from a respectable family. But she was not theirs by genetic inheritance. Just where she did originate, genetically, seemed to be a mystery—or a secret, impervious even to his sources.

"That," said Rose, with amusement, "is one well-guarded secret, then!"

This conversation fascinated me. It was pleasurable to hear, like the taste of Dally's sweet cakes, like the aromas of roses and tea. Feeling very alive, I wanted to be a ranger among rangers forever.

"I want dirt," Kluge said. "If any. Does she do anything but tactics and politics?"

Dally grinned wickedly and filled us in. Plerion had left in her wake at least two distraught lovers (both male.) One of the two attempted suicide. The other talked wildly about taking a vow of celibacy and joining a priestly order.

"That's terrible!" Kluge exclaimed. "She sounds like a black widow!"

"You're in no danger. She won't spin a web for your ugly face." Dally could get away with saying things like that. "On the other hand, a handsome single fellow like Zeph. . . ."

Zeph had a sharp, brooding air about him. "She's crazy," he said. "She's spinning a web of dangerous ideas."

"Speaking of spiders," Rose pointed at me, "I think she's related to you, Cobby."

I dumbly stared at her.

"That Plerion is part Guardian in the genes," said Rose, "Or I'm an onion! The same sense of righteousness, insisting on the true and the right. Mind you, she has her own ideas about what is true and right."

"Our Cob isn't stuffy like most of the Guardians." Dally hugged me. I grinned. These people, the core crew of *Dragonfly*, were close as family to each other. Tonight, finally, I felt almost like one of them.

I ventured, "The High Admiral's even more, well, conservative than the rest of the family. All the family says so."

"Reactionary, perhaps," said Rose. "But Plerion underestimates him, if she thinks he's just an old fossil."

Zeph looked grimmer than ever. "I hope he doesn't underestimate *her*."

"Are you afraid her ideas are wrong?" asked Dally innocently. "Or that they're right?"

"I don't want to know."

Rose said serenely, "This is Sinter's ship and mine. We won't permit anything bizarre to happen."

And Rose was wrong.

Most of a night ago, our dinner and our merry gossip had taken place in one end of the refectory. Now, night-dark, the whole hall smelled of the roses in the vase. The Dawn Icon glimmered its eternal message of ceaseless change. Looking for food, I found some of the basic stuff that Dally had not made beautiful yet. I should not have been so hungry, I thought, since I had stuffed myself at dinner. I didn't understand then how stress burns calories and drives appetite up.

Dragonfly trilled, its communication net signaling that we were under way again. That meant I ought to go report to Zeph. The trill's echo in the refectory had hardly died away when Sinter came in, looking for me. "Cob, I've a question for you." In the darkness, he loomed, a tall gaunt man, with an unreadable expression. But his voice sounded hard. "Why did we change course—toward the multiple star?"

I choked down my last mouthful of food. "Plerion—" But I knew that there was never an acceptable time for covering up one's own fault. "I mean, I redirected the ship," I said in a voice not much above a whisper.

"Under what circumstances?"

Raggedly I described what had taken place on the starbridge after Plerion arrived. Sinter listened with his arms crossed.

When I finished, he said, "And you thought she had the right to do that?"

"I thought so."

"Think some more, then!"

"She's military, and a tactician—"

"The military do not rank over rangers! Not now. We're not at war yet however much some of them want it! I captain this ship. Plerion may dictate a major course change only in the presence of the Enemy —or in a situation of tactical practice—and even then only with my approval. Or if I am completely incapacitated. Didn't we teach you these things?" Sinter sounded angrier than I'd ever heard him.

I hung my head. "Yes sir."

"Did she charm you into doing what you knew to be wrong?"

"I really wanted to direct the ship," I confessed.

"That's natural to want. The problem is that you did it." He was silent for a while. Hardly able to breathe, I waited for my doom, expecting him to banish me from *Dragonfly* effective as soon as we got back to *Parhelion*.

"At least you didn't tell me it was all her fault. You owned up to your part in this debacle." Then Sinter said, "If anything like this ever happens again you are out of *Dragonfly* for good!"

I caught my breath. "Sir—do you mean I'm not out now?"

"Hell, no. You're on probation. That's all."

That was when I did cry. Sinter waited for me to get the sobbing under control. He said gravely, "You don't want to be a standard-bearer for tradition like most of your relatives. Fine. Then you have to think for yourself about what's right and what's wrong."

"I thought it was always right to explore."

"For *Dragonfly* it is. That's what starexplorers are built to do. For human beings, things aren't so simple."

I asked, "Should I go back to my duty station?"

He nodded. "We're on our way back to *Helion*. I think Plerion is staying at the astrogator's window. She's trying to figure out how her tactic went wrong. That's correct on her part. You should report to her. Just don't do anything for her that you shouldn't!" he said sternly.

I hurried up to the starbridge. Plerion sat in front of the astrogator's window, brooding. I thought about how she had gotten me into trouble and *Dragonfly* into danger. I scuffed a foot.

Plerion said sharply, "What do you want?"

"My watch back, or your leave to return to my quarters for the night," I said stiffly, "Tactician."

Not for the first time, and not for the last time, she surprised me. "Mad at me?"

"Sinter just reprimanded me. But he is a just Captain."

"Meaning you're not in serious trouble, and I am. Yes, I guessed that there might be a nest of Enemy at the multiple star. It was the kind of place where they like make their nests. I really expected to get *Dragonfly* out of there dramatically and easily." One of her hands rested on the console, by the controls. "Unfortunately for me, your Captain is right. *Flyer* did not fail. I did." She called the starexplorer by our nickname for it. "I failed to take into account that *Flyer* is not a military ship. Most of which are new and incurious."

Because we were moving, stars streamed across the panoply. A nebula went with them: a tangle of shining gas, the remnants of an old supernova, the kind of nebula called plerion. "*Flyer,*" said the woman called Plerion, "is programmed to warn of Enemy ships, but that programming is relatively superficial. There is absolutely no reflex, deep down in *Flyer*, to avoid the Enemy or anything else in all creation with the exception of star-massive black holes. On the contrary. *Flyer's* most basic reflex is to investigate things.

"There was an uncertain constellation radiating out around the Enemy warship—generated by the warship's engines, its black holes. *Flyer* just crossed that uncertain constellation to the source—like stepping stones—proceeded to investigate that significant entity— our Enemy!—up close!" Plerion's laughter had a bitter edge. "I failed to exclude that option when I sent *Flyer* into the unknown constellations. I should have gotten to know *Flyer* better before trying the tactic."

It sounded like a confession of sorts. Approving, I nodded sagely.

"Do you have string on you? Do something with it."

The starbridge did not strike me as the right place to play with string. But it wasn't wrong—not like redirecting *Dragonfly* for her had been wrong. Taking the long, supple loop of string out of my pocket, I sat down, cross-legged, and did a complicated figure, turning the string into a patterned web between my hands.

"Ah. You're good at that."

My people did stringfigures as something of a national pastime. We found much entertainment value in our pieces of string. I was better at it than most, and my nickname meant a spider of the orb-weaving kind. "That's why people call me Cob."

Plerion said, "Thought so! I play too. I seem to need to toy with things, string, puzzles, when I think. I should not have left my puzzles at home on this trip! May I borrow that?"

I held up my hands for her to take the string. She picked some strands up and pulled them, transforming my figure into another.

She squinted at the string. "Ah, damn it. I need more light." She switched on the bridge light. Her green eyes were slightly defective, not good for seeing in the dark. She laced the string into yet another figure. Somewhat absent-mindedly, she frowned at it.

I looked away from the light. On the panoply, the plerion dwindled. I wished we could have explored it, could have seen how it spanned the night sky of a planet.

"Plerion" was a nickname too, an uncommon one among my people. Sinter, Rose, Kluge were nicknames—Rose a very common one. Sinter sometimes called her Rosy. Nicknames, of which most people had several, surrounded the lives of my people, like electron orbitals, bonding us to each other. The nucleus of one's life, one's soul, was a different matter. Every adult had one true name, a Name. As a rule, someone's Name was neither common knowledge nor an undiscoverably deep secret. I wondered what Plerion's true name might be. It would have been uncouth to ask her outright. Sinter knew what it was. She had to give her name to him, the Captain, when she first came aboard this ship. But it would be hard to pry her name out of Sinter, on account of his rectitude.

Plerion said, "My theory's almost perfect. The application under field conditions is—harder than I expected!" She twisted the string. Then she said dryly, "When experts tell you that something is easier to theorize than to do in real life, you ought to believe them, even if they aren't as smart as you."

Rose had friends who knew what Plerion had been like as a child. She had run her caretakers ragged, seeming to need no more than a few hours of sleep a night. And she had terrorized her teachers: knowing all of the answers to their questions, asking questions for which they knew no answer. Now she had no one but herself to ask. Sweat beaded on her forehead, dampened the fringes of red-gold hair against her dark skin.

"The beauty of it—" Plerion murmured, "is that *they* trust the old constellations just as much and just as blindly as we always have. Earlier, when I took *Flyer* into the unknown constellations, we disappeared from the Enemy's windows. *They could not detect us.* I don't doubt they finally saw us when *Flyer* had that close encounter with the warship. Before they decided what to do about it, I took *Flyer* into the uncertain constellations again, and we vanished as far as the Enemy could tell. If I can only master the unknown constellations— we can resume the war with the Enemy. And win it once and for all. Do go," she said. "I'm thinking, and I'll keep your watch."

In astonishment, I left my string with her. I went to my own room in the living quarters, where I unrolled the sleeping mat. I lay down and then stared at the darkness. After the light on the bridge, the darkness in the narrow room bothered me—it made shapes indistinct. The ordinary things—a small low table, the box that contained my few dearest possessions—looked shapeless and strange.

In my heart of hearts I felt indistinct. I felt shapeless. Tonight I had directed *Dragonfly*—into near disaster. Before that, I had astrogated for half a night. And even then, I realized, well before anything at all went wrong, *it did not feel right*.

I tossed and turned. Did I really want to be an astrogator? No, I admitted to myself. No. The constellations, certain or uncertain, interested me, but not enough to make me want to live them the way Zeph did. More attractive to me was the hope of exploring strange worlds under new suns. All of my life, all fifteen years of it, I had been dreaming about worlds with skies and seas, life and color.

But the rangers were not exploring planets anymore. Not since my people stumbled across the Enemy, to our collective horror and consternation. For my nation's security, for military reasons, the highest priority had been placed on mapping constellation space. So astrogators were needed. I could be trained to astrogate, but not to explore planets. That vocation was precluded because my people had found the Nameless Ones but not yet decided what to do.

Exhausted but sleepless, I recalled fragments of the ongoing and bitter debate of my people with itself.

"Maybe the Nameless Ones have changed."

"They can not change! That's why they're evil!"

"The universe ought to be cleansed of them."

"Are we the wrath of God??"

264

"Why not?"

"No. We will wait and watch until we understand these things." That voice, that finality, belonged to the old man who was the High Admiral of our starfleets, my great-uncle.

"Maybe we had to find them sooner or later." Sliding into a dream, I heard Sinter sounding serious and sad. "But I wish it hadn't happened in my day. We're being co-opted by the military."

Plerion's words: "We can resume the war with the Enemy. And win it once and for all!"

And Kluge's terrified cry: "They want us!"

Something hit me in the stomach. I woke up with a start and a strangled scream, and the ship's cat sprang away. Hiss had jumped down onto me from the air duct which served her as a cat path. Shaking, I coaxed Hiss back to me and gathered her into my arms. She purred uneasily.

I had to think about something else besides Nameless Ones. And what presented itself, to preoccupy my thoughts, was how I had failed tonight. At a crucial moment I had unthinkingly done exactly the wrong thing, and directed the whole ship into danger. I had let the rangers down. I had unwittingly betrayed them.

Hiss crawled under the coverlet. I curled around her. Cats were called by nicknames like Hiss. The cat knew its Name and would never tell it, or have to. In slightly more than a year, I would be old enough for a true name. My Name. My life's shape. And I could not imagine what it would be. I felt like a shapeless and useless portion of personhood. Apart from the soft purring warmth against my stomach, I was miserable and slept neither long nor well.

A sharp trill roused me. It was the summons that meant all-hands-on-deck. Leaving Hiss under the coverlet, I hastily made myself presentable, and dashed to the starbridge. We were preparing to rendezvous with *Parhelion*. I desperately wanted to redeem myself. With my face scrubbed, clothes on straight, I stood by Zeph, ready to be his third hand—though not a very gifted third hand—when he needed me. But he did not even speak to me.

Dragonfly hummed, its engines working hard. The astrogator's window was full of constellations, sparkling with the rapidity of our travel.

Plerion was unimpressed. "A thousand years of this," she said. "No innovation."

The voice of Rose spoke from midair over the starbridge. Rose said, "A thousand years of exploring the stars."

Plerion's mouth twisted into a frown. "Not very well. These old constellations access a very small part of space."

"Quite enough to keep five hundred generations of humans busy exploring. Or five hundred thousand generations."

Evidently the calm, disembodied voice bothered Plerion. She snapped, "That's a hell of a long time to live a collective lie!"

"Lie?"

"The constellations!"

Zeph jerked. He was rigid, muscles of his jaw knotted. Without saying anything, Sinter put a hand on Zeph's shoulder.

Plerion went on, "They don't exist! They are a comfortable delusion. Out of line with the reality of the universe."

"No. The constellations are quite but not ultimately true," the voice said. "People can't live with the ultimate truth, in its totality. No more than the human eye could stare at the blazing sun in the blue sky of old Earth. We need our limiting conventions."

"And our grand illusion?"

"And what is that?"

Rose sounded pleasant. Plerion, on the other hand, was losing her temper. She gestured at the panoply, even though Rose, in the distant engine ring, could not see the gesture. Kluge suppressed a snicker. Plerion said, "The illusion of the whole galaxy around us—the relative motion of the stars—as if we're going faster than light, in a straight line, in real space! It's false!"

"The panoply is true, but it isn't about *us* at all. Think of it as a hymn of praise for the Maker of the stars."

Steaming, Plerion started to retort. Sinter said, "Peace! You can hash it out with Rose once we're safely home." *Dragonfly* had begun the final approach to the location of *Parhelion*.

Then the warning sounded, ringing *Enemy!* A Dire Icon appeared on the edge of the astrogator's window.

"Go faster," Sinter said shortly.

Dragonfly's sturdy engines hummed more vigorously. The starexplorer flew so fast that Zeph's constellations scintillated.

"When we encountered them yesterday—" Sinter said tightly, "That might have stirred them up. Tactician?"

Plerion nodded shortly. "It's possible. At this rate we'll reach *Helion* very soon."

Sinter said, "If something of hostile origin appeared in a fleet under my command, and got away, I'd go looking for it and for where it came from!" Sinter and Plerion had both moved close to the astrogator's window, crowding by me to watch it.

Suddenly a cluster of Dire Icons spilled onto the window, at the rim of it. The alarms in *Dragonfly* rang and rang again. With a sharp intake of breath, hissing between his teeth, and a wave of his hand, Sinter gave *Dragonfly* to Plerion. Plerion fired off new coordinates and Zeph made *Dragonfly* sidle away from what the cluster of icons represented. Not all of the icons were Dire. In the midst of the red triangles we saw a single green spindle, flashing urgently. Sinter said in an unsteady voice, "*Helion's* under attack."

Rose heard that. "Please," she said. "No!"

Plerion said bleakly. "Yes. We stirred the Enemy up—I stirred them up with *Flyer* —they swarmed and found *Helion!*"

Smaller flecks darted around the constellation of Dire Icons. Then one fleck dissolved. "That was one of *Helion's* patrol boats!" Sinter groaned. "They're outgunned as all hell! Where are our warships?!"

Plerion shook her head sharply. "Still far away. This area was thought to be clean."

Her words came to me remotely, as if through a plate of glass, a pane of unreality. I could not believe this: *Parhelion*, with its gardens, and my best friend—everyone and everything I loved most in all the universe—attacked by the Nameless Ones. Worst of all, had happened because I thoughtlessly did what Plerion asked!

Then Plerion said, "Sinter, Captain, we can try to save *Helion*."

"We don't have weaponry. None!"

"We have Five."

Sinter said, "I've heard of that tactic. No. We can't get that close before the Enemy sees us coming—unless—" He nodded slowly.

Rose spoke up. "To the extent that I understand your game, I've the impression that we can't play it without Five."

Plerion said, "Correct, but right now we have a better than even chance to save *Helion*. A less than even chance to save ourselves afterwards," said Plerion. "A fighting chance."

"Rangers aren't fighters," said Sinter.

"Except when they have to be," said Rose. In the heart of *Dragonfly* the engines shifted to maximize the available energy.

"Zeph?" Sinter asked.

The astrogator mutely shook his head.

Kluge exploded at Zeph. "Man, this is no time to freeze! *Helion*'s in danger and we have to—"

"He can't help it," said Sinter. Taking Zeph by the shoulders, he removed him from the astrogator's chair.

"I don't have enough hands to do it all myself!" said Plerion.

"I can astrogate." Sinter took the seat himself. Nodding, Plerion reached over Sinter's shoulder to make the uncertain constellations fill his window. Sinter stared at them.

"The old constellations are there. The brightest that flicker the least," I whispered. I had to force the information out. I felt like screaming, *It's all my fault—I'm sorry!*

"I see. In?"

Plerion answered, "Not directly." She gave him directions, unemotionally, already absorbed in the tactical challenge.

Sinter had some captaining to do first. Using the communication net, Sinter spoke to Dally. "Dal, pray for us," he said bluntly.

"I will," Dally's voice came to the bridge, soft and calm. Through whatever happened next, Dally would stay in the refectory, kneeling in prayer under the Dawn Icon.

Then Sinter called Plerion by her true name. "Tazalha, do whatever you can to save *Helion*."

In our language, *tazalha* meant supernova. Literally, glorystar. Sinter wanted the rest of us all to know Plerion's true name, because it implied brilliance of mind—genius that might save *Parhelion*.

We skirted *Parhelion*'s terrible peril. I tried to keep my eyes on the window, but stole glances at the panoply anyway, rubbernecking. The image horrified me. *Parhelion* maneuvered. The Enemy swarmed after it like angry bees. Another green fleck dissolved. Another patrol boat annihilated. Sick, I turned away from the window. Zeph stood to one side, staring fixedly at the panoply. There was something sickening about him too. I wanted to shake him and turn him back toward his window, his life, the crisis that needed his expertise.

"When?" Sinter whispered.

"Not yet." The window flowed, it snowed with uncertain constellations. But Plerion was still using the old ones—threading us into the Enemy's midst surreptitiously but not undetectably.

Rose's voice asked, "Can't we jump in from this distance, your way?"

"Not if you want to keep your Five under any kind of control."

"Understood," said the engineer.

"Your new ways aren't very reliable," Kluge grumbled.

"No, or they would have been known and used a thousand years since!" Plerion snapped. "Fourcon, six-zee-ten!"

Sinter obeyed Plerion. He piloted *Dragonfly* from point to point to point. Close to him as I was, I saw that Sinter was sweating in his tense concentration. For me, last night, directing *Dragonfly* had been thoughtlessly easy. It had been child's play, because I had no idea what the stakes were. Sinter understood the stakes better than any of us.

Staring at the window, Sinter said, "*Helion* is cornered now."

The Enemy had seized positions at all other points of *Parhelion*'s last constellation. *Parhelion* had nowhere to jump.

"I see that," Plerion said. "When we go out of the normal constellations, I will make the move myself. The timing is crucial to the instant."

"If it's missed?"

"We cease to exist in this universe," she murmured, so that only Sinter, and I, heard.

Suddenly we found that we had attracted the Enemy's attention. It took the form of two attack boats, wicked long thin shards of ship, coming after us. Plerion called, "Rose! Here goes—maxenergy!" She touched the astrogator's controls. The sphere went dark but not blank, had a sketch of stars on it. *Dragonfly* hummed intensely.

I heard Kluge murmur, "Holy mother Terra. . . ."

We came out at a new point in the old constellations. The Enemy boats that had been charging us flew away, bearing down on a position other than ours.

"Well," said Plerion, standing straight. "I seem to have reached an understanding with *Flyer*. It did what I asked! And made some sense of it." She gestured at the panoply. This is a good ship. Reconstellate."

Kluge studied the scene on the panoply. "Look at 'em. No idea where we went to."

Dragonfly resumed its zigging and zagging toward *Parhelion*, engines' hum intensifying and slacking. I stared at the astrogator's window. The deadly constellation around *Parhelion* was getting more complicated. Finally I could stand it no longer. "Why are there so many more things around *Helion*?" I asked.

Plerion said, "The Enemy is letting their attack boats out in force. To close in for the kill. So now there are lots of little starships flying around. Rose! Can we max again now?"

"Yes."

Plerion took us into the uncertain constellations again. The stars on the panoptic sphere faded to a sketch with one tiny red blotch on it. That red blotch swelled huge. Then the panoply normalized. We had jumped across uncertainty to reach a constellation point already occupied by one of the warships. Two or more ships could occupy the same point, more like a zone than a true point. But we ended up appallingly close to the warship.

The panoply showed it to us. *The Shapeless.* Huge, rotating, the eidolon had angles, as of something artificial. It also had turgid and branching parts like something organic—and pulsing surfaces. It was an unholy amalgam of the mechanical and the biological—as though miscegenated from the art of the Creator and the craft of the rational creature. *Uncreated.*

Data scrolled across the panoply under the image of the eidolon. *Dragonfly*—dwarfed but not intimidated by the warship's monstrous bulk—was busy investigating. "Kluge," said Sinter, sounding shaken, "Monitor the information we're collecting. Think military intelligence."

"Right." Kluge's voice cracked. He was scared but still functional.

Plerion said intently, "Rose, get ready to let Five go!"

A vibration came through the ship's structure. In the maximum-energy configuration, the fifth black hole could slide, shift position, endanger the ship. So it could be ejected out of the engines. That was intended to be a last-ditch, dire-emergency option, with no fine control, just getting rid of the thing. "Less than one minute and it goes," Rose reported. "Can't stop it now."

"Hold, hold for thirty seconds!" The seconds fell slowly and heavily. "Hold fifteen more seconds!"

"I'll try!"

The Enemy warship rolled by, bigger and uglier than ever. Every second increased the likelihood that it would notice *Dragonfly* as an intruder. A vast indentation in the warship came into view, a rift in the armor. "Star gate!" Kluge crowed.

"Rose, let it go!" called Plerion.

"Done." *Dragonfly* shimmied as it ejected Five from its engines, or more truly, *Dragonfly* stepped on the massive object to jump away from it.

The eye could not have seen Five in normal space; *Dragonfly* depicted it as a shiny black egg. The egg fell toward the warship's star gate, even as several slivery ships streaked out of the gate. They were the tail end of the warship's emission of attack boats. It was impossible for them not to see us.

"Away!" Plerion said urgently. She named a coordinate. Sinter guided the ship reflexively. We scurried away from the warship, Plerion hoping to thread our way out of the Enemy fleet before they got a fix on our path. There would be no more disappearing tricks without out fifth black hole. We could not even use the highenergy constellations without Five.

On the panoply the misbegotten warship split apart. Great cracks in it let out brilliant momentary flashes—fires extinguished by the vacuum of space—and vents of outgassing vapors. It broke into ragged pieces.

Some of the rangers laughed and shouted. I hated the Nameless Ones for attacking *Parhelion* and for killing some of my people. I shrilled a curse. Sinter called out, "Engines stable?"

Rose answered, "Yes. Did we get the bastard?"

"Yes! *Helion*'s free!" With one warship gone, one constellation point clear, *Parhelion* could escape from the Nameless Ones' trap.

The Enemy warship dissolved into a mass of wreckage. The ruination swirled, whirlpools forming in several places. Black holes, including the warship's own, loosed from the engines that had contained them, were feeding. The whirlpools emitted fitful radiation from matter being ripped into elementary particles.

In the next moment *Dragonfly* cried alarm. Attacking Enemy were closing in on us. We could afford no more concern for *Parhelion*, whether it got out of its doom or not. We were running from our own. Plerion made *Dragonfly* dodge, skip, eluding the Enemy. There was no physical sense of accelerating or turning—inertia is a function of normal space, not starflight. Abandoning communication silence, Kluge sent out distress calls to our people.

Three Enemy boats closed in on us from different directions. Plerion found a point to jump to, left the Enemy veering away from a collision with each other. This time, though, they saw exactly where we went. They reconstellated and kept coming.

Plerion clenched her fists. "I hate running!"

Sinter said evenly, "Keep it up. Where now?" In reply she rattled off a string of new coordinates.

The Nameless started shooting at us. They had weapons of the type we called starbolts. *Dragonfly*'s brain painted the bolts on the panoply, spears of red light.

A starbolt glanced on the surface of *Dragonfly*. It glazed the panoply. The astrogator's window went crazy, incoherent. Zeph suddenly shook off his paralysis and leaped to the controls. He made *Dragonfly* tumble away from the Enemy. Somehow he and Kluge, between them, damped out the oscillations in its astrogating instruments, got the constellations back in the window. I could do nothing. I bit my lip so hard against wanting to cry out, *I'm sorry!* that I tasted blood.

Then we made a calculated jump. Starbolts lashed the point where we had just been. Sinter moved away, giving the astrogation back to Zeph, without comment, except to say, "That was an attempt to disable us. It failed."

A pealing tone sounded and new icons appeared at the rim of the window: blue spindle shapes. That meant our people, better yet, our battleships, among them the flagship *Solaris*. Plerion and the rangers were busy keeping us alive. I alone had an opportunity to watch the fighting. My people began as enemies of the Enemy, warriors who lost their homes while winning the war. A thousand years later we still had the skill and the will to fight. Flanked by smaller attack ships, *Solaris* broke the first rank of the Enemy that it found in its way.

With such vengeance bearing down on them, the rest of the Nameless ships began to scatter and run. In one last gesture of enmity, a parting shot, they tried to obliterate *Dragonfly*. Starbolts hailed across our constellation.

Plerion almost got us out intact—almost. We took a direct hit. *Dragonfly* quivered. Damaged, part of the hull contracted, automatic mechanisms trying to seal a rupture by telescoping the hull. *Dragonfly*'s convulsion knocked me off my feet. Scrambling up, I noticed the *Dragonfly* -hologram over the starbridge. It flashed red in the middle of its long thin shape. "Almost severed," Plerion said tonelessly. "It's over for us."

Sinter called, "Rose! *Rose!*" She did not answer. The starbolt had broken *Dragonfly*'s communication net. He whirled toward me. "Find out what's happened back there!"

I bolted. In the middle of *Dragonfly* I found the axis bent and buckled. Air escaped into space with a thin scream. Scared, I hesitated and screamed, "Rose! Dally!"

A faint reply came from far ahead and down. "Help!"

I had to go down there. I skidded on the wall of the axis. The remaining dyads of black holes had been dislocated—or the ship dislocated around them. They caused a strange misaligned sense of gravity. The well down to the engine room slanted, the ladder in the well canted crazily.

It was dark in the engine ring, almost too dark for me to see anything. I cried out, "Where are you?!"

"Here!" Twenty feet away from me, Dally moved something with a clatter. "Debris fell on her! Help me get her out!"

The engine ring was not a place of clean smooth tectonic shapes anymore. I stumbled across wreckage. Some of it had sharp edges. Cryogenic liquids' vapor steamed from broken lines. When I reached him, Dally was standing on a brace, trying to keep his balance and struggling with a massive plate—a big broken piece of engine plating. Grudgingly it shifted only a little bit.

Thinking like a child, I looked at the plate hopelessly. Then I remembered that I was taller and stronger than Dally. And I saw how the plate was situated. "I'm going to lift right here because I think the whole thing'll move if I do!" I took hold of a corner of the plate. Rough frost covered it. Straining, I lifted with all my strength. The plate tilted up.

Dally reached under it. Then he went completely in. "Don't let go!"

"It wants to snap back," I gasped. "Hurry!"

Dally scrabbled in there. I panted with exertion and my fingers ached from cold. Finally he pulled Rose out. She moaned. Crying, tears icy on my face, I let go and the wreckage crashed back into its place. "We've g-got to go back up," I stammered, with numb lips. "*Flyer*'s almost broken in two and if this end f-falls off—"

Dally was already trying to carry Rose up the crazy ladder. I leaped up after them, caught hold of her, and added my efforts to his and hers. Rose seemed uncoordinated. Her arm slipped, slick with blood, in my hands. She said something unintelligible. The cocked gravity in the well seemed worse than before, and it tried to make us slide down. Dally said, "Stop! She's bleeding too much—" He had a bandana in his pocket. We tied it around Rose's arm above the gash, as a tourniquet.

Trying not to jolt her too much, we thrashed up toward *Dragonfly*'s broken back. The axis slanted so badly that we put our feet in some of the handholds, using them like stairs. The night lights flickered on and off like candles in a wind—blown by gusts of electricity through the damaged ship's circuits.

Dragonfly shivered. Dally cried, "What was that?"

"That," said Rose, faintly but clearly, "was leaving go of the rest of the holes. Automatic. I hope the Enemy runs into them." She held one hand to her head.

Where the axis was buckled, the whistle of escaping air sounded louder than before, rising to a howl. We plunged past the howling air that stirred our hair. Then we found a portal shutting in our faces. *Dragonfly* was trying to seal itself against losing more air.

"No!" Dally hissed. "Open! Open!" I fumbled with the manual override. The portal relented just enough to let us get through. "Alright, now close, you twit!" Dally fumed.

I wheezed. My chest ached from lack of oxygen.

The three of us retreated into the refectory. There we huddled together, under the Dawn Icon. Nothing could be heard from the communication net: silence. Dally loosened the tourniquet on Rose's arm. "Where else does it hurt?" he asked her.

"Headache. And—there—doesn't hurt, doesn't even feel."

"Frostbite, I think," Dally said, probing her forearm with his fingers.

I listened to them. I worried about the Nameless Ones. Had our people rescued us, or was *Dragonfly* adrift in space, mute and helpless? Could the Nameless Ones have wormed their way in through the damaged hull, boarded *Dragonfly*? I went looking for Dally's longest kitchen knife. He kept it very sharp. With that in my hand I guarded Rose and Dally. If anything alien came in, I meant to stab it.

Something big charged into the galley. I raised the knife. Sinter caught my arm and lowered it. Recognizing him, Rose stood up, and he swept both of us into a hug. Dropping the knife, I clutched his shirt like a baby.

"We're being towed," Sinter said thickly. "By *Helion*."

Rose fainted in her husband's arms. Gently he lowered her to the floor.

"She got hurt and lost a lot of blood, but she'll be OK," Dally whispered.

The communication net crackled back to life. "Testing, testing, can you hear me?" said the net in Kluge's voice.

Dally answered, "Your voice is music to our ears, old man!"

Then we heard the attention signal, unmistakable, from the flagship of our fleet, followed by the High Admiral's voice. The Admiral wanted to know who had eliminated the Enemy warship to let *Parhelion* out of the deadly trap. He waited for an answer. Had they not survived? Did anyone know the truth of the matter?

"Plerion—?" Dally whispered.

"May not be ready to talk to the Admiral," Sinter said. "She fell apart as soon as we were we were safe. When I left the bridge she was crying. Kluge, transmit this." He said in a firm clear voice, "Sinter of *Dragonfly* here. *Dragonfly* did it."

There was a pause on the other end. "*Dragonfly*?" the Admiral echoed. "The starexplorer?"

"At the time, *Dragonfly* was commanded, by Plerion, Tactician." Sinter stated.

It was time for day to begin. The daylights came on, starting with a gentle glow, a luminescent dawn. The light revealed the refectory in jumbled disarray and bright red blood all over Rose. Sinter crouched beside her until the paramedics arrived.

Space tugs hauled *Dragonfly* in through the star gate of *Parhelion*. With its stern almost disconnected, airless and inert, *Dragonfly* was bundled into drydock. This transmitted strange little jolts and shocks through the starexplorer. A few more things fell apart. The ship's day brightened into a morning with wavelengths slightly out of kilter.

The medics rushed Rose away to *Parhelion*'s hospital. Dally went with them, holding her hand. The rest of us left in a slightly more ceremonious fashion, first asking the Captain for leave to go. Tears rolled down Zeph's stony face as he made his way out of *Dragonfly*. Kluge carried away some delicate, damaged circuitry to fix at home.

Sinter called me into the refectory last after the rangers. The Dawn Icon dominated the far wall, the spindle shining gold. Sinter had picked up the vase and its roses, which had been knocked down, and placed them back into the niche in the wall.

Sinter bowed, to me. "She might have bled to death down there if you hadn't gotten here out," he said.

I blurted, "I'm so sorry it all happened and that I ever had a part in helping Plerion start it—!"

"As far as I'm concerned, you've made amends. *She* has not." He scowled. "Hell, she's gotten what she wanted and more! A chance to show her stuff. A starring role as a genius and a hero. She may have even triggered the war that she and her faction have been looking forward to! It still wasn't right to get *Dragonfly* into the nest of Enemy in the first place. And she ought to be made to do some kind of penance for that. I don't know how. At this point I doubt that formal charges would stick to her. If this is war, even if it's victory, I hate it. I wish I could talk to Rose."

He seemed wrung out and bitterly unhappy. I felt that I had to take Rose's place, to give him wise advice. At least I had to try. "Plerion has a will to righteousness as she sees it," I said. "I think she'd really do penance—if it was something that seemed right to her way of thinking."

"Maybe. Go get her for me."

Plerion, like the rest of us, was supposed to ask the Captain for permission to leave the ship. She seemed edgy as a cat when she came into the refectory.

"Sit down." Sinter seemed stronger, sterner now; he had pulled himself together. "We have unfinished business, we three. You," he fixed Plerion with a steady gaze, "started this."

"I did not intend all that has happened!"

"I don't approve either of what you intended, or of what you did," said Sinter. "But I want to know why, Tazalha." Using her true name like that told her that he meant very serious business. "You have your faction behind you. You and your militant friends will outlive the High Admiral even if you don't tip the scales of public opinion away from him. Why rush it?"

With her arms crossed defensively, she refused to reply.

"Cob, what do you think? Why did she have you to redirect *Dragonfly* last night?"

"She wanted to show off."

"Were you showing off?" he asked Plerion.

Putting it that way disagreed with her. "No!"

"No, Tazalha?"

She burst out, "I cannot wait for the Admiral to watch and wait, test me, test my ideas, for a decade or two. I can't wait for him to die, either!"

"Why not?" Sinter shot back.

"Being able to unravel the secrets of the constellations—it's a mathematical talent of a kind that peaks early in life. I can feel it burning bright and burning out. I've got a few more years. That's all!"

I listened, electrified. This implication of her name had not occurred to me. Tazalha: glorystar, supernova. Such a star blazes brighter than the rest of the galaxy, but not for long. A supernova fades fast. What remains is a dense, dull, fast-spinning neutron star in a shroud of nebulosity—a plerion—where the glorystar had been. It must have been painful to have a nickname reminding her that the bright blazing core of her being would die. And yet supernovas are the forge of the heavy elements of which worlds and living things are made. A plerion is the visible sign of that life-giving mystery of creative destruction.

Sinter said, "You are the smartest person I've ever met—but putting *Dragonfly* into that danger, confident that you could levitate out of it—was stupid!"

"What else was I to do?" she flared. "Would you waste my talent, while the old man ruminates—and while we lose the chance to settle our old score with the Enemy?"

She was right about the High Admiral. The Admiral would let her talent flare and fade and gutter, unused, before he would put our people on a new and unprecedented course.

"I would have you looking into the mysteries of creation," Sinter said evenly, "and leave the Enemy alone. The uncertain constellations must go somewhere else besides war."

"Then I respect you. You are a truth seeker. Not like so many." She spoke with the bitterness of old, festering frustration. "The Admiral, immersed in ancient military texts. —The purblind astrogator of yours!"

"Not blind—blinded!" Sinter said harshly. "Believe me, he saw what you've uncovered, more clearly than anyone else, the Admiral included, I believe. It seared his mind's eye. It shocked his spirit. Zeph is brittle. That's not his fault." Sinter heaved a deep sigh. "I asked him to keep the truth about what happened on the starbridge last night to himself."

"You did?!"

"I did. Cob. Can you keep a secret too?"

I hastily stood up and bowed assent.

He said, "All of us will say that I decided to investigate the multiple star—plausible enough—Plerion being absent from the starbridge at the time."

That startled Plerion. "A military commander with his ship broken around him and his engineer in the hospital—"

"She's my engineer and my wife. And my astrogator is on the brink of a nervous breakdown."

"A military commander in your place would try to have me court-martialed!"

"I'm not military and I can't imagine what good it would do."

"I—then I have to thank you!" she said awkwardly.

"That's optional. What I really want is for you to make amends."

"Like what?" she said warily.

"You used *Dragonfly* in order to get what you want. Hereafter, leave us out of your war," he told Plerion. "Use your influence in military circles to keep us uninvolved. No more tactical missions. No scouting and errand-running for the military, not even if we're at war. The rangers' calling is exploration for its own sake. I want you to see to it that *Dragonfly*, at least, is free to do that."

Plerion considered. Then she announced, "It's fair. I agree!"

Sinter gave me an almost imperceptible, approving nod. He let Plerion leave then. "Go—Tazalha."

"Oh, wait." Plerion turned to me, holding out my string. "This is yours. Thank you." Then she said, "He's quite right. The uncertain constellations do go somewhere besides war."

"Where?" I asked.

Plerion placed the string in the palm of my hand. With a dazzling smile, she said, "Earth!" and on that note she left.

For a moment I fantasized vividly, imagined crossing uncertain constellations, not to clash with the ugliness of the Shapeless, but to seek our paradise lost, our Earth.

Sinter waited. With a jolt, my attention came back to the here and now. *Dragonfly* was ruinously damaged. And I, as a fledgling crew member, had succeeded at being a hero but failed at being an astrogator. I dreaded never going to the stars with *Dragonfly* again. Finally I forced the words out. "May I leave?"

"Only until we get *Dragonfly* repaired." He smiled. "Go in peace, my friend."

But I did not go alone. Sinter went with me. He took one rose from the refectory, carefully holding its thorny stem in his fingers. On our way out of *Dragonfly* we collected Hiss the cat. Then I helped him deactivate the ship. We turned off the communication net, the life support systems, everything except the machine intelligence and the daylights. In the bright light of day, repair crews would assess the battle damage and start making plans to rebuild *Dragonfly*.

PART II

The beginning chapters of *Witherspin* (Avendis Press, December 2019)

THE FAIR GAME

The interstellar city-state Wendis presents an amusing face to the stars, especially during its annual Ascendance Fair, when visitors come from all the other worlds on that end of human space and time to enjoy games, re-enacted ancient battles, exotic ancient food, and festivities. But some of the games are perilous; some of the reasons for the Fair are very serious; and someone like Nia Courant can find herself facing the choice to be a pawn or a player.

1

GREENING DAY

The Great Wall of Wendis loomed over Nia like a glass cliff. Her footfalls echoed on the Wall's wide fauxstone stairway. On the other side of the clear Wall was the space shield, with complicated metallic corrugations the size of ravines. She climbed upward in the space shield's shadow, in cold and stillness. Except for her, the Great Wall seemed deserted tonight.

The absence of other people puzzled but also pleased her. There was no one else around to witness her missteps. As she climbed higher, the spingravity lessened, but the tendency to misplace her feet increased. Wendis was an enormous, solitary, spinning cylinder in deep space. Spingravity held everything in Wendis in place, but it was a tricky facsimile of gravity. For someone like Nia, who had grown up on a terraformed planet, spingravity and stairs were a bad combination, and the vast whorl of stairways inside the Great Wall of Wendis posed a severe test. Every year she lived here, though, it got easier.

The proximity of space chilled the air. Nia's breath condensed into white wisps. Now faint starlight glazed the fauxstone steps. Higher up, the concave rim of the space shield glittered with reflected starlight, and starlight flooded the steps. Encouraged, Nia dared to run up the rest of the way. She reached the High Landing breathing hard, but victorious.

Then she realized that someone was already there, turning around in an irritated flicker of motion at the sound of her footsteps. He was shirtless and pale as white marble. He had the slim-hipped build of a boy. But behind his shoulders, transparent membranes with red veins angled over his head and slanted down beside his torso—he had diaphanous wings, tented like the wings of a bug. Nia froze. She knew Wendis harbored two or three of his kind, but she'd never seen one before. She didn't like meeting one here.

They were called angels, a flattery intended to placate them, because everyone was afraid of them. The rumor of an angel on the Great Wall would clear everyone else away in a hurry. That explained why the Wall was deserted tonight. And it meant she might be in danger. She suppressed an urge to bolt back down the stairs. For her, that could be more dangerous than the angel. Instead she sidled away along the High Landing. Apprehension made her skin prickle.

The angel stared at her with large dark eyes. Then the angel said, "Azuri."

Nia stiffened with anger on top of her apprehension. A person from the planet Azure was an Azurean. *Azuri* meant a *thing* from Azure. "Shandy," she retorted. A thing from Shandy.

The angel responded with a cold flicker of a smile.

Nia circled around the High Landing, taking slight, low-energy steps lest she accidentally launch herself over the guard rail in the scant spingravity. Above her, starlight shone on a latticework of metallic beams and gratings. When Nia reached another stairway, a third of the way around the Landing, the angel was distant and lost in silvery light. She breathed easier.

The angels had been human before they were changed to live in low-gravity artificial environments in deep space. According to Wendisan lore, they were the creatures of a merciless interstellar god named Shandy.

Nia scanned the landing. No sign of the angel. Fact: all he had done was toss an insult at her. Another fact, one she knew too well: rumors can mutilate the truth. The angel had been looking out at the stars before he heard her coming. Maybe all he wanted was the view. Nia stretched to ease her leg muscles and let the view claim her own attention.

The Great Wall of Wendis was the transparent western end of the spinning space cylinder. Above the glittering rim of the space shield, around the spin axis, the Great Wall was a window on the universe. All around Wendis, starships and star bubbles flickered like fireflies in an eternal night. Arriving starships re-entered real space with flares of light. Lesser flashes heralded bubbles containing messages and small goods from other worlds. Fading, the ship-lights and bubble-lights sorted themselves out. The ships maneuvered toward the Port on the other end of Wendis. The bubbles streamed into the Mailyard net below the Great Wall. And the backdrop of it all was starry space, rotating with the incessant spin of Wendis.

Wendisans had their own constellations. Nia didn't know most of those. But she recognized the Raptor, the seven stars of the Faxen Union. Above the Raptor's back—in the safest position that close to the Raptor—wheeled the sun of Azure. Her home. So far away that the blue seas and white continents were only a trace of photons in the spark of light of that distant star.

Homesickness rolled over her like a cold, heavy wave. At this moment, the dawn of Greening Day was sweeping over Azure. Once every year for three years, Nia had climbed the Great Wall of Wendis when it was Greening Day on Azure, observing the holiday in her own lonely way from here. With a hollow feeling in the pit of her stomach, she remembered her last Greening Day at home. It came just after her career crashed down in ruin along with her father's ambitions for her. They had an argument wracked with pain and anger on both sides. He had finally shouted at her. *"You made an inter-stellar fool of yourself! Admit it!"* She fired furious words back at him. Unspoken, yet ringing in the air at a psychologically deafening volume, was their family history. The Courants were descendants of the starship astronauts from Earth, the star voyagers who first brought green hope to a barren ice world. From her childhood on, much had been expected of Nia Courant. Before the end of her last Green Holidays on Azure, she had argued with everyone in her family. Was it still homesickness, if you'd been sick of home and they of you when you left?

Behind her, a voice said, "Hello, Inanna."

She whirled. The landing was empty. But the angel knelt on a metal beam overhead, intently regarding her. Nia felt chill fear. She hadn't realized that with wings, in low gravity, he could glide this far. "How do you know my name?"

"Don't be surprised," the angel answered. "You're famous."

Nia retreated to the stairway. She found the first step by feel. Her heart pounded. Acutely aware of how steeply the stairs curved down, she hesitated. The angel flexed his wings. Stars shone though translucent membranes with ruby-red veins. Unnerved, Nia said, "Enjoy the view," and turned away from the angel to the stairs.

Down was safety. But safety was a long way down.

One step. One more. One after another. Fear of falling and fear of the angel crowded out her breathing. Her overtaxed leg muscles quivered, but she pushed herself until she reached the Low Landing.

A tube train flashed by, pedestrians and delivery bots shared the sidewalk, and never had the populous nocturnal hum of Wendis sounded so reassuring to Nia. She halted and leaned on a railing for support. If the Great Wall was an annual, self-imposed test, she passed with flying colors this time.

But the angel came as a very unwelcome complication. How did he know her name? Very few people in Wendis knew that "Nia" was a lifelong nickname and her real name was Inanna. And what did the angel mean by *famous*? She was an interstellar lawyer, recently promoted to Assistant Counsel at Avend University in Wendis. That didn't qualify as fame. Wendis had plenty of interstellar lawyers, most of them more accomplished than she was.

The angel's voice had been soft and yet cold, so cold it burned in her memory.

Suddenly the signal pod on her bracelet trilled. The contour of the trill told her that she had a bubble in the Mailyard. For a moment Nia just stared at the trilling pod. A bubble for her just when it was Greening Day on Azure? That was almost as unexpected as the angel.

In more peaceful times, the space shield stayed irised all the way down to the Low Landing, where people could watch star bubbles come and go in the Mailyard. The mail station was located just off the Low Landing on a street called the Milky Way. A uniformed mail official queried the identity pod on Nia's bracelet. Satisfied by her identity, the official produced her bubble. Automated scanners had already screened and approved it, and it rested on the scanner tray, like a giant pearl. The bubble split open and folded down to reveal its cargo—a glass bottle full of liquid the pale pink of dawn on Azure.

The gift tag flashed on the scanner screen. *Nia dear, have a happy Greening Day, and all our love. Eirene and Vim.* Nia was so surprised that she felt light-headed. She knew better than to expect Greening Day gifts from her parents, but she'd never dreamed that Grandmother Eirene and Grandda Vim would send her a bottle of aquarel.

The mail official said genially, "It's good to get a bubble when you're far from home."

Nia nodded.

"Do you know about the Ascendance Fair? It's the most wonderful event in Wendis. Visitors come from all the terraformed planets for the Fair. It starts tomorrow, and this year it will be better than ever."

"So I understand. I work with Hiro Hiroshi Low," Nia answered.

The mail official beamed. "Hiro Hiroshi is a Wendisan of faultless patience and politeness, a true son of the Service Guild! That's my own Guild. He's bringing honor to us all."

Hiro was Nia's invaluable legal assistant. Serving on the Fair Committee was an important civic responsibility for him, and he had been carrying it well. Unfortunately for Nia, though, Hiro was patiently, politely, and honorably determined to cast her in a ridiculous role in the upcoming Ascendance Fair. She could imagine news about that getting back to Azure during the Green Holidays. Just thinking about it made her tense up. With a mental jolt, Nia wondered if the *Fair* had been what the angel meant by "famous." Wendis was a small world, its connective social tissue was gossip, and the most exciting annual event in the world was the Fair.

The mail official deftly knotted the ends of Nia's carry-cloth over the bottle. Cradling the cloth-wrapped aquarel in her arms, Nia left the mail station with her thoughts churning. She could well imagine whatever Hiro had told the Fair Committee about her percolating into the social aquifer of Wendis. Complete with her real name—Inanna—and the fact that she had been named after a Wendisan great-grandmother. *Oh no.* The last thing in the universe Nia wanted was fame as an actress in a tourist-attracting carnival in Wendis.

For most of her three years here, her mind had been elsewhere: mastering interstellar law, grappling with the legalities of the University's relationships with the Faxen Union as well as the Alliance of Starmark. That might not be good enough. She'd surrendered her Azurean citizenship when she came here. Her family bridges, if not burned down, were badly charred. She didn't want to remain an outsider in Wendis indefinitely. Especially not an outsider who was fair game for casting in the Ascendance Fair. She had to find a way to be at home here. But how? With Azurean looks and planet-born awkwardness in spingravity, her chances of seamlessly fitting in weren't much better than the angel's.

Nia crossed a civic plaza to its far end.

Slender arches framed a view of the interior of the cylindrical world. Tonight Wendis was full of fog and erratic winds that tattered and twisted the fog or let it pool in sheltered places. She could barely make out Avend University's glassbrick spires and the hilly park uphill from the University. The park was dotted with lanterns and pavilions set up for the Ascendance Fair. Bobbing in a breeze, the lanterns looked pretty, like cottony fireflies. Nia had never attended the Fair. She'd stayed too busy with work. Unremitting work had gained her the job of Assistant Counsel at the University.

Wendis was a hard place to get to know. It showed foreigners a polite and entertaining face which turned out to be practically inscrutable. After three years Nia knew less about Wendis than the average Wendisan child. The Fair, on the other hand, was designed expressly for visitors. It might be fun, if you could just be an entertained visitor.

As though the signal pod on her bracelet had read her mind, it chirped a call from Hiro. Nia stepped into a nearby commcube to hear what he had to say. When she put the pod into the signal slot, one wall of the commcube melted away to show the foggy, lantern-lit park close up. Hiro appeared in front of her, holding a butter-yellow daffodil.

"No," Nia told him.

He was a slender Wendisan with golden skin, curly black hair, and a pleasant, expressive face. Now his forehead wrinkled slightly. "No?"

"No, I will not play the part of the Queen of Europa in your Fair."

"The Fair Committee just had a long meeting. Almost the only item on the agenda everyone agreed on was that you would be the best choice for the role in all of Wendis! We have so few people with authentic Europan skin tones, and like most lawyers you're good at acting." Behind Hiro, people struggled to inflate a large pavilion, with a breeze making the transparent material twist and flap. "And this year our Fair happens to coincide with your home world's Green Holidays, commemorating your astronaut ancestors. Surely that would be propitious."

More like *conspicuous*. Torn between admiration and irritation at Hiro's persistence, Nia used the Wendisan triple-negative. "No, no-no. Is this why you called?"

Hiro opened his hands; the daffodil disappeared. It was a virtual flower. "Not really. We have a legal emergency."

He explained. On the other end of Wendis tonight, in the Port, a xen-ecology professor bringing a newly discovered alien species back to the University had run afoul of Customs in the Port. Customs balked after the professor checked both *plant* and *animal* in the declarations form.

A window in the commwall flashed on, showing six small tangles of leaves and tendrils. They looked like thinnings from Grandda Vim's garden greenhouse. All six specimens had been impounded at the Port.

Nia told Hiro, "I'm sure the Port officials don't want anything dangerous getting past them into the Fair. But Professor Zeng is a reputable xen-ecologist. He wouldn't bring in something dangerous. Our best tactic is a provisional waiver of identity, like for people, when their gender is ambiguous, but irrelevant. An identity waiver will put the matter into a different department in the Port—away from anyone heated up by arguing with Zeng."

"I'll transmit the waiver within the hour. Should the creatures be provisionally animal or vegetable?" Hiro had a twinkle in his eye. "Or mineral?"

"Vegetable. The Wendisan fondness for plants may predispose the Port authorities favorably." A vine-and-flower design bordered the walls of Nia's commcube. "I wonder if the plant-animals bloom? That would be an interesting twist in your flower code."

A luminous daffodil winked into the flowery border of the commwall. That much of the flower code she knew. A daffodil symbolized the offer of an unexpected yet delightful opportunity. On the verge of saying *for the last time, NO*, Nia found her attention caught by the inflated pavilion behind Hiro. Someone had turned on a string of colored lights along its spine. The pavilion reminded Nia of Greening Eve, of phospho-lights blazing in niches carved in ice outdoors, bright chandeliers in a lofty cathedral, singing and giving gifts. Being a gifted member of a happy family. The pavilion blurred with Nia's tears.

"Counselor?"

If he'd directly asked her what the problem was, she might have told him. It tied into things she hated to think about, but tonight had brought everything closer to the surface than usual. With a direct question she would have explained. But it was Wendisan custom not to ask direct, personal questions.

Silence stretched out uncomfortably.

"I'm not rejecting your Fair." The thought of staying at work while all of Wendis was having a festival made the pit of her stomach feel hollow. "I'm sure it's wonderful."

Maybe Hiro picked up on the emotional freight in her words. "I would be honored to show you the Fair on Opening Day. Let me give you an insider's view of the Fair."

It was an attractive offer, but Hiro had ulterior motives.

Then Nia realized what was going on. Space games. In all space ships and stations everywhere, people invented innumerable little games—weightless food games, clever new uses for tools, subtle exercises in marking territory—ways to stay sane and cooperative in close quarters in a patently hostile universe. As huge and old as it was, Wendis was a space habitat too. For her to ever be at home here, she would have to learn to play intricate Wendisan space games. Her choices were to be a player or to be a pawn. Being an unknowing pawn was how she had once made an interstellar fool of herself. She did not like being a pawn.

She'd rather be a player. She would play well and to win. Starting with the Fair. The bottle of aquarel felt cool and heavy inside the carry-cloth. In a way that had nothing to do with the brain chemistry involving ethanol, it gave her courage. *Here goes.* "Mattis and Vijay-Kol each asked me to go to the Fair. To be even-handed, I'll go with both of them, and you can show us the Fair, but you'll be free to leave if Committee duty calls you away."

It was a reasonable counteroffer, and Hiro knew it. "I will be honored," he said politely.

Nia felt pleased with herself. She suspected that Mattis and Vijay-Kol, given the interest each of them had been showing in her lately, and given an opportunity to attend the Fair with her, would outdo each other trying to monopolize her. At best, everyone would have a reasonably good time. At worst, Hiro would have very little leeway to maneuver her into the unwanted role of Queen of Europa.

The rational side of her mind asked, *would playing that role really be so bad?*

A different part of her mind countered with the slashing swiftness of a reflex burned in by pain. *Looking like a fool is always bad. It wrecks your life. Never again.*

2
_____

FAIR PLAY

"**W**elcome to Parhelon Fair" glittered on a soaring gate the color of gold.

This was the oldest and grandest of all the Ascendance Fairs in Starmark. The Fairs all celebrated that singular age of invention and violence that formed the modern human universe—the age of the Ascendance, when rockets first launched from the face of Earth and soon spacecraft streamed away from the home planet and, finally, starships left never to return.

A chattering crowd streamed through admission portals in the golden gate, but Hiro directed Nia to an inconspicuous side door. He waved his Fair pass and let them both into the Fair grounds. "What would you most like to see?" Hiro asked.

Nia answered, "My Wendisan great-grandmother was very old and I was very small when she died. But I remember her having soft wrinkles and white hair like a cloud, and telling me about the Fair in Wendis, that it meant playing make-believe games, having good things to eat, and putting on costumes. It sounded wonderful."

"Then we'll look for your great-grandmother's Fair today," Hiro said warmly.

A few minutes later, two familiar youthful professors strode through the Golden Gate. "It should be 'Perihelion Fair,'" said Mattis, the disheveled but brilliant physicist. "Right now Wendis is at perihelion in orbit around its sun."

Vijay-Kol parried with a criticism from his own field. "As I tell my Elementary History class, this Fair distorts history to a ludicrous extent. The real Golden Gate is thought by most scholars to have been a bridge."

"Those are functionally different things," Mattis said.

Nia smiled at them. Evidently, they were going to be every bit as possessive of her attention as she had expected. *Let's see Hiro get around that!*

Hiro said, "Most visitors go to the Mall first of all."

"To get to the Mall we follow the yellow brick road," Vijay-Kol said, reading a sign post.

"It's interesting that people in the Twentieth Century favored yellow bricks for roadway paving material," said Mattis.

T he Replica Factory sold precious plastic toys, letter-openers shaped like prehistoric swords, and model rockets. Mattis and Vijay-Kol found those things more fascinating than Nia did. Hiro suggested, "Just a few doors down is the shop with the best garb in the whole Fair. Let me show you." Intrigued, Nia followed Hiro out of the Replica Factory, into the center of the Mall, which surrounded an ice-skating rink under a skylight.

It gave Nia an odd twinge to think of ice-skating on the fevered world that Earth had been at the Ascendance. Here, though, the ice rink was a playground. Neophytes in bright clothes lined up at the rail on one side of the ice, released the rail, and coasted toward the opposite rail, pushed by the spingravity. Advanced skaters glided through circles reshaped by spingravity, carving rococo lines on the ice. In a separate area, fenced off by an elastic barricade, people from terraformed worlds scooted across the ice on their backs and bottoms, laughing and gasping at how spingravity made them swerve or slow or accelerate, depending on which way they launched themselves from the rail.

The Timely Emporium occupied a prime location facing the ice rink. Nia felt a flash of alarm when Hiro revealed that the shop belonged to Bess Elzebet Seller, the Chairwoman of the Fair Committee. She was away, though. Busy running the whole Fair, she had left a niece in charge. So instead of encountering the Fair's Chair, Nia met her goods.

Folded bandannas and neckties filled small bins. Brightly colored Twentycent garb dangled from high racks. Exquisitely crafted pieces of jewelry were displayed in transparent cases, and on top of the cases, glass and stone beads were artfully heaped like lustrous moraines. Oh my, Nia thought, I could have a wonderful time playing dress-up in here. She discovered thick, soft sweaters. "This is real wool. It's first quality," she said told Hiro.

Vijay-Kol materialized at her elbow. "I'll buy one for you."

"None of these are my color," Nia said sweetly. Ten points off for lack of originality.

Vijay-Kol was from Faxe, the prime world of the Faxen Union: the single most powerful polity at this end of human history. He was a product of the Faxen ruling class—physically nearly perfect, certain that anything could be bought, certainly able to afford it. Azureans, however, knew not to be unduly influenced by Faxen wealth. That was good political strategy, and good personal strategy too. Nia had to admit, though, that Vijay-Kol was attractive. He wore his physical perfection well, like an expensive but familiar, tailored suit of clothes. Mattis had a much different charm—he was as engaging as an unabashed young dog.

It was customary for visitors to the Fair to buy bits and pieces of antique costume. Vijay-Kol donned a green beret which complimented his sharply tailored coverall. Mattis selected a paisley tie that clashed with his tunic. Nia shared a dubious look with Hiro and then they both suppressed laughter.

Exiting the Mall, the small group boarded an aerial tram. As the tram purred upward through the foggy air, Hiro explained the layout of the Fair. "During the Fair, much of the inside surface of Wendis is turned into Fairgrounds. The plain around the central part of the Celadon Sea depicts the Twentieth Century, but the Fairgrounds reach up onto Mount Zaber. There, and east of the Sea as well, are recreations of eras even further back in ancient history."

"That's historically lax," said Vijay-Kol. "It's supposed to be the Ascendance, the twentieth and twenty-first Centuries."

"It's a game, and the rules are what they are," Nia said.

Hiro nodded approvingly.

I'm catching on, Nia thought.

The fog thinned. Now they could see the misty foothills of Mount Zaber. A wide valley opened up out of the bulk of the mountain. Tall, slim towers stood in the center of the valley. That, Hiro said, was Rocket Park. Finally the tram slanted down into a box canyon where stood a cluster of flimsy-looking buildings. Mattis called out, "Wild West, here we come!"

The buildings were made of distressed fauxwood. Papier-mâché horses in various poses stood next to fauxwood rails beside the street. Food vendors offered fry bread, curry and doughnuts. "Curry is good on the fry bread," said Mattis, waving a piece with his mouth full. Hiro bought Nia a cup of strong, tasty kavva, and a piece of a gingery cake. "I know which foodstuffs are authentic, such as gingerbread," he confided.

The Edge of Town overlooked a brushy gulch where Cowboys and Indians were scheduled to have a war over possession of an oil well. It began with a staged scuffle between a Cowboy and an Indian. The actors rolled around in a flurry of feathers and faux-leather fringes. They were University people who had spent many hours rehearsing. Hiro glowed with approval.

Unfortunately, Mattis and Vijay-Kol pulled each other into an argument about the historicity and fluid mechanics of oil wells. Vijay-Kol's voice slid into the tones of a lecturer. Mattis responded as though in a scientific dispute, waving his hands. Nia, for whose benefit the two were putting on their sideshow, did not feel benefited.

Hiro asked, "Would you like to come behind the scenes with me?"

In fact, Nia would have preferred to simply enjoy the Fair. But avoiding the fair game was no way to win it. *Here goes.* She interrupted Mattis and Vijay-Kol to say, "Enjoy the show. We need to see to University business." True enough, since Hiro's role on the Fair Committee was University Liaison. She followed him to an inconspicuous door in the low cliff that bounded the canyon. A brief translating elevator ride brought them to the six-sided control room for the Fair. "Welcome to the Hexagon," said Hiro.

Nia looked around curiously. Everyone in here wore Fair garb as they sat under holovision screens or conferred around tables.

A bulky man in a long brown coat intercepted them. Hiro said, "This is Security Chief Echt, and that's an F. B. I. trench coat he's wearing, Fair Bailiffs and Investigators—"

The Chief growled, "Drat these highhanded foreigners! Hiro, some Faxi bodyguards roughed up a couple of Albian University students. The Albis *were* calling the Faxis names having to do with passenger pigeons and dodo birds, but the Faxis overreacted. We squared the situation away, but it left a bad taste in some mouths, including ours."

"Faxens and Albians would think that Wendis is neutral territory," Nia observed.

"It is, ma'am, but the Fair has its own rules."

A man wearing a white coat and spectacles with heavy plastic rims joined them. Hiro said, "This is Jake Isoroku Genner, the Fair's Liaison from the Engineer's Guild. He's garbed like a Rocket Scientist."

"Honored," Nia said correctly.

"This is your University lawyer?" Genner asked.

Hiro said, "She is Nia Inanna Az-Courant."

"Honored!" the Fair-garbed men chorused.

Nia was floored. Her complete Azurean surname was Az-Courant, "Az" signifying astronaut ancestry. She didn't go by that name form here. And on top of that, Hiro had used "Nia" like a Wendisan social nickname. That was a huge compliment to her.

"Are we getting rid of the chaff with purple hair?" Genner asked.

Hiro explained, "The woman cast as Europan Queen insists on purple hair. Bess Elzebet Seller was the Queen of Ethiopia in her younger days, and is a stickler for authenticity. She deems purple hair authentic Twentycent, but not role appropriate. They've argued about it."

Nia gestured toward her own hair. "Silver may be even less authentic than purple."

"Bess Elzebet wondered about that," said Genner. "But since the quicksilver hair on Azure is early genetic engineering from Earth, everyone agreed it's essentially authentic."

Nia stared at him. That was an Az family secret. Or so the Az families thought. Wendis, though, had been finding out and filing away stray secrets for two thousand years. She knew that by now, and kept learning it all over again.

Swelling with the importance of what he intended to say, Chief Echt intoned, "Permit me, ma'am, to suggest that it would bring honor to your astronaut ancestors if you were to step into the luminary role. . . ." Nia was about to be put in the awkward position of flatly turning down admirers. But then the Chief's wrist pod chimed. The Chief held that wrist to his ear, listening to a report coming through on his pod. His face darkened. "Hiro! There's a missing student."

"Just one?" Hiro sounded annoyed.

"This one is a high-lordling from Goya. Has a head stuffed full of fairy tales and daring plans, no doubt, and your Proctor can't account for him."

Hiro replied, "Don't rely on our Proctor. He's a useless political appointee. Find the boy's friends, roommates, rivals, and ask them if they know where he might be."

Nia said, "Point out that anyone who withholds information about a fellow student engaging in prohibited activities is violating the Honor Code themselves."

The Chief asked Hiro, "Should the spooks search for him?"

Nia said, "It looks like you have an emergency. I better get out of your way."

"Not yet," said Hiro, answering both Nia and the Chief. "The Goyan boy may be in the amusement park. I'll direct our group there and look for him."

In the translator back to the Wild West, Nia said, "You knew introducing me with the Wendisan social nickname form would charm them. Too bad your Fair duties derailed your intentions."

He scowled at the floor of the translator. "I wish the wargamers would use Proctor Kugel for target practice. It will be a public relations nightmare for the Fair and the University if a student from a prominent Goyan family gets into trouble on the dark side of the Fair."

"What dark side? I thought the Fair was supposed to be safe and visitor-friendly."

"Nia Inanna, the Fair has never been as safe as we make it seem. And this year it's more dangerous than ever."

Riding the roller coaster with Mattis left Nia windblown and laughing. Mattis was ecstatic. "In the straightaway it was velocity perfectly counteracting the spin of Wendis! No spingravity. We were weightless. We are in space, we really are."

Still breathless, Nia gasped, "Those swooping curves made the whole world seem to rock back and forth! And the corkscrew—!"

"Made us oscillate between microgravity and double gee. Wow!"

"I'm dizzy." Nia clung to Mattis to steady herself. Extra credit for making her enjoy spingravity for once.

Jealousy flashed across Vijay-Kol's chiseled features.

Hiro had not seen the missing Goyan boy in the amusement park. Nia wondered what in the Fair would most attract a Goyan boy— specifically, an aristocrat's son from the feudal kingdoms in the interior of Goya's single large continent.

Hiro directed his little group through short cut in a fence to Everyville. He glanced around searchingly while pointing out Elm Street, with boxlike little houses, and Main Street, with City Hall and other edifices. Nia doubted that the Goyan boy would be here. Mattis, on the other hand, excitedly called out, "Look! A car!" Ancient vehicles lined one block of Main Street. The ambulance, fire truck and taxicab were superficial facsimiles. The garbage truck, complete with working collection mechanisms and being demonstrated by uniformed actors, was surrounded by curious Wendisans. Denizens of a tightly closed environmental loop, Wendisans were highly interested in ancient dealings with waste matter.

The cherry-red roadcar had its hood invitingly open to reveal real Ascendance automotive technology. After many minutes, Mattis had to be pulled away from his contemplation of the internal combustion engine.

"The vehicles will be in the March of History," said Hiro. "The March starts in the Rift Valley beyond the other end of the Sea. Participants come down the Silk Road, and up the Roman Road, and some descend the East and West Highways from the mountains. When it reaches full strength, the March ends at Rocket Park at midnight."

Hiro led them to Town Square, where a large lawn surrounded a Courthouse. Food vendors ringed the Square. Besides kebobs and curry buns and twists of salted baked dough, there were tubes of meat in long white buns with bright red, green and yellow condiments. "Hot dogs!" Hiro said. "Twentycent people enjoyed eating dog. This is synthmeat, though."

"I should hope so!" Nia chose a surimi shrimp kebob instead.

Beyond the buildings of Town Square rose a slender spire. Pointing with the shrimp kebob, Nia asked, "Is that a make-believe church?"

"At Fair time it pretends to be a stage set pretending to be an antique church," said Hiro. "But it's really a church, the only one in Wendis, St. Delaney-By-the-Sea."

Nia frowned. She'd been only vaguely aware that there were a few Catholic Orthodox believers in Wendis. Fine. They had to worship somewhere. Wendis also had at least one sect of Hades-worshipers. There was no reason for her to cross paths with either group.

Hiro led their little group to the Town Square lawn, where they picnicked on springy grass dotted with yellow flowers. "This is the best lawn in Everyville," Nia said.

"It's been tended for years by one of our University people," Hiro said. "Lee, the drama professor. For this year's Fair, he's directing an ancient play called 'A Streetcar Named Desire'."

"He's done a good job directing this lawn," said Nia, noting healthy crabgrass, dandelions, and clumps of lush chickweed—all standard terraforming species. None of them grew outdoors on Azure except in rare sheltered spots. Nia became aware of feeling comfortably warm. Wendis always seemed cold to her, colder than Azure. On Azure, you lived in warm greenhouses and stonebuilt habitats with good heating systems. Wendis tended toward energy conservation and cool, clammy fogs. But this was summer in Wendis, perihelion, when Wendis orbited closest to its sun and the Engineers tuned the weather to make it balmy.

Mattis and Vijay-Kol were arguing about something again, but in a fair and spirited way, like the professors they were. Hiro quietly conferred with the Hexagon about the still-missing Goyan student. Meanwhile a Marching Band worked its way past the food vendors on Main Street, putting forth brisk horn and drum music. Nia liked sitting here with friends, pretending to be at home in the first home of all, on Earth in the summer.

———

A hollow boom, and then another, echoed in the air. "The war games," said Vijay-Kol, and scrambled up. "We don't want to miss this." He took Nia's arm.

"What about the physics of bullets?" Mattis crowded close to Nia's other side. "A bullet launched anti-spinwise would break loose from the spingravity and fly free."

"They use beams of light and mesh vests that register hits," said Hiro.

It was late morning. The sunball in the heart of Wendis had

almost reached the midpoint of its crystalline spar. Fair visitors congregated at the City Limit where Everyville ended on the brink of one of the Celadon Sea's great slosh cliffs. Below, a plain stretched between the cliff and the pale green water. Usually it served as sport fields, but today the Darkling Plain framed the main war game of the Fair. The program was detailed in an information kiosk. "The cliffs on Aven Island are painted white," Nia said. "That's supposed to be a place called Britain that had white chalk cliffs. Where we're standing is called Normandy."

"I know what war it is," said Vijay-Kol. "Mid-Twentycent. They had rifles, bayonets, artillery cannons—no lightguns, no atomics until the very end." The plain and the sea swarmed with re-enactors, foot-soldiers on the Plain and sea-going soldiers in boats on the water. The game plan was clear enough: an invasion of the land from the sea. Artillery boomed again. "Half a million prehistoric humans died or were wounded at Normandy," Vijay-Kol lectured. "Pitiful really, because there was no human speciation in those days. Any of them could have interbred with each other's wives. Yet they had differences worth a world war. Such was old Earth in the last days before it went to seed and sowed the stars with starships."

He's hard-hearted, Nia thought. Many Faxens were nice people, though naive—Mattis being a good example on both counts—but Vijay-Kol knew what kind of toll history had exacted. It didn't move him. He felt all of the pain and toil and waste of history justified because Faxe now rested at its pinnacle.

"There aren't half a million re-enactors down there," Mattis said. He swept the plain with his hand held at arm's length, then announced, "Maybe fifty-five hundred."

Hiro said, "That's a very good estimate. Counting supporting players, there are almost six thousand participants. The makeup artists under the bushes will use many liters of red paint making the wounded look wounded."

Eager, interested, Mattis was a shiny slate where pain and disappointment had never written anything. He and Nia were about the same age, but Nia felt older.

She became aware of warm radiance on her arms. "The fog burned off."

"The Engineers promised the Fair Director clear weather at noon," said Hiro.

For once, the interior of Wendis was clear. In the center of the cylindrical world loomed the Wend Range, three mountains that rose up like frozen waves, curved spinwise. The middle mountain, Spectre, rose so high that it curled around the sunspar at the center of the world. The radiant sunball in its crystal spar had already glided past the jagged crest of Mount Chance. The sunball was approaching tall Spectre, after which it would pass over broad Mount Zaber.

Re-enactors flowed onto the Darkling Plain. They formed up into opposing forces, armed with glinting guns and bayonets, shielded by sharp wire, sturdy boat hulls and the long metal snouts of the artillery weapons. The two sides of the war confronted each other across the glistening edge of the sea. When they came to blows it would ring to the eaves of the world, even though it was all a show. Nia found herself holding her breath. She expelled it in irritation as she realized that Vijay-Kol meant to deliver a lecture on ancient military history here and now, stifling Mattis' attempts to lecture on the physics of antique weaponry.

The armies moved. Ranks of combatants crashed into each other, falling into chaotic patterns, regrouping. Artillery throbbed. Land mines blossomed like thunderous flowers. Spectators cheered. Vijay-Kol and Mattis fell silent. With horrified fascination, Nia noticed scores of wargamers playing dead, splashed with blood-red paint.

Then the sunball reached the summit of Spectre. The tallest mountain's shadow fell on the Darkling Plain. It happened every day, but the world was usually so full of bright fog as to make the noontime eclipse hardly noticeable. Not today. Obscuring the sun, Spectre loomed tall and dark, and the summit that curled around the sunspar evoked the hooded face of a menacing, supernatural figure. The shadow sweeping the Darkling Plain from west to east was its terrible cloak, and fear swept with it. Nearby, a child sobbed.

Nia backed away. She couldn't stand watching the war under the eclipse. It was only shadow and show, but it felt too real. She slipped away through the crowd.

I n the quiet, dim interior of St. Delaney-By-the Sea, Nia had her head in her hands when she sensed someone sitting down next to her. She murmured, "Hiro, I thought your Fair was all farce and games, but that was about real history." And it had made her instinctively seek a place that felt safe, and she'd come here. Old habits die hard. But St. Delaney *did* feel safe. It was silently empty—no priests, no congregation, and Hiro was here with her.

"The Director of the Fair is a profound man," Hiro said. "His Fairs point toward truth, while being entertaining. No one's ever seen anything quite like today, though. I think the Director means to suggest a shadow falling on our own time in history. Just as it must have seemed to people in the Twentieth Century, a happy outcome is not yet certain."

Nia shook her head. "Earth going to seed and throwing off starships that germinated on new worlds—that's easy to say, and happy for us, but the Twentieth Century was blood and terror and death for millions. History almost ended before it began."

"Some people believe Faxe is throwing a dark shadow on our day," said Hiro.

"My father, for one." She looked up at windows radiant with scenes of Earth and serene human figures. The window near the altar depicted Saint Delaney in his spacesuit among the asteroids. "See the saints, Hiro? They glow because they lived in dark times."

Hiro diplomatically answered, "I'm Buddhim, but all faiths in Wendis have holy people."

"Are there any holy people in the March of History?"

"The role of Gautama Buddha is played by a Buddhim priest. An equally irreproachable priest plays Attila the Hun. Three friends of mine play Popes. They adore the gorgeous garb."

Nia had an incipient headache. "So the Fair is a farce except when it isn't."

"The garb isn't at all farcical for those who have key roles. It's as authentic as possible, and very nice. For example, the Queen of Europa wears an authentic lovely dress—"

Nia could hardly believe her ears. "And you want me to play that role? Nobody in space places wears dresses—except the hookers in the port! What do you take me for?"

"I can explain, Counselor—"

"Look, if you're going to tell people Nia is my social nickname, just call me Nia!" If she'd known how emotionally ragged she'd be today, she would have skipped the Fair.

Hiro said, "The Fair includes those Popes in robes, and a phalanx of Old Roman warriors in skirts, all of them dignified, none of them going near the zero-gravity realms until they change into sensible shorts or coveralls."

His wrist pod whistled frantically. With obvious irritation, he punched a stud on the pod. Nia heard the consternated voice of Chief Echt. "We know where that Goyan lord's son is. He's in the Siege of Jerusalem and so is a hereditary enemy of his family—a University upperclassman also from Goya. They intend private combat."

Tension etched into Hiro's face. "Please tell me the other Goyan is a Saracen re-enactor."

"No. He's a Crusader." The Chief signed off.

Hiro ran his hand through his hair. "If a student from a prominent Goyan family gets hurt, the consequences will be awful. Scandal. Hospital expenses. Other Goyan families pulling their children out of the University!"

"People are re-enacting the *Siege of Jerusalem*?"

"The Fair Committee was opposed, since it's a thousand years too early. But those putting the idea forward made a case for the Crusades being key background for Twenty-First Century history, and the Committee was overruled. I must go. I'm sorry."

So *that* was what a Goyan lord's son most wanted to do in the Fair. "I'm coming with you," Nia said. "You may need a University lawyer."

3
THE PLAIN OF PAIN

The nearest commcube was camouflaged as an archaic telephone booth. Nia messaged Mattis and Vijay-Kol to say that she and Hiro had been called away to urgent University business but hoped to rejoin them later. Then Nia and Hiro caught a train at the transit tube station. They had a compartment to themselves, with a low table on which Hiro spread out an insider's map of the Fair. It was more detailed than the maps in the hands of Fair guests, and updated in real time. East of the Celadon sea and west of its terminal slosh cliff, Hiro's map showed an area called the Plain of Pain. Moving dots surrounded an icon labeled "Jerusalem."

Several of the dots were red. "Casualties," Hiro admitted.

"Make-believe?"

Hiro shook his head unhappily. "They'll be taken to the hospital and put back together. I didn't want you to see this part of the Fair." His shoulders sagged.

The tube train coasted into a station where the signage flashed ZONED PARK: HEADQUARTERS AND VISITOR CENTER. A dozen visitors filed off the tube train. Nia said, "Never mind what I think about the Fair. Who's who around Jerusalem?"

"The Saracens are honorable fighters, with notable exceptions.

There are also Byzantine mercenaries looking for trouble, and some Zulu warriors siding with the Saracens. The Crusaders, I'm sorry to say, draw from the worst element in Wendis. They usually find their recreation in the high Zones in the Park."

The tube train slowed and stopped again. PARK ZONE 5: INFERNO.

Additional signage flashed under the station announcement. RESTRICTED ACCESS: MUST HAVE REQUIRED PERMITS AND WAIVERS FILED WITH PARK RANGERS.

The aching tension in Nia's head seemed to flow into her shoulders. From perplexity to dread. "I like the Zoned Park up to Zone Four. I know any zone higher than that has real danger. But I'm one of few foreigners who've ever read the whole Wendisan Legal Code. Wendis has legal immunity from an explicit variety of bad outcomes to visitors in the Park, as long as the waivers are in order. I thought some of the waiver wording was fanciful and the signage was phrased to serve notice of danger in a titillating way. But now I suspect that terrible things do happen in the Park. Am I right?"

Hiro sighed. "People from all the terraformed worlds in Starmark pay well to take part in dangerous and, sometimes, terrible games in the Zoned Park. Danger pleases some people. It makes them focused, or alive, or superior to those who avoid danger. Or superior to those don't survive."

Nia shivered.

The next brief stop flashed in red letters. PARK ZONE NINE: THE MOST DANGEROUS GAME: HIGHLY RESTRICTED: ENTER AT YOUR OWN RISK. Nia had seen that signage before. Today it made her skin crawl.

Hiro's voice was quiet and bitter. "The Fair Council has to negotiate with the vested interests of the Zoned Park. This year they drove a hard bargain. As a result, we reserved the Plain of Pain for the Park's most dangerous elements, so they can come out to play with history too, in return for not killing, robbing, exploiting, or scaring tourists in the Fair."

Nia felt numb. *Parts of Wendis aren't as bad as I thought. They're worse.*

"Still, the players on the Plain of Pain must follow the Fair rules," Hiro said.

"Fair rules?"

"Everyone has a role, and every role has rules. There are rulers—Popes, Queens, Presidents—but their authority is limited by continent and ethnic or religious group." Hiro seemed happier to slant the conversation back to the Fair as a whole. "The inhumans have secret rules, and everyone who plays a magical being has the magic rule set. It's all old school."

"Old what?"

"In Wendisan secret rhyming talk, school means rule."

"Why do I sometimes hear the phrase 'rotten onion' in a very unlikely context?"

Hiro smiled conspiratorially. "Faxen Union."

His wrist pod whistled. The latest news from Chief Echt yanked Hiro back to his immediate problem. Apparently the Goyan boy had arranged to meet a Crusader in private combat in front of Jerusalem's Gate, today in the early afternoon. Hiro shook his head glumly. "There are five gates. We don't have enough free safety officers to check all those gates in the next hour. We dare not send less than three together."

The signage in the tube car flashed again. PARHELON FAIR: SIEGE OF JERUSALEM: NO CHILDREN OR PETS ALLOWED.

This wasn't going to be her great-grandmother's Fair. Or Nia's own idea of a fun game. But it sounded like a perfect place for a foolhardy young man to get into trouble. "Since they're University students, would they recognize me?"

"Yes. You have very distinctive looks."

"Then we take a likely Gate. Get a safety officer to meet us. That makes three and frees up someone else to check the other gates."

Hiro shook his head. "Your citizenship has never been my business, and I assume it's ex officio. That's not good enough to approach Jerusalem."

"I'm a full legal citizen of Wendis," Nia told him. "Out of all of her descendants, my great-grandmother bequeathed her citizenship to me."

Hiro's eyebrows went up. Then he said, "Just don't forget that citizenship makes no difference to a flying spear."

The view of Jerusalem from the bleachers was safe. Unfortunately, it was also distant. The stage-set city called Jerusalem brooded behind thick, high walls. In front of the west wall, attackers clustered in two groups. Fighters wearing tabards over suits of mail congregated under a vermillion banner. A separate, grubbier group surrounded an ungainly catapult.

A rider mounted on a horse cantered from one group to the other, attracting a hail of arrows from the city. *A horse?* Nia shook her head in amazement. The horse must have been bred in Wendis, or it would be even clumsier here than she was, since it had more feet. Nia tiredly rested her chin on her hand. "We aren't getting anywhere. And the fighting isn't either."

"It isn't scripted," Hiro pointed out.

Mounted Saracens thundered around the northwest corner of the city. They tore through the Crusaders around the vermillion banner, cutting off and circling around a third of them. The rest of the Crusaders shouted and surged that way. The banner rocked and rippled. Then the details disappeared in cloud of dust. Nia said, "We've got to get closer."

"Even for a citizen, it's dangerous to be a spectator on the ground here."

"Where does that leave our student?" Nia retorted.

They climbed out of the bleachers. Spectators on the ground stood closer to the action. Hiro was less than average height for a Wendisan, and he could barely see the action going on near Jerusalem, but he slipped through a crowd as easily as an eel through seagrass. Nia stuck to him and they forced their way toward the battleground.

Nia was taller than most Wendisans, and for once it was an advantage to her. Over the spectators' heads, she watched a detachment of mounted Crusaders racing toward the fracas in progress. Their swords and maces glinted in the sunlight. They rode into the dust cloud stirred everything up. Flailing weapons and running feet could be glimpsed in the dust.

Nia didn't see any blue-robed Saracens around the West Gate, or anywhere else.

The skirmish subsided. The two sides separated, dragging away their bleeding casualties. It looked like real blood, not paint. Of all things in all of history for Wendis to make a game of, the Siege of Jerusalem had to be one of the worst, and—with horses—most logistically difficult. It was absurd. Unless the psychological logic was to hammer away at a crooked place in history, trying to make it right. What it said about Wendis, harboring a game this elaborately brutal and historically compulsive, Nia did not want to wonder.

Nia and Hiro reached a huge flat rock, a good vantage point, just in time for there to be no action to see. Hiro called the Hexagon. He learned that the Security Officer who was supposed to meet them— Chief Echt—had been delayed by a fracas. Spectators were breaking through the sidelines south of Jerusalem for a better look at the fighting between Zulus and Byzantine mercenaries.

They sat down on the big flat rock to wait for the Chief. Nia drew her hand across her brow. "Why is it so awfully hot here?"

Hiro wiped his own face with a fauxsilk handkerchief. "This is a heat dump for the environmental systems. It's historically apt, as ancient Jerusalem was in a desert."

"The Darkling Plain is smooth. Why do the stones here have sharp edges?"

"Many years ago, in the Great Tumble, a coal-black asteroid glanced off the hull of Wendis. In the catastrophe that followed, a section of Mount Chance fell down. The Plain of Pain is the debris field."

Staging the Siege of Jerusalem on a sharp-edged field of ruin seemed weirdly apt. It also made Nia more uneasy than ever. She didn't like this place or this war.

Enemy groups glared at each other. Nia felt dangerous anticipation in the air like the electric tension before a thunderstorm. She and Hiro had to find that Goyan boy—and soon, before the storm broke. Hiro, though, was too fundamentally decent and gentle to decipher the black heart of a game like this. *When in doubt get good advice.* But who in Wendis could advise her about a vicious war game? Not University professors or officials! Then who?

Ah. Maybe Nia knew the right person. She told Hiro, "We've got to do something. I think Robard Benedet is probably involved in this. Do you think we could contact him?"

To Nia's surprise, Hiro bristled. "You only know him from tedious University functions where he's a more sophisticated and witty companion than anyone else, and you're the most attractive and exotic woman there. He has his reasons to be attentive and charming to you at such times. It would be stupid to seek his help here."

Nia suppressed an impulse to say *YOU seem to have paid inordinate attention to MY social life.* He was still bristling. Suddenly she knew why. "You're afraid of Robard."

Hiro's fist clenched on his map. "There are nasty rumors about his sexual dealings with men. You've never seen that, since you are only social friends, in public. I'm sure you haven't been alone with him—"

"Don't be sure," Nia snapped.

"Great Heaven! How could you?" Hiro's voice rose.

"What you just said!" Her voice rose too. "And how intriguingly Wendisan he is!"

Hiro gasped. "His sort isn't a true Wendisan!"

"Like the Zoned Park isn't Wendis and the Siege of Jerusalem isn't the Fair?" she shot back. She'd never argued with Hiro before. The atmosphere here was laced with hostility. "There may be Wendisan things and people that you're too nice to understand."

Hiro glanced around, taking in the spectators closing in around them. He said stiffly, "Behind his back people call him Bent Robard."

"That doesn't surprise me. I only thought we might be able to get information from him. I didn't say I trust him to help us, because I don't. He keeps a monster caged in the basement of his soul. I know because I've seen it."

Hiro looked startled. "*Seen* it?"

"Not under intimate circumstances," she said before Hiro's imagination could run wild. "It was when he showed me his collection of replicas of ancient weapons."

Robard Benedet displayed his weapons in the hall of his house— by Wendisan standards, a large and expensively furnished house. What he took out of its display case to show her was a spiked ball attached by a chain to a short stick. Unlike the swords, daggers and lances, which were things of severe beauty, this thing, called *morning star,* had looked ugly and cruel. Yet he'd held it gently—almost caressingly. At that moment she'd seen behind his eyes a shadowy, monstrous, barbaric mood very much at odds with his urbane exterior.

Even in the heat here, the memory made Nia shiver. The monster at the bottom of Robard's soul would like the Siege of Jerusalem. It might even be let out of its cage to play.

Hiro's wrist pod whistled. "Hiro?" It was Security Chief Echt. "The locator puts you at the Rock By The Hard Place. Stay put—I'm on my way. We have new information. The spooks think he's on the west side of the city!"

"We see no sign of the boy near the western gate," said Hiro.

Nia jumped up onto the rock and looked toward Jerusalem. "The battle lines are forming up again. Are you sure the city has only five gates?"

Hiro smoothed out the map and laid it on his knees. "This shows a great gate on the northwest corner, and one in each direction of the compass."

"The original city had a tiny gate called the Needle's Eye."

Hiro traced the wall of Jerusalem with his finger. "Yes! Near the northwest corner!"

Nia squinted, trying to see across the field. "I think I see it under that minaret."

"There are so many moving dots on this map that they look like trails of ants! A column of Crusaders is marching from the north and Saracens are streaming out of the major gates to meet them. The west side of Jerusalem is no place for private combat—it looks as though a battle will break out there!"

Nia shook Hiro's shoulder. "What if a foreigner who shouldn't be here at all gets killed? There'd be no way to pin the blame on anyone."

"Killed?" Hiro clutched his hair. "That would be a disaster for the Committee and the University!"

And for the boy. Nia turned back toward Jerusalem. A flutter of bright blue cloth caught her eye. "I see him!" She leaped off the rock and ran toward the Needle's Eye.

"Nia! Wait!"

Nia wove through spectators crowding toward Jerusalem. Beyond the spectators she glimpsed a blue-robed Saracen and a Crusader brandishing swords at one another, close to the wall. The Crusader wore a coat of mail—not the heavy authentic sort, but lightweight, bright synthetic mail that gleamed under the ragged sleeves of his tabard. If the Crusader was a University upperclassman, he'd been in Wendis several years longer than the younger Goyan. That gave him a deadly advantage in the spingravity of Wendis. Fighting moves would make the boy in blue robes lose his balance, more likely sooner than later. If Nia's own experience was any guide, he'd been here just long enough to *think* he could handle himself in spingravity.

The noise in the background escalated, and it had ominous sharp edges. Over her shoulder, Nia registered Crusaders and Saracens converging on the great Northwest gate, with splinters of battle spilling this way. The struggling blue Saracen seemed fixated on his adversary, heedless of the war looming toward him. Behind the two combatants, the Needle's Eye stood open, only a little taller than a man, a port in the breaking storm of combat. Nia gestured toward it, hoping Hiro got the idea.

The Saracen staggered backward. He clutched his bleeding sword arm with his free hand. The Crusader pressed toward him. Nia caught the Crusader's trailing cloak and gave it a hard yank. When he turned toward her, she ignored his sword and shook her finger in his face. "Are you trying to throw the Honor Code out into space in broken pieces? I'll see you in University Court!"

He backed away. Good. He did recognize her. From the corner of her eye, she saw Hiro dragging their Saracen away toward the Eye of the Needle. Even better!

In front of the wall, Crusaders and Saracens collided like clashing tides and surged this way, yelling and bashing weapons against weapons. Panicky spectators, running, blocked Nia's retreat toward the Needle's Eye. The University Crusader ran away with the spectators.

A big brown warhorse angled out of the fighting. The horse carried a menacing mailed rider. Scattering spectators left and right, the rider made for the blue Saracen robe. In a split second, Nia guessed that the Crusader had never meant to kill his family's enemy personally. Instead he'd arranged with another Crusader to make sure it happened—*now*.

Side-stepping on polished hooves, the horse covered the ground at a terrifying rate. Nia sprang aside. But the spingravity snared her feet. She fell. It seemed to happen in slow motion clogged with dread. She hit the rocky ground hard, flat on her face, and froze. The horse lunged over her. Its rear hooves thudded on each side of her head.

Hiro's voice screamed, "Citizen down! Citizen down!"

The swirling action eddied, space opening around Nia. She sat up, feeling the sting of cuts from sharp rocks, but nothing that hurt enough to indicate a blow from the horse's hoof. She seemed to be the center of interrupted action that rippled outward a stone in a pond. Wargamers called out, "Citizen down!" Stray spectators yelled, "Where?" "What citizen?" "That one!"

A mailed knight on a tall sorrel mare cantered up and stopped short. He leaped off, flinging the reins to a follower on foot. He tossed his helmet to another follower. Nia recognized Robard and saw that he was furious. He seized Nia's wrist and roughly hauled her to her feet. "Citizen *interfering,* you mean."

The morning star hung from his belt, caked with blood. Nia instinctively knew that this was a very bad way to encounter Robard. She drew in a breath, intending to tell him that it was a University matter. Before she could speak, he backhanded her. The mail on the back of his hand scraped her cheek. The pain brought tears to her eyes.

He'd never seen her in pain before. It changed something. She saw the monster in his soul uncoil behind his eyes. And look back at her. Icy terror shot through Nia's nerves.

Behind Robard, Saracens had rushed out of the Eye of the Needle to carry the blue-robed boy back into the City. Instead of melting away with them, Hiro stepped forward. His voice shaking, Hiro told Robard, "Let her go. She's a citizen!"

Keeping his grip in Nia's wrist, Robard shook his head. "If your Committee comes for her under a parley flag—we'll parley. Until then, she's mine." Crusaders ringed around them. The expressions obscured behind helmets and masks looked like glee.

Dread crushed Nia's breath. Robard liked men more than women, but he could like a woman well enough. What she had already known about him and what Hiro had said today about Robard's reputation fused in an awful realization. Who Robard liked, he loved to hurt. If she couldn't get away from him, he would hurt her and savor her pain.

Desperation spurred Nia to think fast. Rules worked in the Fair. Rules were how Robard usually kept his monster locked down. She stood straight and said, "No. I am your queen."

"What?"

"I am the Queen of Europa."

Robard shot Hiro a daggery glance. Hiro's head bobbed up and down. "The Fair Committee's unanimous choice!"

Robard let go of Nia's wrist. He snatched a painted piece of wood out of a pocket and hurled it onto the ground. "Tell your servant to pick that up. It's a token to get out of hell free. Show it if anyone tries to stop you. Now get out of my war." Robard gestured, and his Crusaders handed him his helmet and the reins of his sorrel mare. And he swung up onto the horse and led the Crusaders away like a magnet pulling iron filings.

———

The token got them past straggling Crusaders on foot and through a band of smirking mercenaries. Nia was trembling, but she kept her head up. Better act regal until out of sight of the Crusaders. As she and Hiro reached the bleachers, a ragged roar went up on the battlefield behind them. The combatants were at it again. When they ducked behind the bleachers, Nia and Hiro clung to each other. Hiro gasped, "I had no idea he would try to take a woman hostage!"

"I guessed the right rule to use on him!"

"Thank Heaven," Hiro said faintly.

Chief Echt barreled behind the bleachers. "I said stay put at the Rock!" he bawled. "If I hadn't seen her silver hair over the crowd, I'd never have found the two of you!"

"The boy is with the Saracens in the city," Hiro said, "and hurt badly enough to stay wherever they put him."

"Then both of you clear out of here!"

The roar of battle seemed louder, closer, studded with distinct crashes and thuds and whinnies from horses. Spectators started jumping off the back of the bleachers to flee. "To the tube station!" Hiro took Nia's hand and led her at a full-out run past indecisive spectators and curious ones who stopped to look back. They dodged a squad of Fair Bailiffs pouring out of the train with stun guns in hand

Hiro and Nia jumped into a train car just before it pulled out of the station. The tube train was packed with Fair visitors on their way to points West. Every seat was taken. Everyone stared at Nia and Hiro as they thumped down to sit on the floor. Hiro put his arm around her. "There was no time to find out if that beast stepped on you, should we go to the hospital?"

"It didn't step on me and I'm not really hurt. What about you?" His shirt bore streaks of reddish-brown color that wasn't paint.

"That boy was bleeding profusely and pale as a scallop when I got to him. Are you sure you aren't hurt?"

"I've been in worse shape the times I fell off a horse at home. This was just falling under one." Then the bigger picture sank in. Nia shuddered. "It's bad enough to be conspicuous and trip on stairs all the time. How many people are going to hear how I fell under a horse?"

"Everyone in Wendis," said Hiro.

4

ROCKET PARK

In the Hexagon, Fair Committee members and workers clustered around Nia and Hiro. The excited attention made Nia shrug awkwardly while the medic on duty assessed the bruises and cuts on her face, hands and knees. Was she *certain* the horse hadn't stepped on her? "It didn't," she insisted. "Horses know where their feet are, and I knew to stay still." Cold dismay coiled in the pit of Nia's stomach. Hiro was right. The foreigner falling under the horse would be the talk of the Fair.

A heavy-set, dark-skinned woman hurried into the Hexagon. Garbed in bright geometric-patterned cloth, she parted the Fair workers like an angelfish scattering the lesser species of a coral reef. She announced, "Everything is witherspin on the Plain of Pain! The Jerusalem war went out of control and I just heard that Hiro's Az was run over by a horse!"

This was Bess Elzebet Seller, the Chair of the Fair.

Nia and Hiro gave her a more accurate account of events, including Nia's narrow escape from Robard. Elzebet had a wide, kind face, and Nia told her about Robard's motives. Elzebet threw her hands up in horror. "Durzy, go get some peppermint tea for this woman!" she ordered one of the Fair workers and snapped at the medic, "Put that bottle of brown bandage away. This is Wendis and you can find a shade that matches her skin. Do you think she'll want this unpleasantness to jump out of every mirror at her?"

The cool air in the Hexagon chilled Nia. "*Everything has gone witherspin on the Plain of Pain,*" Elzebet Seller had said. Nia had abstractly known that "witherspin" meant things going wrong or falling apart. Now Nia knew how it felt: everything spinning the wrong way and the all-pervasive force of spin unpredictably, perilously skewed. She shivered.

Elzebet wrapped a fluffy blanket around Nia's shoulders. "We'd have had terrible trouble if that University student had been murdered, and I have you and Hiro to thank! But what in the name of Tumble was Bent Robard thinking? The nerve of him presuming to take an uninvolved citizen hostage, while he's standing in the bloodiest war game anyone has ever seen! I've already had three calls from the hospital and the last one was Dr. Tsuda herself complaining about how things are going. The Normandy Invasion swamped them with sprains and broken limbs—and then the half dead from the Plain of Pain started pouring in. I'm filing charges against that Proctor of yours, Hiro. It's his job to make your students stay inside the rules. He let that boy sneak away into the worst corner of the whole Fair, and the Bailiffs found three more University students in the Den of Iniquity! Drink this, dear, peppermint tea is just the thing after an upset."

The tea tasted sweet and comforting, but Nia felt the skewed spin of circumstances forcing her in a direction she didn't want to go. "The March of History must have started by now. Is it too late?"

Hiro answered, "No, the Twentycent actors haven't joined it yet—"

"Then I have to do what I told Robard I would."

Elzebet drew herself up to her full height and width, as dignified as the Ethiopian Queen she had once played. "That was said under duress, and that's not how we do business."

"I won't be a liar," Nia insisted. She gingerly touched her left cheekbone, which felt sore. "I may look worse for wear, but I don't dare go back on my word."

"She's right," said a man's calm voice. "If she is the Queen, Bent Robard can't take refuge in fury that he was publicly deceived. He may have no choice but to face the truth."

"What truth, Ban Hayao?" Elzebet asked.

"If he'd taken a citizen hostage and tortured her, he would have crossed the line into criminality in the eyes of everyone in Wendis." Detaching himself from the background, the calm-voiced man gently tilted Nia's face. "My makeup artists can conceal your injuries."

Hiro told Nia, "This is Ban Hayao Pannister, the Fair Director."

Hayao Pannister had the clearest eyes Nia had ever seen, reminding her of still water in a deep pool. On impulse, Nia asked him a question that had been blazing in the back of her mind all afternoon. "I don't understand your Fair. It's illogical, it's entertaining, it's beautiful in places, and it can be serious as death and murderous as hell. Why?"

He smiled; a network of crows-feet framed his eyes. "You have just described human history. But watch what happens at midnight tonight."

———

To make sure she wouldn't lose her nerve, Nia sent Hiro back to her apartment for the bottle of aquarel, while Elzebet Seller fitted Nia with a Twentycent dress and jacket. The knee-length skirt had an elegant cut and soft drape. The jacket felt like friendly armor, and the mauve fabric complimented Nia's complexion. "I expected something more ostentatious," Nia said.

Elzebet answered from behind Nia where she was adjusting the hemline. "The Queen of Europa—to be more accurate, *England;* the continent was Europa but the Queen was England's—was a head of state, and she wore first quality Twentycent clothing in the best of taste."

Hiro reappeared with the aquarel. He now wore a Twentycent

business suit and fauxsilk tie. Unlike Fair visitors who adopted pieces of antique clothing at random, he looked comfortable and tasteful. He said approvingly. "Bess, you've outdone yourself."

"Honored for the opportunity," said Elzebet, giving Nia's jacket a final tweak.

Nia and Hiro boarded a serpentine float with other Twentycent dignitaries—a President, a Pope, and the Ethiopian Emperor. To Nia's relief, they all had places to sit. Elzebet had given her high-heeled shoes, and standing in those on a moving float in spingravity seemed like a recipe for disaster. Their float pulled into the March of History behind a float carrying feather-fringed Indians and white-scarfed, goggled Aviators, and just ahead of blue-coveralled Astronauts on a Moon Rover. Nia quickly realized that this wasn't going to be unpleasant in any of the ways she'd feared it would. The crowd along the route applauded. Nia copied the gesture used by the Aviatrix, tilting her hand toward the spectators, who waved back. The friendly attention reminded Nia of when she had been much younger, performing artistic dance and enjoying being on stage. She poked Hiro in the ribs. "Smile!"

"Ah, I wanted this very much. But what you saw today wasn't your great-grandmother's fair. You must be disillusioned with Wendis."

"My great-grandmother's fair didn't bring me to Wendis." Nia spotted Mattis and Vijay-Kol and gave them a more animated wave. Mattis waved back. Vijay-Kol scowled.

Hiro said. "Wendis lives at the heart of interstellar law, and it's only natural that an ambitious interstellar lawyer would situate herself here."

"It was more like a port in a storm for me."

Hiro was a Wendisan's Wendisan. He had always been proper when interacting with Nia. No personal questions. But they were friends now. The rules had changed. "What storm?"

He deserved her honesty, and the March was climbing onto Zaber's knees and leaving the noise of the crowd behind. Nia took a deep breath. "My family on Azure expected me to become a political leader and work to preserve Azure's independence from Faxe. But I got into trouble at the end of law school—in field work. The fallout eventually ended any hope of a political career on Azure. I was blacklisted there. I invoked my great-grandmother's Wendisan citizenship and came here. I didn't want to play the part of the Queen because it sounded too much like a farce of something that I really did dream about—being a head of state someday."

"Great Heaven, I had no idea," said Hiro.

The March wound its way up Mount Zaber toward the wide, bowl-shaped valley that held Rocket Park. The number of participants surprised Nia. There were actors playing dignitaries, but all kinds of other costume too—peasants and nurses, farmers and bureaucrats, courtesans and scribes, converging from all directions. "Is everybody in Wendis taking part in this?"

Hiro smiled. "Every Wendisan. Those who have essential work to do are watching through their friends' and relatives' personal cams."

As the March went up Zaber, its route switchbacked. Participants ran up and down the mountain to have a word with friends in another era. Caught up in the spectacle, Nia didn't notice Robard on his sorrel mare until he pulled up beside the float. Nia felt her heart thud with alarm and anger. She couldn't bring herself to look at Robard. Instead she watched his mare. The way the mare held her head was relaxed, and Robard's hands on the reins light. Robard's mare had never been abused, Nia thought, because she wasn't human, and his sadistic drive was.

"I didn't think you'd do something like this," Robard said. "I underestimated you. Fortunately for me."

Surprised, Nia looked into his face, and saw Robard—not his monster—in his eyes, a grim Robard without the usual glint of sardonic wit. Nia guessed that he already realized what Pannister had said—how close he'd come to crossing the line into criminality.

He said, "May I have my get-out-of-hell-free token back? I might need it tomorrow."

Hiro produced the token. Nia held it out for Robard to take. Then he flicked the reins and his nimble mare climbed the slope, taking him back across a thousand years of make-believe history. Hiro crossed his arms, radiating disapproval at Robard's back.

Their float crested the rim of the Rocket Park valley, and Nia gasped. Everyone who'd been ahead of them in the March of History now surrounded the tall rockets. The marchers were all afoot. Horses, empty floats, the cherry-red roadcar from Everyville, and the Moon Rover ringed the valley. Later marchers were still arriving. They included a large number of people dressed from head to foot in black.

"This way," Hiro said. Peasants and children seemed to be doing fine without footwear, so Nia left the high-heeled shoes in the float and went in stocking feet. The grass felt soft and springy. It was almost midnight. The valley filled with the buzz of anticipatory conversation. Angling toward the rockets, Hiro said, "You are the most able interstellar lawyer I've ever worked with. How in High Heaven's name did you get into trouble in law school field work?"

She'd never told anybody in Wendis. Now she was walking shoeless on grass on a Wendis summer night given over to history. And history had its wicked rulers, its wretched wars, its inglorious Crusades. Her personal past did not seem unduly disgraceful. She took a deep breath. "I defended someone accused of sedition against the planetary authority on Moira."

"But Moira is the Faxen Union's prison world—what a terrible venue for field work!"

"There are people on Moira besides prison colonists—the world has cities and free citizens. It's a rough place for legal field work, but the people need legal help and a young lawyer can learn a lot. I chose to go there. The accused was innocent but the planetary authority wanted him found guilty. I won by going outside of Accepted Interplanetary Law. Moira has a strange legal subcode that's recognized in a treaty with Faxe. Officially, I failed the fieldwork, and it looked like my father had raised an anti-Faxen activist. His enemies were happy to seize on that, so it damaged him professionally." She gritted her teeth. She hated having been an unwitting pawn in that political game. "I graduated with honor anyway and succeeded in everything I did after that for years. Then my name came up for appointment to the Interplanetary Department of Azure's government. Somebody brought up the field work. I was disqualified for any sensitive government post," she ground out, "because of what I had done on Moira. They called it evidence of deeply flawed professional judgment."

Hiro wore an amazed expression. "The innocent man on Moira went free?"

"Yes, and as far as I know he's still alive and well. It cost me my home, my relationship with my family, and the life I intended to lead."

People were sorting themselves into a single spiraling line from the rockets to the rim of the valley. Hiro hooked his arm around hers. "Nia, tumble happens. It even happened to Wendis when the asteroid hit. How you cope is what counts. Like today. You saved that foolish boy, fell under a horse, and made a brilliant escape from Bent Robard. No wonder you're good at recovering from tumble. You've had practice."

Wendisans crowded together, holding hands with family and friends. Nia found Jake Isoroku Genner on her other side. Garbed in his white lab coat, he winked as he hooked his elbow around hers and said, "We descendants of astronauts and engineers should stick together."

At midnight a hush fell. One by one the rockets lit up from inside. Then Nia saw that the rockets were made of paper, and they were trembling and shaking.

With a swishing sound, the rockets rose into the air on exhaust fire made of glittering streamers. Nia wondered where they would go —Wendis was only a mile across.

Above the heads of the Wendisan crowd, the rockets burst into showers of light. Fireworks! The sparks curled, lights shaping themselves into birds, butterflies, flowers, and animals. Nia smelled a trace of acrid combustion on the air. On the ground, the Marcher of History stood around the rocket-liftoff Ascendance with faces illuminated by life drawn in fireworks light.

Above the colorfully garbed Marchers on the valley's slopes stood

ALEXIS GLYNN LATNER

all of the people wearing black. Nia whispered, "I bet they represent the Dead Zone." The vast bubble of depopulated galactic space centered on lost Earth.

Hiro said, "Some are our Children of Bane and other Shades of Human. They have their origins in the Dead Zone. They deserve a place in the Spiral of History too, so they play the role of Dead Zoners."

Nia saw, or imagined, a black-clad, slim-hipped figure with diaphanous wings unfurled. Angels were adapted to low or no gravity —but could wear gravity braces here, just as people born on low-gravity moons did when visiting higher gravity. "Even angels?"

"All sentient beings in Wendis are threads weaving one fabric," Hiro said firmly.

Genner said, "Our adolescents delight in filling out the ranks of the Dead Zoners by wearing black clothes and black masks and pretending to be unimpressed by the fireworks."

She laughed. "They'll outgrow being unimpressed." Wendis was a grand stage for fireworks tonight. The opposite side of Wendis was decked with smooth fog, a featureless dark backdrop. She pointed up at a whirl of colored fire that sketched a distinctive rodent. It even had whiskers. "Is that a marmot?"

"A marmot in honor of Azure," said Genner.

Nia felt happier than she had in years. Let news about me being a Queen in Parhelon Fair get back to Azure, she thought. It didn't matter anymore. What she really wanted was to be home, and she wasn't there yet, but some day she would be. And home would be *here*.

Animals and plants made of light proliferated toward the West end of Wendis. There, just inside the Great Wall, crystal towers— offices, government buildings, and trade centers—radiated from the axis. Now the civic towers lit up. The west end of Wendis shone like a star with coruscating rays. Nia felt a shiver of recognition, from seeing something she already knew, in an unforgettable new light.

Along with a mountain range, a sea, a University, dangerous games, and knowledge as old as history, Wendis had a city, one with a

328

very old name. It recalled the ancient days when the earliest rockets vaulted up from the face of the Earth. To cameras looking up, the rockets finally looked like bright stars. The rockets carried brave spacefarers whose missions began at the place with the same high-reaching name as the city in the western end of Wendis: Star City.

AFTERWORD

If you enjoyed *The Fair Game,* the story continues in *Witherspin,* published by Avendis Press in December 2019.

And the adventure continues in *Starmaze,* to be published in 2020.

You can sign up for my occasional Newsletter about *Starmaze* and other projects here: http://eepurl.com/bvm_Bv.

ALSO BY ALEXIS GLYNN LATNER

The *Aeon's Legacy* Series

Hurricane Moon

Downfall Tide

Star Crossing

Spike, a *Pets in Space* story

Helldive

The *Starways* series

Mascot, a *Pets in Space* Story

Starway, a *Pets in Space* Story

Winter's Prince in Pets in Space 4

Witherspin

Starmaze (2020)

ABOUT THE AUTHOR

Alexis Glynn Latner likes to write tales of romantic adventure that touch readers' hearts and their minds as well. She also writes nonfiction, does editing, teaches and mentors creative writing, and works at Rice University's Fondren Library in Houston, Texas. For fun and real-life adventure she is a sailplane pilot.

Her science fiction and fantasy stories have appeared in *Analog Science Fiction and Fact*, *Amazing Stories*, and many print and online anthologies including the *USA Today* best-selling *Pets in Space*. She's had stories in a couple of mystery anthologies too. Her science fiction novel *Hurricane Moon* was published by Pyr (Prometheus Books) in 2007 and again by Avendis Press in 2014 with the sequels *Downfall Tide*, *Star Crossing*, and finally *Helldive* in 2018. A new romantic science fiction series begins with *Witherspin* in late 2019.

Find out more about Alexis' books and stories:

www.alexisglynnlatner.com
www.facebook.com/AuthorAlexisGlynnLatner/
https://twitter.com/AlexisGLatner